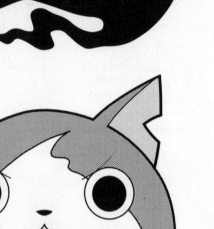

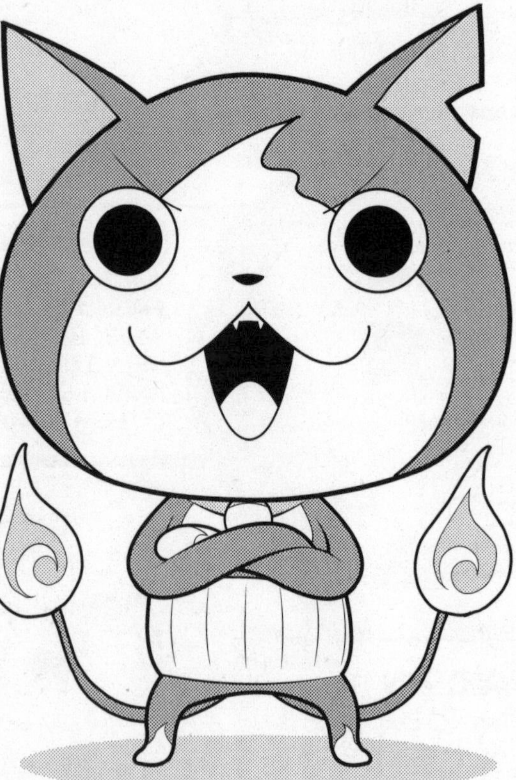

STORY AND ART BY
NORIYUKI KONISHI

ORIGINAL STORY AND SUPERVISION BY LEVEL-5 INC.

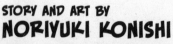

CHARACTER INTRODUCTION

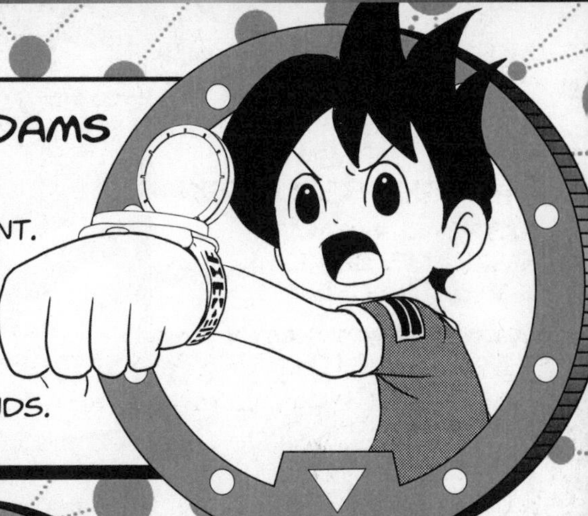

NATHAN ADAMS

AN ORDINARY ELEMENTARY SCHOOL STUDENT. WHISPER GAVE HIM THE YO-KAI WATCH, AND THEY HAVE SINCE BECOME FRIENDS.

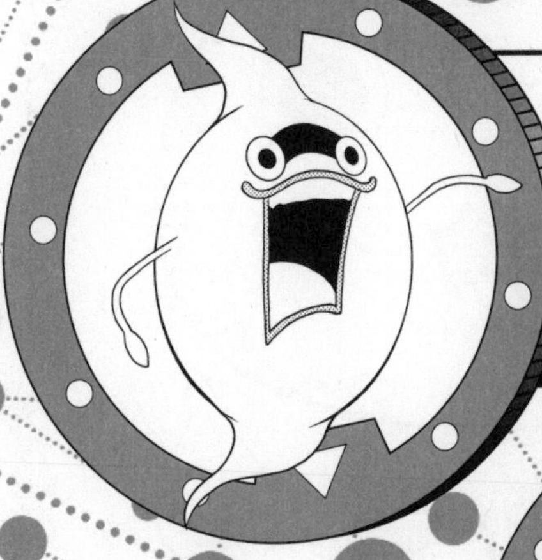

WHISPER

A YO-KAI BUTLER FREED BY NATE, WHISPER HELPS HIM BY USING HIS EXTENSIVE KNOWLEDGE OF OTHER YO-KAI.

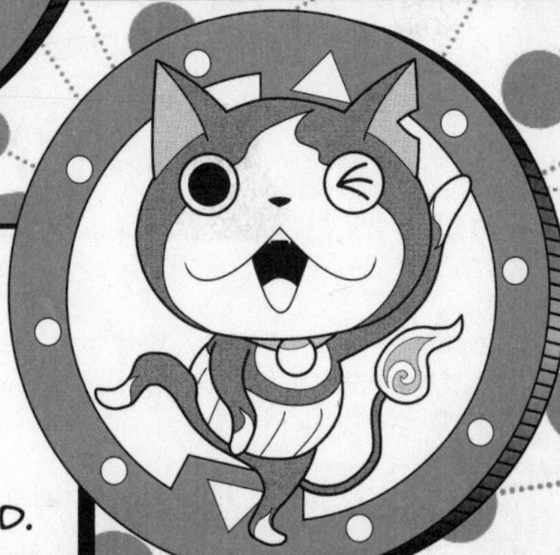

JIBANYAN

A CAT WHO BECAME A YO-KAI WHEN HE PASSED AWAY. HE IS FRIENDLY, CAREFREE AND THE FIRST YO-KAI THAT NATE BEFRIENDED.

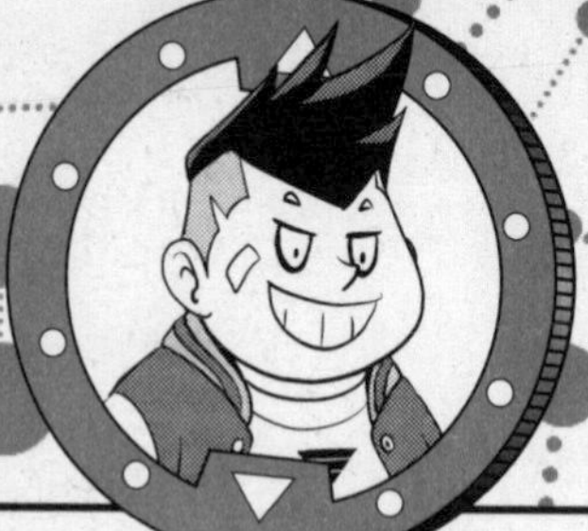

EDWARD ARCHER
NATE'S CLASSMATE. NICKNAME: EDDIE. HE ALWAYS WEARS HEADPHONES.

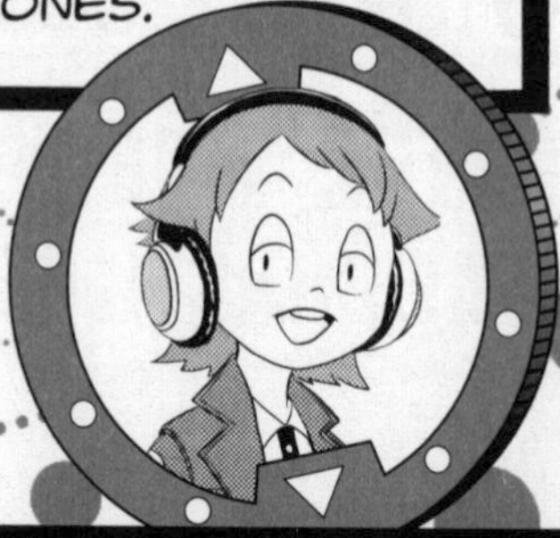

BARNABY BERNSTEIN
NATE'S CLASSMATE. NICKNAME: BEAR. CAN BE MISCHEIVOUS.

TABLE OF CONTENTS

CHAPTER 8:
NATE THE BAD BOY?!
FEATURING REBEL YO-KAI ROUGHRAFF

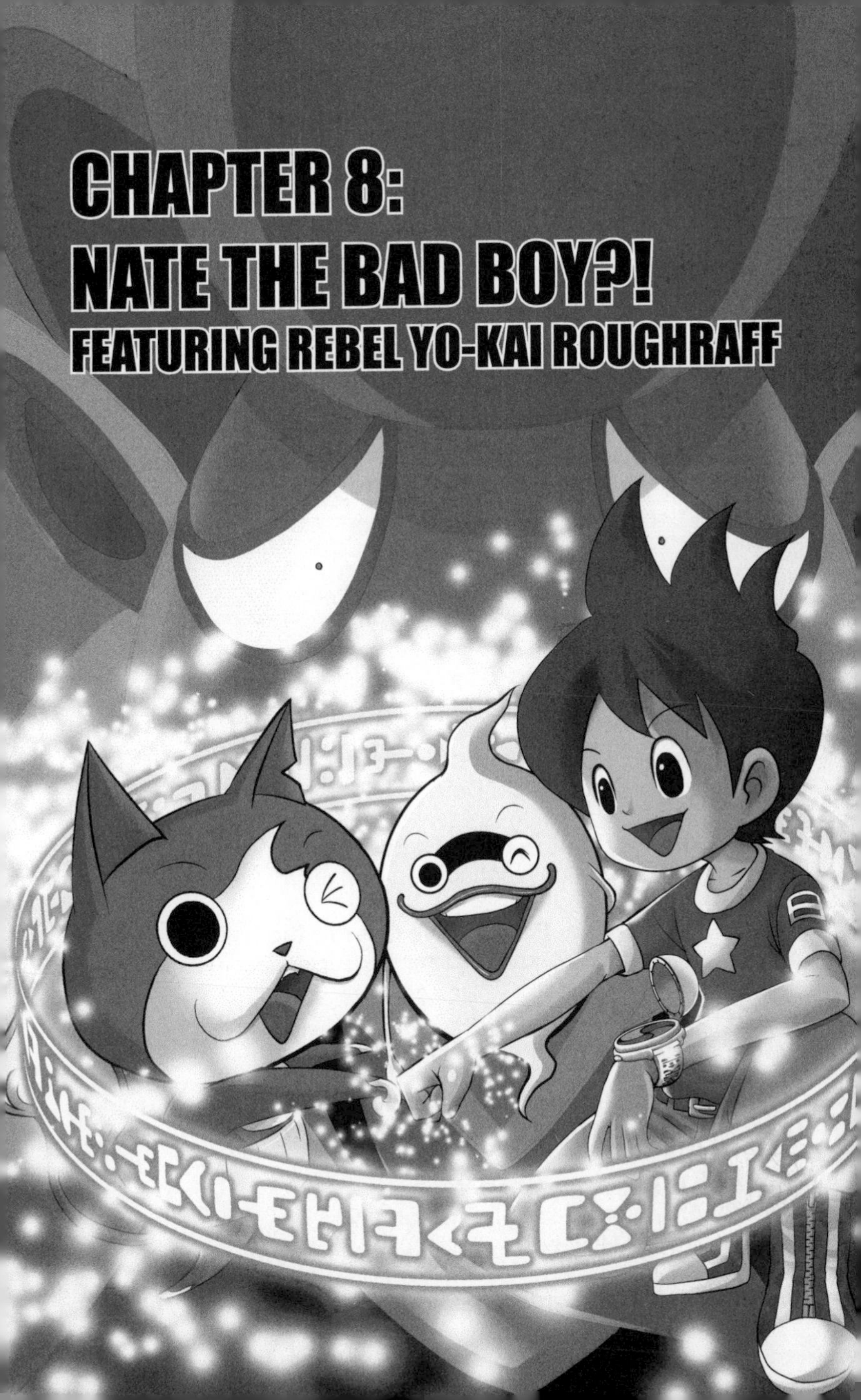

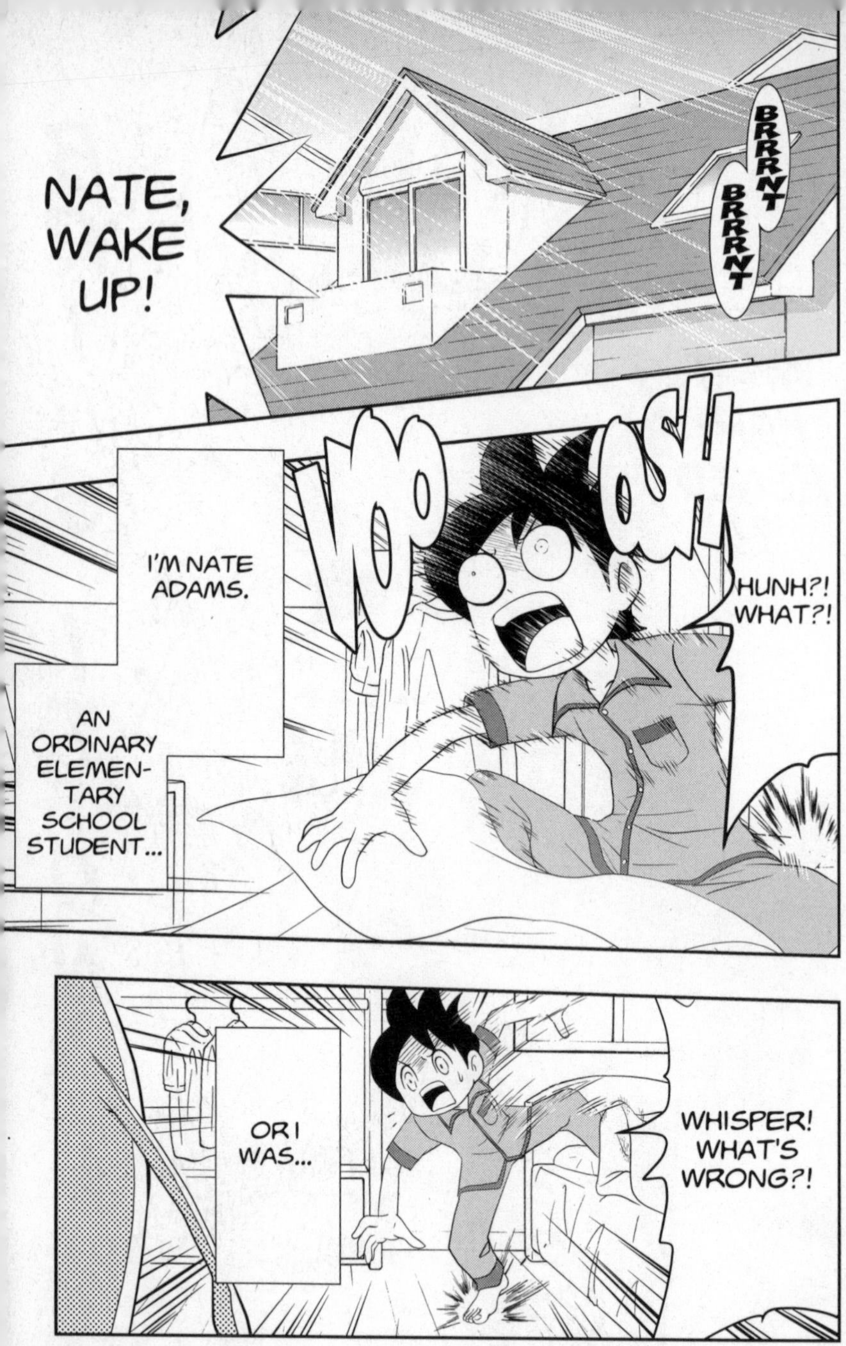
BRRRNT
BRRRNT
NATE, WAKE UP!
VOOOSH
HUNH?! WHAT?!
I'M NATE ADAMS.
AN ORDINARY ELEMENTARY SCHOOL STUDENT...
WHISPER! WHAT'S WRONG?!
OR I WAS...

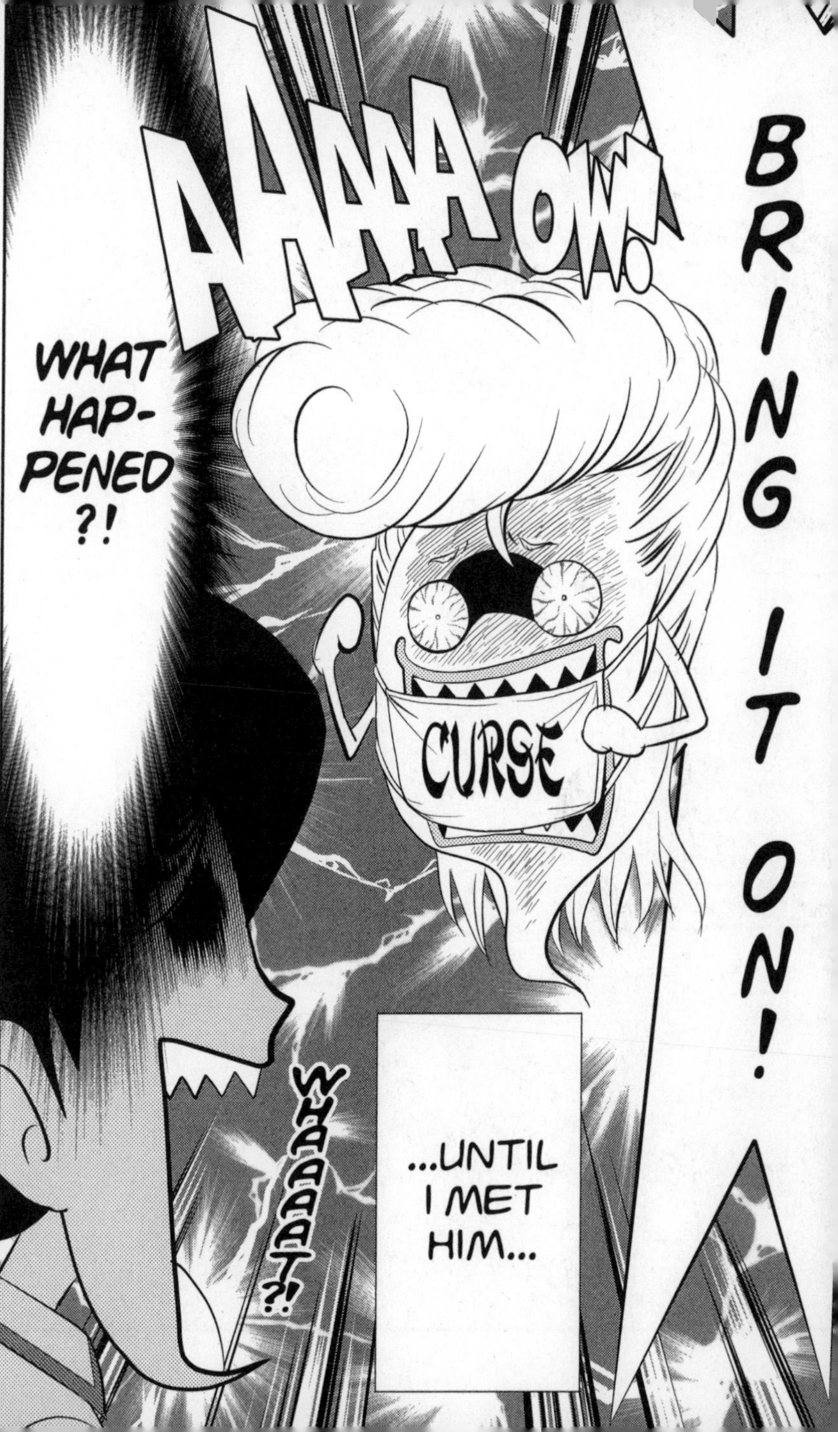
BRING IT ON!!
AAAA OW!!
CURSE
WHAT HAP-PENED?!
...UNTIL I MET HIM...
WHAAAAAT?!

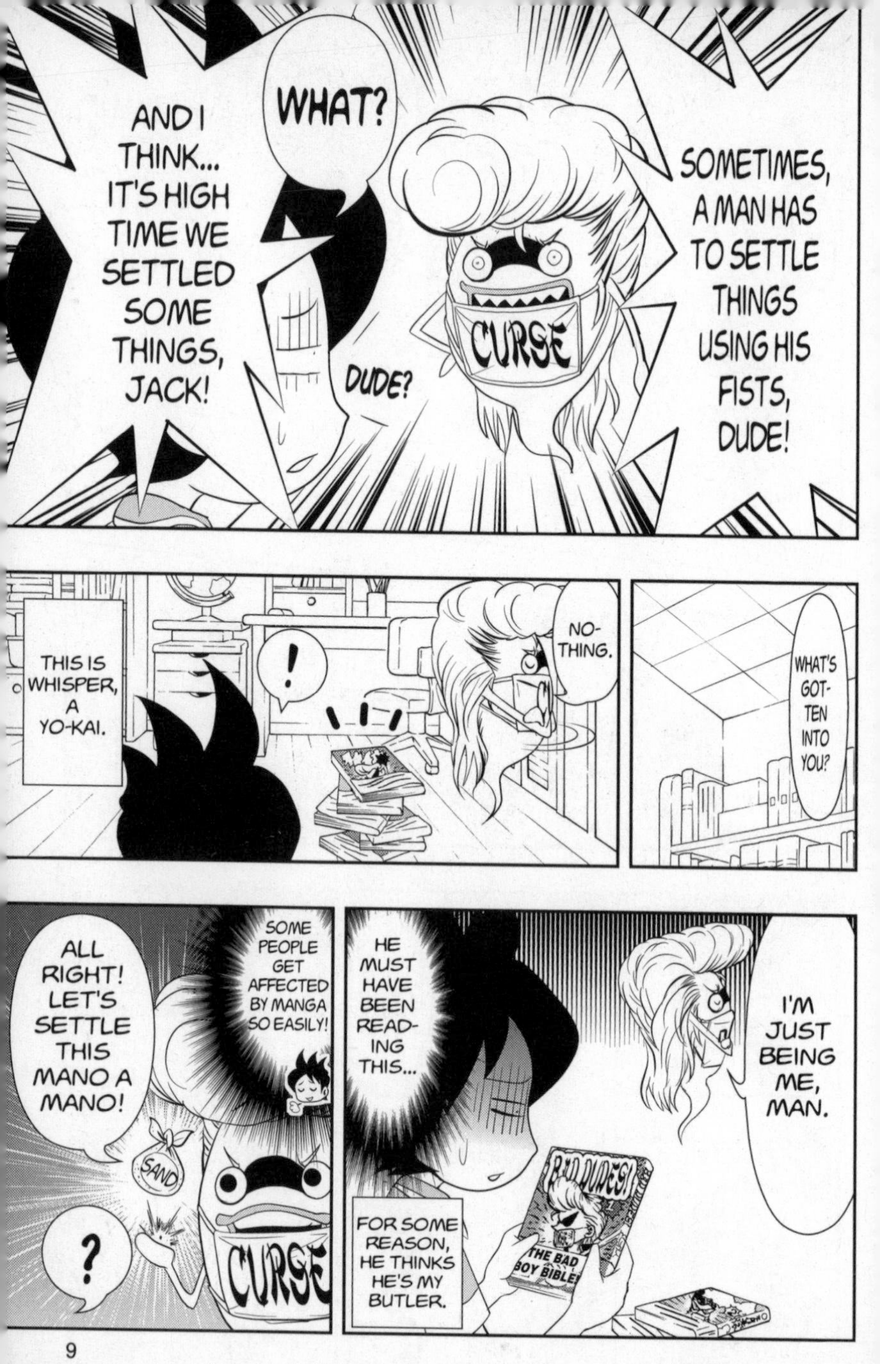
SOMETIMES, A MAN HAS TO SETTLE THINGS USING HIS FISTS, DUDE!
CURSE
WHAT?
DUDE?
AND I THINK... IT'S HIGH TIME WE SETTLED SOME THINGS, JACK!
WHAT'S GOT-TEN INTO YOU?
NO-THING.
!
THIS IS WHISPER, A YO-KAI.
I'M JUST BEING ME, MAN.
HE MUST HAVE BEEN READ-ING THIS...
BAD DUDES!
THE BAD BOY BIBLE!
FOR SOME REASON, HE THINKS HE'S MY BUTLER.
SOME PEOPLE GET AFFECTED BY MANGA SO EASILY!
ALL RIGHT! LET'S SETTLE THIS MANO A MANO!
SAND
?
CURSE

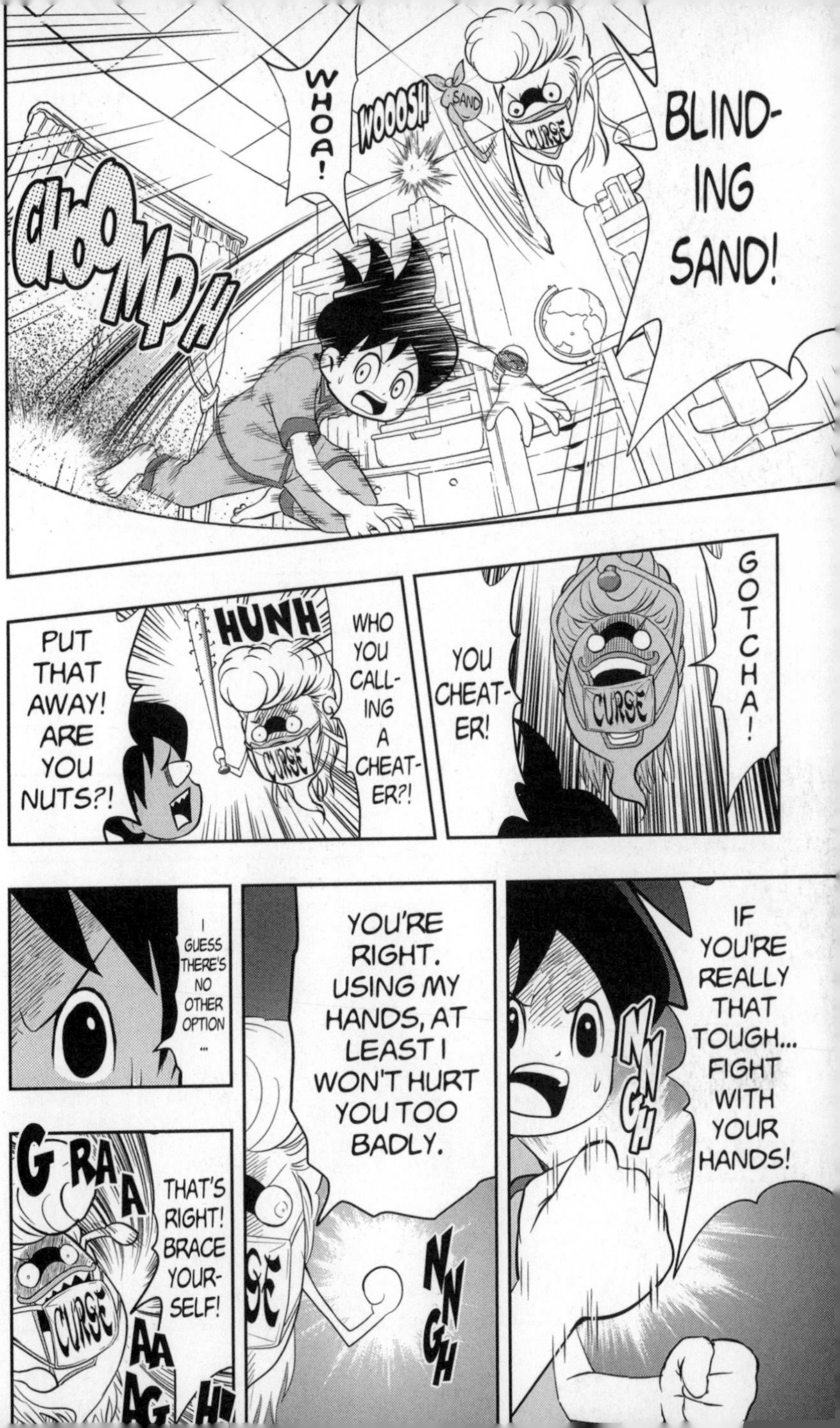
BLINDING SAND!
SAND
CURSE
WOOOSH
WHOA!
CHOOMPH
GOTCHA!
CURSE
YOU CHEATER!
WHO YOU CALLING A CHEATER?!
HUNH
CURSE
PUT THAT AWAY! ARE YOU NUTS?!
IF YOU'RE REALLY THAT TOUGH... FIGHT WITH YOUR HANDS!
NNGH
YOU'RE RIGHT. USING MY HANDS, AT LEAST I WON'T HURT YOU TOO BADLY.
NNGH
I GUESS THERE'S NO OTHER OPTION ...
THAT'S RIGHT! BRACE YOURSELF!
GRAAAAAGH!
CURSE

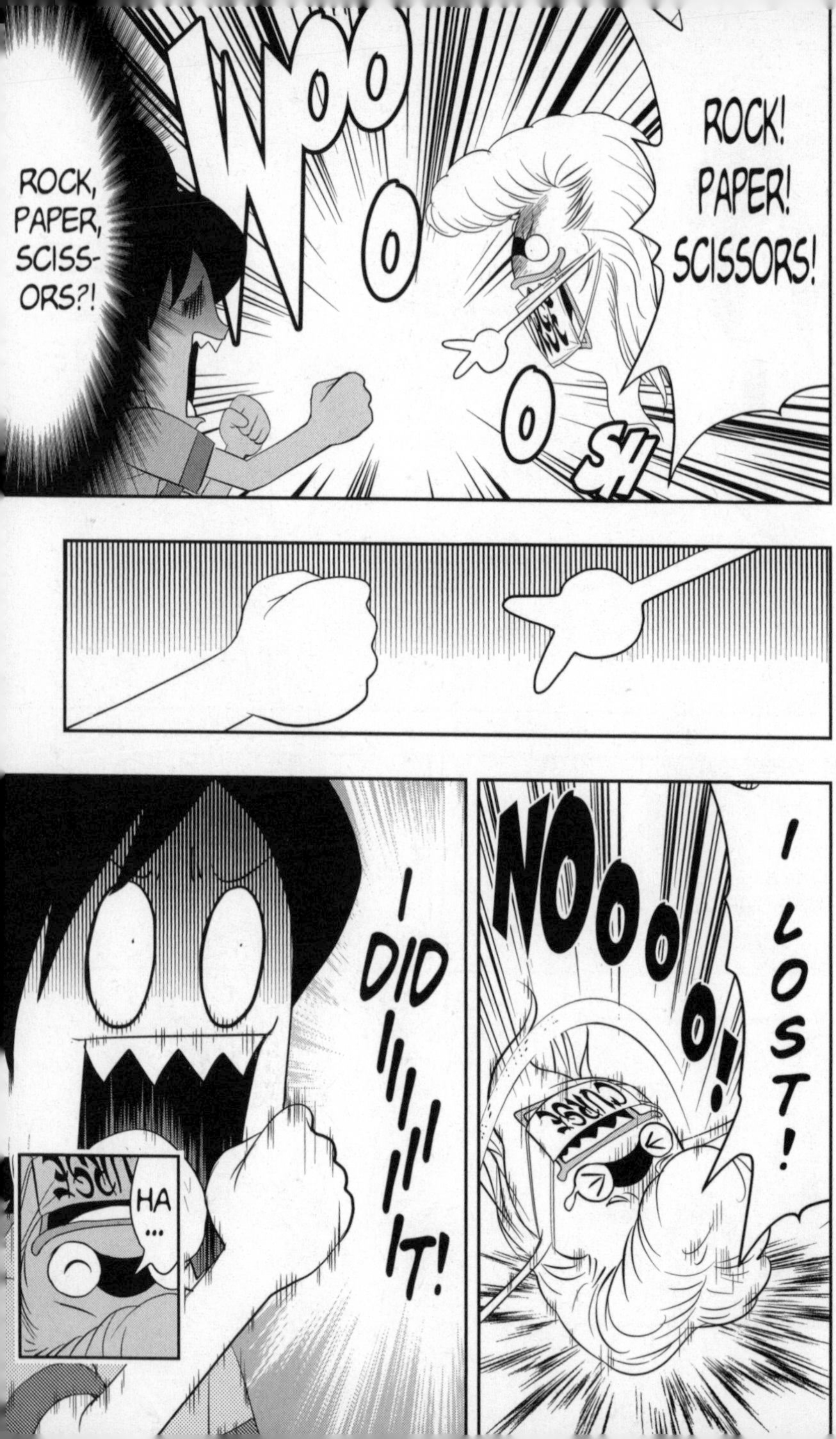
ROCK! PAPER! SCISSORS!
ROCK, PAPER, SCISS-ORS?!
WOOOOSH
NOOOOOO!
I LOST!
I DID IIIIIIIT!
HA...

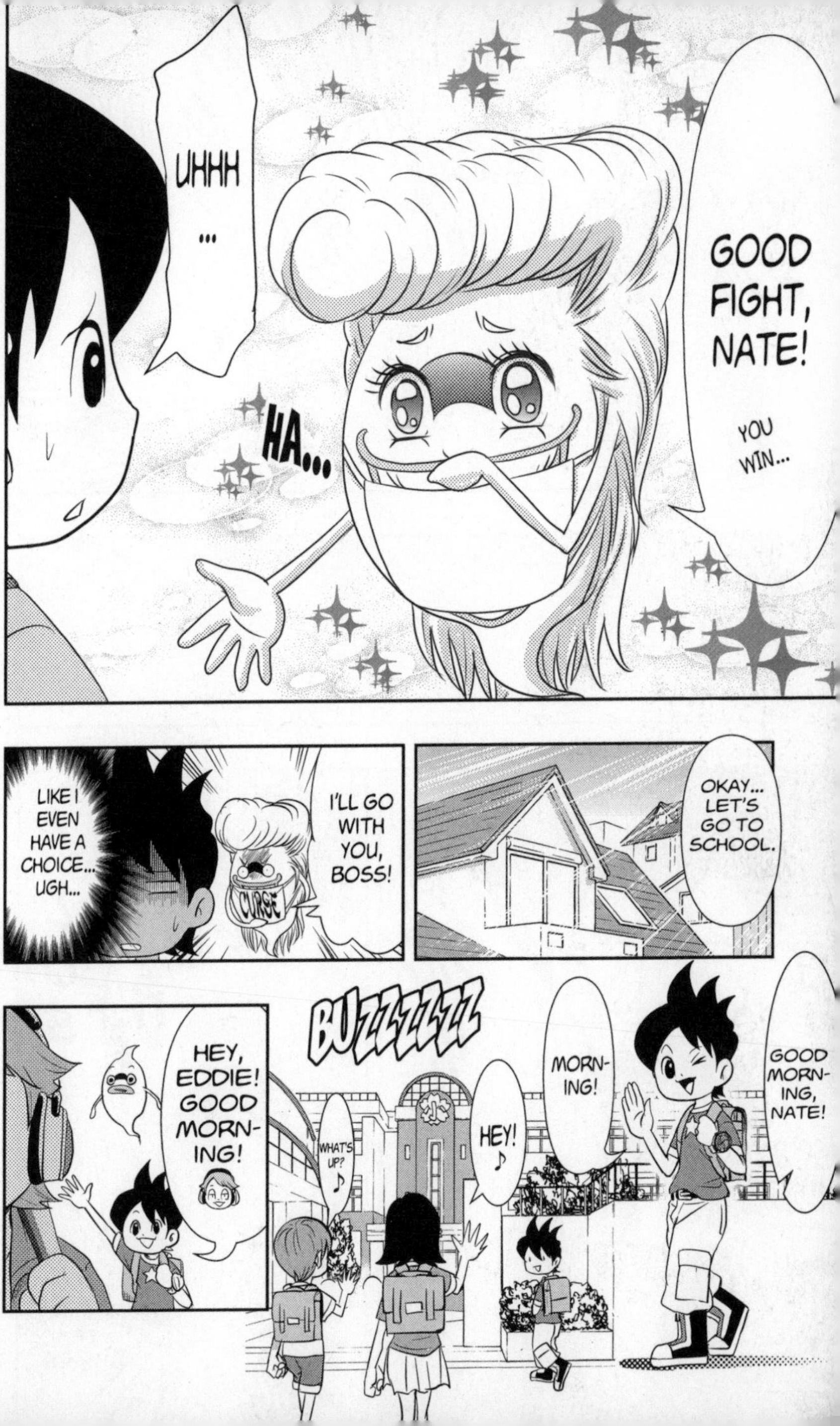
GOOD FIGHT, NATE!
YOU WIN...
HA...
UHHH ...
OKAY... LET'S GO TO SCHOOL.
I'LL GO WITH YOU, BOSS!
CURSE
LIKE I EVEN HAVE A CHOICE... UGH...
GOOD MORN-ING, NATE!
MORN-ING!
BUZZZZZZZ
HEY! ♪
WHAT'S UP? ♪
HEY, EDDIE! GOOD MORN-ING!

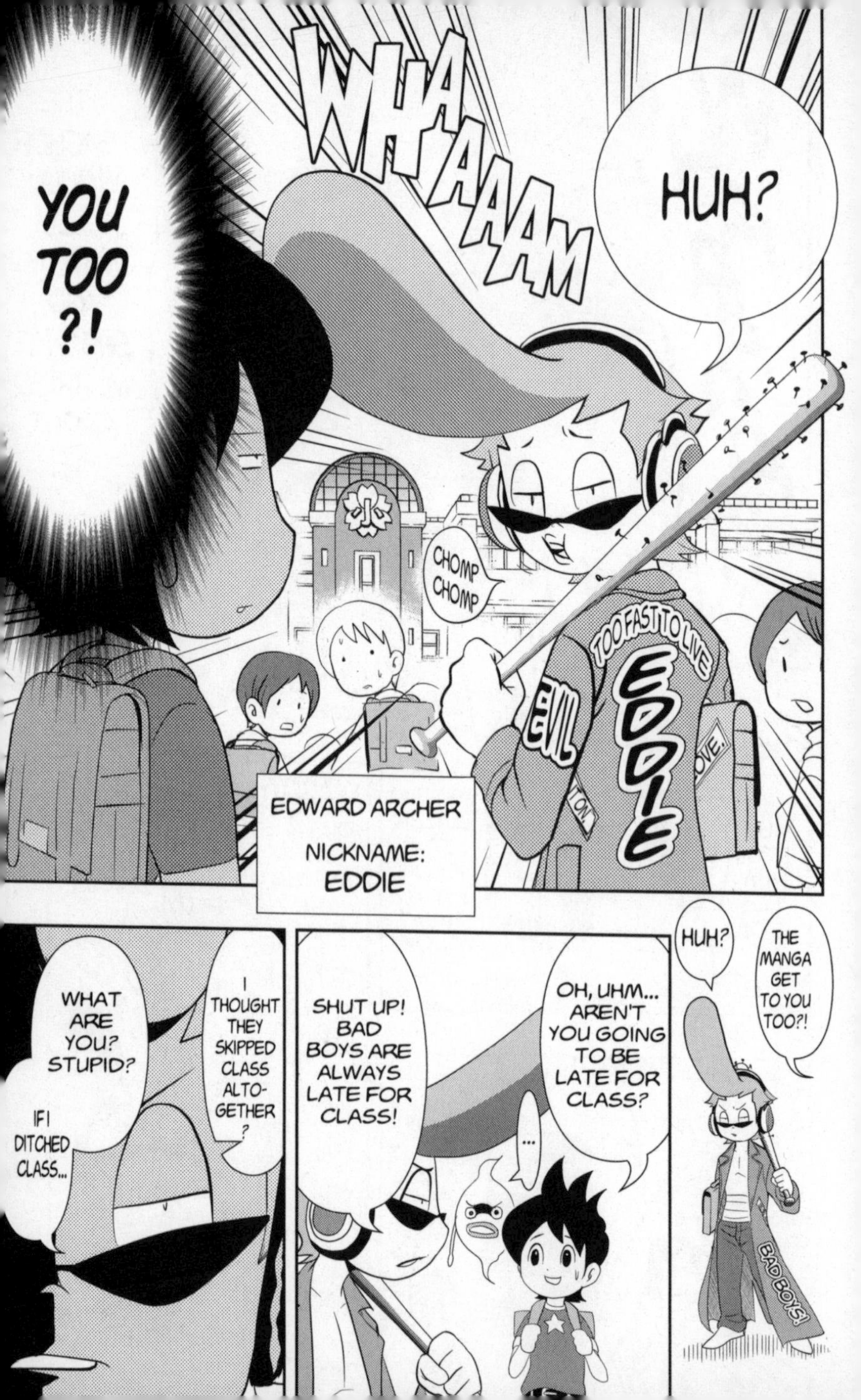
HUH?
WHAAAAM
YOU TOO ?!
CHOMP CHOMP
TOO FAST TO LIVE
EDDIE
EVIL
EDWARD ARCHER
NICKNAME: EDDIE
THE MANGA GET TO YOU TOO?!
HUH?
BAD BOYS!
OH, UHM... AREN'T YOU GOING TO BE LATE FOR CLASS?
SHUT UP! BAD BOYS ARE ALWAYS LATE FOR CLASS!
...
I THOUGHT THEY SKIPPED CLASS ALTOGETHER?
WHAT ARE YOU? STUPID?
IF I DITCHED CLASS...

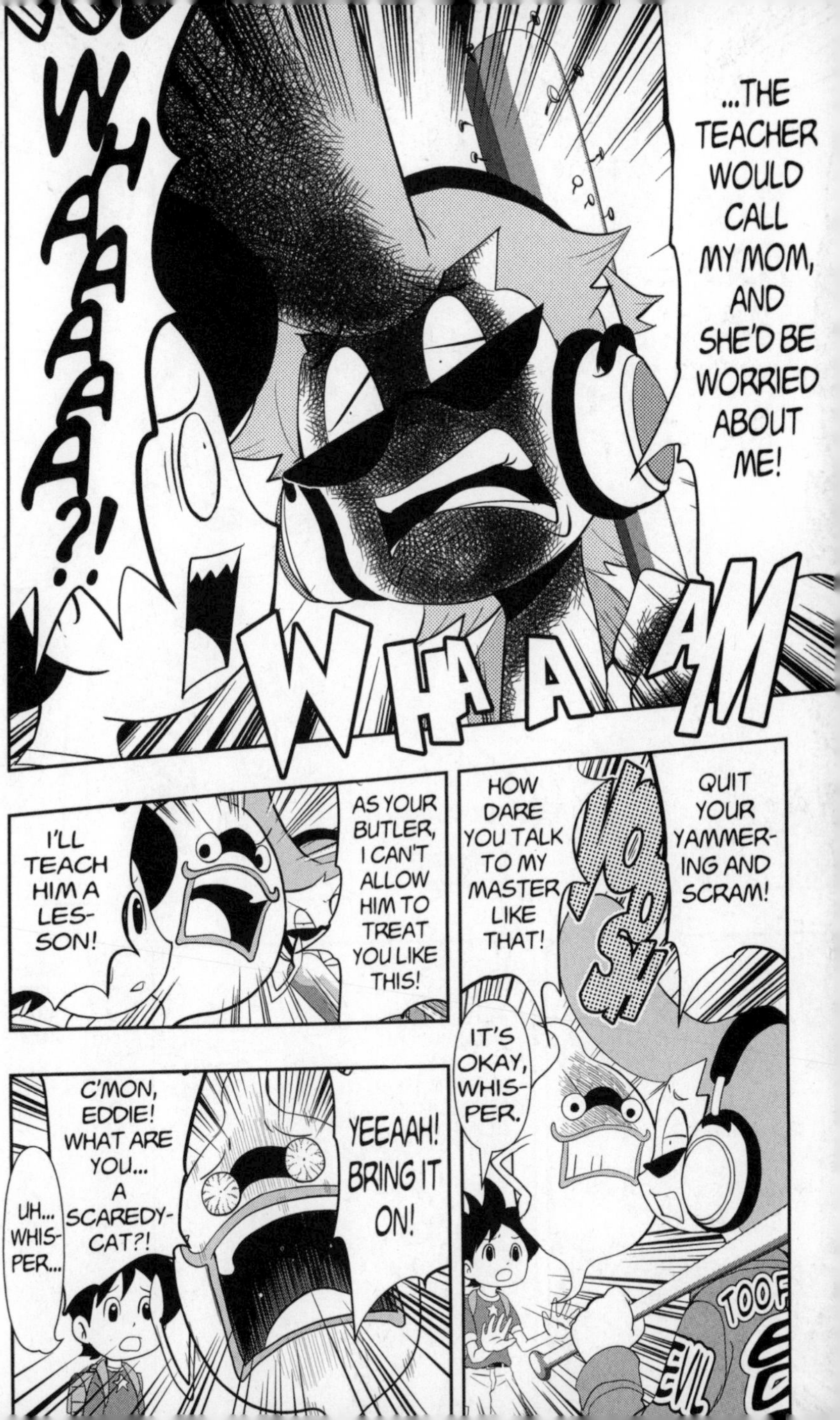
...THE TEACHER WOULD CALL MY MOM, AND SHE'D BE WORRIED ABOUT ME!
WHAAAAA?!
WHAAAM
QUIT YOUR YAMMER-ING AND SCRAM!
HOW DARE YOU TALK TO MY MASTER LIKE THAT!
AS YOUR BUTLER, I CAN'T ALLOW HIM TO TREAT YOU LIKE THIS!
I'LL TEACH HIM A LES-SON!
IT'S OKAY, WHIS-PER.
TOOF
YEEAAH! BRING IT ON!
C'MON, EDDIE! WHAT ARE YOU... A SCAREDY-CAT?!
UH... WHIS-PER...

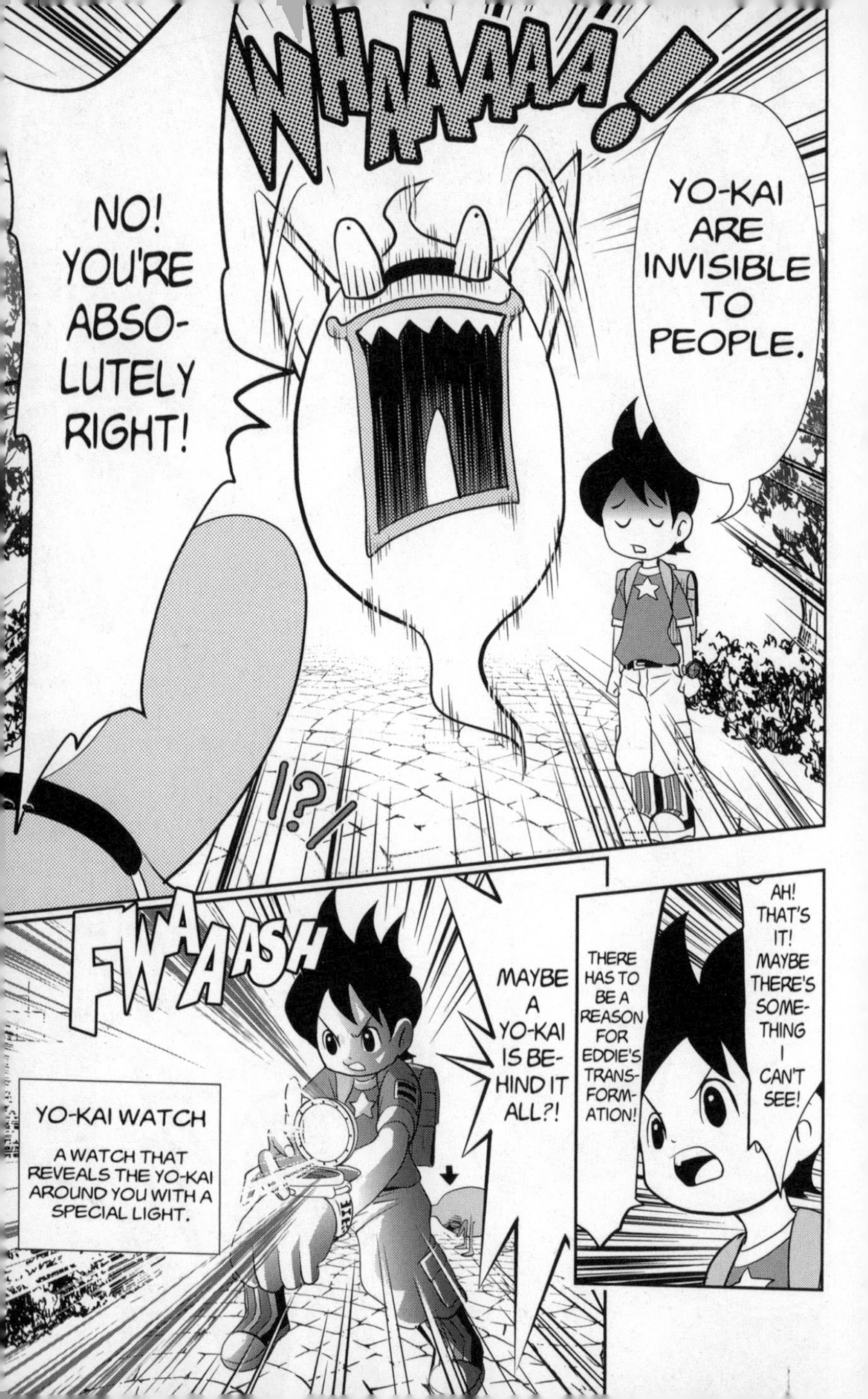
YO-KAI ARE INVISIBLE TO PEOPLE.
WHAAAAA!!
NO! YOU'RE ABSOLUTELY RIGHT!
!?
AH! THAT'S IT! MAYBE THERE'S SOMETHING I CAN'T SEE!
THERE HAS TO BE A REASON FOR EDDIE'S TRANSFORMATION!
MAYBE A YO-KAI IS BEHIND IT ALL?!
FWAAASH
YO-KAI WATCH
A WATCH THAT REVEALS THE YO-KAI AROUND YOU WITH A SPECIAL LIGHT.

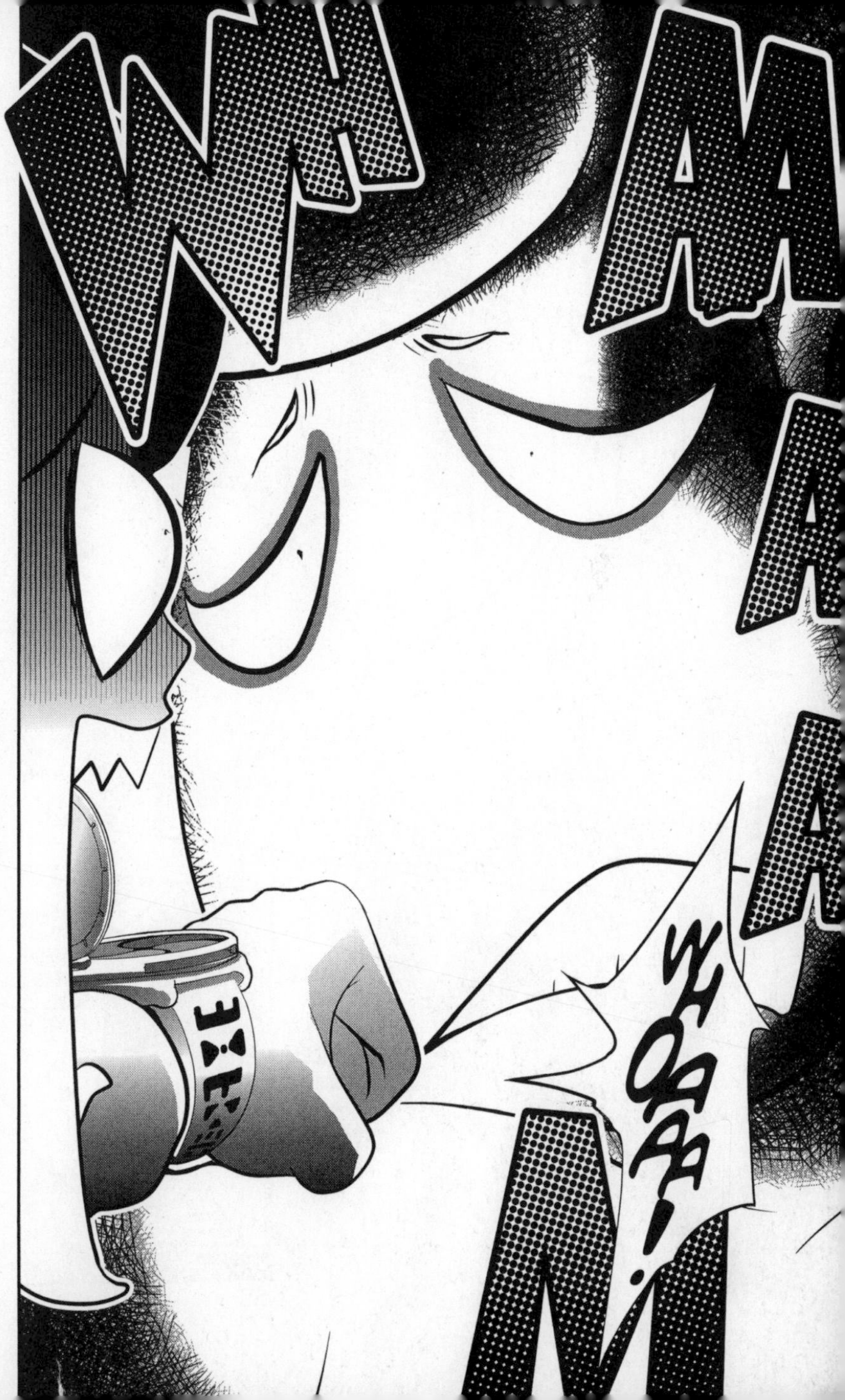
WHAAAM
SHOAA!

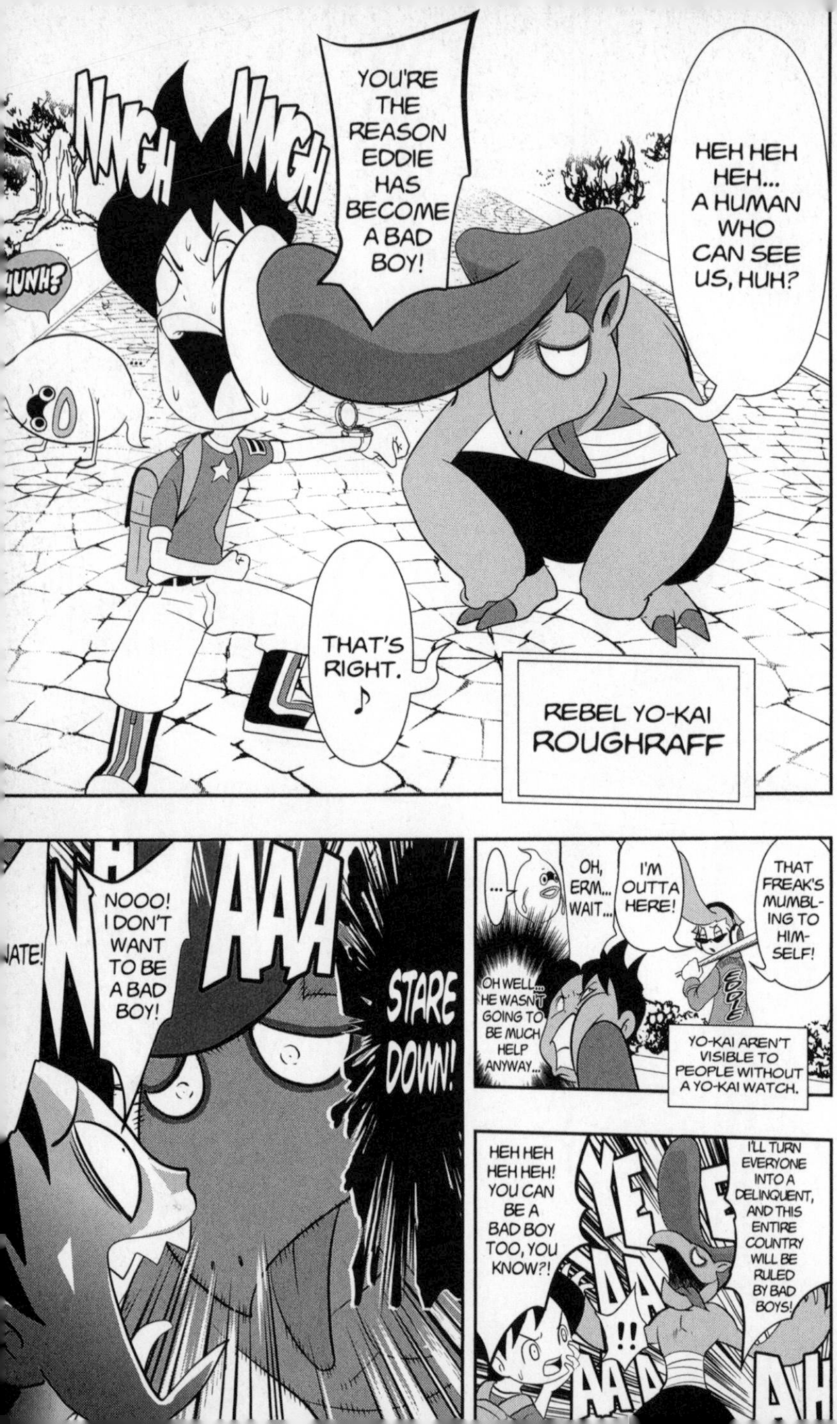
HEH HEH HEH... A HUMAN WHO CAN SEE US, HUH?
YOU'RE THE REASON EDDIE HAS BECOME A BAD BOY!
NNGH NNGH
HUNH?
...
THAT'S RIGHT. ♪
REBEL YO-KAI ROUGHRAFF
THAT FREAK'S MUMBLING TO HIMSELF!
I'M OUTTA HERE!
OH, ERM... WAIT...
...
YO-KAI AREN'T VISIBLE TO PEOPLE WITHOUT A YO-KAI WATCH.
OH WELL... HE WASN'T GOING TO BE MUCH HELP ANYWAY...
I'LL TURN EVERYONE INTO A DELINQUENT, AND THIS ENTIRE COUNTRY WILL BE RULED BY BAD BOYS!
HEH HEH HEH HEH! YOU CAN BE A BAD BOY TOO, YOU KNOW?!
!!
AH
STARE DOWN!
AAA
NOOO! I DON'T WANT TO BE A BAD BOY!

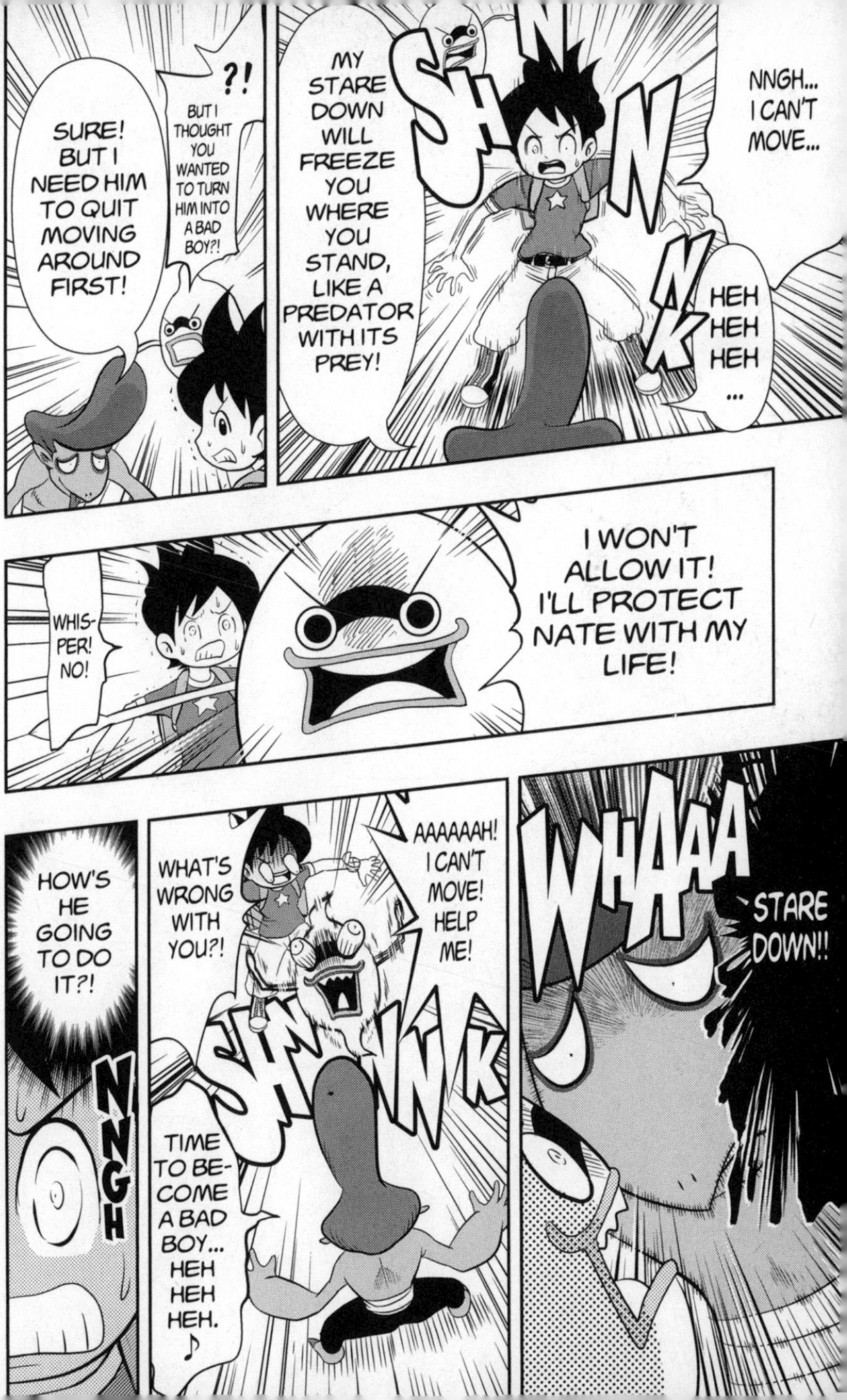
NNGH... I CAN'T MOVE...
SHNNNK
MY STARE DOWN WILL FREEZE YOU WHERE YOU STAND, LIKE A PREDATOR WITH ITS PREY!
HEH HEH HEH ...
?!
BUT I THOUGHT YOU WANTED TO TURN HIM INTO A BAD BOY?!
SURE! BUT I NEED HIM TO QUIT MOVING AROUND FIRST!
I WON'T ALLOW IT! I'LL PROTECT NATE WITH MY LIFE!
WHIS-PER! NO!
WHAAA
STARE DOWN!!
AAAAAAH! I CAN'T MOVE! HELP ME!
WHAT'S WRONG WITH YOU?!
SHNNNK
TIME TO BE-COME A BAD BOY... HEH HEH HEH. ♪
HOW'S HE GOING TO DO IT?!
NNGH

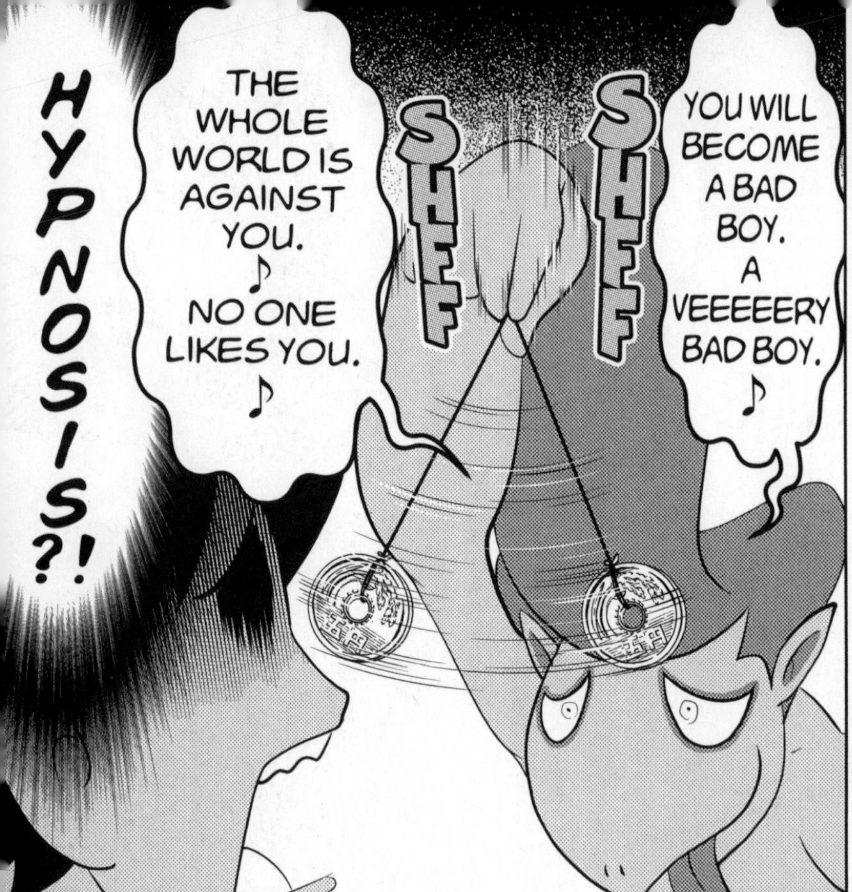
YOU WILL BECOME A BAD BOY. A VEEEEEERY BAD BOY. ♪
SHFF
SHFF
THE WHOLE WORLD IS AGAINST YOU. ♪ NO ONE LIKES YOU. ♪
HYPNOSIS?!
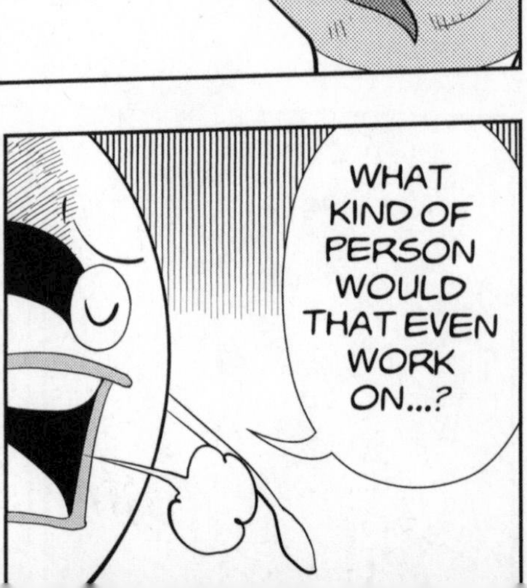
WHAT KIND OF PERSON WOULD THAT EVEN WORK ON...?
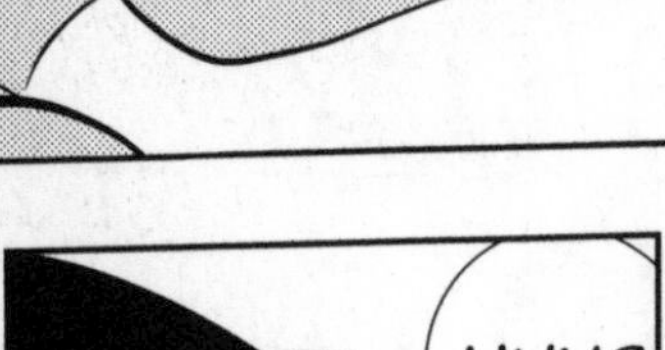
HUH?

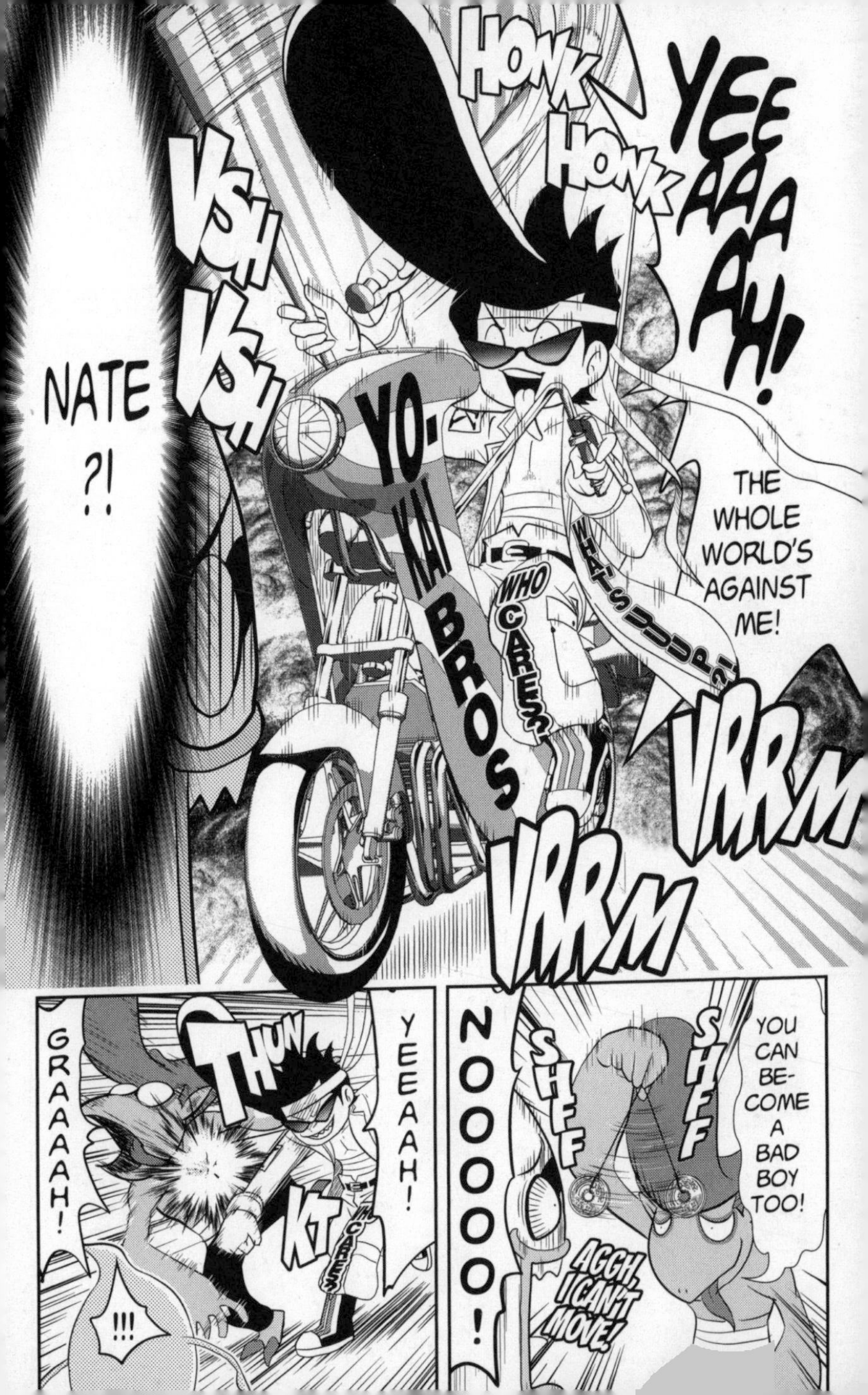
YEE AAAA AH!
HONK HONK
VSH VSH
THE WHOLE WORLD'S AGAINST ME!
WHO CARES
YO-KAI BROS
VRRM
VRRM
NATE ?!
YOU CAN BE-COME A BAD BOY TOO!
SHFF
SHFF
NOOOOOO!
AGGH, I CAN'T MOVE!
YEEAAAH!
THUN
GRAAAAAH!
KT
WHO CARES
!!!

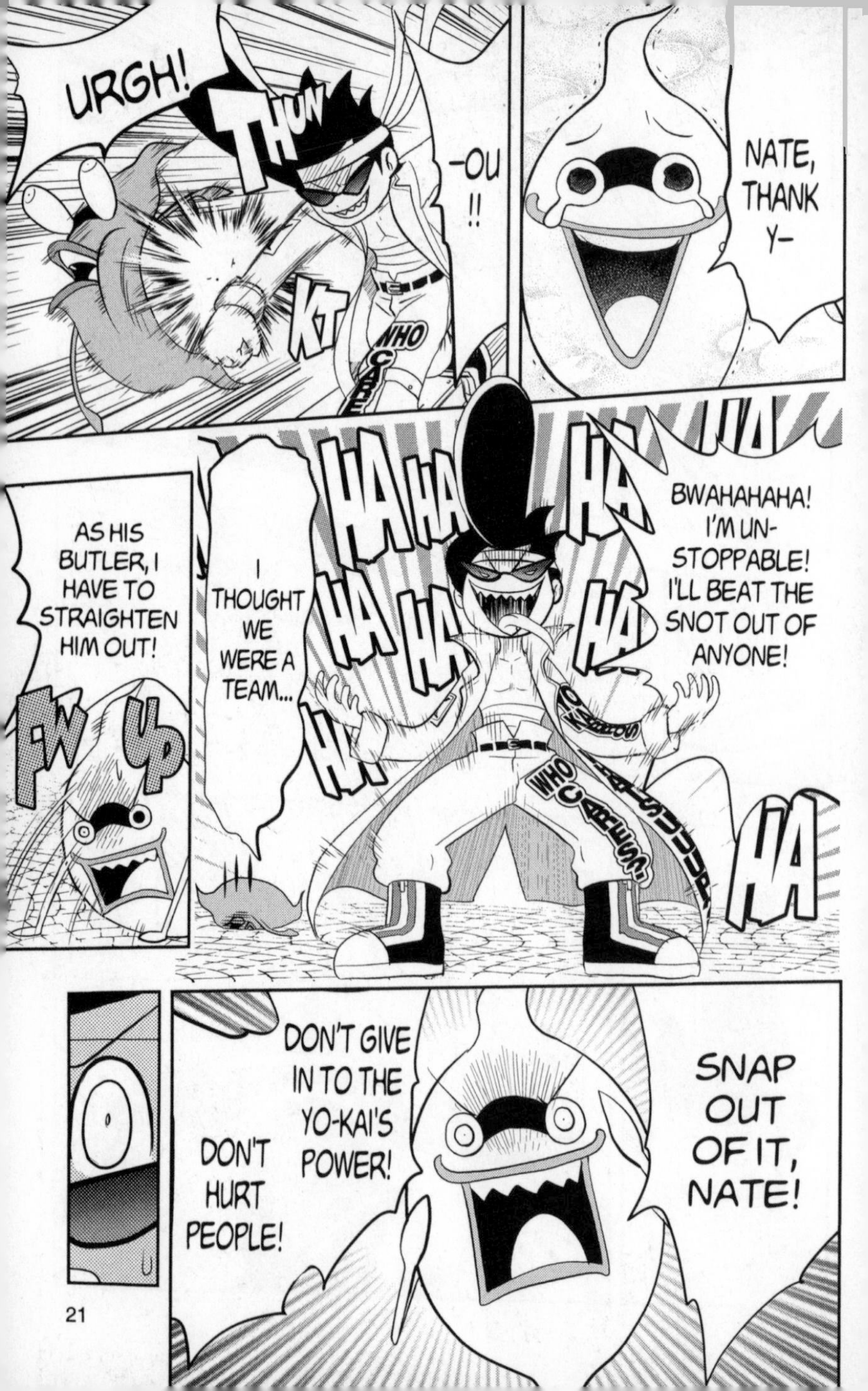
NATE, THANK Y–
–OU !!
THUN
URGH!
KT
WHO CARE
HA HA HA HA
BWAHAHAHA! I'M UN-STOPPABLE! I'LL BEAT THE SNOT OUT OF ANYONE!
HA HA HA HA HA
I THOUGHT WE WERE A TEAM...
WHO CARES
HA
AS HIS BUTLER, I HAVE TO STRAIGHTEN HIM OUT!
FW UP
SNAP OUT OF IT, NATE!
DON'T GIVE IN TO THE YO-KAI'S POWER!
DON'T HURT PEOPLE!

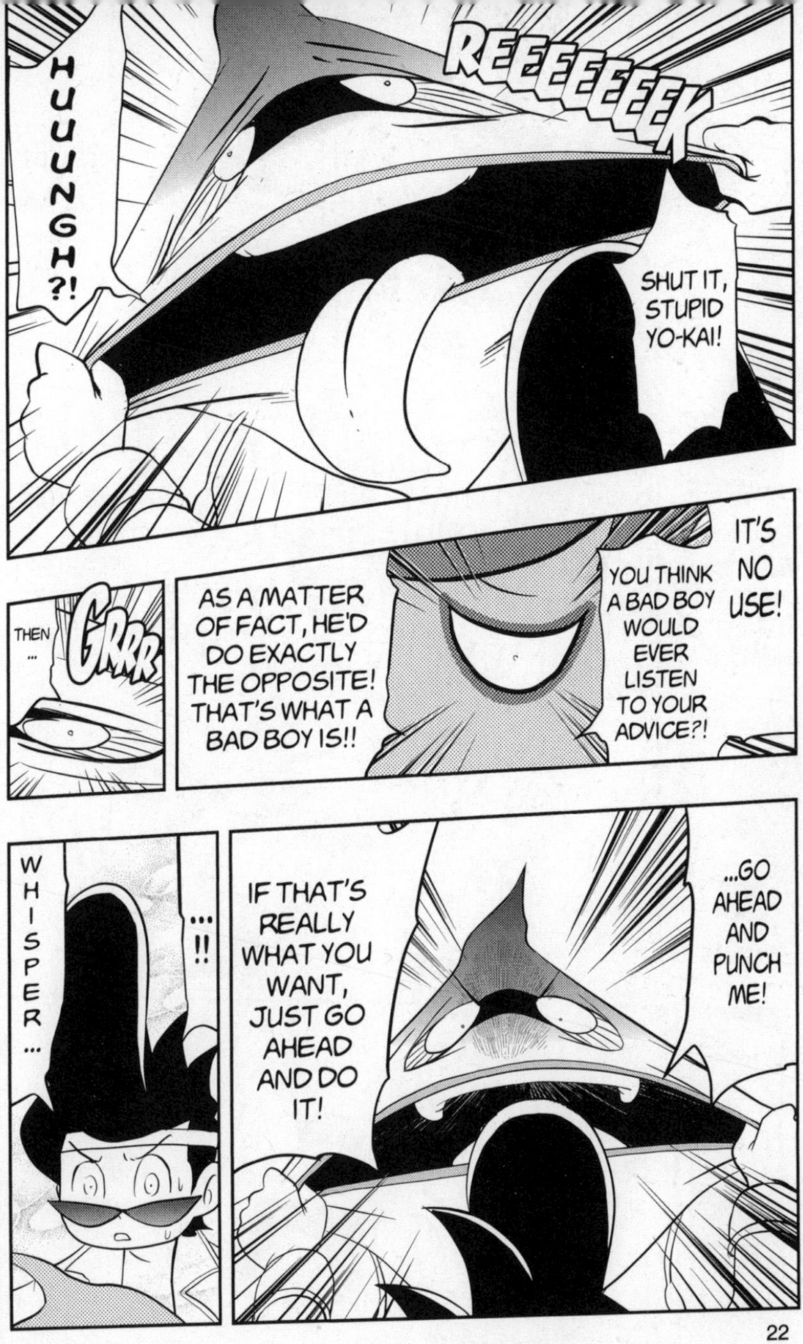
REEEEEEEEK
SHUT IT, STUPID YO-KAI!
HUUUNGH?!
IT'S NO USE!
YOU THINK A BAD BOY WOULD EVER LISTEN TO YOUR ADVICE?!
AS A MATTER OF FACT, HE'D DO EXACTLY THE OPPOSITE! THAT'S WHAT A BAD BOY IS!!
GRRR
THEN...
...GO AHEAD AND PUNCH ME!
IF THAT'S REALLY WHAT YOU WANT, JUST GO AHEAD AND DO IT!
...!!
WHISPER...

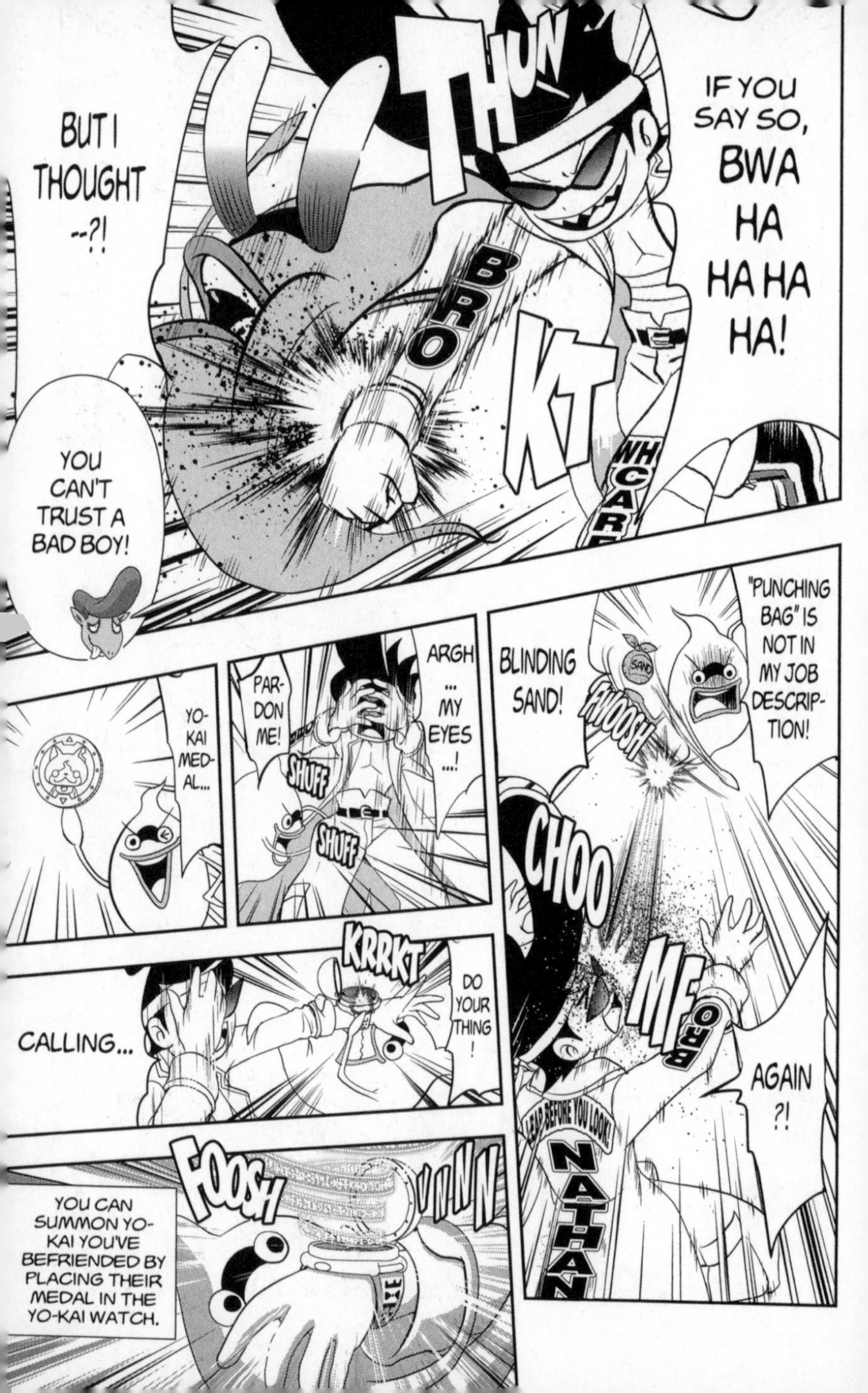

IF YOU SAY SO, BWA HA HA HA HA!
THUN
BRO
KT
BUT I THOUGHT --?!
YOU CAN'T TRUST A BAD BOY!
"PUNCHING BAG" IS NOT IN MY JOB DESCRIPTION!
BLINDING SAND!
FWOOSH
SAND
CHOO
MF
AGAIN ?!
LEAP BEFORE YOU LOOK!
NATHAN
ARGH ... MY EYES ...!
PAR-DON ME!
SHUFF
SHUFF
YO-KAI MED-AL...
KRRKT
DO YOUR THING !
CALLING...
VNNN
FOOSH
YOU CAN SUMMON YO-KAI YOU'VE BEFRIENDED BY PLACING THEIR MEDAL IN THE YO-KAI WATCH.

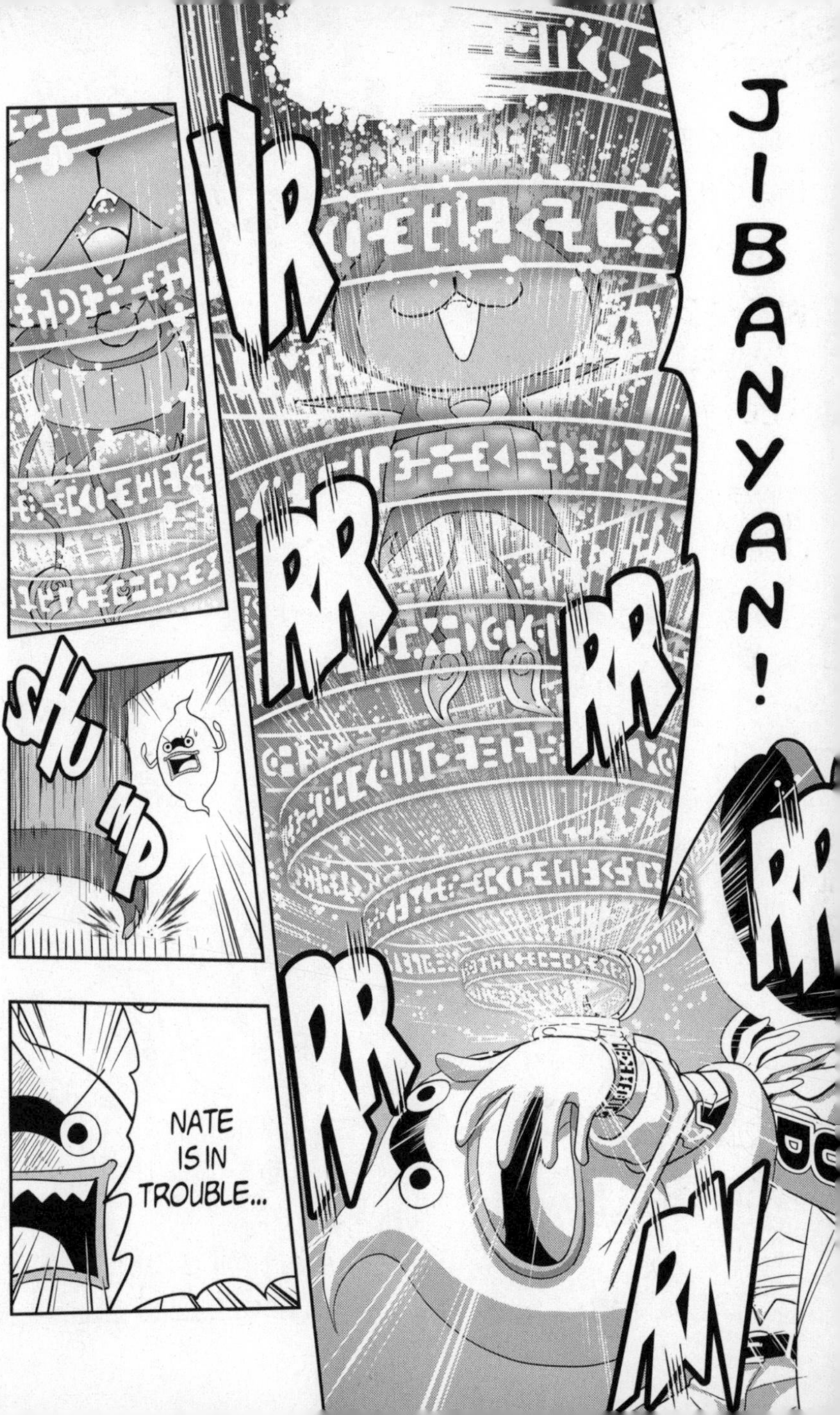
JIBANYAN!
VRRRRRRRRRRN
SHUMP
NATE IS IN TROUBLE...

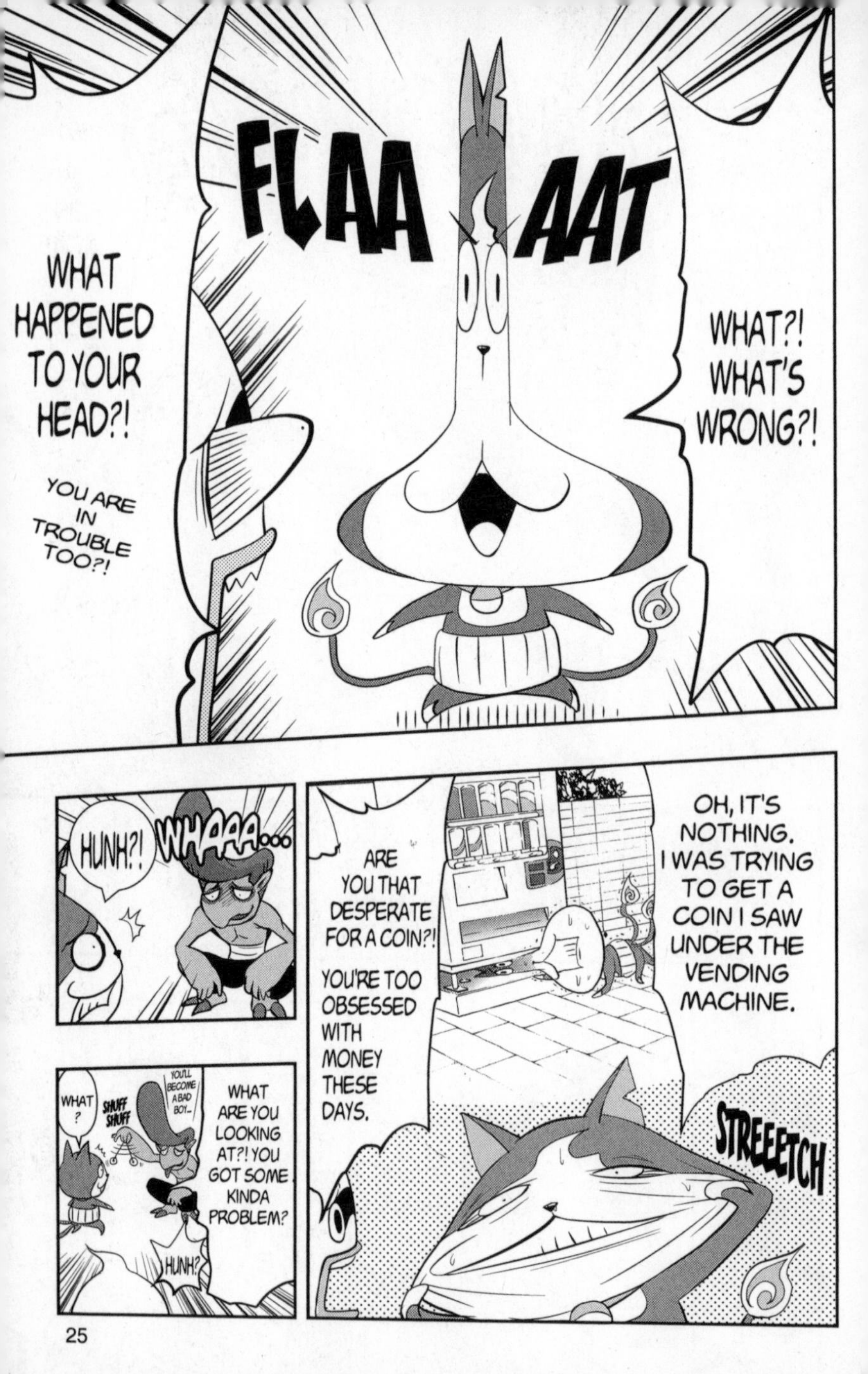
WHAT?! WHAT'S WRONG?!
FLAA AAT
WHAT HAPPENED TO YOUR HEAD?!
YOU ARE IN TROUBLE TOO?!
OH, IT'S NOTHING. I WAS TRYING TO GET A COIN I SAW UNDER THE VENDING MACHINE.
ARE YOU THAT DESPERATE FOR A COIN?!
YOU'RE TOO OBSESSED WITH MONEY THESE DAYS.
STREEETCH
WHAAA...
HUNH?!
WHAT ARE YOU LOOKING AT?! YOU GOT SOME KINDA PROBLEM?
YOU'LL BECOME A BAD BOY...
SHUFF SHUFF
WHAT ?
HUNH?

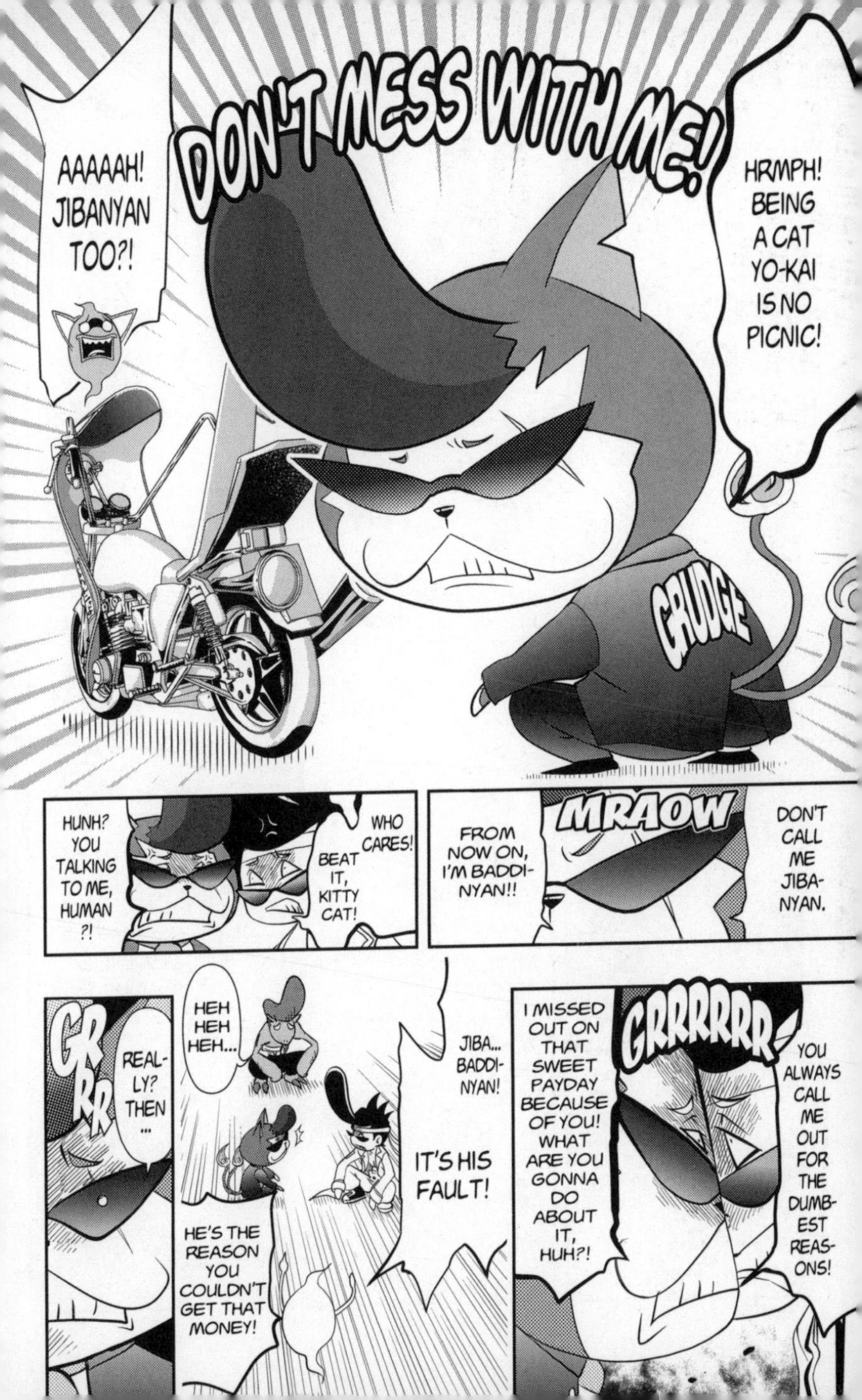
HRMPH! BEING A CAT YO-KAI IS NO PICNIC!
DON'T MESS WITH ME!!
AAAAAH! JIBANYAN TOO?!
MRAOW
DON'T CALL ME JIBA-NYAN.
FROM NOW ON, I'M BADDI-NYAN!!
WHO CARES!
BEAT IT, KITTY CAT!
HUNH? YOU TALKING TO ME, HUMAN?!
GRRRRRR-
YOU ALWAYS CALL ME OUT FOR THE DUMB-EST REAS-ONS!
I MISSED OUT ON THAT SWEET PAYDAY BECAUSE OF YOU! WHAT ARE YOU GONNA DO ABOUT IT, HUH?!
JIBA... BADDI-NYAN!
IT'S HIS FAULT!
HEH HEH HEH...
HE'S THE REASON YOU COULDN'T GET THAT MONEY!
GRRR
REAL-LY? THEN ...

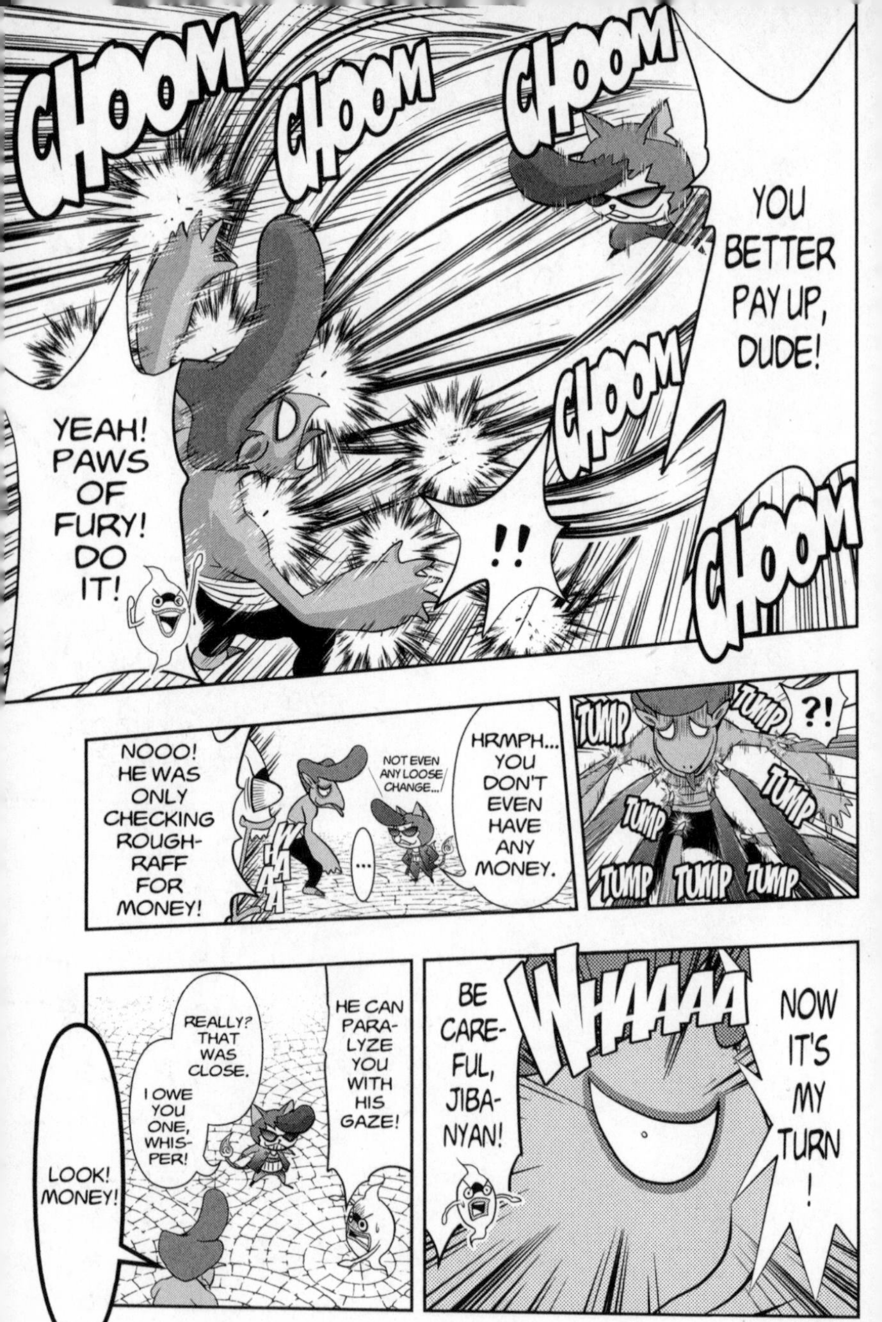
CHOOM
CHOOM
CHOOM
YOU BETTER PAY UP, DUDE!
CHOOM
CHOOM
!!
YEAH! PAWS OF FURY! DO IT!
?!
TUMP
TUMP
TUMP
TUMP
TUMP TUMP TUMP
TUMP
HRMPH... YOU DON'T EVEN HAVE ANY MONEY.
NOT EVEN ANY LOOSE CHANGE...
...
WHAAA
NOOO! HE WAS ONLY CHECKING ROUGH-RAFF FOR MONEY!
NOW IT'S MY TURN!
WHAAAA
BE CARE-FUL, JIBA-NYAN!
HE CAN PARA-LYZE YOU WITH HIS GAZE!
REALLY? THAT WAS CLOSE.
I OWE YOU ONE, WHIS-PER!
LOOK! MONEY!

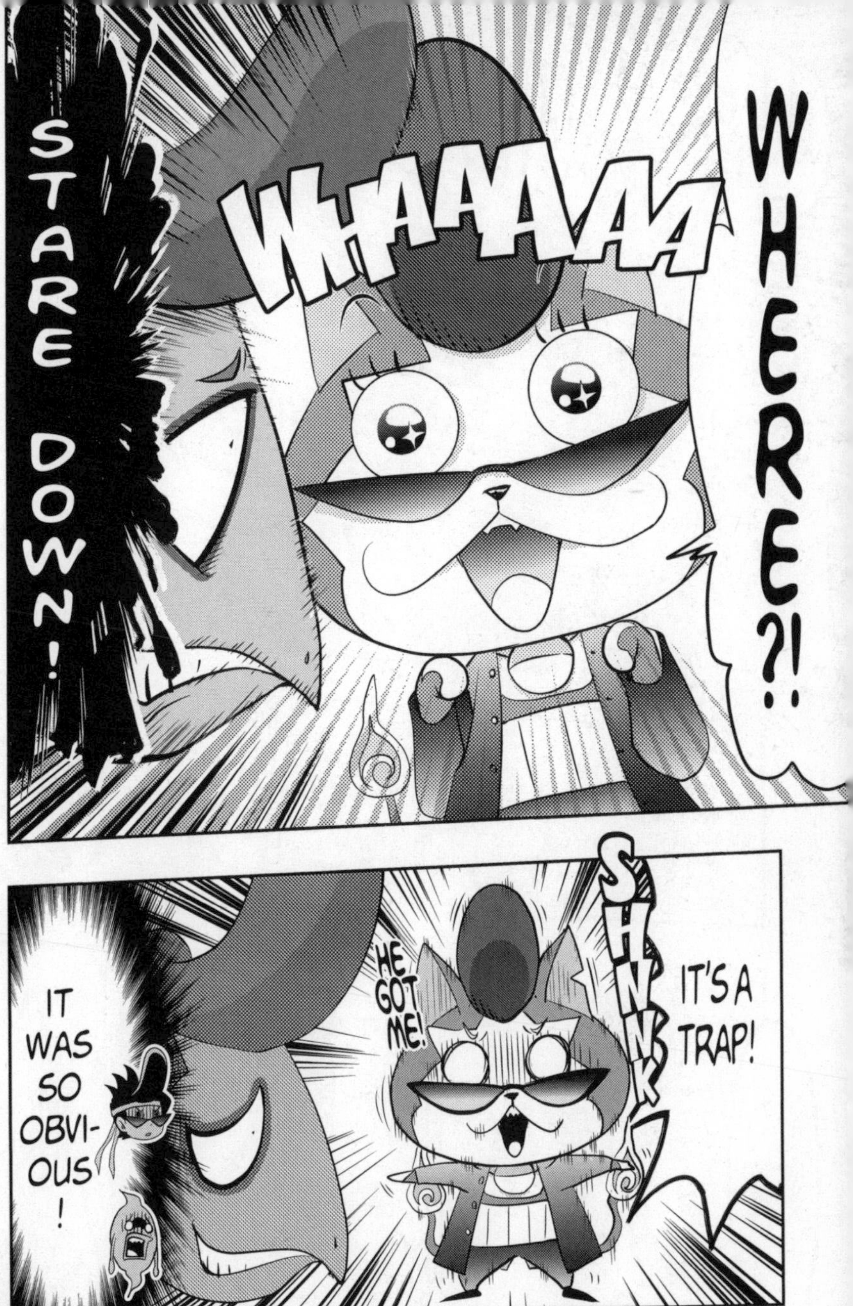
WHERE?!
WHAAAAAA
STARE DOWN!
SHNNK
IT'S A TRAP!
HE GOT ME!
IT WAS SO OBVI-OUS!

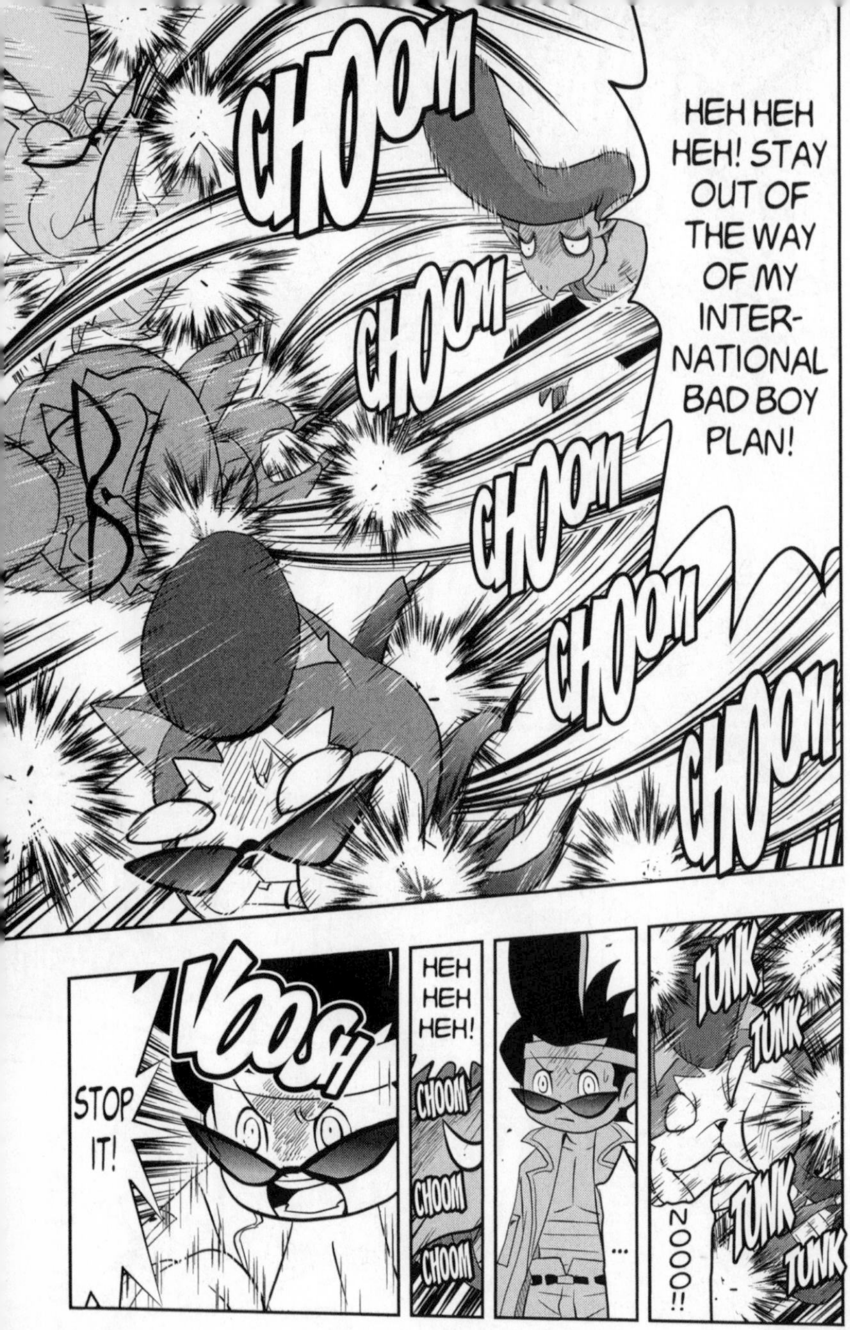
HEH HEH HEH! STAY OUT OF THE WAY OF MY INTER-NATIONAL BAD BOY PLAN!
CHOOM
CHOOM
CHOOM
CHOOM
CHOOM
TUNK
TUNK
TUNK
TUNK
NOOOO!!
...
HEH HEH HEH!
CHOOM
CHOOM
CHOOM
VOOSH
STOP IT!

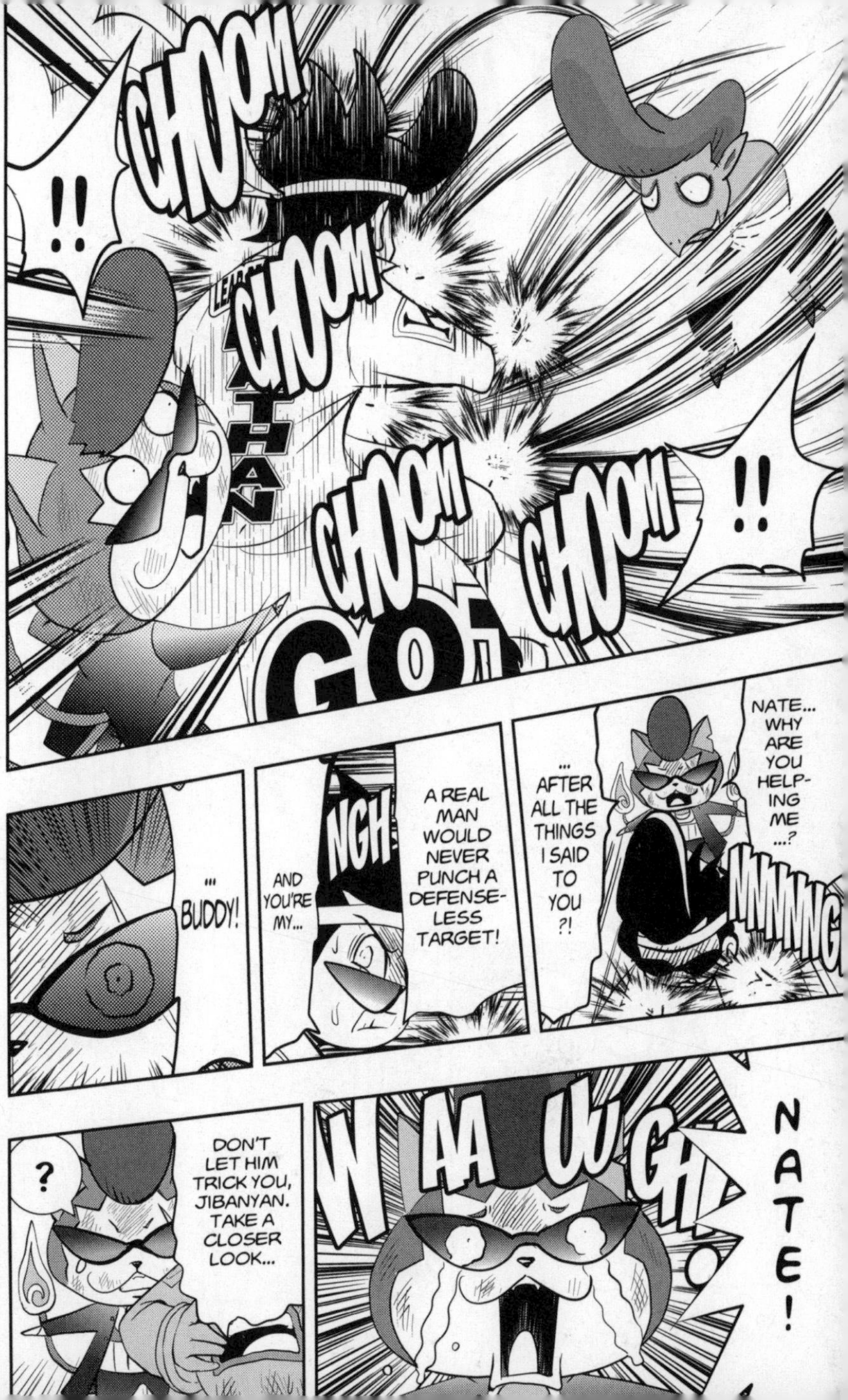
CHOOM
!!
CHOOM
CHOOM
CHOOM
!!
NATE... WHY ARE YOU HELPING ME ...?
MNNNNG
... AFTER ALL THE THINGS I SAID TO YOU ?!
A REAL MAN WOULD NEVER PUNCH A DEFENSELESS TARGET!
NGH
AND YOU'RE MY...
... BUDDY!
NATE!
WAAUUGH
DON'T LET HIM TRICK YOU, JIBANYAN. TAKE A CLOSER LOOK...
?

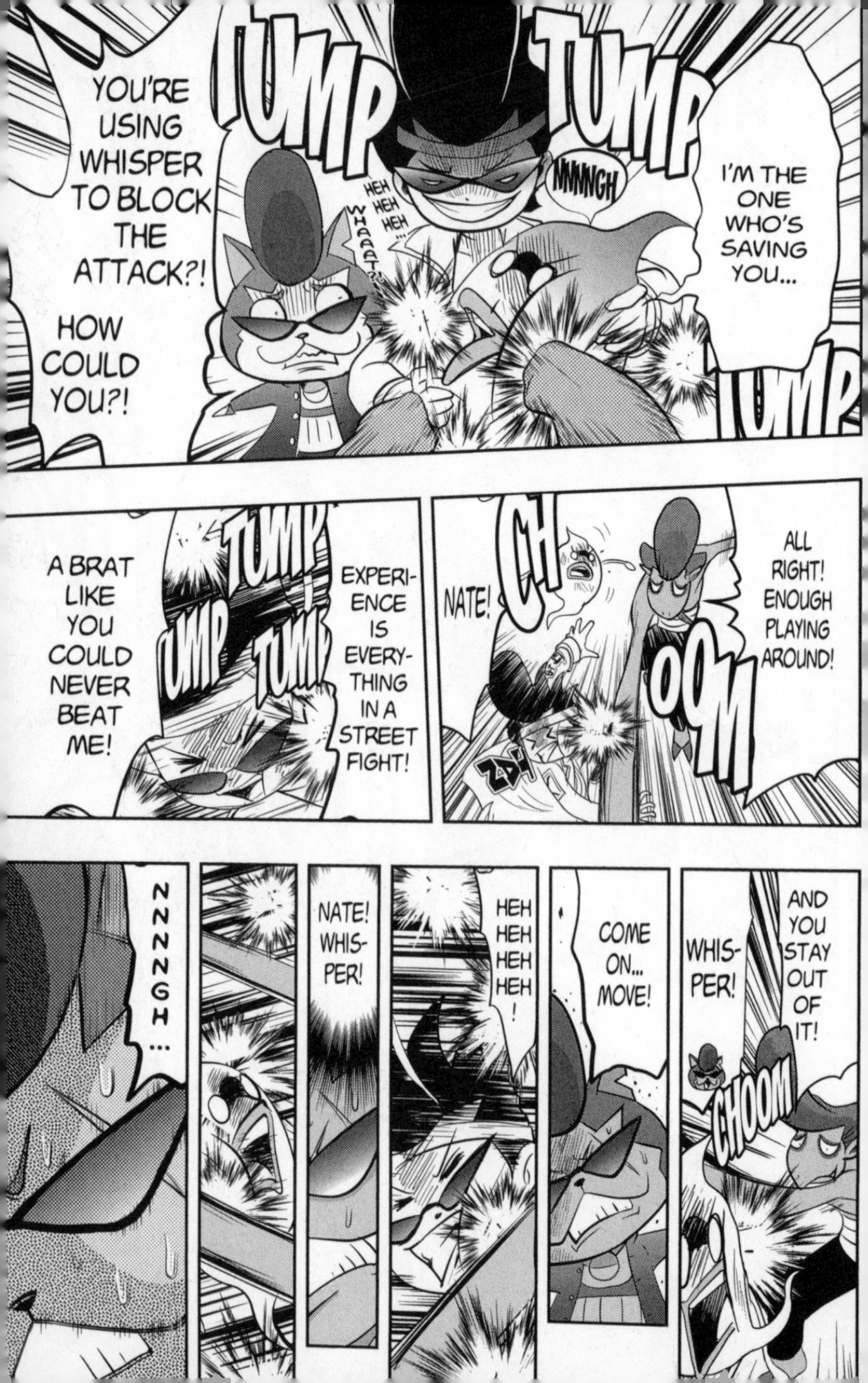
TUMP
TUMP
I'M THE ONE WHO'S SAVING YOU...
MNNNGH
HEH HEH HEH...
WHAAAAT?!
YOU'RE USING WHISPER TO BLOCK THE ATTACK?!
HOW COULD YOU?!
ALL RIGHT! ENOUGH PLAYING AROUND!
NATE!
TUMP
EXPERIENCE IS EVERYTHING IN A STREET FIGHT!
A BRAT LIKE YOU COULD NEVER BEAT ME!
AND YOU STAY OUT OF IT!
WHIS-PER!
CHOOM
COME ON... MOVE!
HEH HEH HEH HEH!
NATE! WHIS-PER!
NNNNNGH...

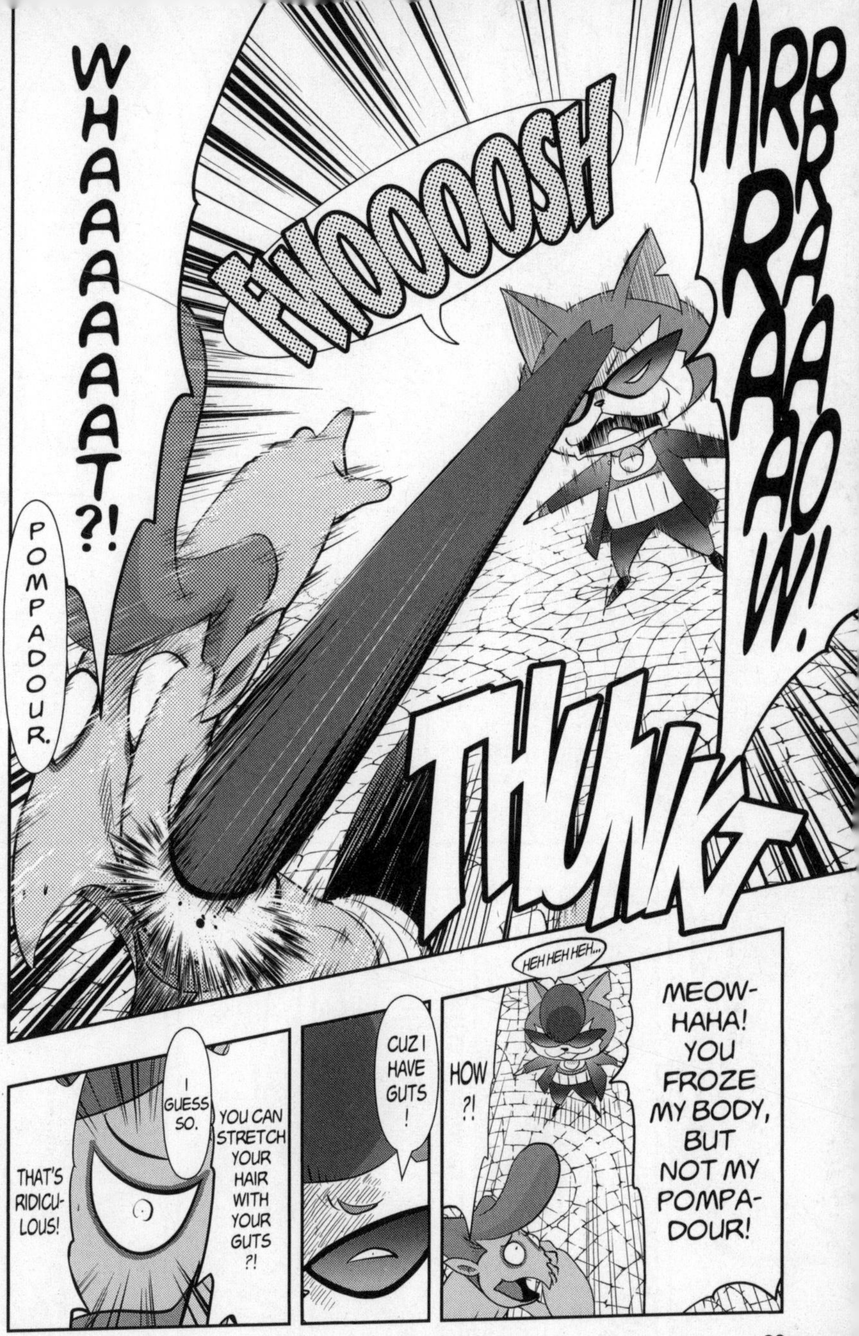
MRRRRRAAAAAOW!
FWOOOOOSH
WHAAAAAAAT?!
POMPADOUR.
THUNK
HEH HEH HEH...
MEOW-HAHA! YOU FROZE MY BODY, BUT NOT MY POMPA-DOUR!
HOW?!
CUZ I HAVE GUTS!
YOU CAN STRETCH YOUR HAIR WITH YOUR GUTS?!
I GUESS SO.
THAT'S RIDICU-LOUS!

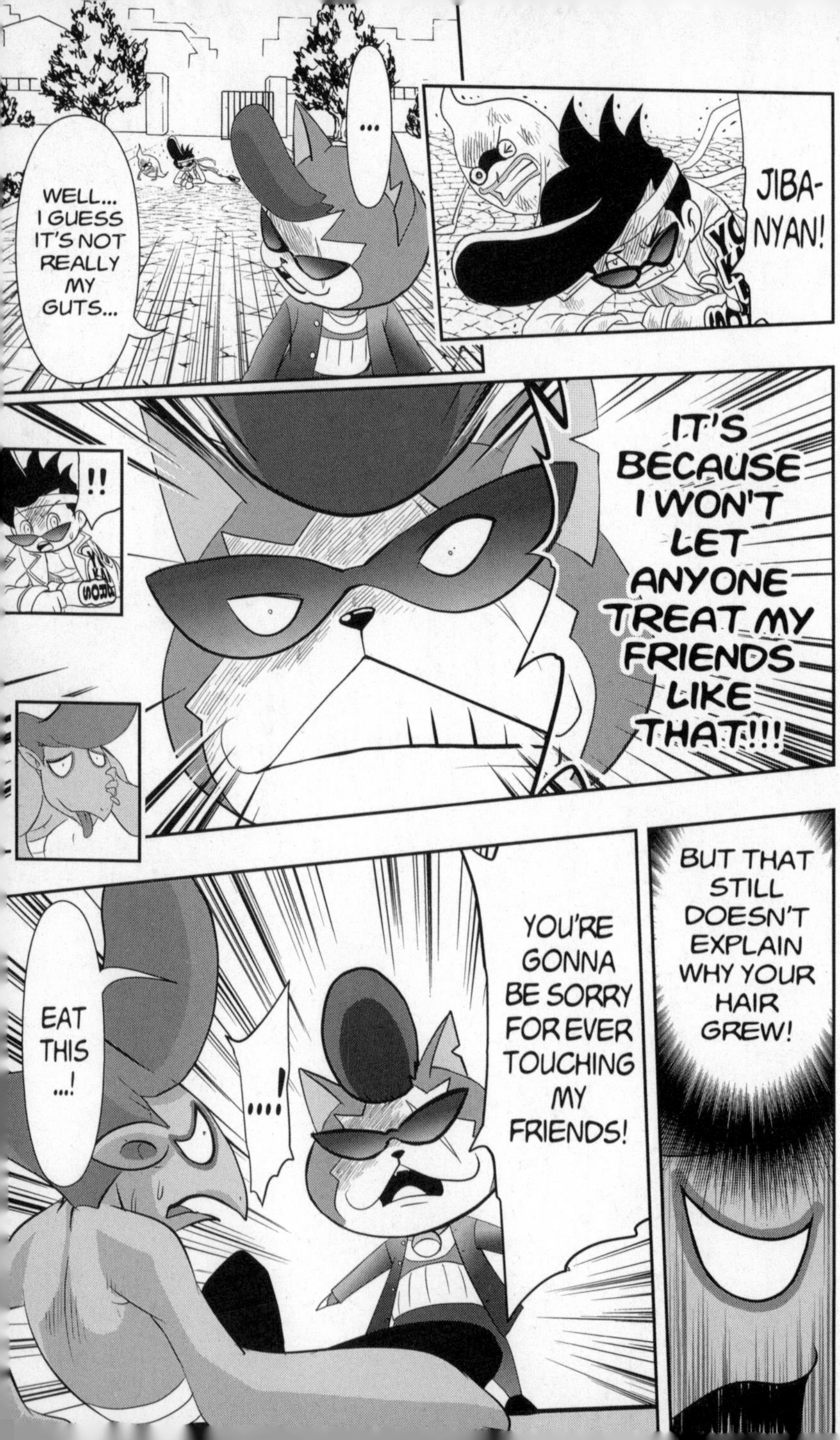
JIBA-NYAN!
...
WELL... I GUESS IT'S NOT REALLY MY GUTS...
IT'S BECAUSE I WON'T LET ANYONE TREAT MY FRIENDS LIKE THAT!!!
!!
BUT THAT STILL DOESN'T EXPLAIN WHY YOUR HAIR GREW!
YOU'RE GONNA BE SORRY FOR EVER TOUCHING MY FRIENDS!
....!
EAT THIS ...!

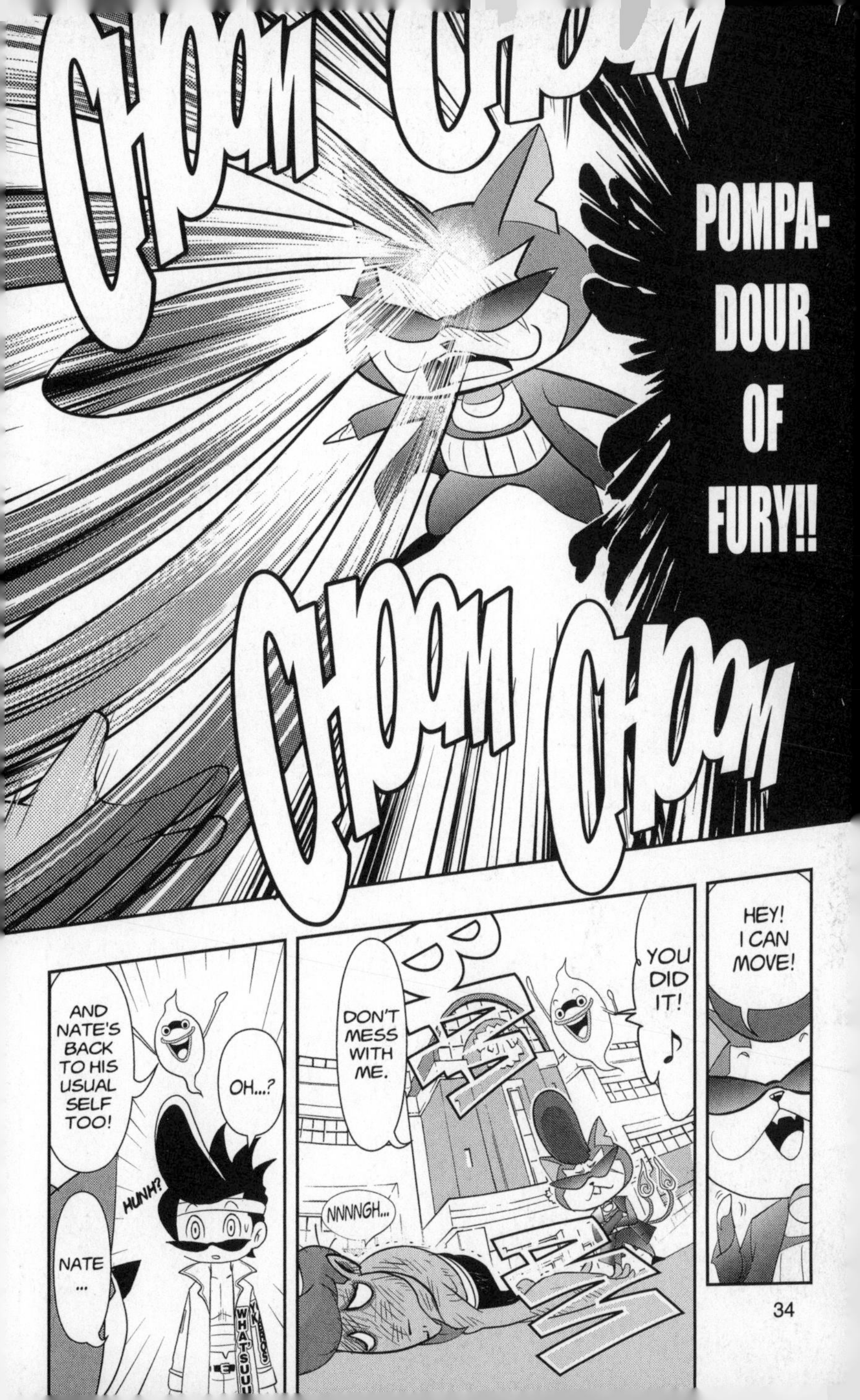
CHOOM CHOOM
POMPA-
DOUR
OF
FURY!!
CHOOM CHOOM
HEY!
I CAN
MOVE!
YOU
DID
IT!
♪
DON'T
MESS
WITH
ME.
NNNNGH...
AND
NATE'S
BACK
TO HIS
USUAL
SELF
TOO!
OH...?
HUNH?
NATE
...

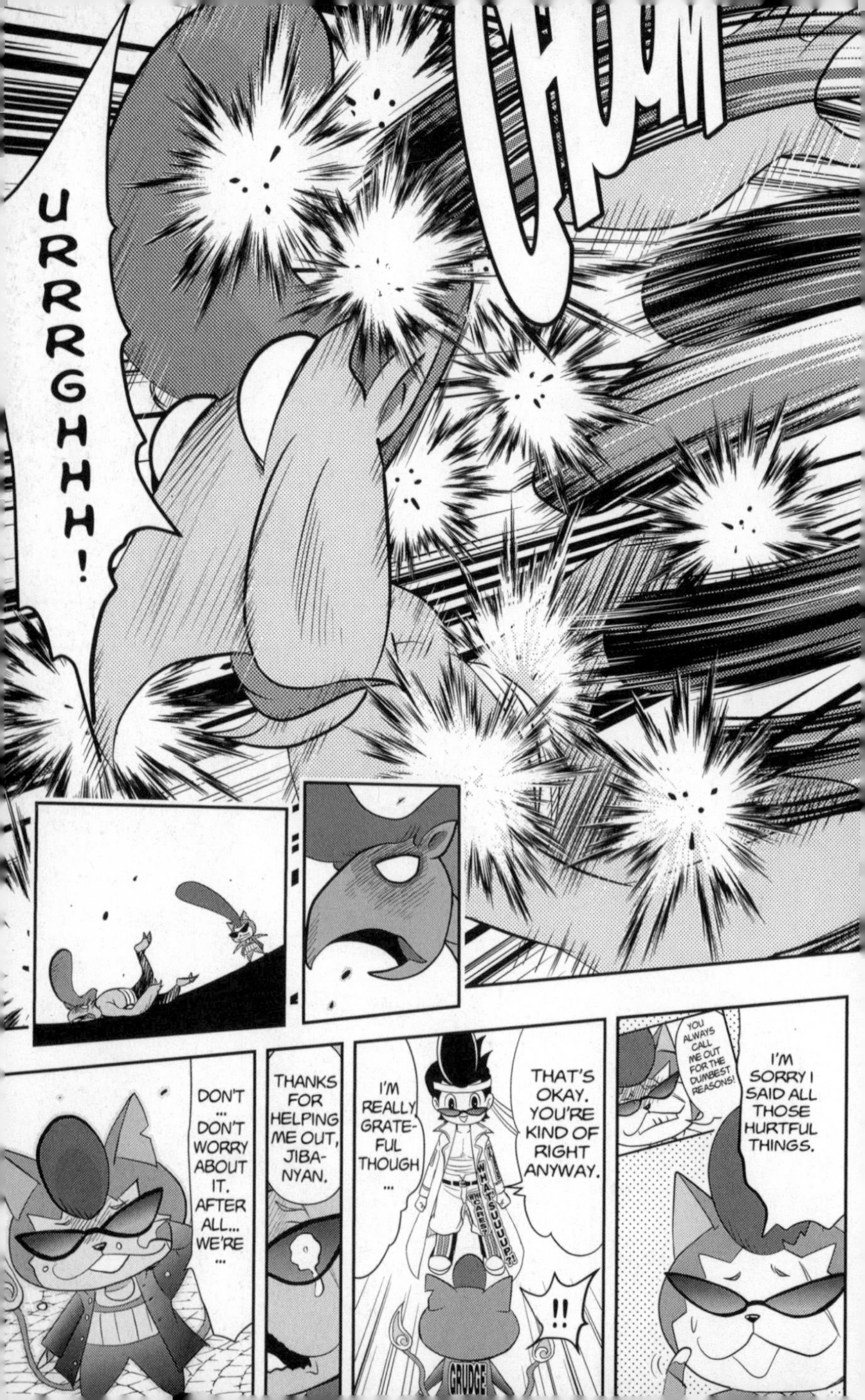
URRRGHHH!
I'M SORRY I SAID ALL THOSE HURTFUL THINGS.
YOU ALWAYS CALL ME OUT FOR THE DUMBEST REASONS!
THAT'S OKAY. YOU'RE KIND OF RIGHT ANYWAY.
I'M REALLY GRATEFUL THOUGH...
!!
GRUDGE
THANKS FOR HELPING ME OUT, JIBANYAN.
DON'T... DON'T WORRY ABOUT IT. AFTER ALL... WE'RE...

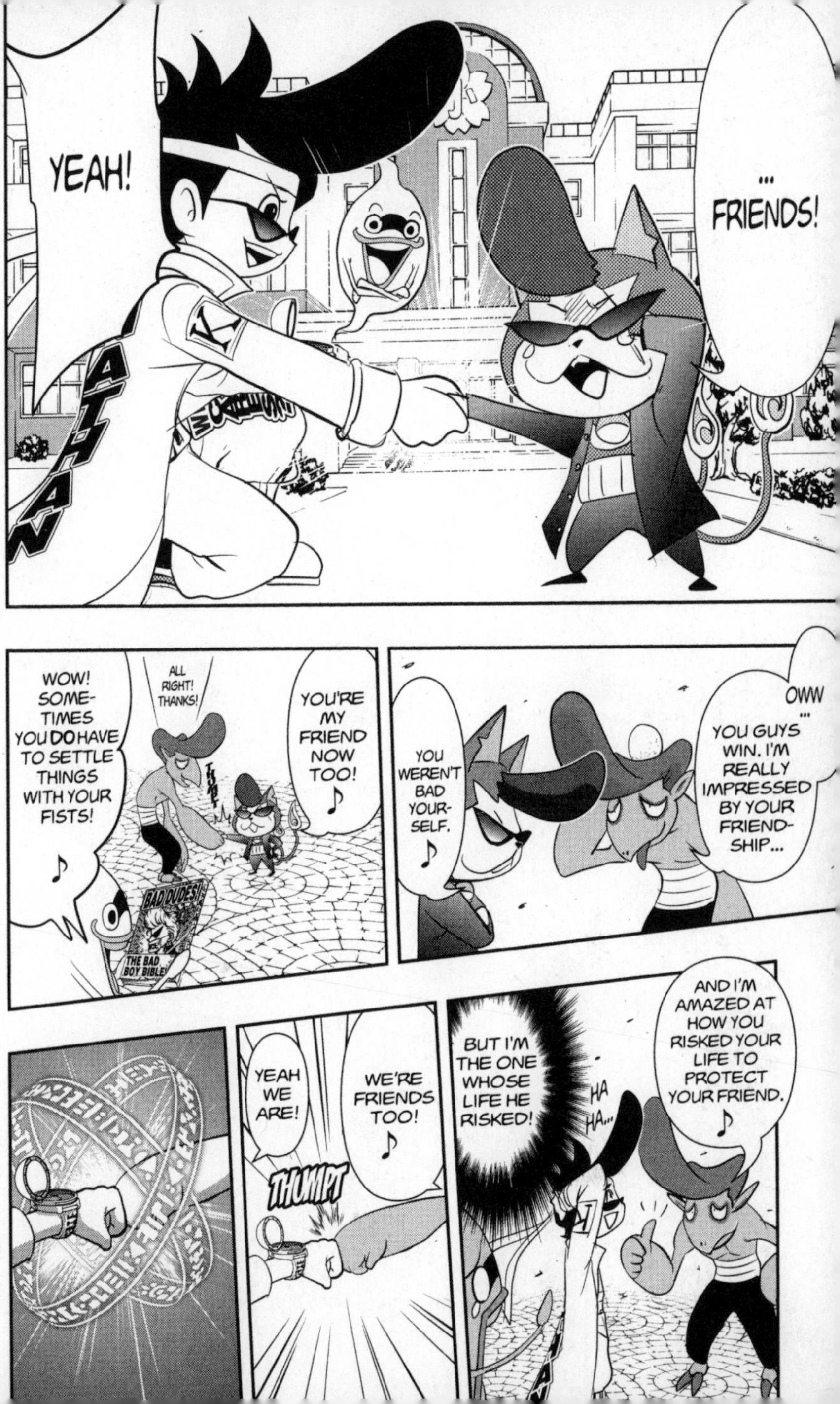
... FRIENDS!
YEAH!
OWW ... YOU GUYS WIN. I'M REALLY IMPRESSED BY YOUR FRIEND-SHIP...
YOU WEREN'T BAD YOUR-SELF. ♪
YOU'RE MY FRIEND NOW TOO! ♪
ALL RIGHT! THANKS!
THUMP
WOW! SOME-TIMES YOU DO HAVE TO SETTLE THINGS WITH YOUR FISTS! ♪
BAD DUDES!
THE BAD BOY BIBLE!
AND I'M AMAZED AT HOW YOU RISKED YOUR LIFE TO PROTECT YOUR FRIEND. ♪
HA HA...
BUT I'M THE ONE WHOSE LIFE HE RISKED!
WE'RE FRIENDS TOO! ♪
YEAH WE ARE!
THUMPT

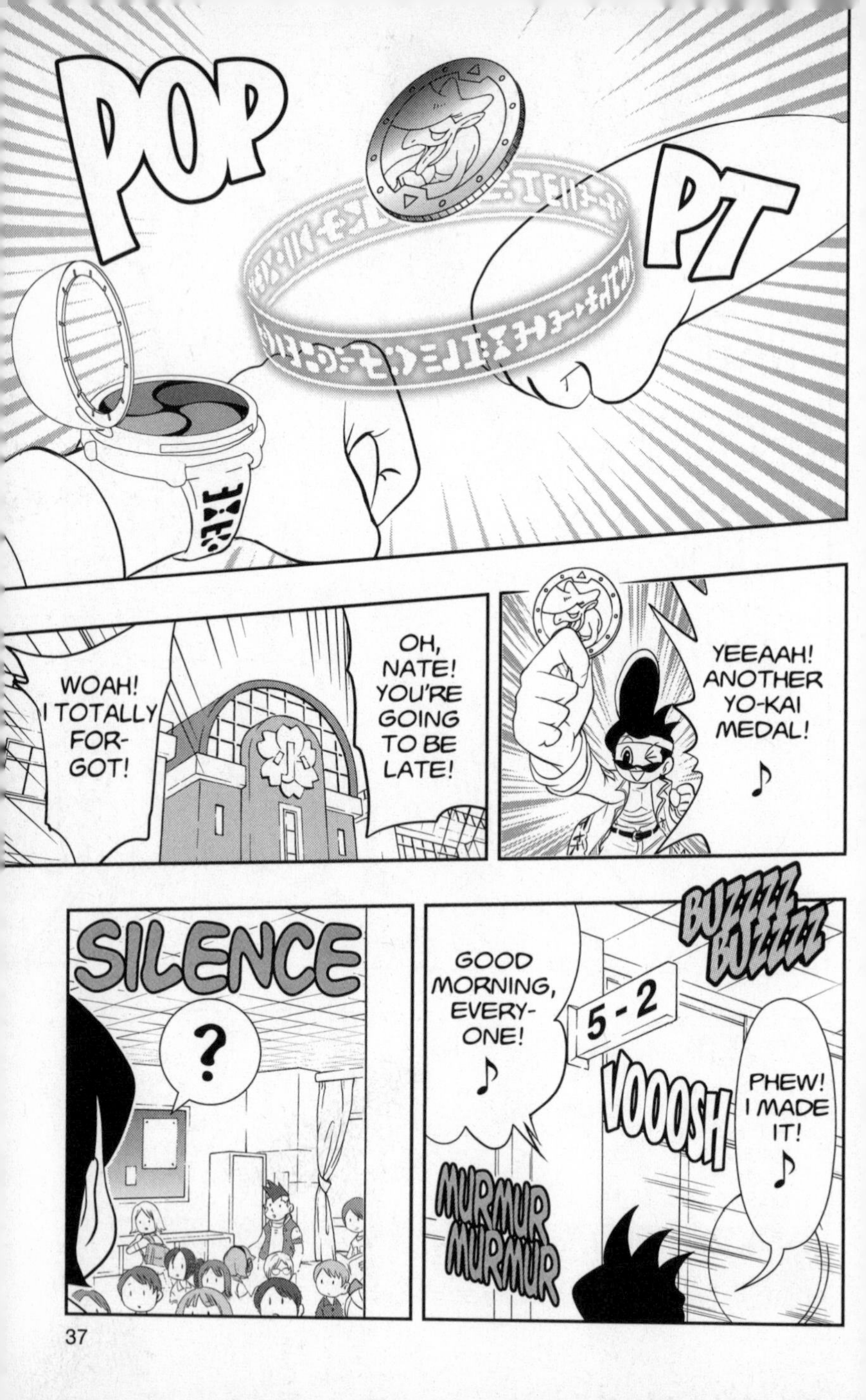
POP
PT
YEEAAH! ANOTHER YO-KAI MEDAL! ♪
OH, NATE! YOU'RE GOING TO BE LATE!
WOAH! I TOTALLY FOR-GOT!
BUZZZZ BUZZZZ
PHEW! I MADE IT! ♪
5 - 2
VOOOSH
GOOD MORNING, EVERY-ONE! ♪
MURMUR MURMUR
SILENCE
?

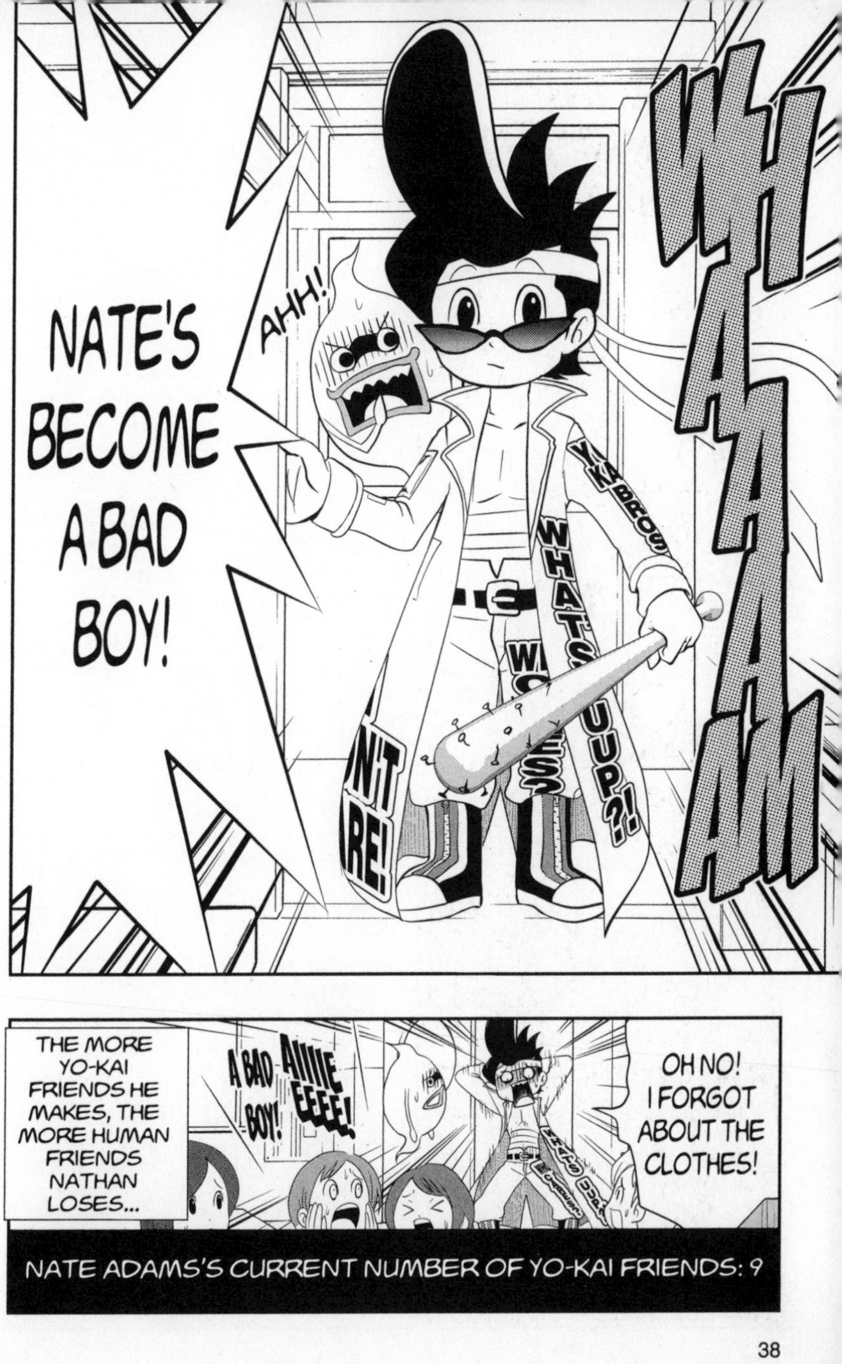
WHAAAAM
AHH!
NATE'S BECOME A BAD BOY!
WHAT'S UUP?!
OH NO! I FORGOT ABOUT THE CLOTHES!
AIIIIEEEEE!
A BAD BOY!
THE MORE YO-KAI FRIENDS HE MAKES, THE MORE HUMAN FRIENDS NATHAN LOSES...
NATE ADAMS'S CURRENT NUMBER OF YO-KAI FRIENDS: 9

SUMO

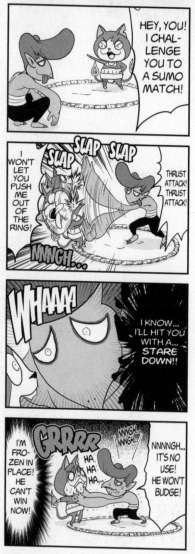

HEY, YOU! I CHALLENGE YOU TO A SUMO MATCH!
SLAP
SLAP
THRUST ATTACK! THRUST ATTACK!
SLAP
I WON'T LET YOU PUSH ME OUT OF THE RING!
NNNGH...
I KNOW... I'LL HIT YOU WITH A... STARE DOWN!!
WHAAAA
NNNGH... NNNGH...
NNNNGH... IT'S NO USE! HE WON'T BUDGE!
GRRRR
HA HA HA...
I'M FROZEN IN PLACE! HE CAN'T WIN NOW!

CHAPTER 9: JUST SNAP OUT OF IT!

FEATURING SPACED-OUT YO-KAI DAIZ

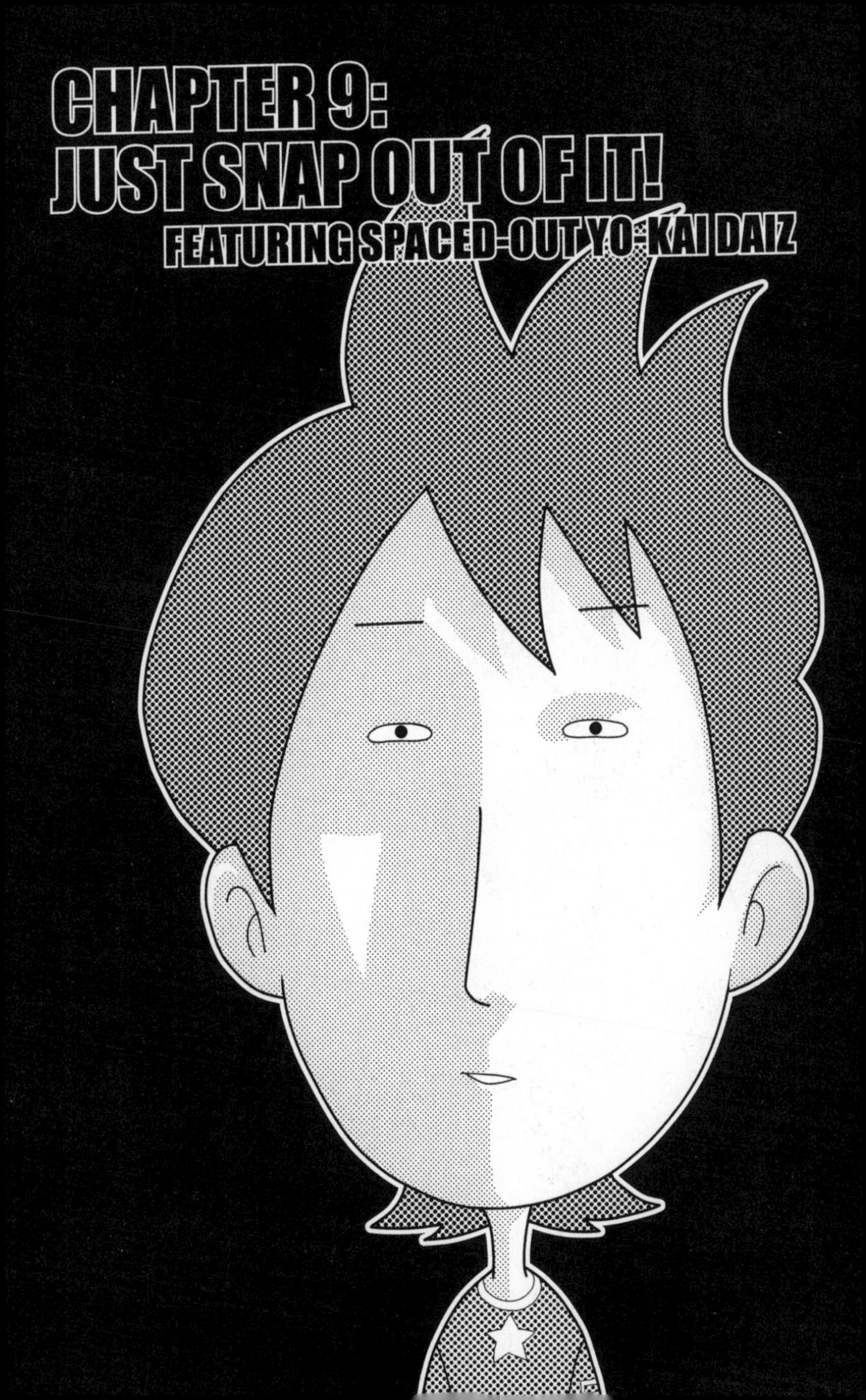

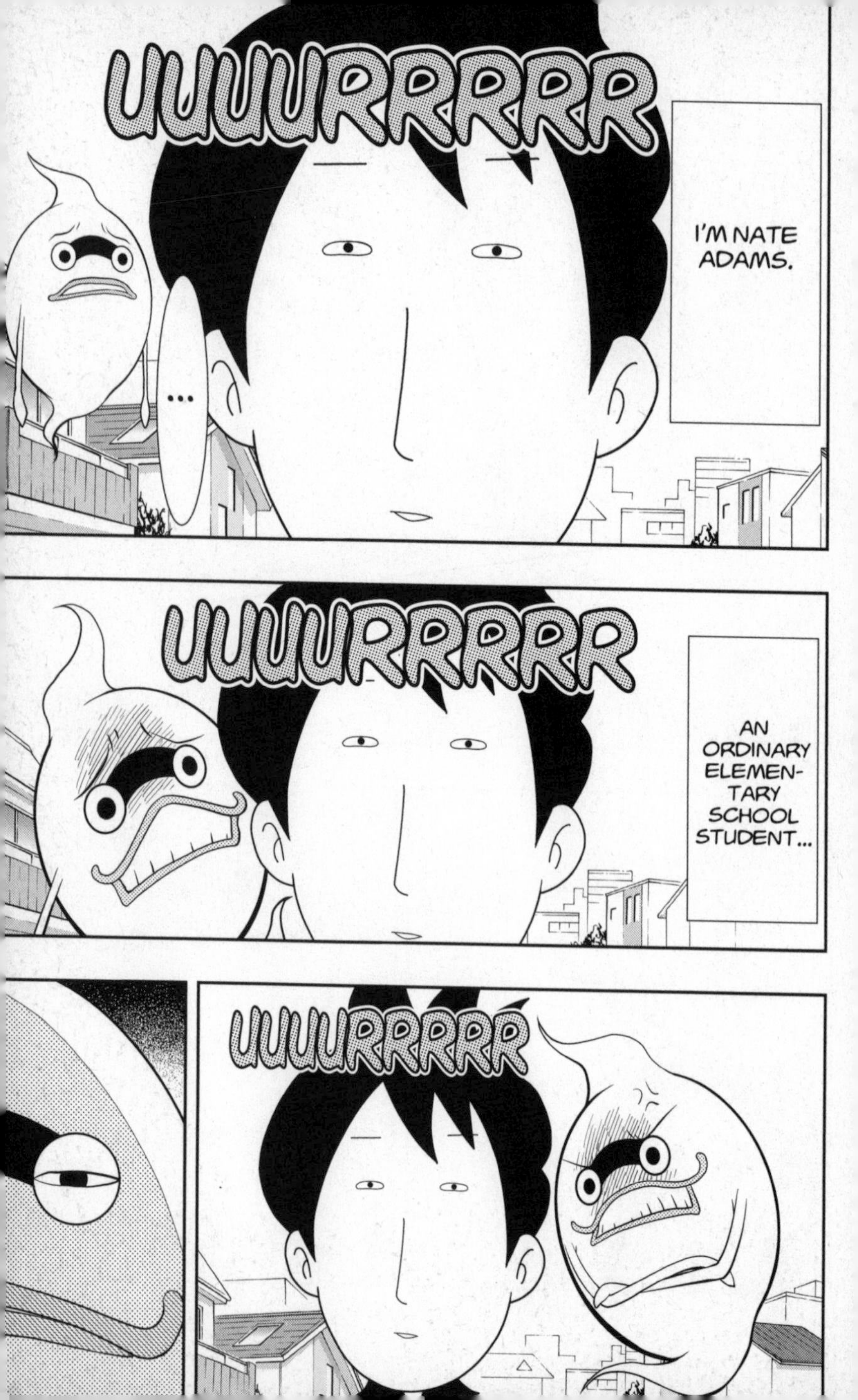
I'M NATE ADAMS.
UUUURRRRR
...
AN ORDINARY ELEMEN- TARY SCHOOL STUDENT...
UUUURRRRR
UUUURRRRR

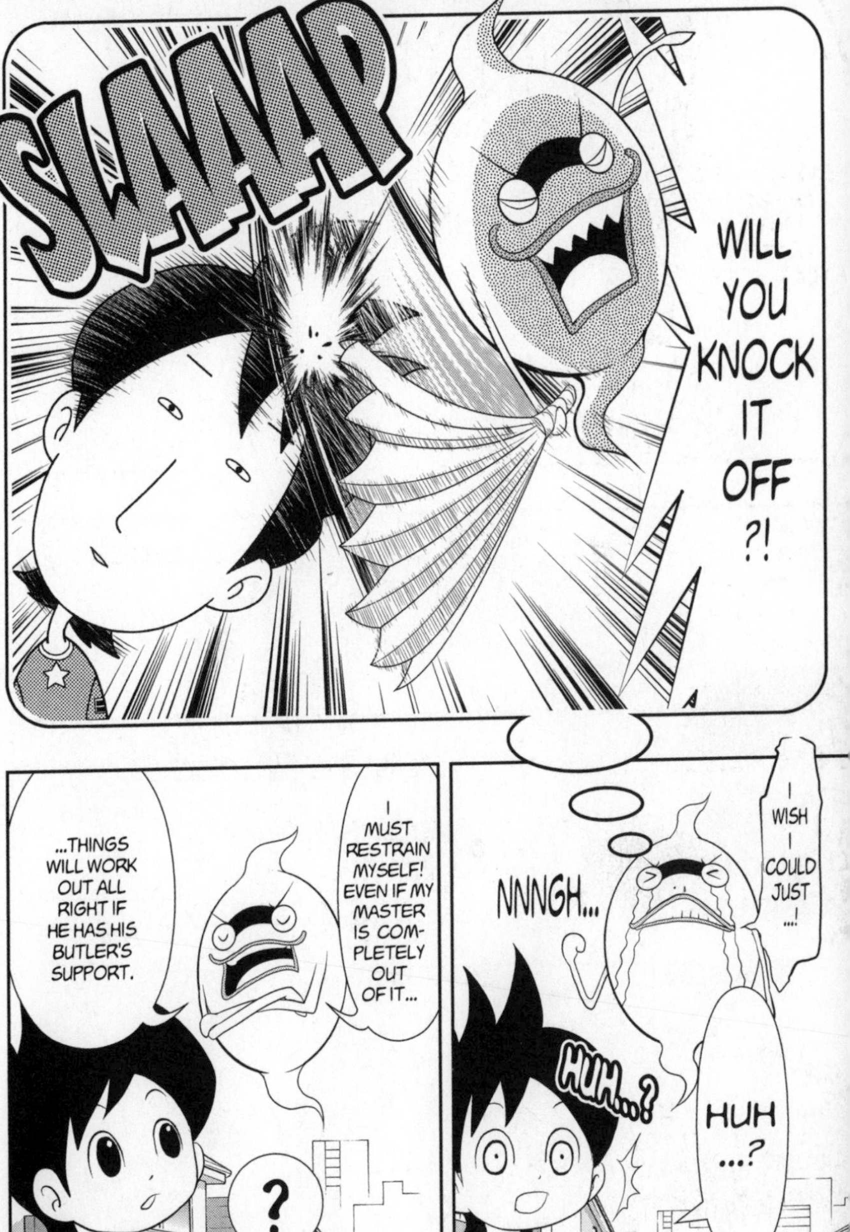
SLAAAP!
WILL YOU KNOCK IT OFF?!
I WISH I COULD JUST ...!
NNNGH...
HUH...?
HUH...?
I MUST RESTRAIN MYSELF! EVEN IF MY MASTER IS COMPLETELY OUT OF IT...
...THINGS WILL WORK OUT ALL RIGHT IF HE HAS HIS BUTLER'S SUPPORT.
?

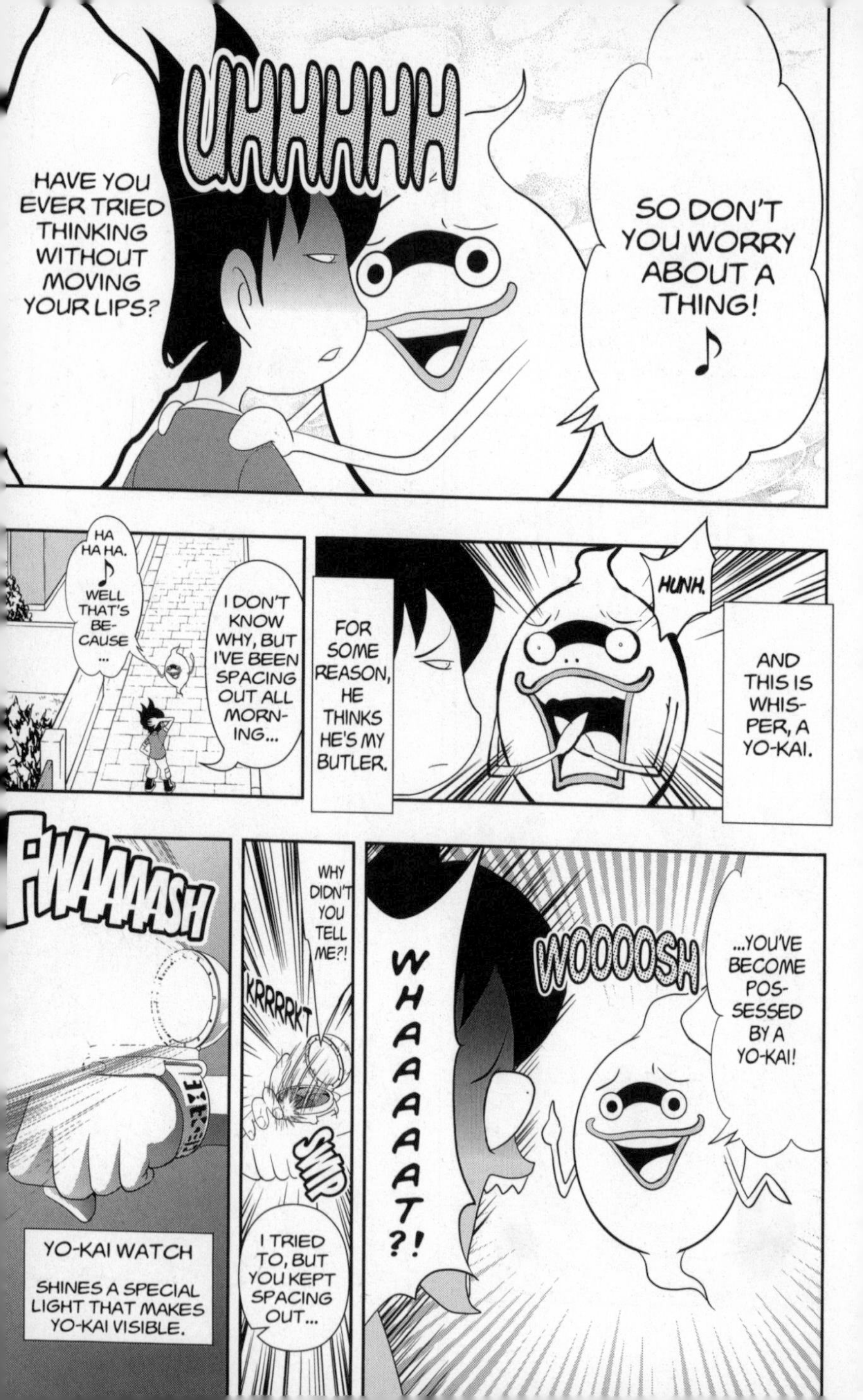
SO DON'T YOU WORRY ABOUT A THING! ♪
UHHHHH
HAVE YOU EVER TRIED THINKING WITHOUT MOVING YOUR LIPS?
AND THIS IS WHIS-PER, A YO-KAI.
HUNH.
FOR SOME REASON, HE THINKS HE'S MY BUTLER.
I DON'T KNOW WHY, BUT I'VE BEEN SPACING OUT ALL MORN-ING...
HA HA HA. ♪ WELL THAT'S BE-CAUSE ...
...YOU'VE BECOME POS-SESSED BY A YO-KAI!
WOOOOSH
WHAAAAAAAT?!
WHY DIDN'T YOU TELL ME?!
KRRRRKT
SWIP
I TRIED TO, BUT YOU KEPT SPACING OUT...
FWAAAAASH
YO-KAI WATCH
SHINES A SPECIAL LIGHT THAT MAKES YO-KAI VISIBLE.

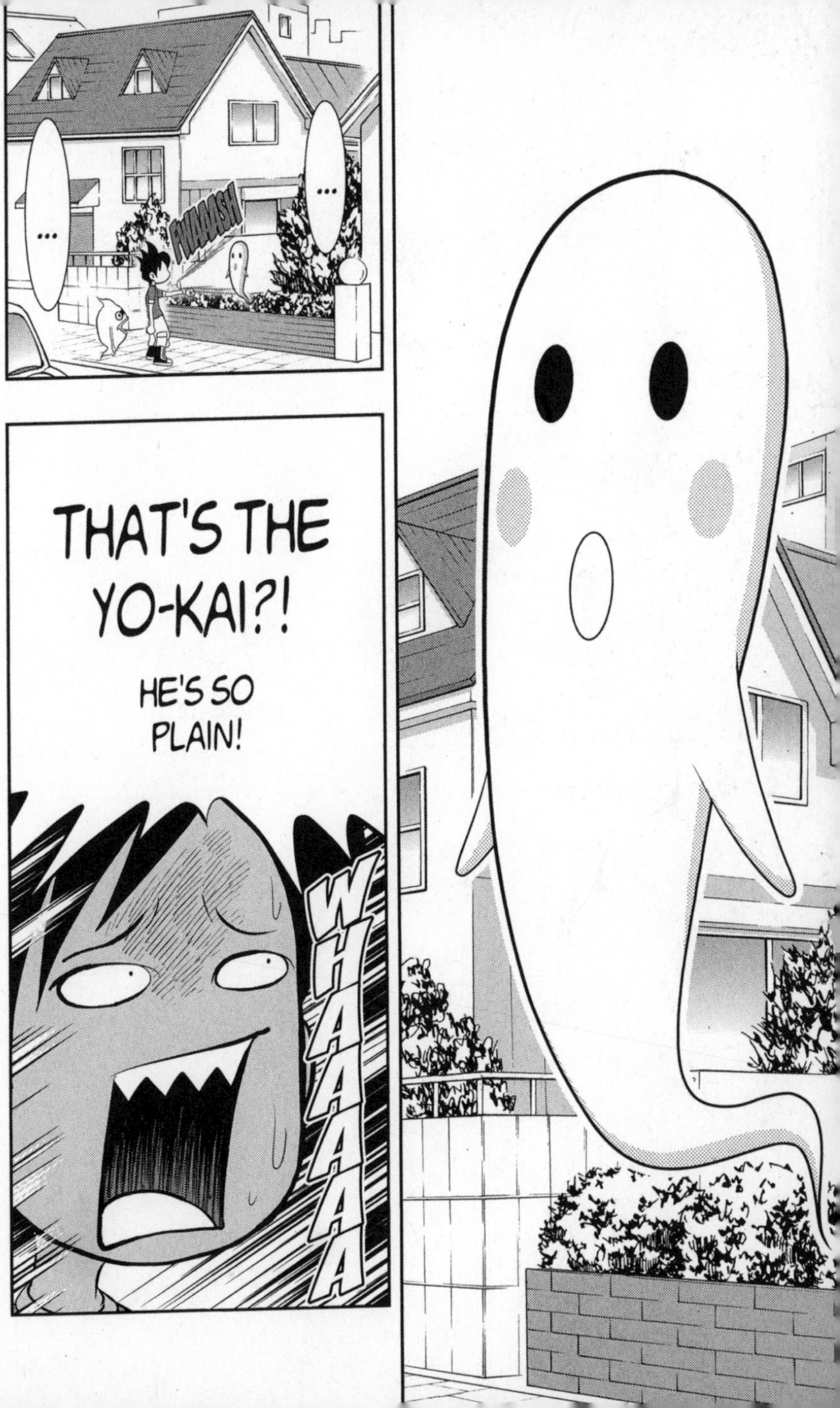
...
FWAAASH
...
THAT'S THE YO-KAI?!
HE'S SO PLAIN!
WHAAAAAAA

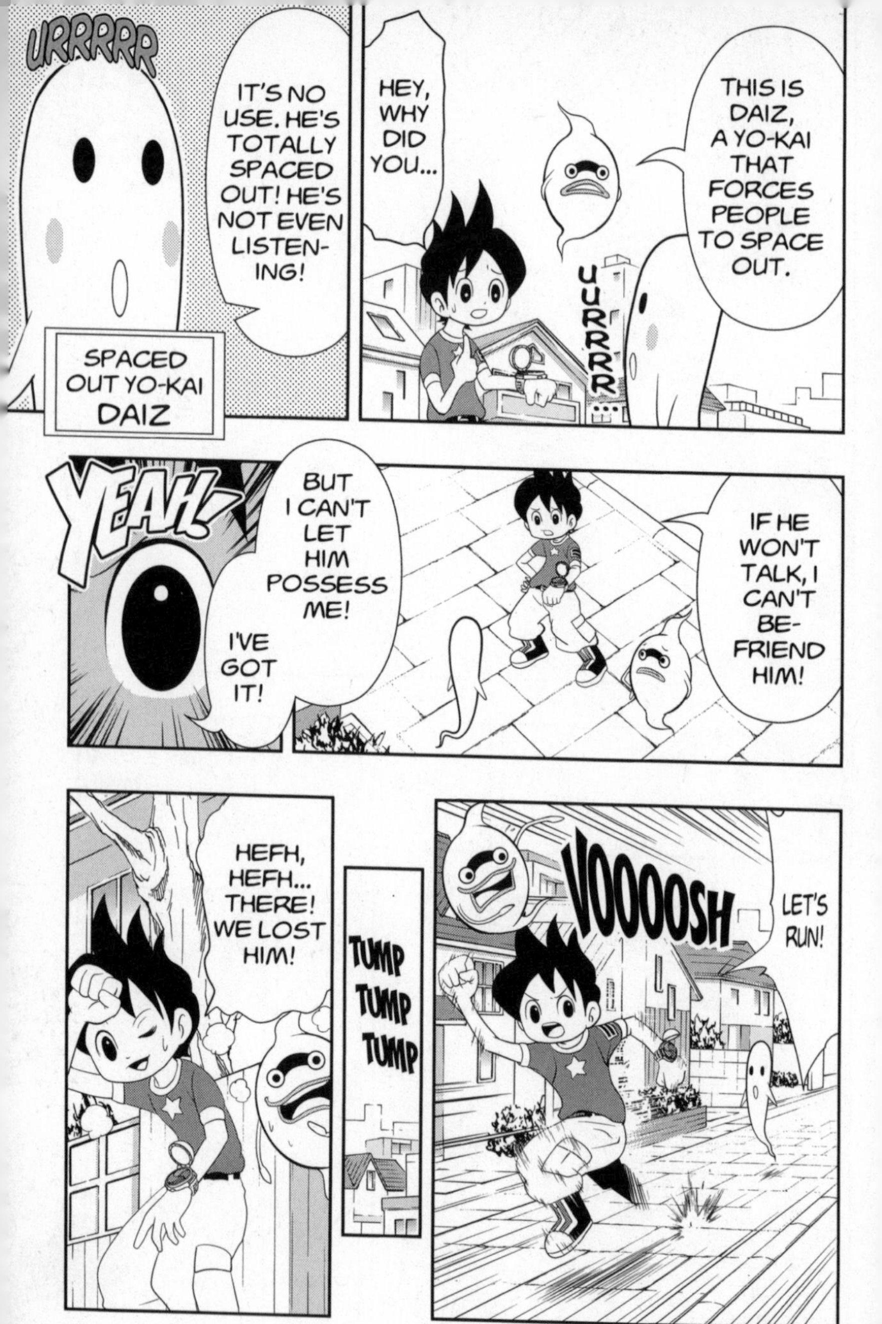
THIS IS DAIZ, A YO-KAI THAT FORCES PEOPLE TO SPACE OUT.
HEY, WHY DID YOU...
UURRRR
URRRRR
IT'S NO USE. HE'S TOTALLY SPACED OUT! HE'S NOT EVEN LISTENING!
SPACED OUT YO-KAI DAIZ
IF HE WON'T TALK, I CAN'T BEFRIEND HIM!
BUT I CAN'T LET HIM POSSESS ME!
YEAH!
I'VE GOT IT!
LET'S RUN!
VOOOOSH
TUMP TUMP TUMP
HEFH, HEFH... THERE! WE LOST HIM!

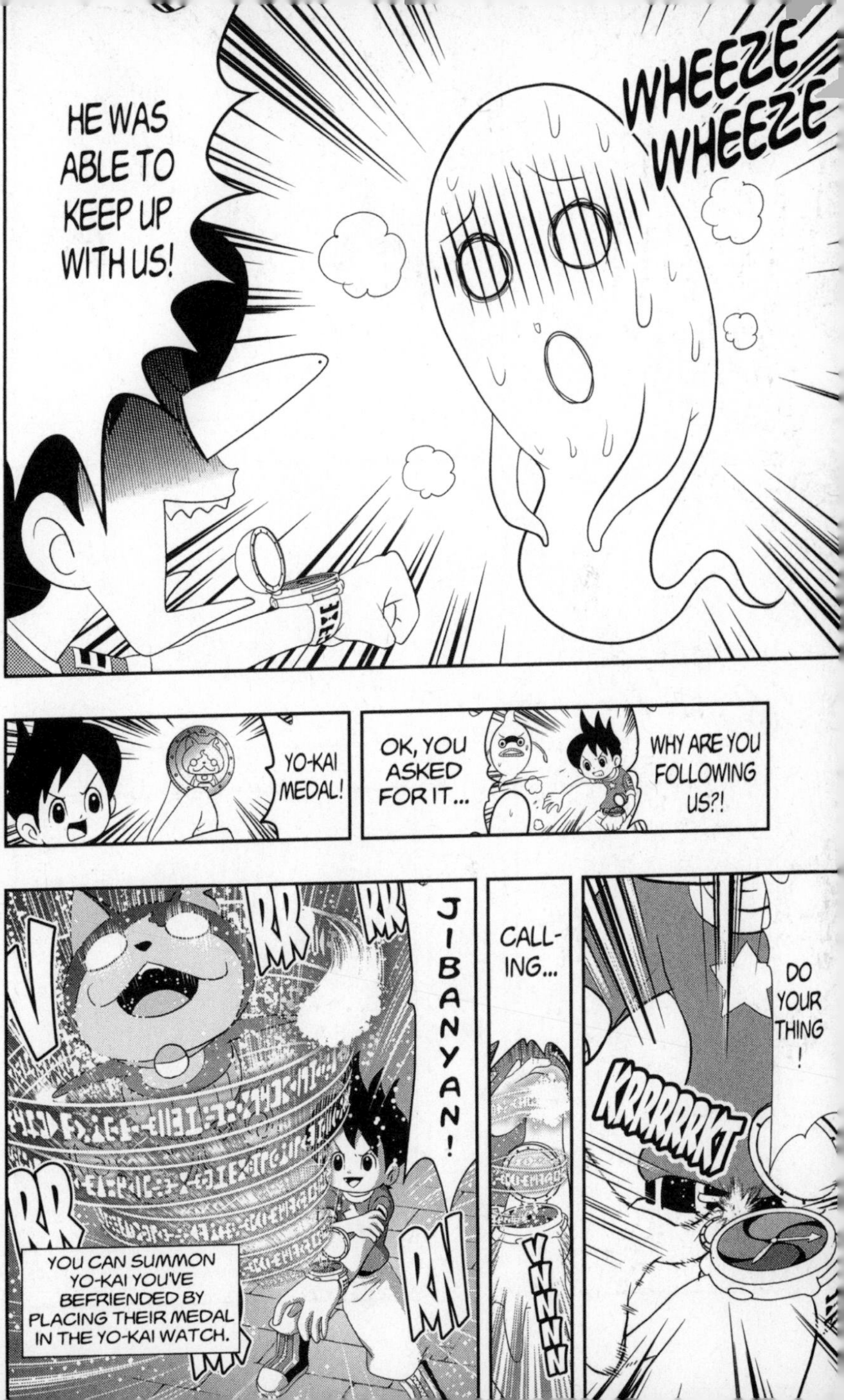
WHEEZE WHEEZE
HE WAS ABLE TO KEEP UP WITH US!
WHY ARE YOU FOLLOWING US?!
OK, YOU ASKED FOR IT...
YO-KAI MEDAL!
DO YOUR THING!
KRRRRRKT
CALLING...
VNNNN
JIBANYAN!
RR
RR
RR
RN
YOU CAN SUMMON YO-KAI YOU'VE BEFRIENDED BY PLACING THEIR MEDAL IN THE YO-KAI WATCH.

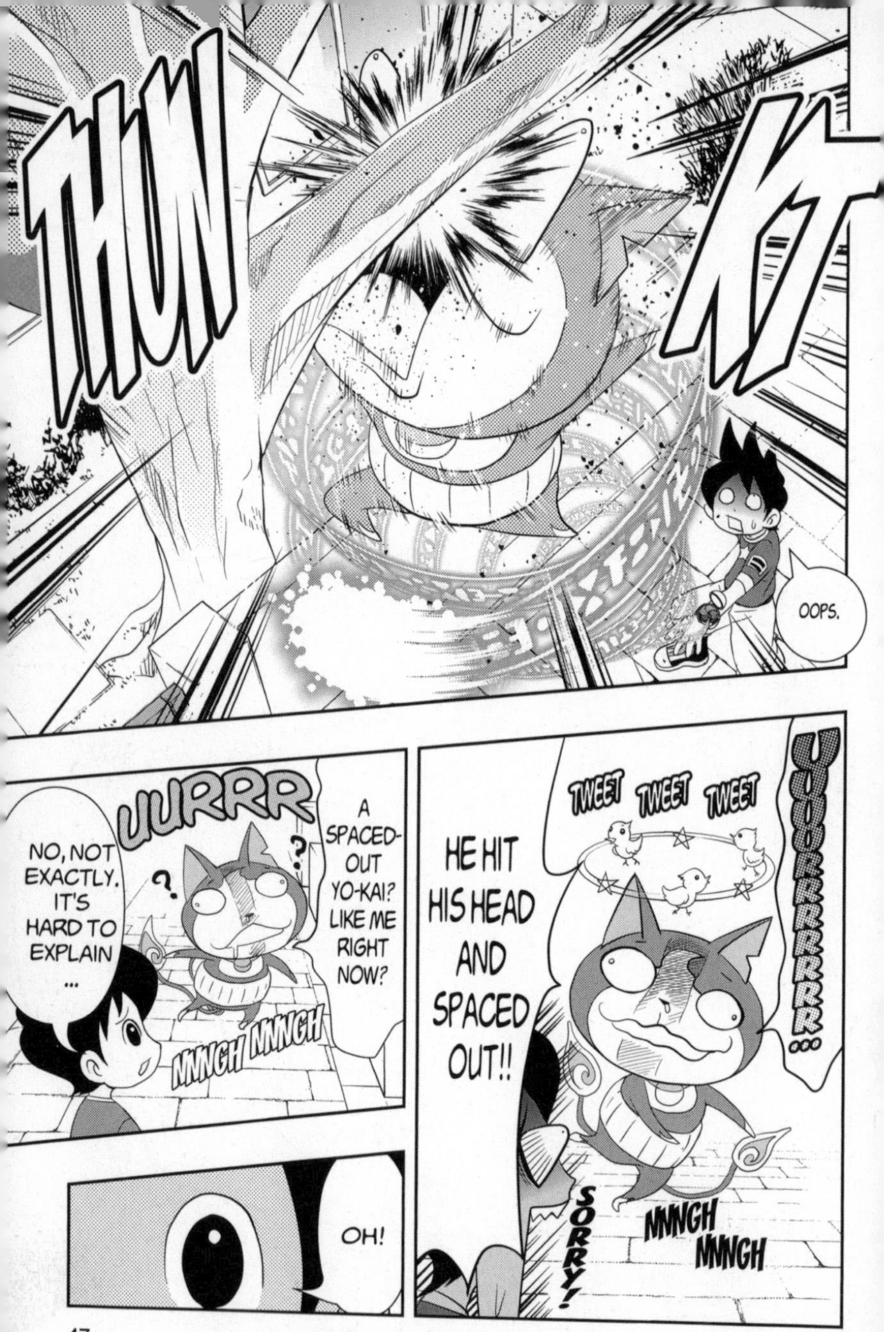
THUNK
OOPS.
UUURRRRRRR...
TWEET TWEET TWEET
HE HIT HIS HEAD AND SPACED OUT!!
SORRY!
NNNGH NNNGH
UURRR
A SPACED-OUT YO-KAI? LIKE ME RIGHT NOW?
NO, NOT EXACTLY. IT'S HARD TO EXPLAIN ...
NNNGH NNNGH
OH!

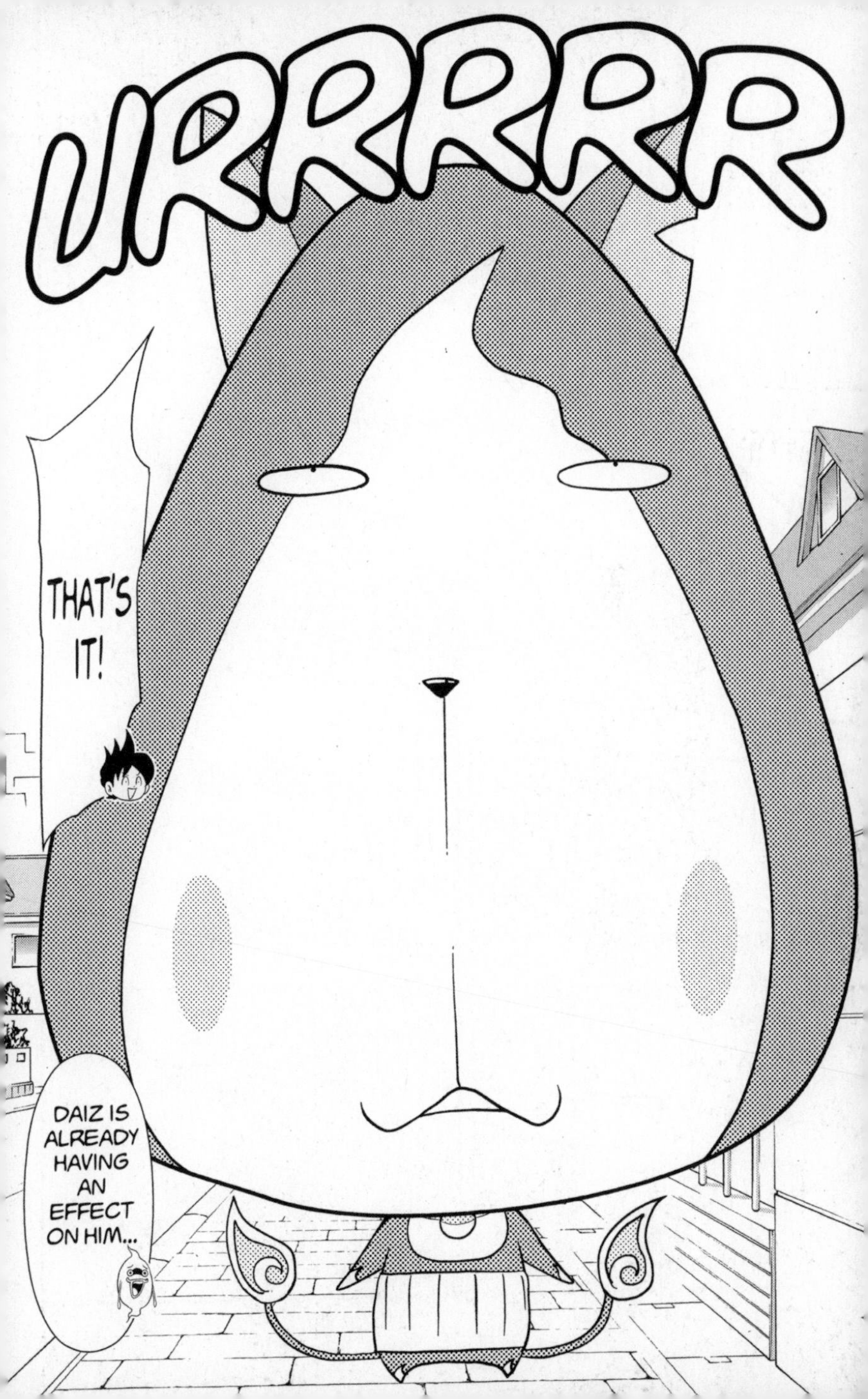
URRRRRR
THAT'S IT!
DAIZ IS ALREADY HAVING AN EFFECT ON HIM...

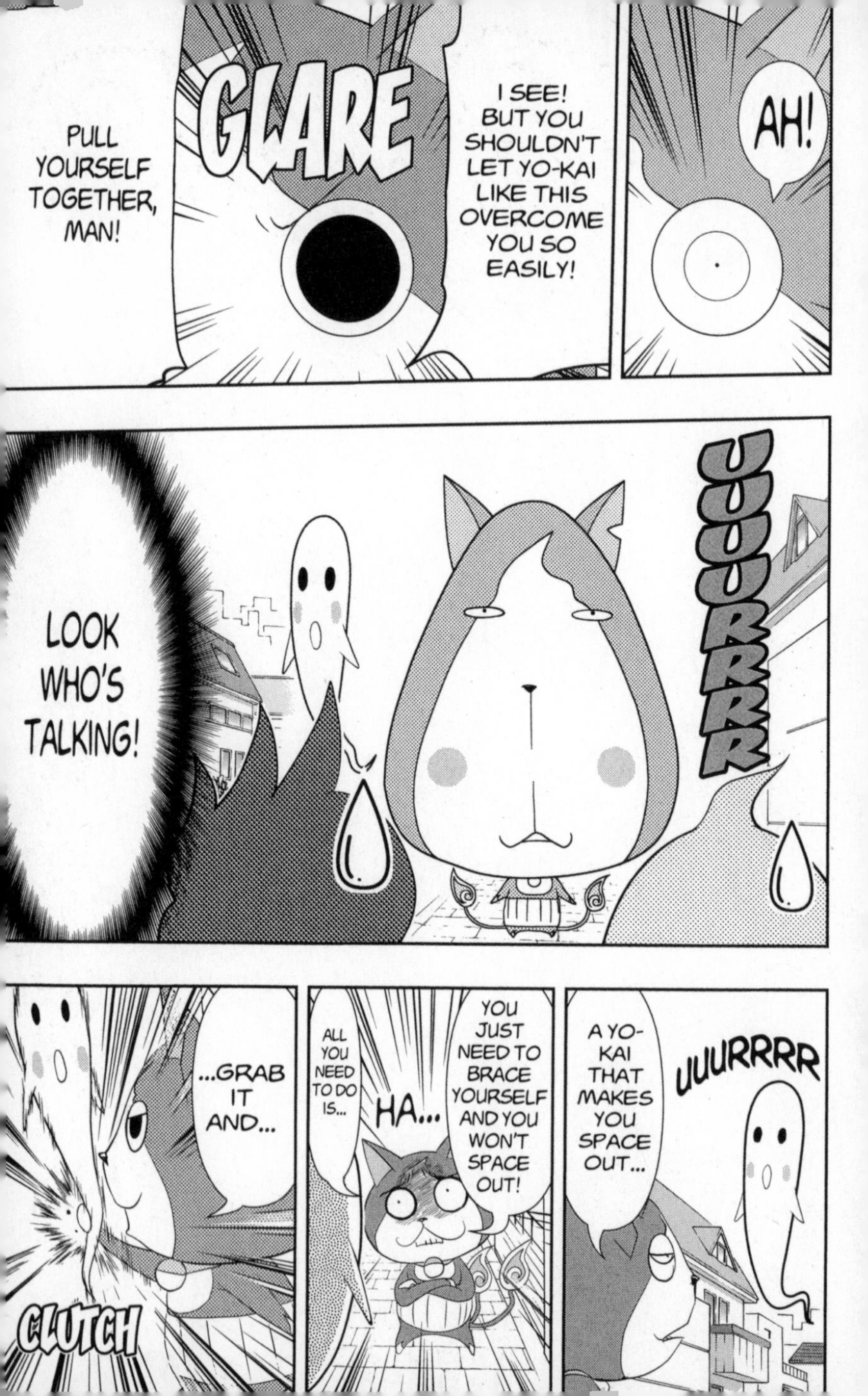
AH!
GLARE
I SEE! BUT YOU SHOULDN'T LET YO-KAI LIKE THIS OVERCOME YOU SO EASILY!
PULL YOURSELF TOGETHER, MAN!
UUUURRRR
LOOK WHO'S TALKING!
UUURRRR
A YO-KAI THAT MAKES YOU SPACE OUT...
YOU JUST NEED TO BRACE YOURSELF AND YOU WON'T SPACE OUT!
HA...
ALL YOU NEED TO DO IS...
...GRAB IT AND...
CLUTCH

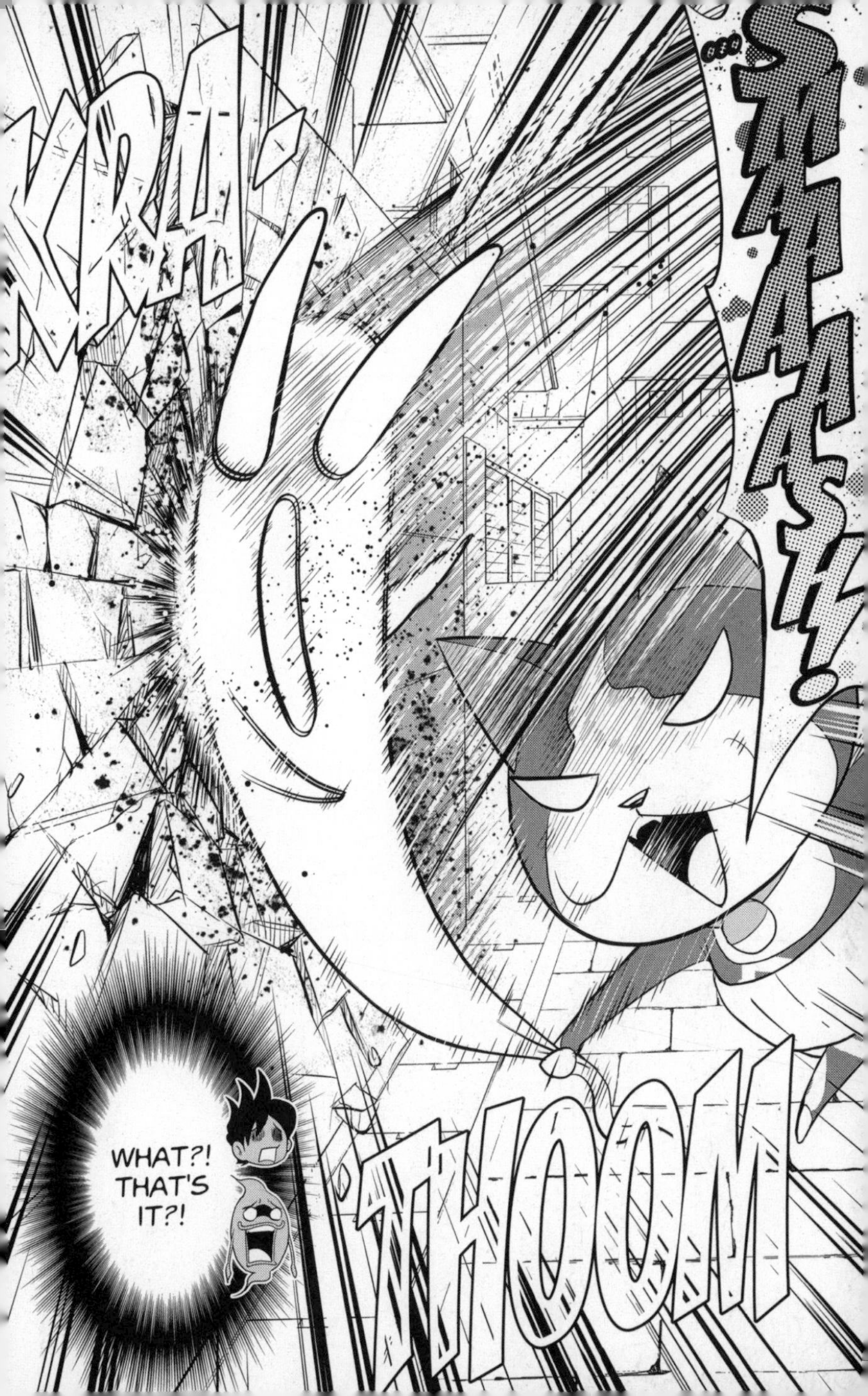
SMASH!
KRAK
THOOM
WHAT?! THAT'S IT?!

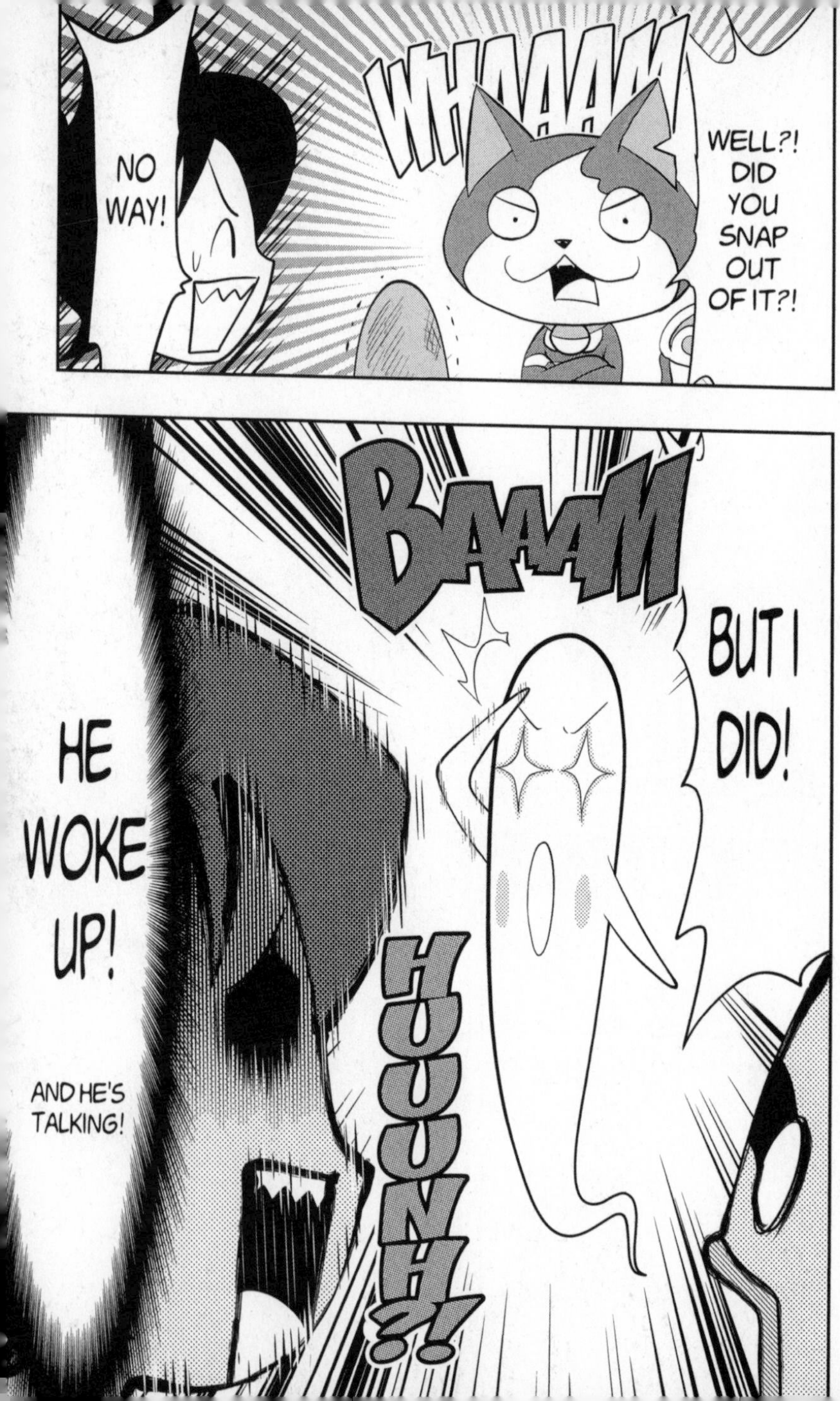
WHAAAM
WELL?! DID YOU SNAP OUT OF IT?!
NO WAY!
BAAAM
BUT I DID!
HUUUUNH?!
HE WOKE UP!
AND HE'S TALKING!

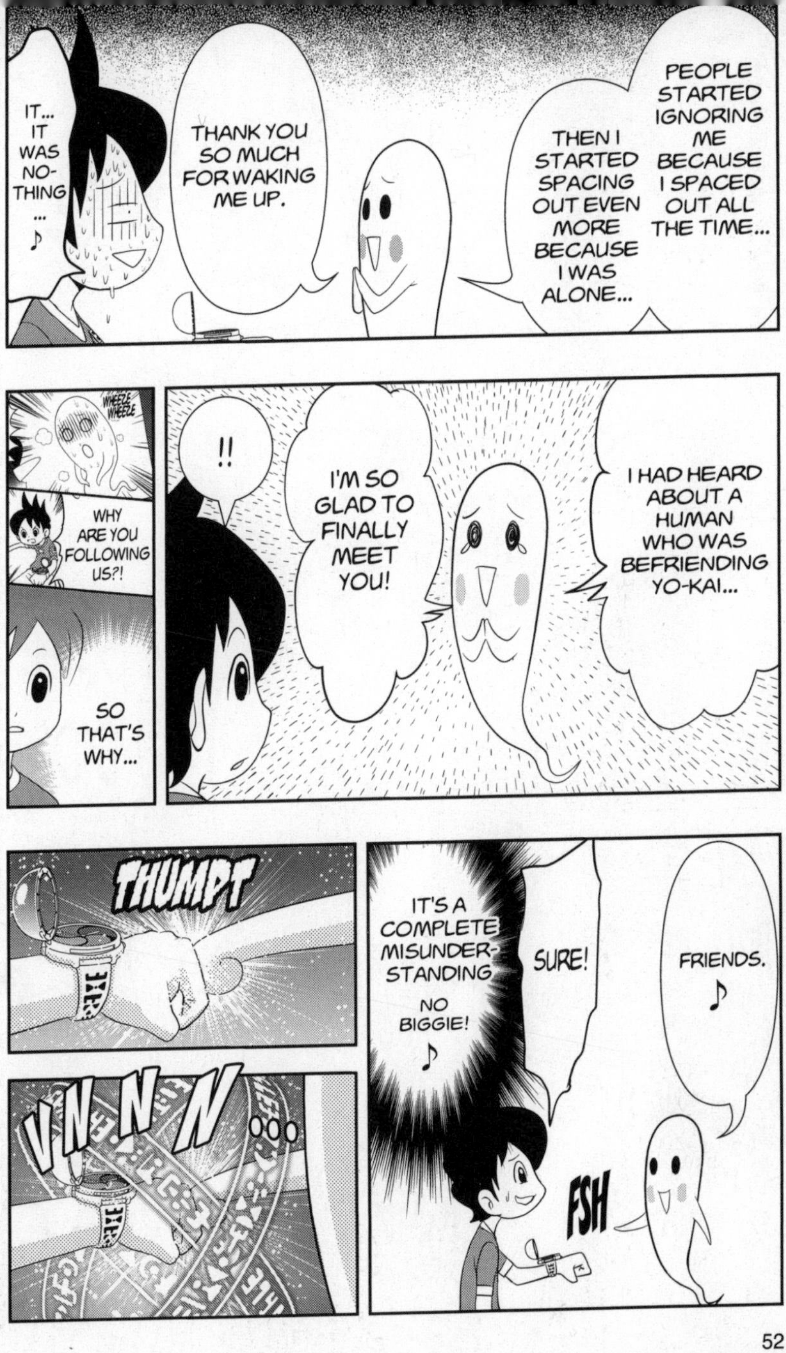
PEOPLE STARTED IGNORING ME BECAUSE I SPACED OUT ALL THE TIME...
THEN I STARTED SPACING OUT EVEN MORE BECAUSE I WAS ALONE...
THANK YOU SO MUCH FOR WAKING ME UP.
IT... IT WAS NO-THING... ♪
I HAD HEARD ABOUT A HUMAN WHO WAS BEFRIENDING YO-KAI...
I'M SO GLAD TO FINALLY MEET YOU!
!!
WHEEZE WHEEZE
WHY ARE YOU FOLLOWING US?!
SO THAT'S WHY...
FRIENDS. ♪
SURE!
IT'S A COMPLETE MISUNDER-STANDING
NO BIGGIE! ♪
FSH
THUMPT
VNNN...

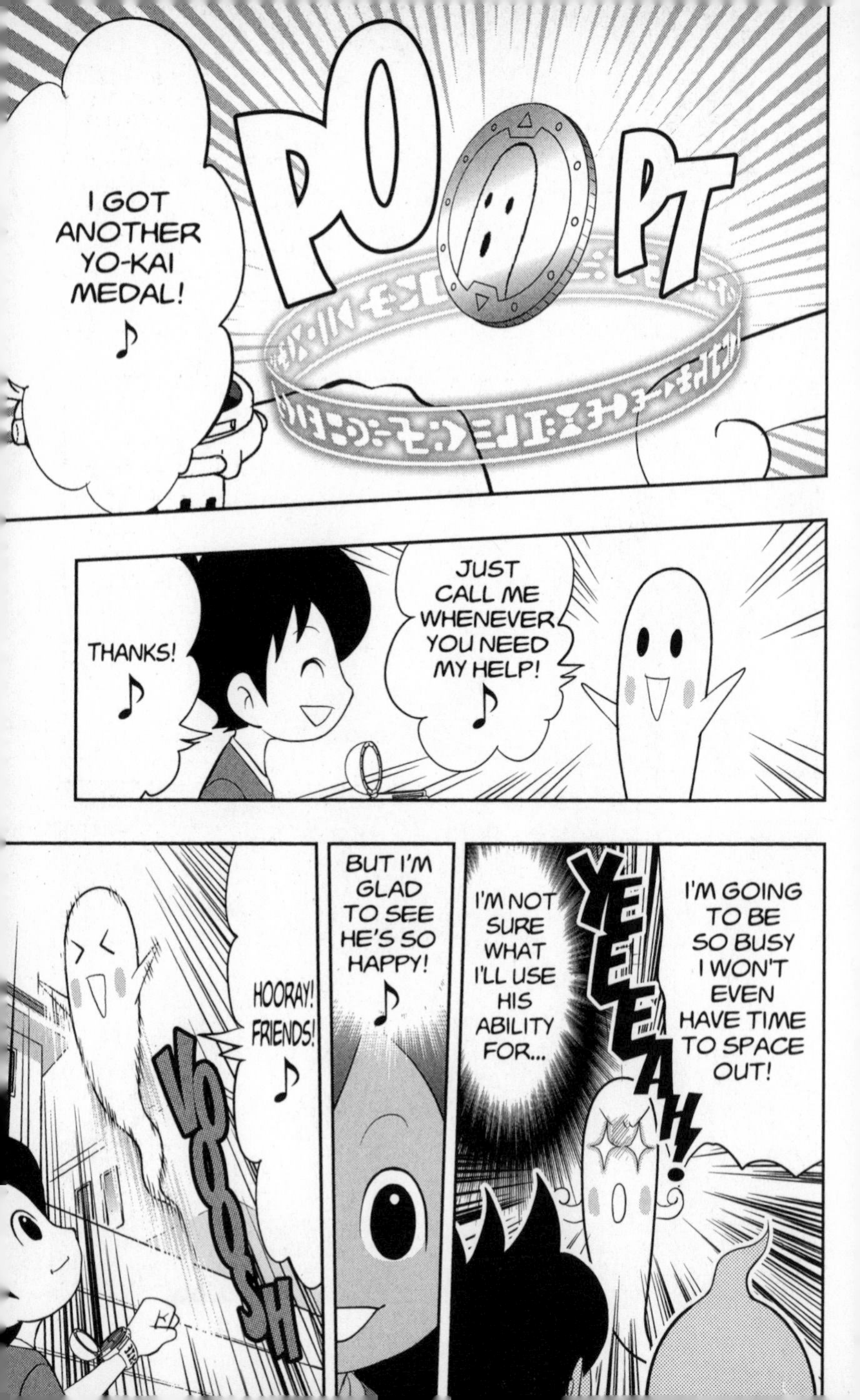
POOPT
I GOT ANOTHER YO-KAI MEDAL! ♪
JUST CALL ME WHENEVER YOU NEED MY HELP! ♪
THANKS! ♪
I'M GOING TO BE SO BUSY I WON'T EVEN HAVE TIME TO SPACE OUT!
YEEEEAH!
I'M NOT SURE WHAT I'LL USE HIS ABILITY FOR...
BUT I'M GLAD TO SEE HE'S SO HAPPY! ♪
HOORAY! FRIENDS! ♪
VOOOOSH

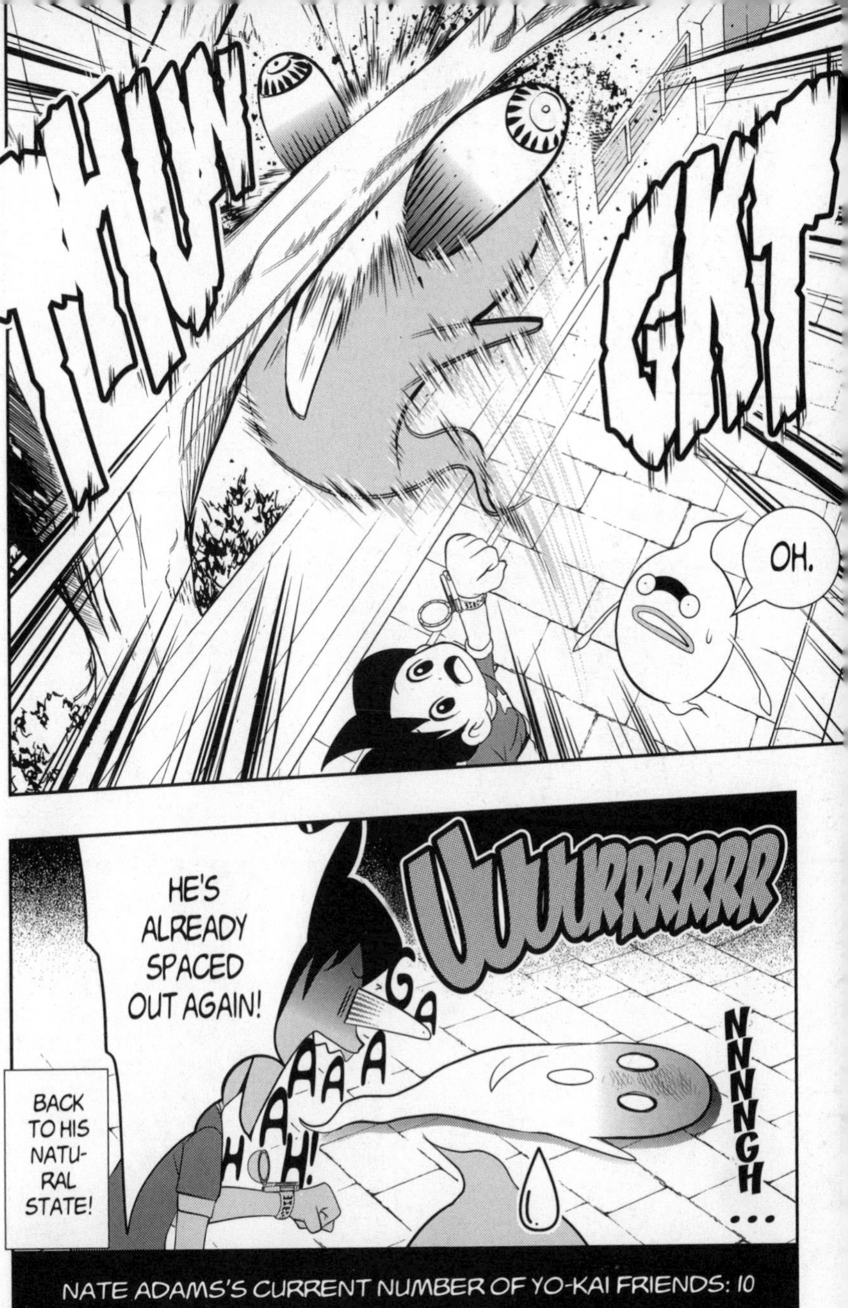
OH.
NNNNGH...
GAAAAAHH!
HE'S ALREADY SPACED OUT AGAIN!
BACK TO HIS NATU-RAL STATE!
NATE ADAMS'S CURRENT NUMBER OF YO-KAI FRIENDS: 10

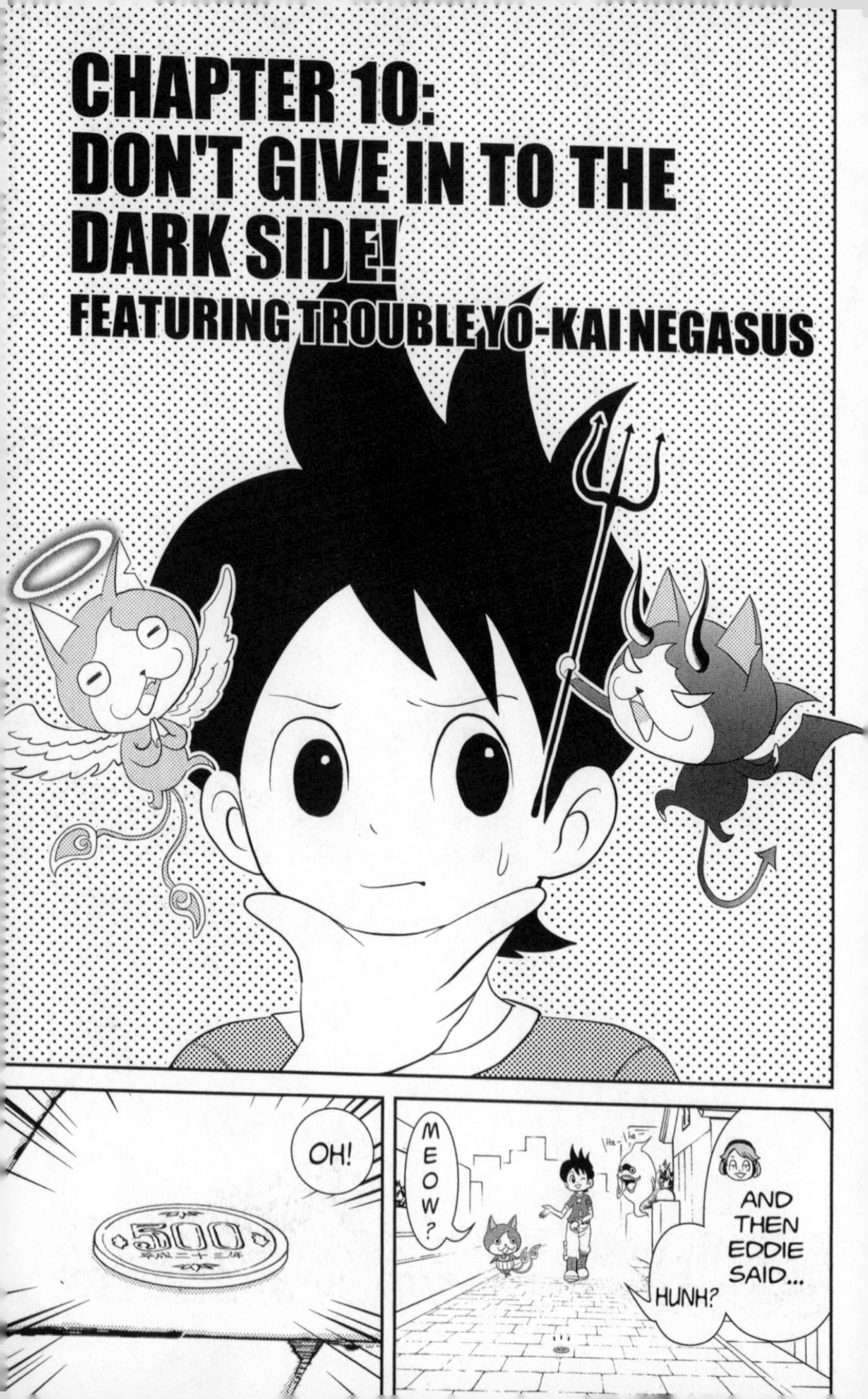
CHAPTER 10:
DON'T GIVE IN TO THE DARK SIDE!
FEATURING TROUBLE YO-KAI NEGASUS
AND THEN EDDIE SAID...
MEOW?
HUNH?
OH!
500

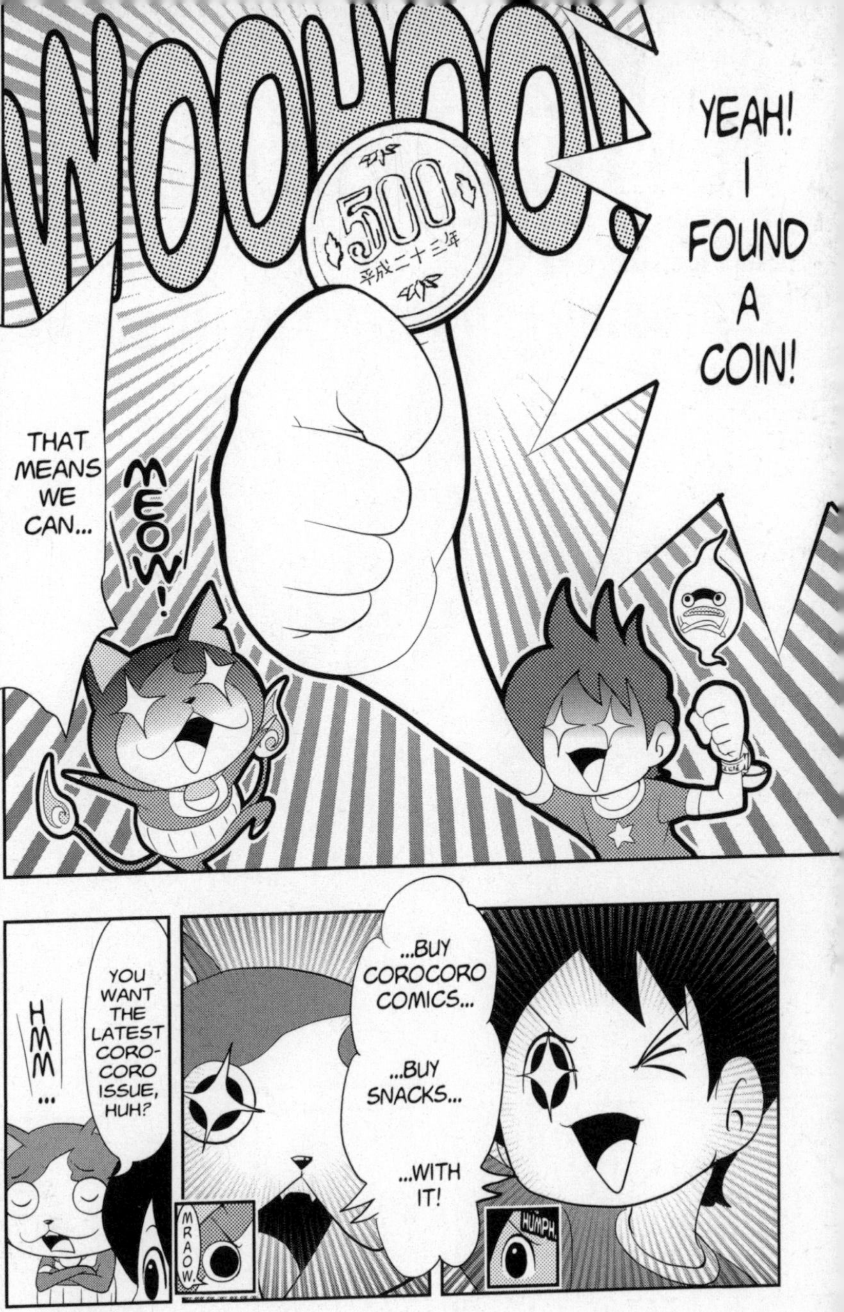
WOOHOO!
500
平成二十三年
YEAH! I FOUND A COIN!
THAT MEANS WE CAN...
MEOW!
...BUY COROCORO COMICS...
...BUY SNACKS...
...WITH IT!
HUMPH.
MRAOW.
YOU WANT THE LATEST CORO-CORO ISSUE, HUH?
HMM...

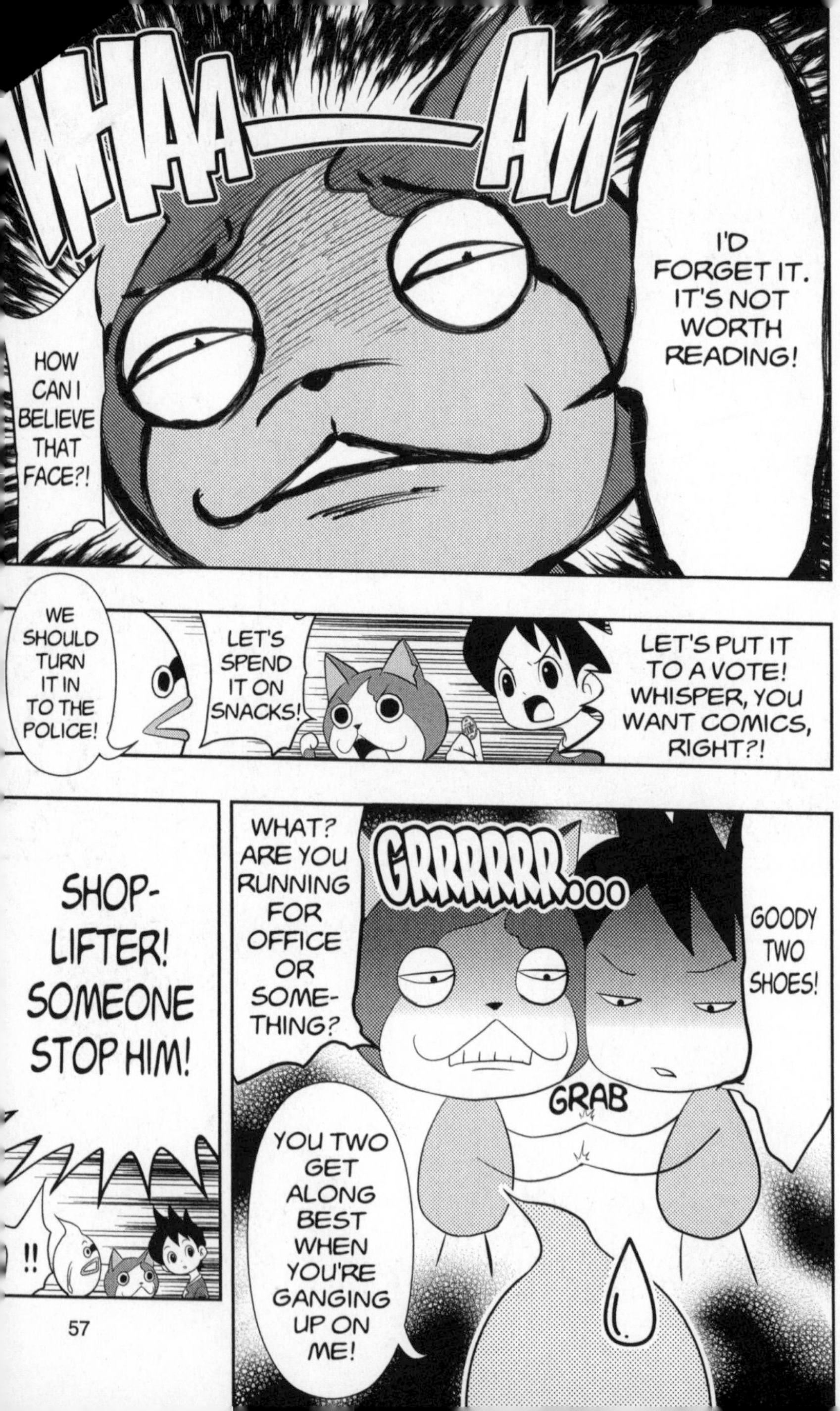
I'D FORGET IT. IT'S NOT WORTH READING!
WHAA—AM
HOW CAN I BELIEVE THAT FACE?!
LET'S PUT IT TO A VOTE! WHISPER, YOU WANT COMICS, RIGHT?!
LET'S SPEND IT ON SNACKS!
WE SHOULD TURN IT IN TO THE POLICE!
GOODY TWO SHOES!
GRRRRRR...OOO
WHAT? ARE YOU RUNNING FOR OFFICE OR SOMETHING?
GRAB
YOU TWO GET ALONG BEST WHEN YOU'RE GANGING UP ON ME!
SHOP-LIFTER! SOMEONE STOP HIM!
!!

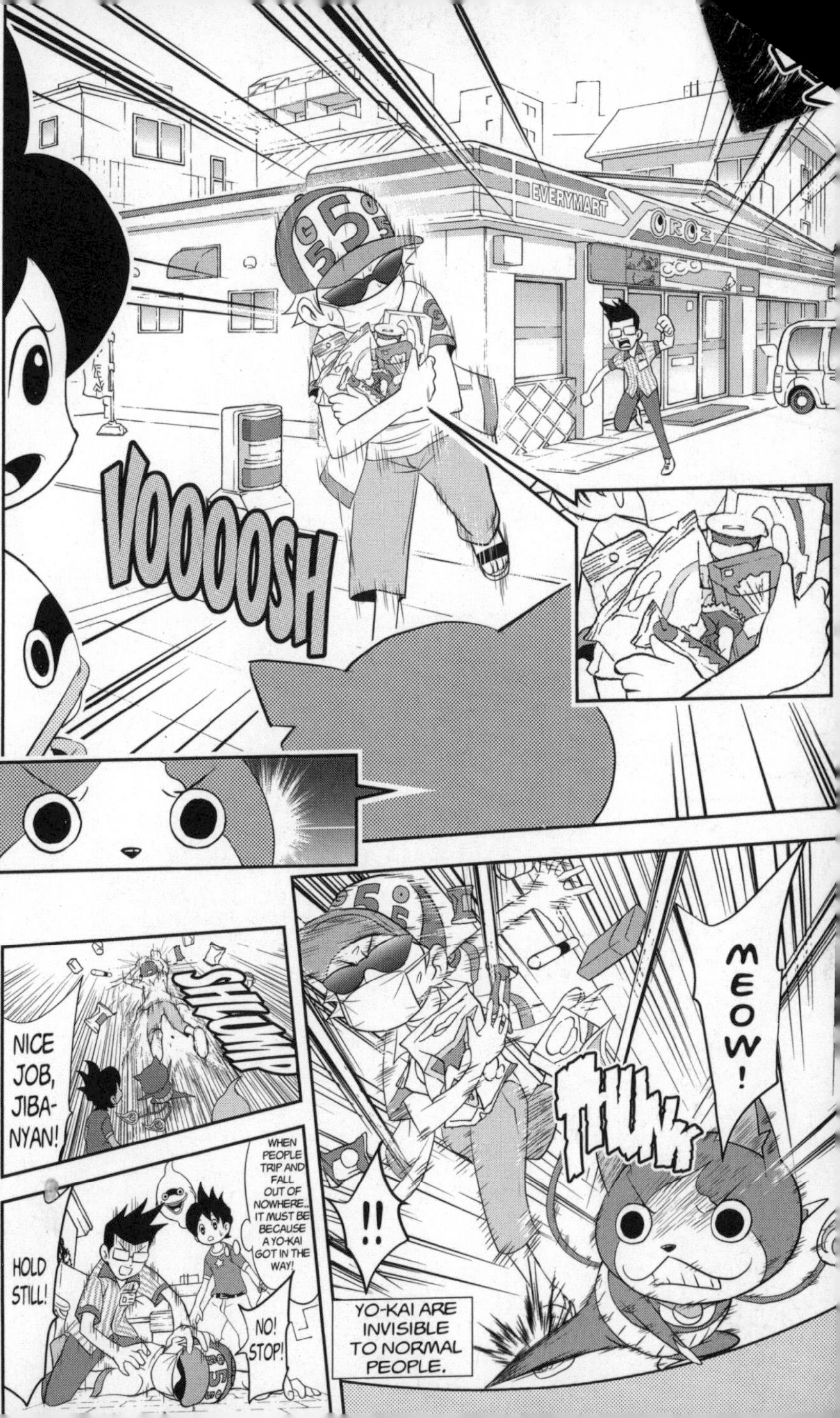
EVERYMART
VOOOOSH
MEOW!
THUNK
!!
YO-KAI ARE INVISIBLE TO NORMAL PEOPLE.
SHLUMP
NICE JOB, JIBA-NYAN!
WHEN PEOPLE TRIP AND FALL OUT OF NOWHERE... IT MUST BE BECAUSE A YO-KAI GOT IN THE WAY!
HOLD STILL!
NO! STOP!

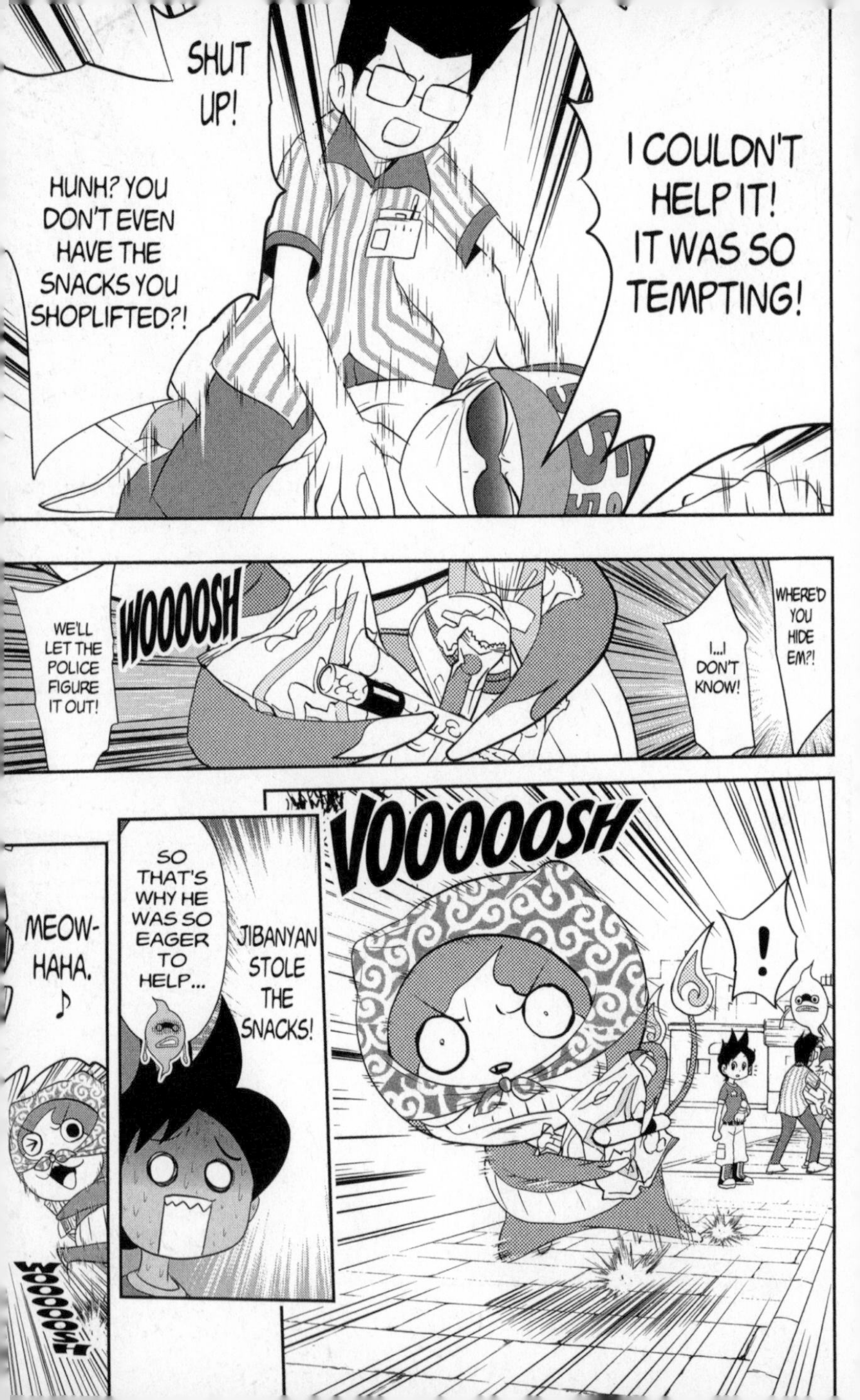

I COULDN'T HELP IT! IT WAS SO TEMPTING!
SHUT UP!
HUNH? YOU DON'T EVEN HAVE THE SNACKS YOU SHOPLIFTED?!
WHERE'D YOU HIDE EM?!
I...I DON'T KNOW!
WOOOOSH
WE'LL LET THE POLICE FIGURE IT OUT!
VOOOOOSH
!
JIBANYAN STOLE THE SNACKS!
SO THAT'S WHY HE WAS SO EAGER TO HELP...
MEOW-HAHA. ♪
WOOOOOSH

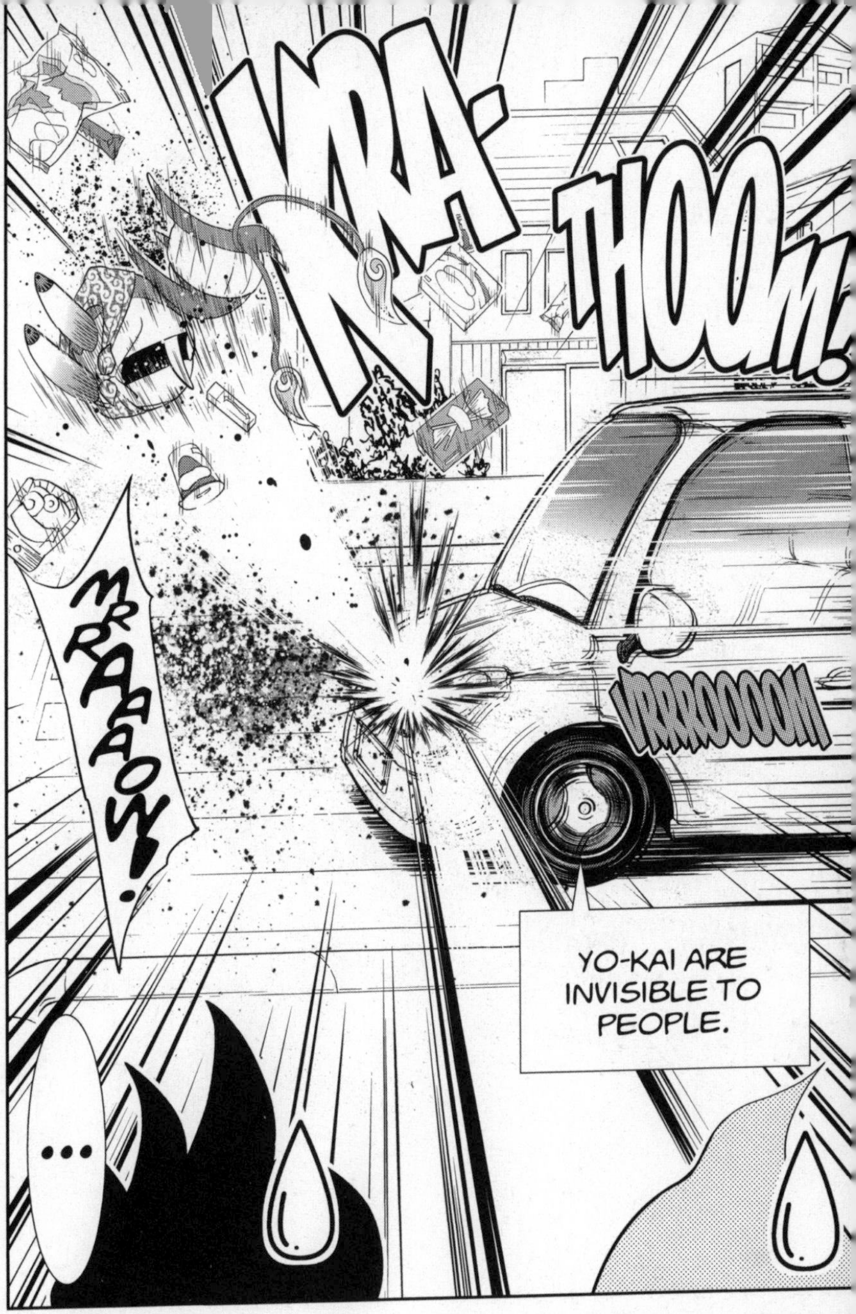
KRA-THOOM!
VRROOOOM
MRRAAAOW!
YO-KAI ARE INVISIBLE TO PEOPLE.
...

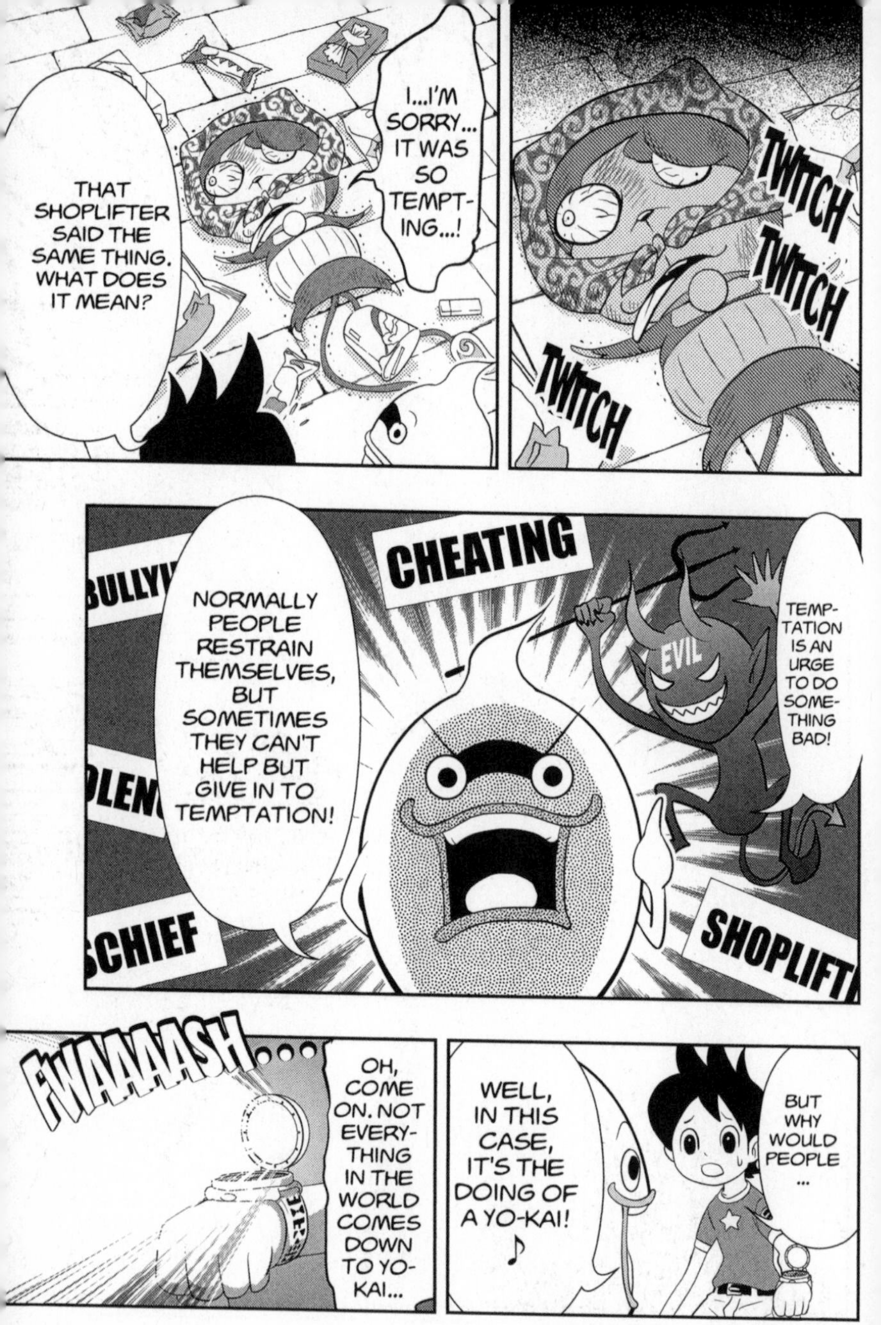
TWITCH
TWITCH
TWITCH
I...I'M SORRY... IT WAS SO TEMPTING...!
THAT SHOPLIFTER SAID THE SAME THING. WHAT DOES IT MEAN?
CHEATING
TEMPTATION IS AN URGE TO DO SOMETHING BAD!
EVIL
NORMALLY PEOPLE RESTRAIN THEMSELVES, BUT SOMETIMES THEY CAN'T HELP BUT GIVE IN TO TEMPTATION!
BULLYI
OLENC
SCHIEF
SHOPLIFT
BUT WHY WOULD PEOPLE ...
WELL, IN THIS CASE, IT'S THE DOING OF A YO-KAI! ♪
OH, COME ON. NOT EVERYTHING IN THE WORLD COMES DOWN TO YO-KAI...
FWAAAASH...

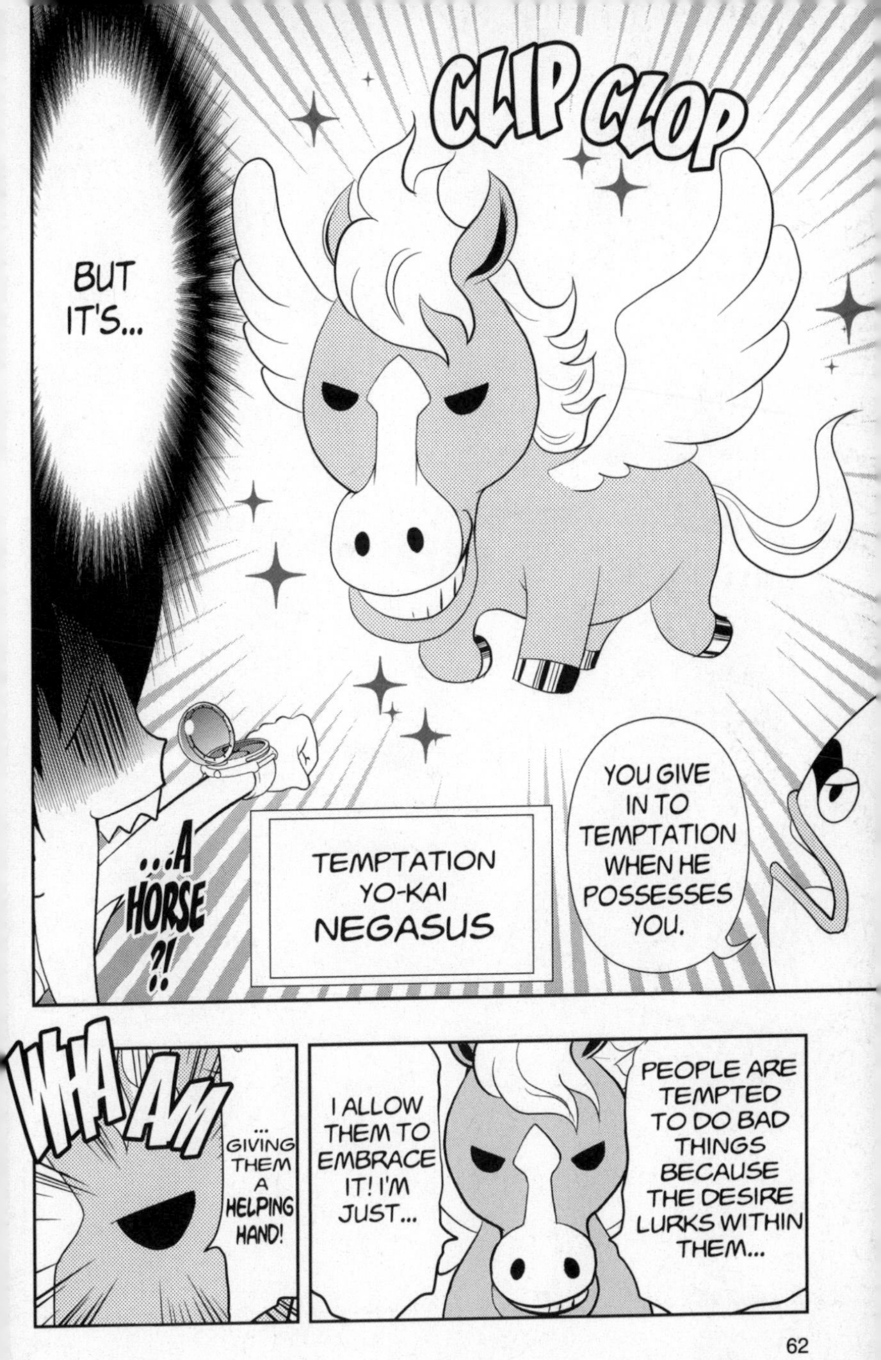
CLIP CLOP
BUT IT'S...
...A HORSE?!
TEMPTATION YO-KAI NEGASUS
YOU GIVE IN TO TEMPTATION WHEN HE POSSESSES YOU.
PEOPLE ARE TEMPTED TO DO BAD THINGS BECAUSE THE DESIRE LURKS WITHIN THEM...
I ALLOW THEM TO EMBRACE IT! I'M JUST...
WHAAM
...GIVING THEM A HELPING HAND!

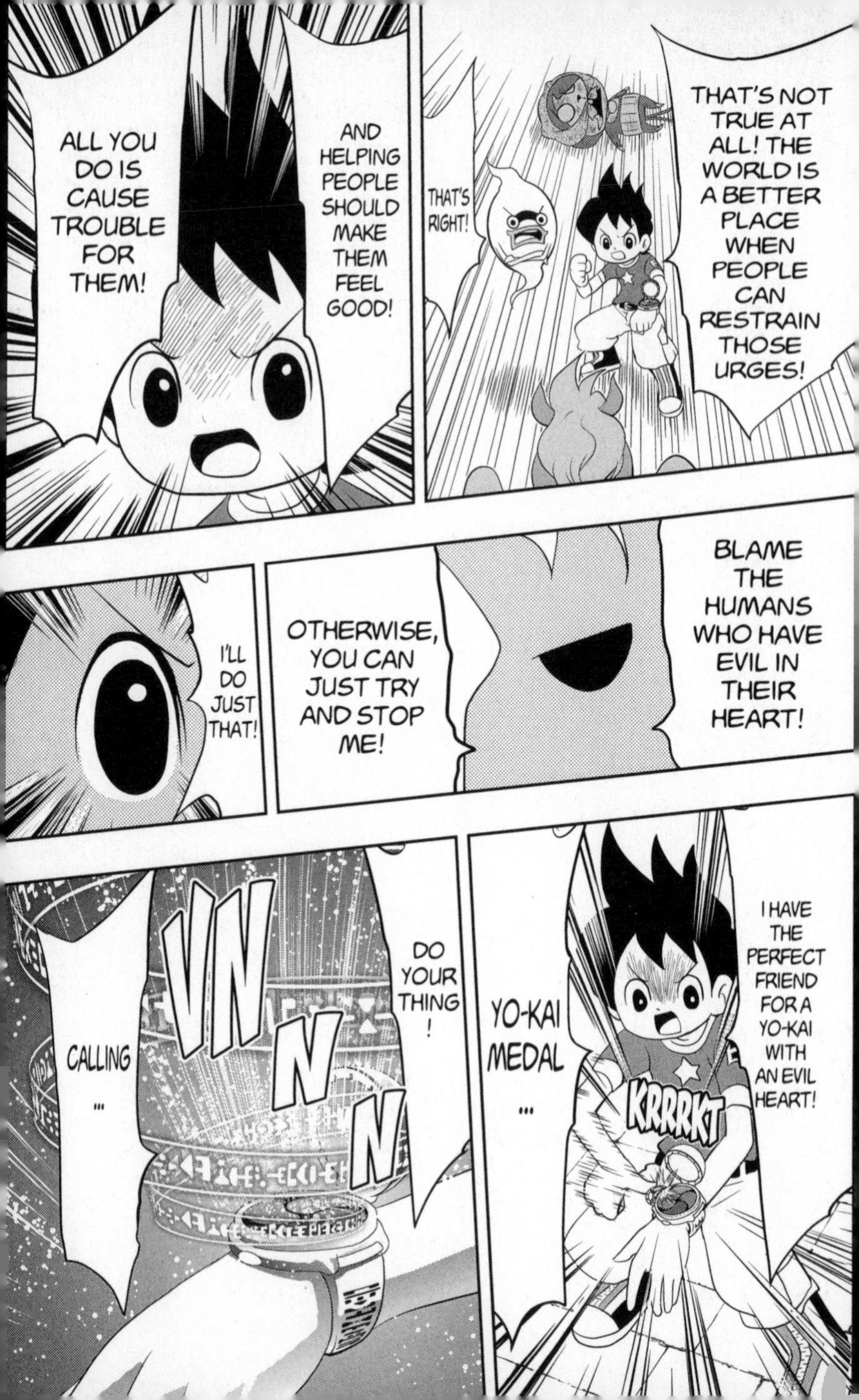
THAT'S NOT TRUE AT ALL! THE WORLD IS A BETTER PLACE WHEN PEOPLE CAN RESTRAIN THOSE URGES!
THAT'S RIGHT!
AND HELPING PEOPLE SHOULD MAKE THEM FEEL GOOD!
ALL YOU DO IS CAUSE TROUBLE FOR THEM!
BLAME THE HUMANS WHO HAVE EVIL IN THEIR HEART!
OTHERWISE, YOU CAN JUST TRY AND STOP ME!
I'LL DO JUST THAT!
I HAVE THE PERFECT FRIEND FOR A YO-KAI WITH AN EVIL HEART!
YO-KAI MEDAL ...
KRRRKT
DO YOUR THING!
VNNN
CALLING ...

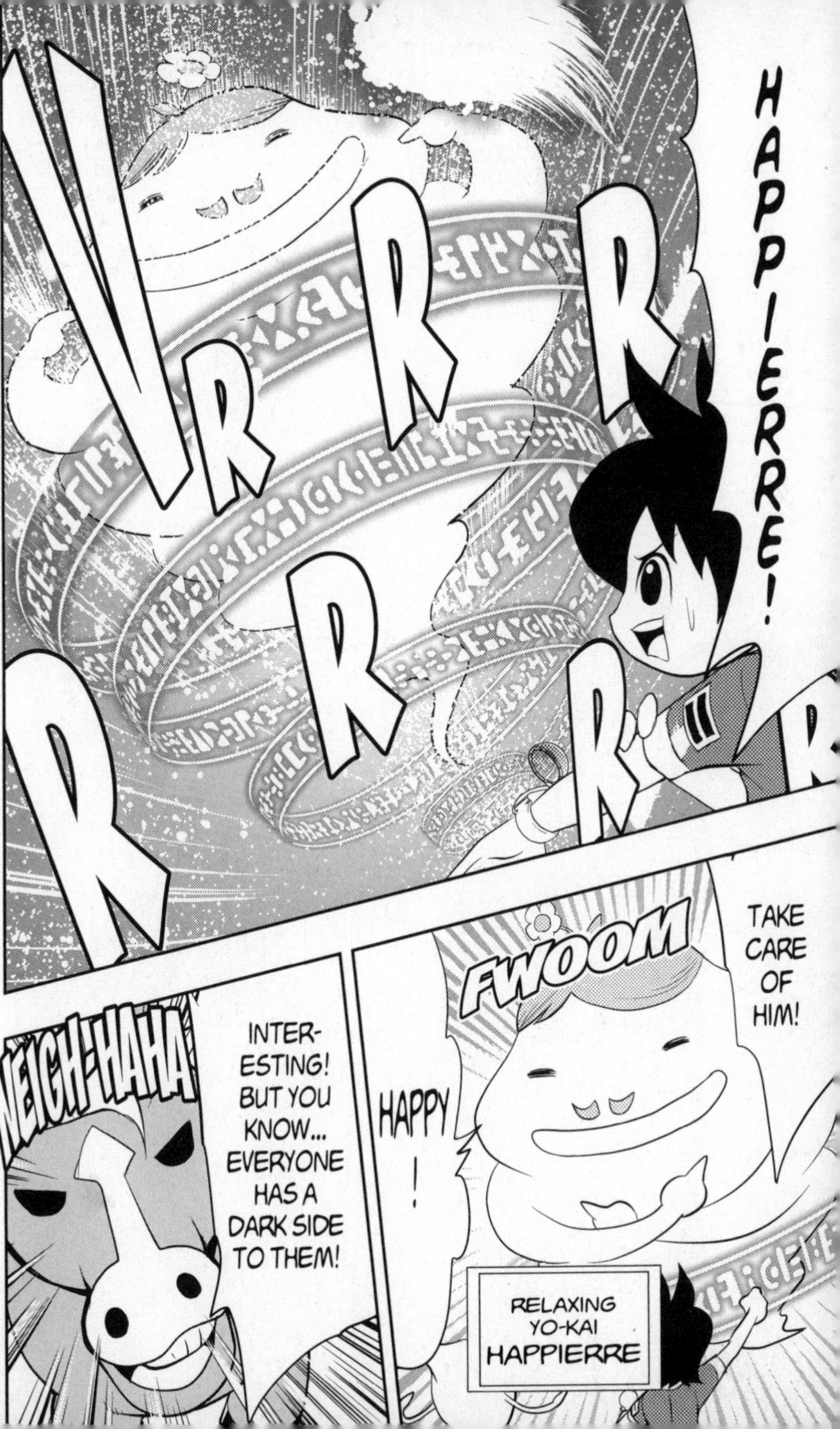
HAPPIERRE!
VRRRRRRR
TAKE CARE OF HIM!
FWOOM
HAPPY!
RELAXING YO-KAI HAPPIERRE
NEIGH-HAHA
INTER-ESTING! BUT YOU KNOW... EVERYONE HAS A DARK SIDE TO THEM!

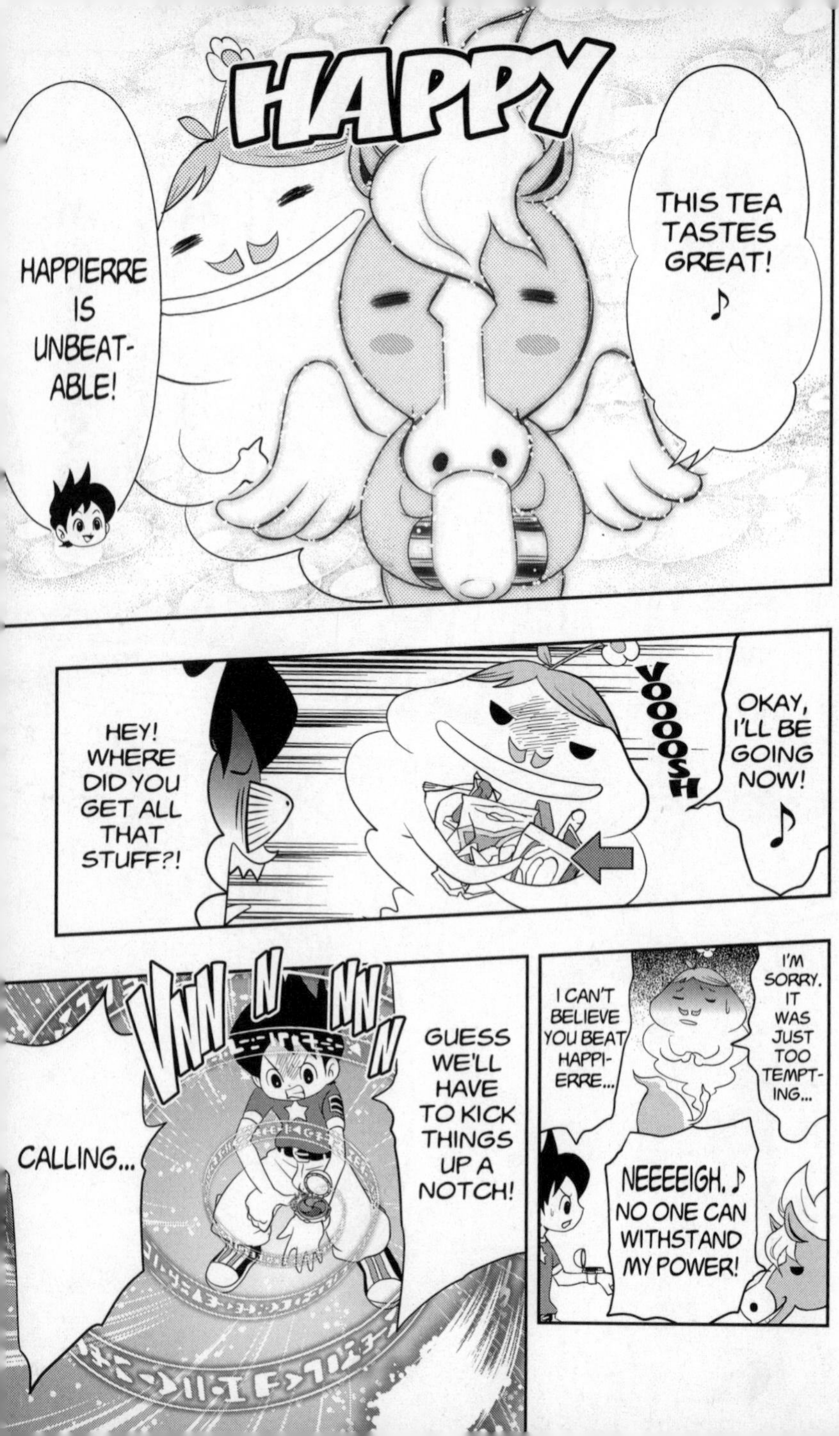
THIS TEA TASTES GREAT! ♪
HAPPY
HAPPIERRE IS UNBEATABLE!
OKAY, I'LL BE GOING NOW! ♪
VOOOOSH
HEY! WHERE DID YOU GET ALL THAT STUFF?!
I'M SORRY. IT WAS JUST TOO TEMPTING...
I CAN'T BELIEVE YOU BEAT HAPPIERRE...
NEEEEIGH. ♪ NO ONE CAN WITHSTAND MY POWER!
GUESS WE'LL HAVE TO KICK THINGS UP A NOTCH!
VNN N NN N
CALLING...

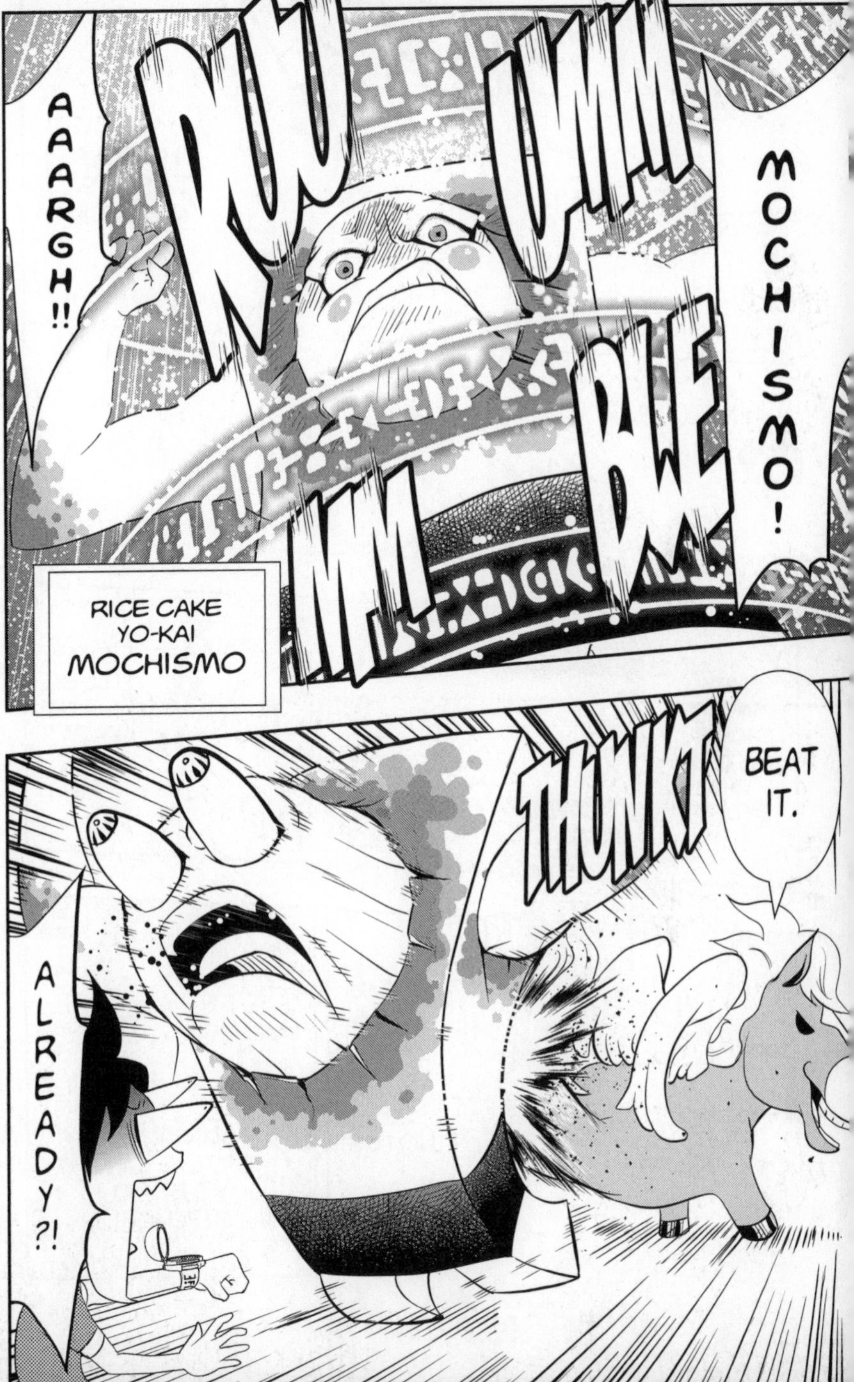
MOCHISMO!
AAAARGH!!
RICE CAKE YO-KAI MOCHISMO
BEAT IT.
THUNK!
ALREADY?!

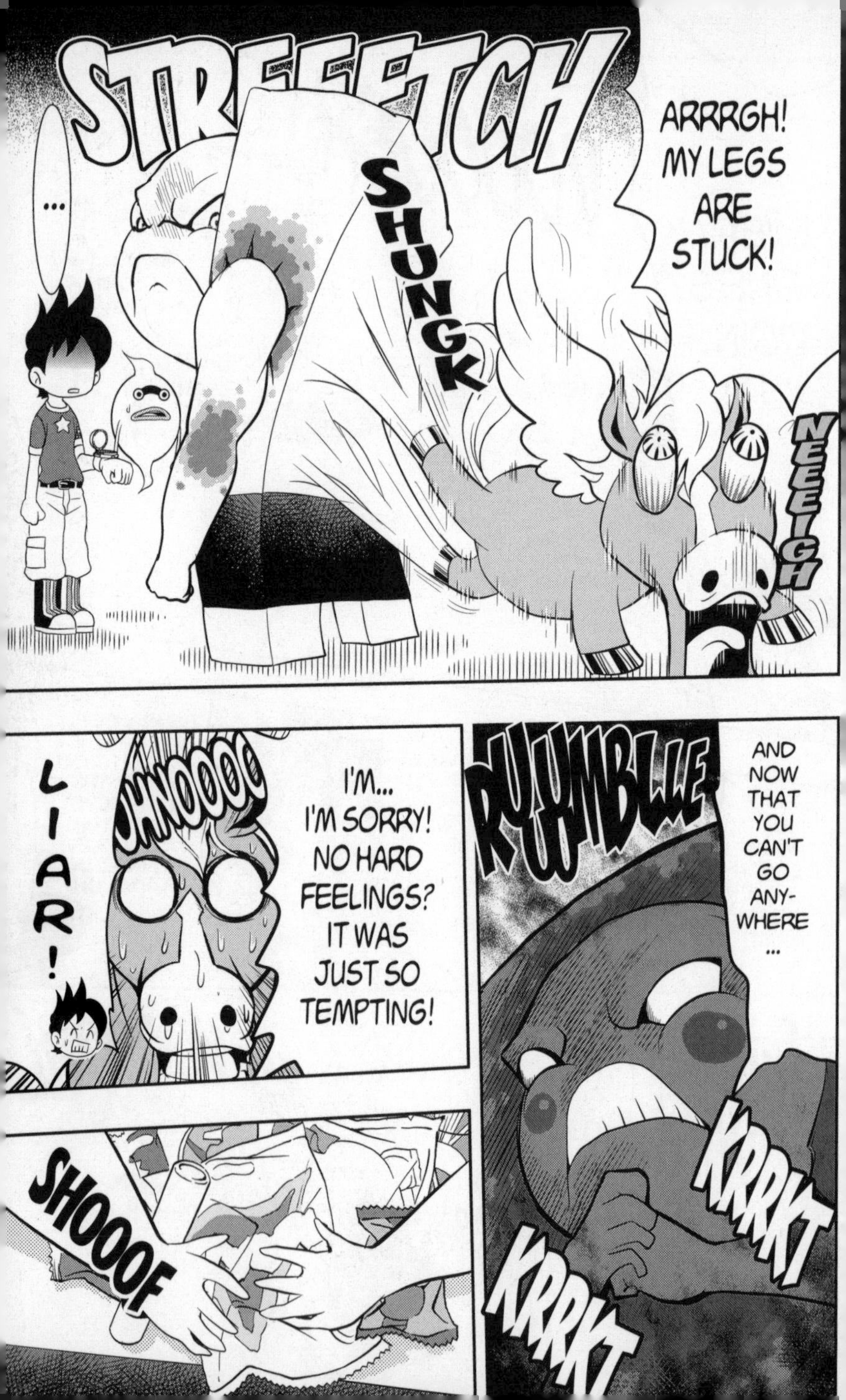
ARRRGH! MY LEGS ARE STUCK!
STREEEETCH
SHUNGK
NEEEEIGH
...
RUMBLLE
AND NOW THAT YOU CAN'T GO ANYWHERE...
KRRKT
KRRKT
I'M... I'M SORRY! NO HARD FEELINGS? IT WAS JUST SO TEMPTING!
OHNOOOO
LIAR!
SHOOOF

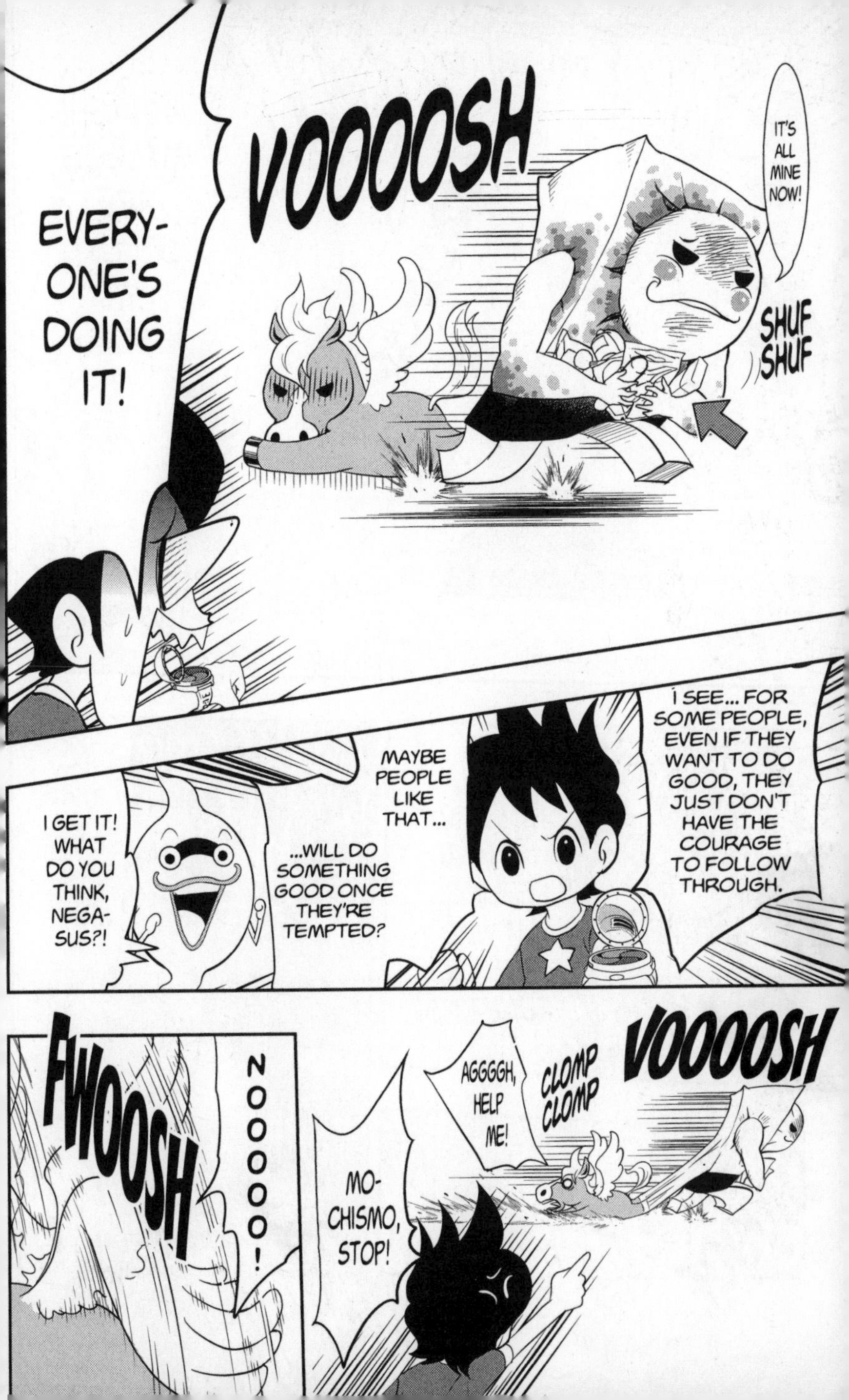
IT'S ALL MINE NOW!
VOOOOSH
SHUF SHUF
EVERY-ONE'S DOING IT!
I SEE... FOR SOME PEOPLE, EVEN IF THEY WANT TO DO GOOD, THEY JUST DON'T HAVE THE COURAGE TO FOLLOW THROUGH.
MAYBE PEOPLE LIKE THAT...
...WILL DO SOMETHING GOOD ONCE THEY'RE TEMPTED?
I GET IT! WHAT DO YOU THINK, NEGA-SUS?!
VOOOOSH
CLOMP CLOMP
AGGGGH, HELP ME!
MO-CHISMO, STOP!
NOOOOOO!
FWOOSH

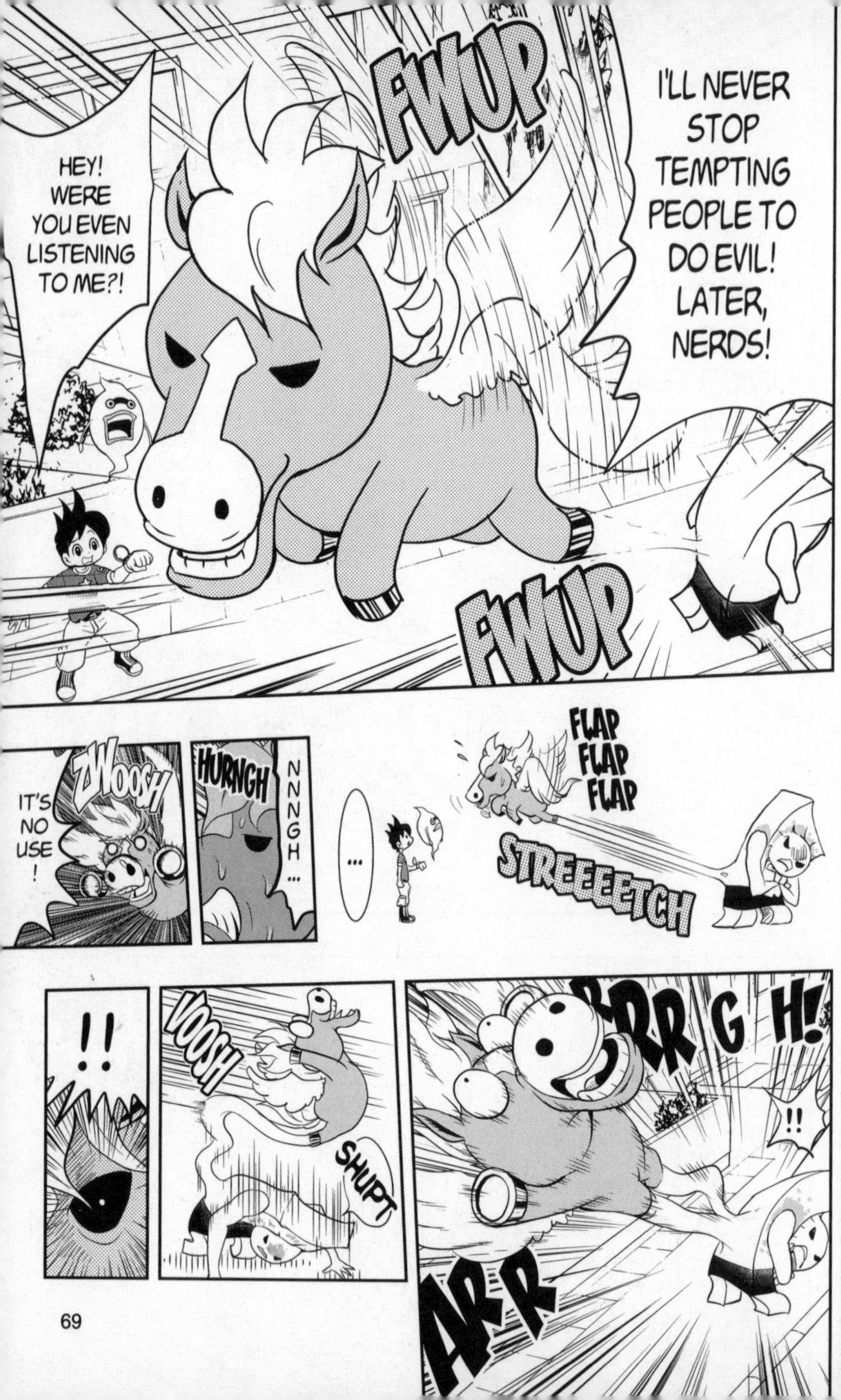
I'LL NEVER STOP TEMPTING PEOPLE TO DO EVIL! LATER, NERDS!
FWUP
HEY! WERE YOU EVEN LISTENING TO ME?!
FWUP
FLAP FLAP FLAP
STREEEEETCH
...
HURNGH
NNNGH...
ZWOOSH
IT'S NO USE!
BRRRGH!
!!
ARR
VOOSH
SHUPT
!!

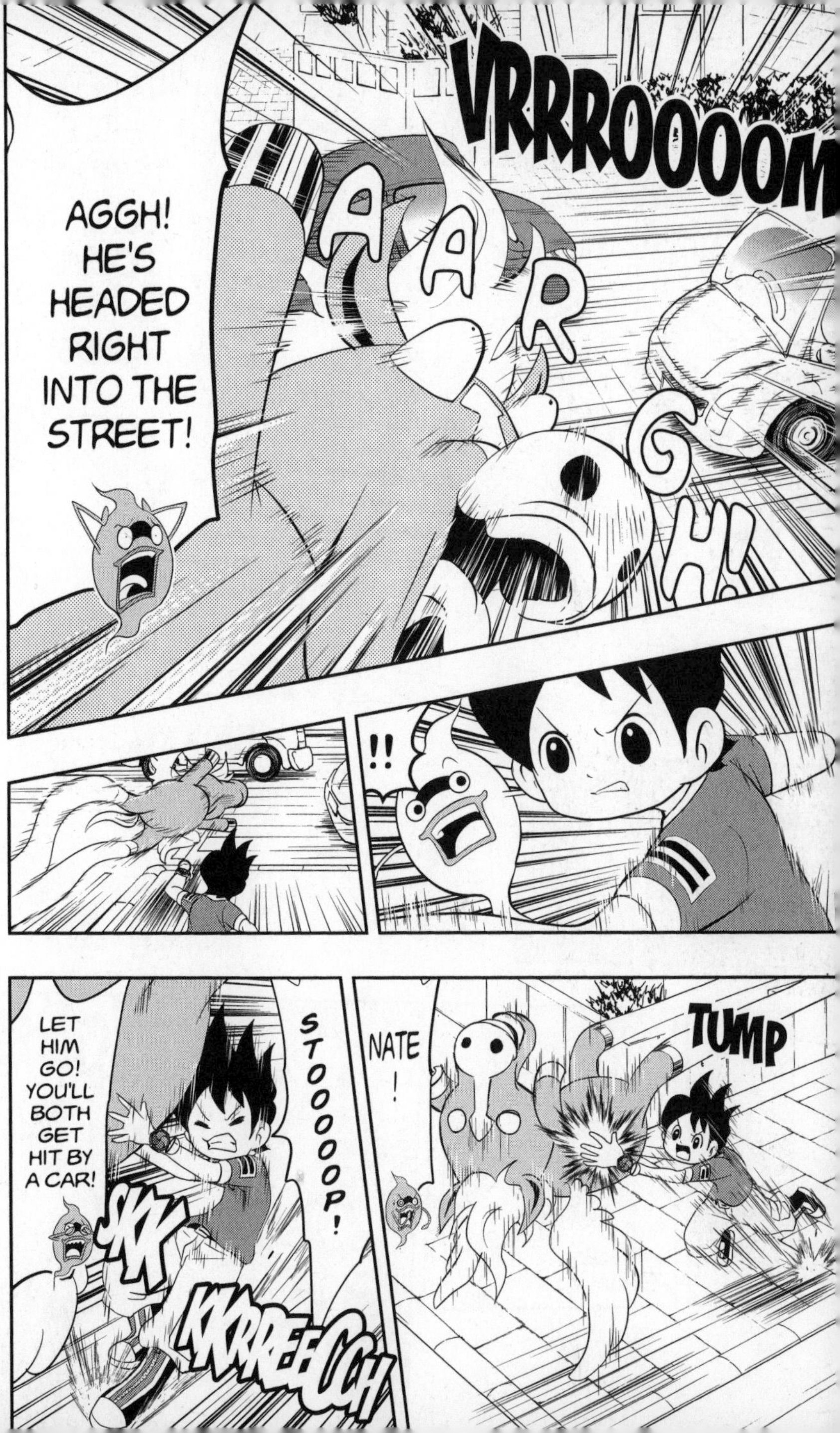
VRRROOOOM
AAARGGH!
AGGH! HE'S HEADED RIGHT INTO THE STREET!
!!
TUMP
NATE!
STOOOOOOP!
LET HIM GO! YOU'LL BOTH GET HIT BY A CAR!
SKK
KKRREECH

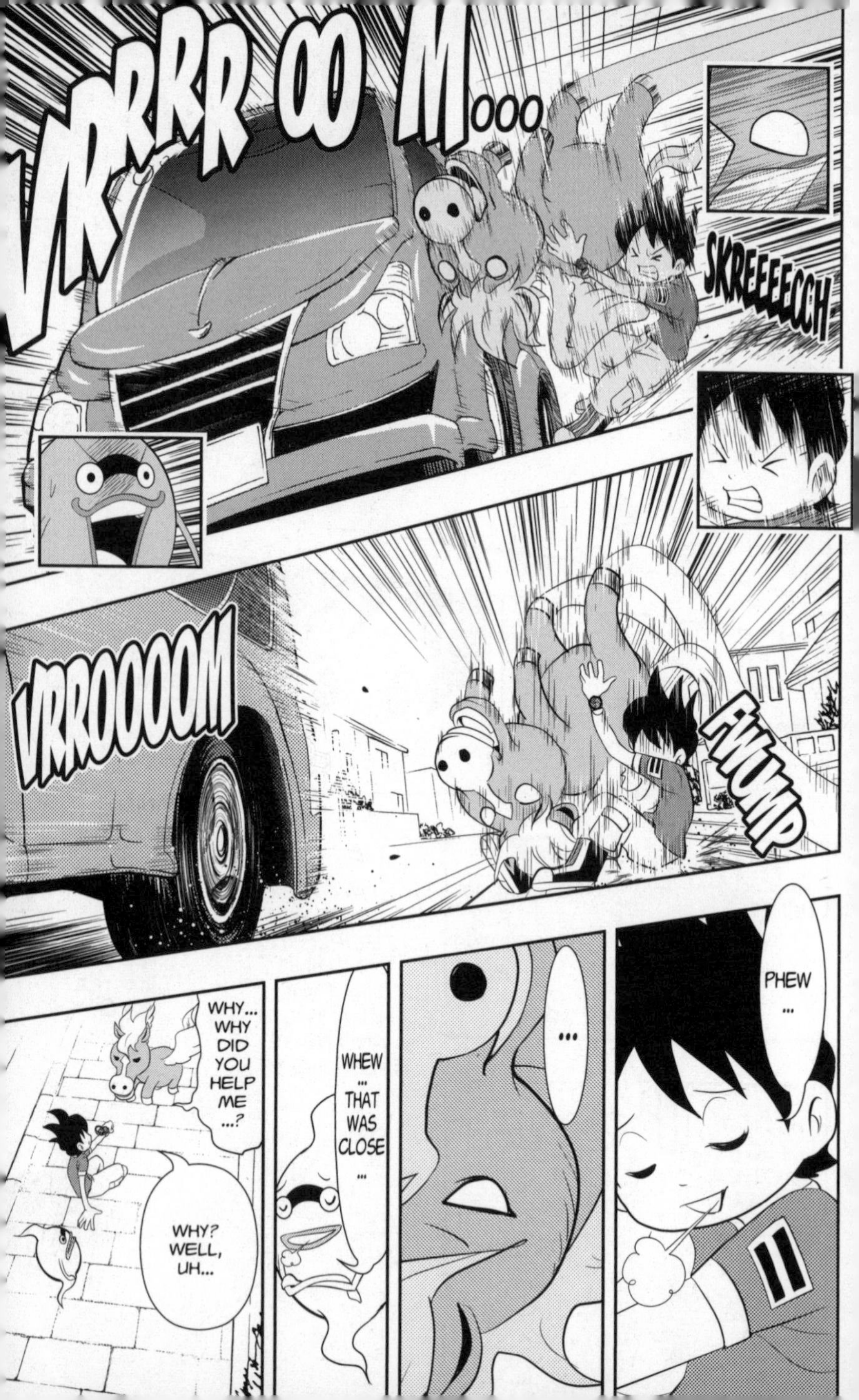
VRRRR OO M...
SKREEEECCH
VRROOOOM
FWUMP
PHEW ...
...
WHEW ... THAT WAS CLOSE ...
WHY... WHY DID YOU HELP ME ...?
WHY? WELL, UH...

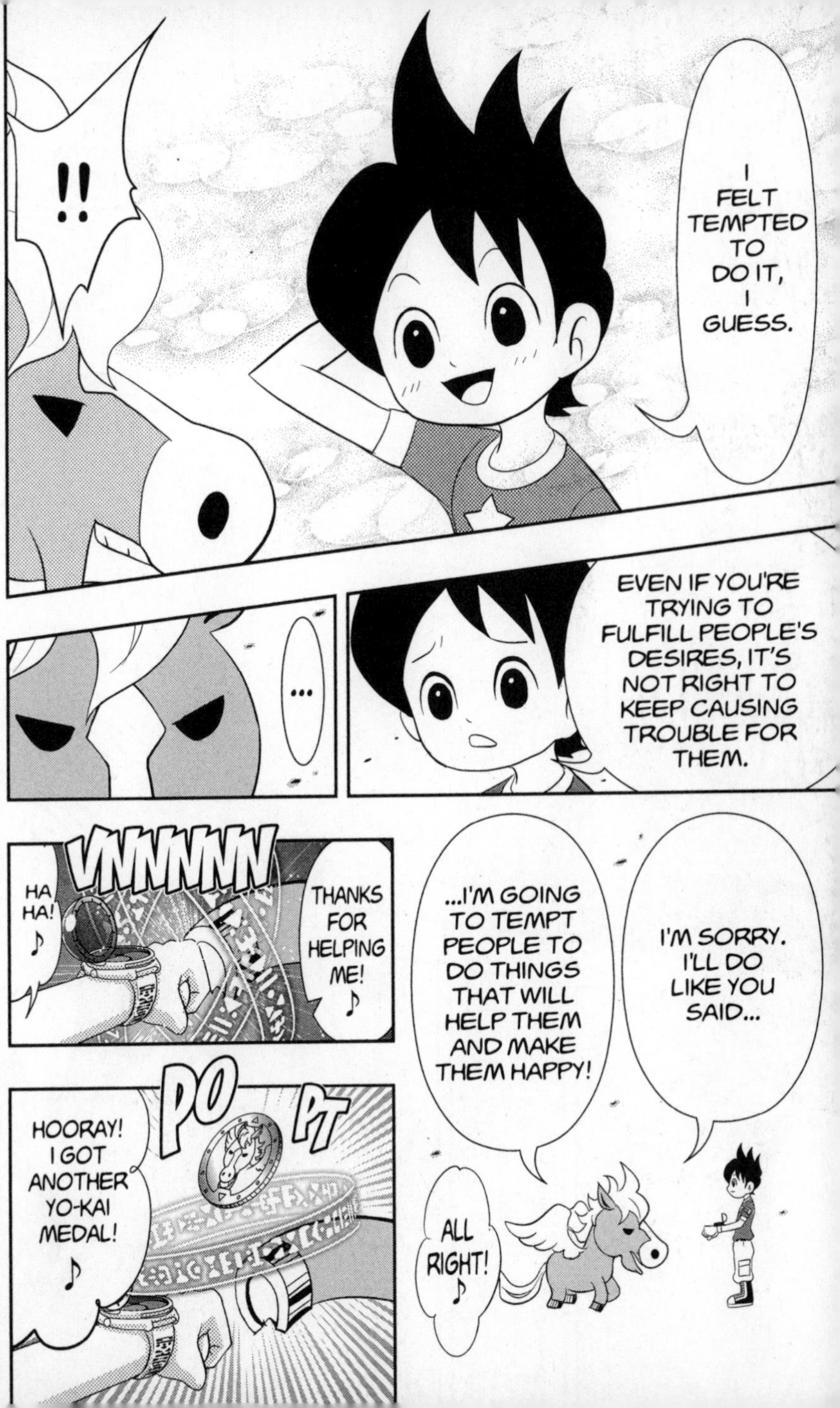
I FELT TEMPTED TO DO IT, I GUESS.
!!
EVEN IF YOU'RE TRYING TO FULFILL PEOPLE'S DESIRES, IT'S NOT RIGHT TO KEEP CAUSING TROUBLE FOR THEM.
...
I'M SORRY. I'LL DO LIKE YOU SAID...
...I'M GOING TO TEMPT PEOPLE TO DO THINGS THAT WILL HELP THEM AND MAKE THEM HAPPY!
ALL RIGHT! ♪
VNNNNNN
THANKS FOR HELPING ME! ♪
HA HA! ♪
POPT
HOORAY! I GOT ANOTHER YO-KAI MEDAL! ♪

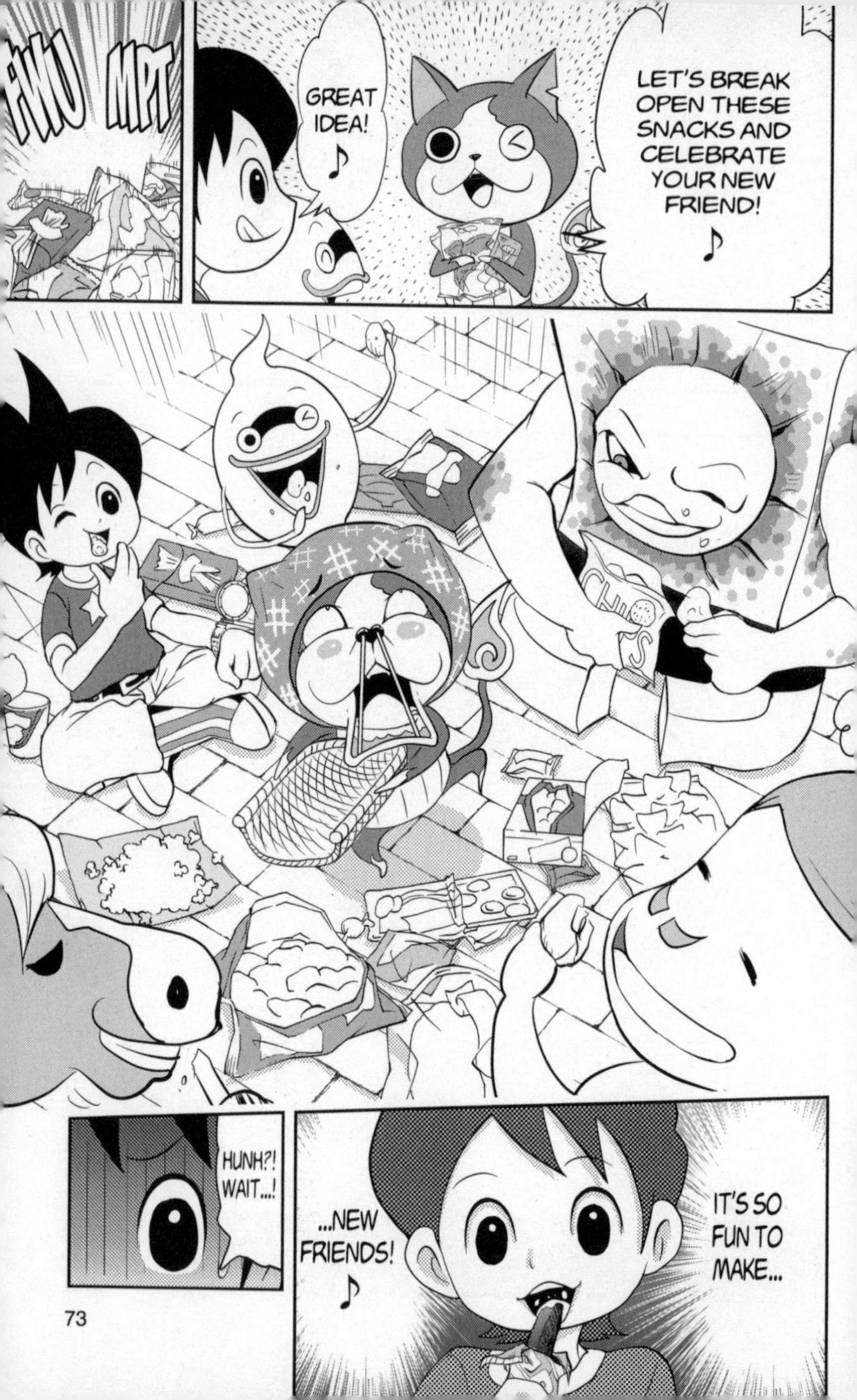
LET'S BREAK OPEN THESE SNACKS AND CELEBRATE YOUR NEW FRIEND! ♪
GREAT IDEA! ♪
MPT
IT'S SO FUN TO MAKE...
...NEW FRIENDS! ♪
HUNH?! WAIT...!

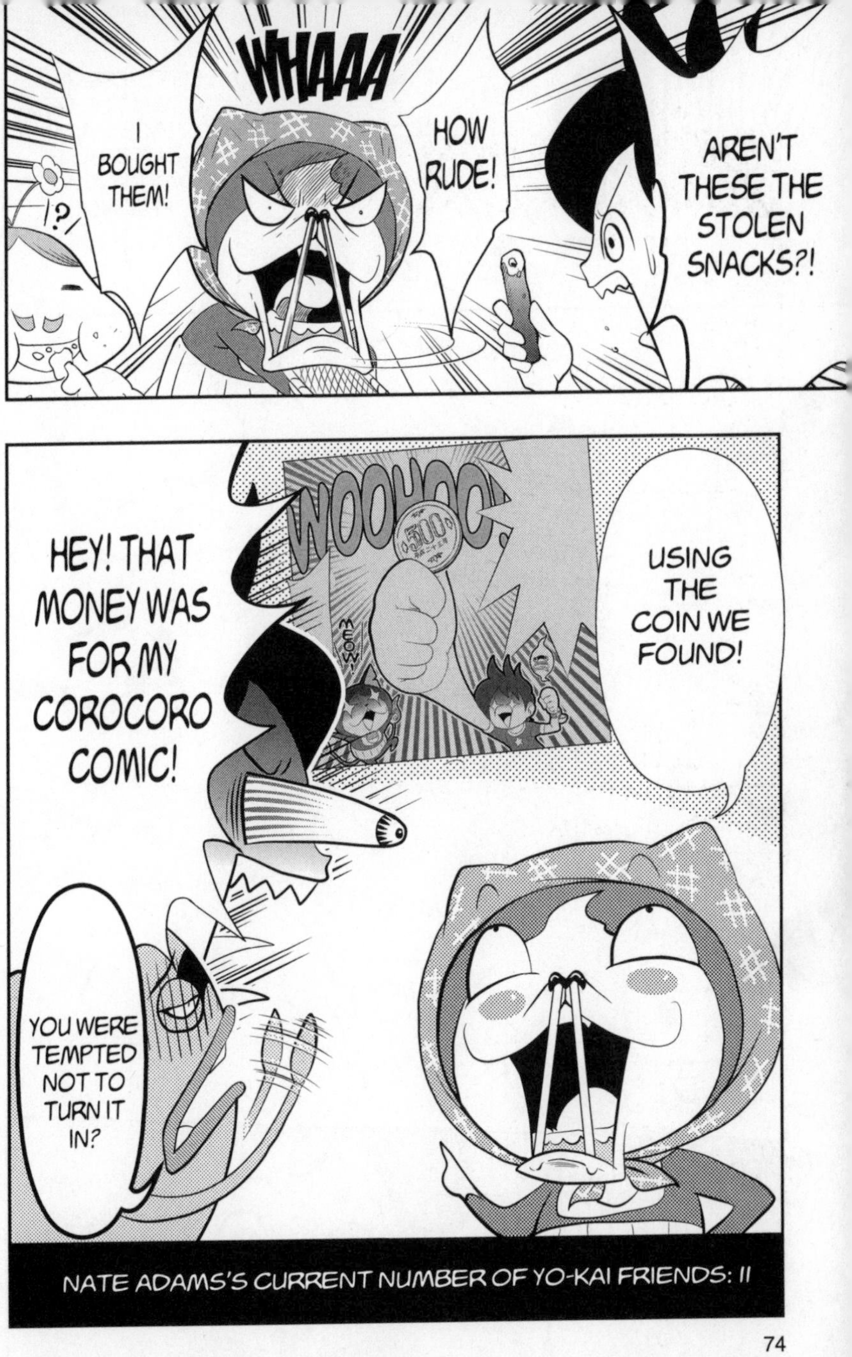
AREN'T THESE THE STOLEN SNACKS?!
HOW RUDE!
WHAAA
I BOUGHT THEM!
!?
USING THE COIN WE FOUND!
WOOHOO
MEOW!
HEY! THAT MONEY WAS FOR MY COROCORO COMIC!
YOU WERE TEMPTED NOT TO TURN IT IN?
NATE ADAMS'S CURRENT NUMBER OF YO-KAI FRIENDS: 11

OPEN MIC NIGHT: DAIZ & NEGASUS

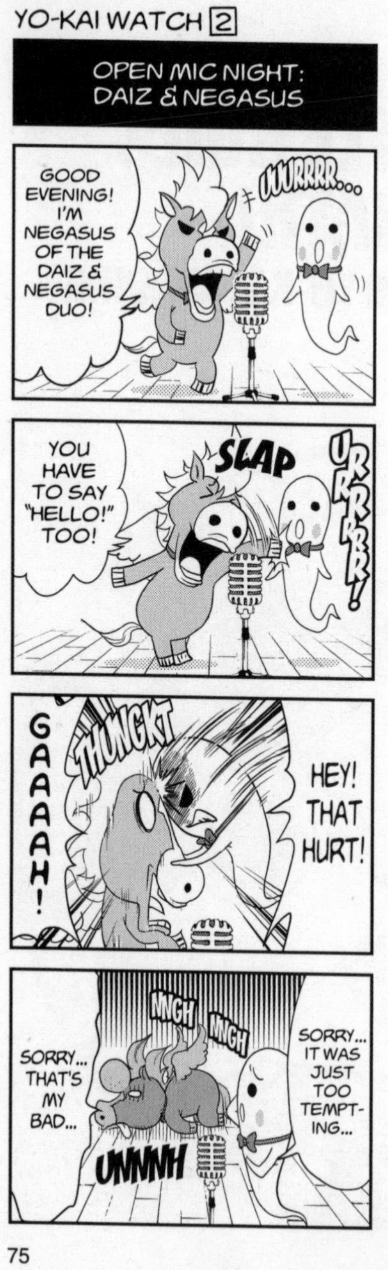
UUURRRR...
GOOD EVENING! I'M NEGASUS OF THE DAIZ & NEGASUS DUO!
URRRRR!
SLAP
YOU HAVE TO SAY "HELLO!" TOO!
HEY! THAT HURT!
THUNGKT
GAAAAAH!
SORRY... IT WAS JUST TOO TEMPT-ING...
MNGH
MNGH
SORRY... THAT'S MY BAD...
UNNNH

CHAPTER 11: A YO-KAI BATTLE BOILS OVER IN THE BATH!

FEATURING GYM-LOVER YO-KAI SPROINK

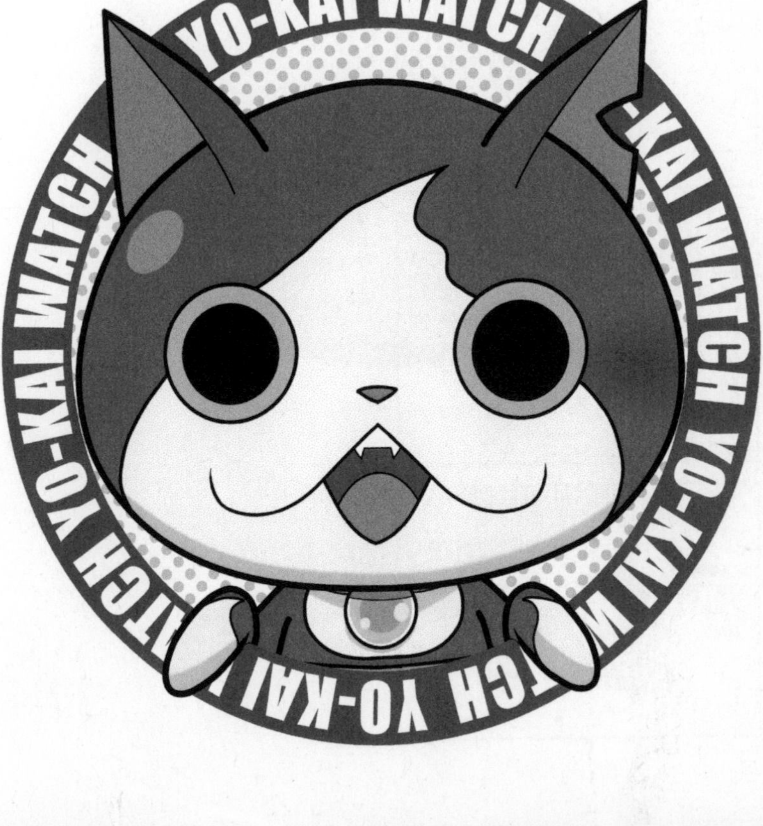
YO-KAI WATCH

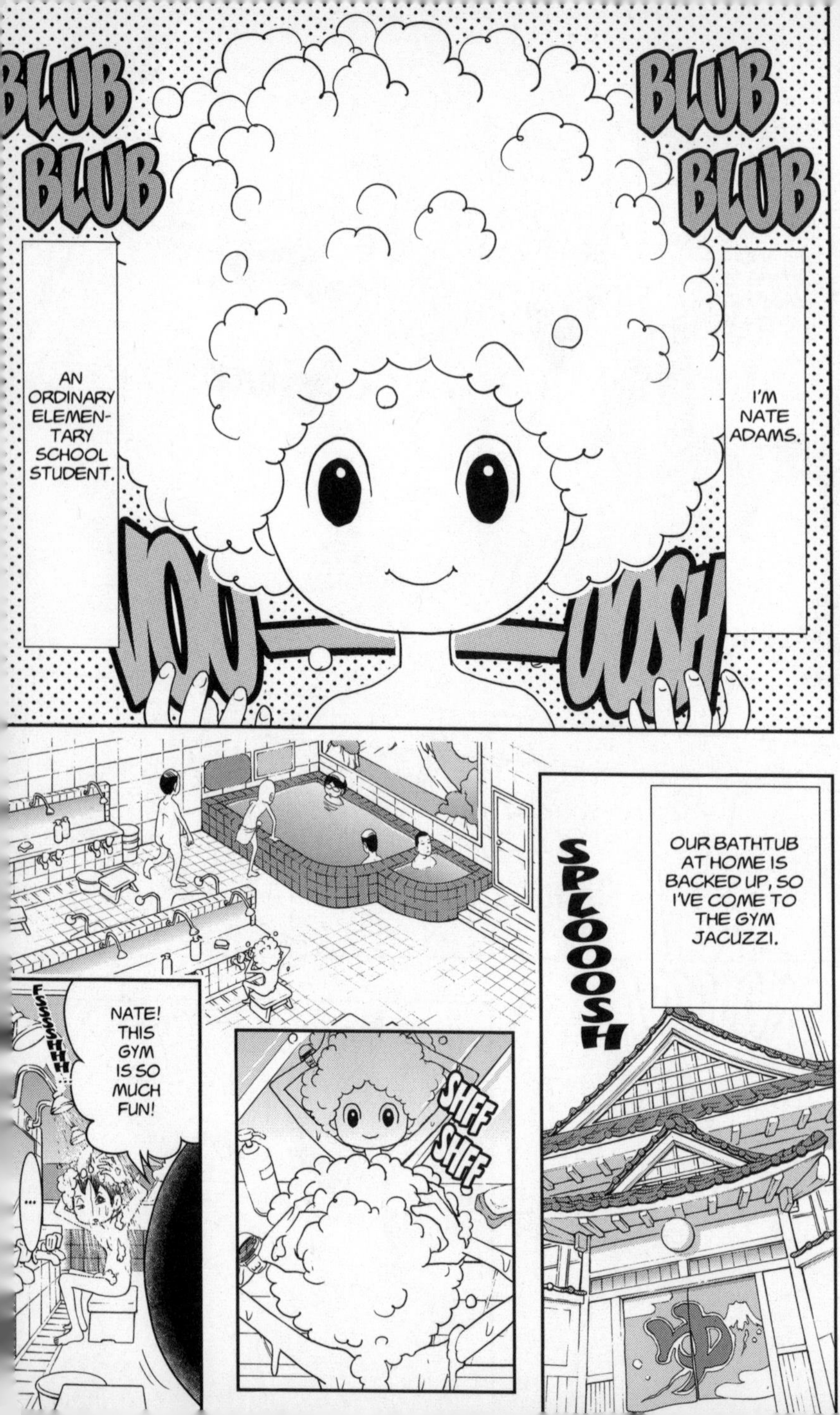
BLUB BLUB
BLUB BLUB
I'M NATE ADAMS.
AN ORDINARY ELEMENTARY SCHOOL STUDENT.
VOO
UOSH
OUR BATHTUB AT HOME IS BACKED UP, SO I'VE COME TO THE GYM JACUZZI.
SPLOOOOSH
SHFF SHFF
NATE! THIS GYM IS SO MUCH FUN!
FSSSSHHH
...

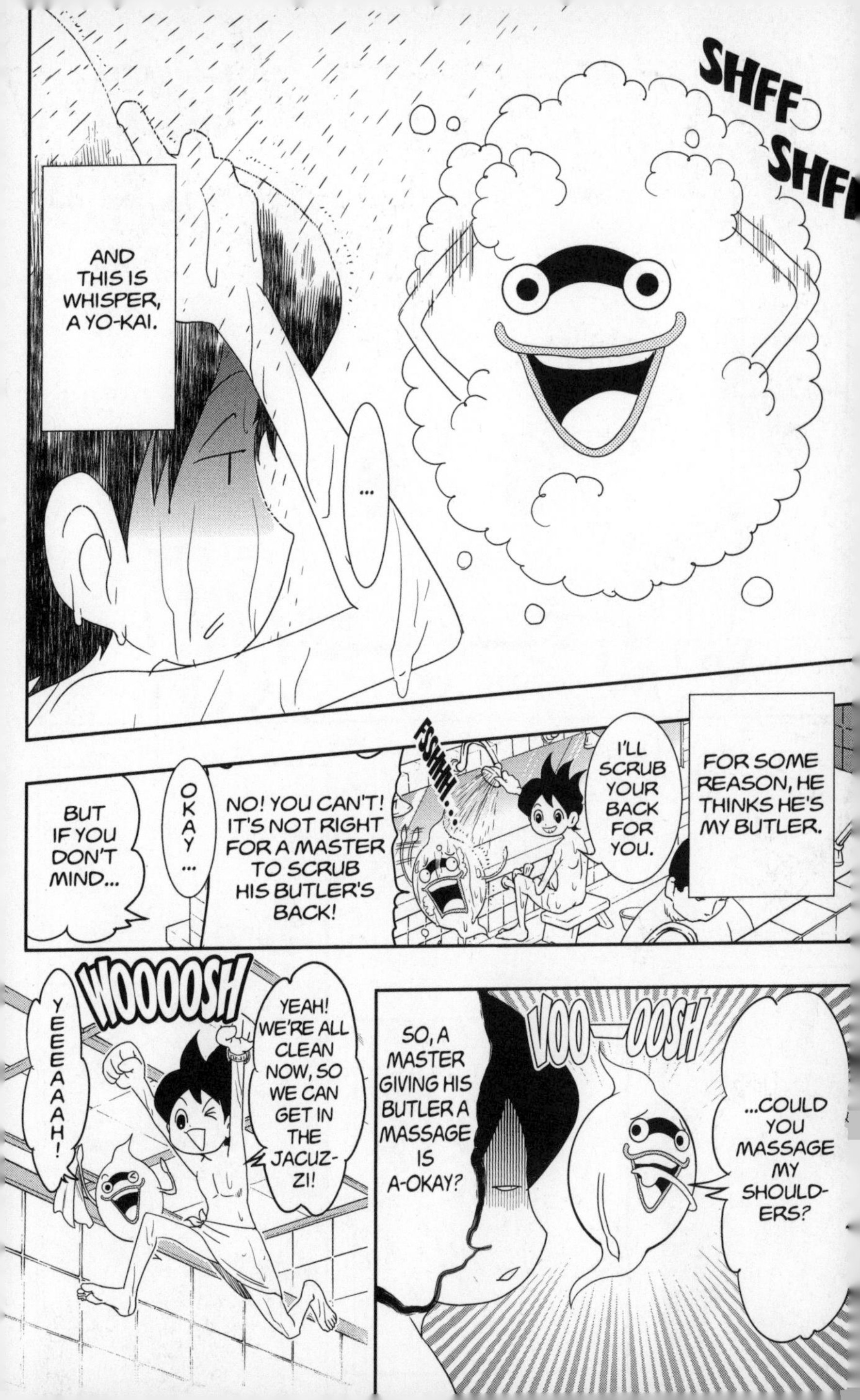
SHFF SHFF
AND THIS IS WHISPER, A YO-KAI.
...
FOR SOME REASON, HE THINKS HE'S MY BUTLER.
I'LL SCRUB YOUR BACK FOR YOU.
FSSHHH...
NO! YOU CAN'T! IT'S NOT RIGHT FOR A MASTER TO SCRUB HIS BUTLER'S BACK!
OKAY...
BUT IF YOU DON'T MIND...
...COULD YOU MASSAGE MY SHOULDERS?
VOO—OOSH
SO, A MASTER GIVING HIS BUTLER A MASSAGE IS A-OKAY?
YEAH! WE'RE ALL CLEAN NOW, SO WE CAN GET IN THE JACUZZI!
WOOOOSH
YEEEAAAAH!

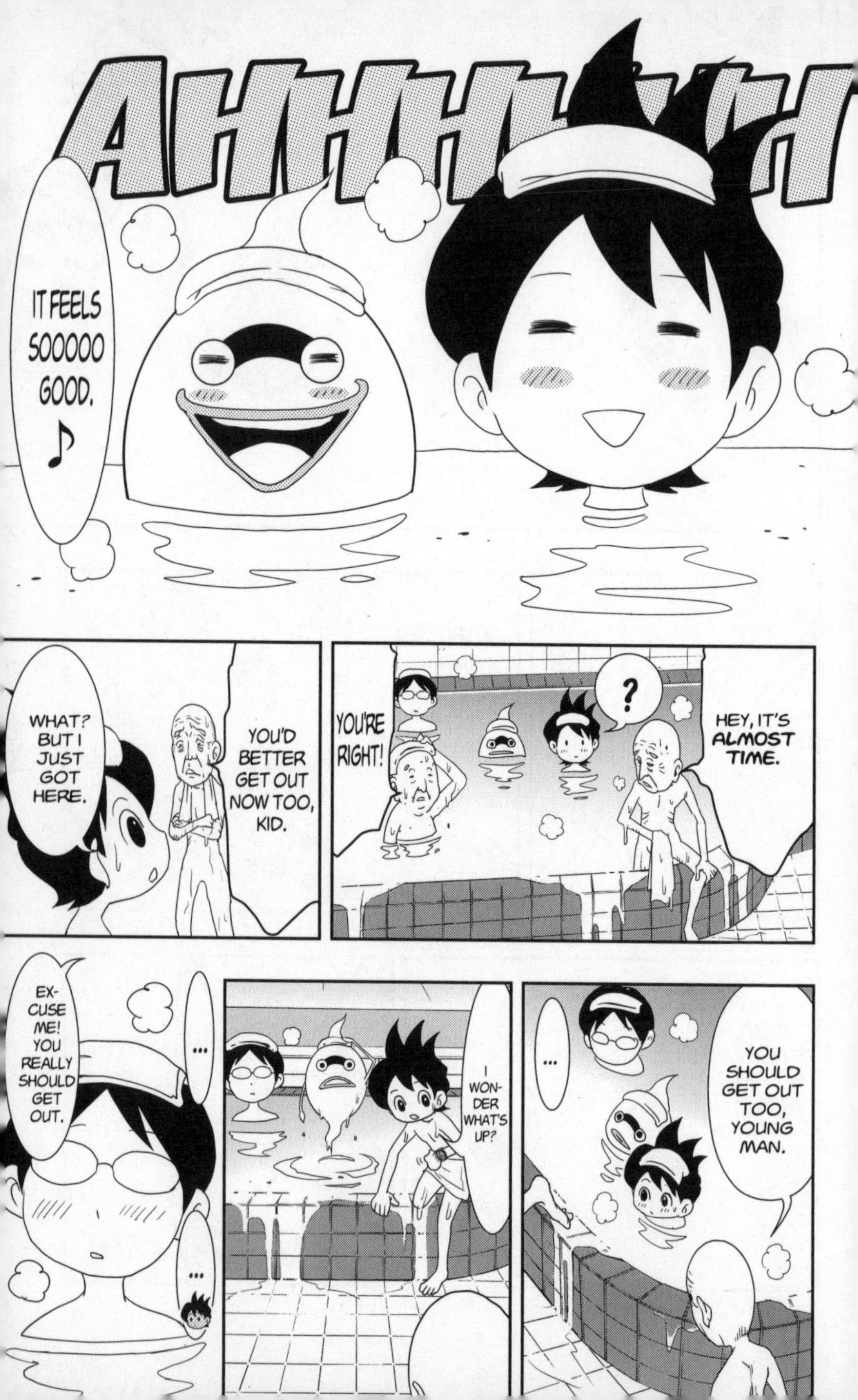
AHHHHHHH
IT FEELS SOOOOO GOOD. ♪
HEY, IT'S **ALMOST** TIME.
?
YOU'RE RIGHT!
YOU'D BETTER GET OUT NOW TOO, KID.
WHAT? BUT I JUST GOT HERE.
YOU SHOULD GET OUT TOO, YOUNG MAN.
...
I WONDER WHAT'S UP?
...
EXCUSE ME! YOU REALLY SHOULD GET OUT.
...

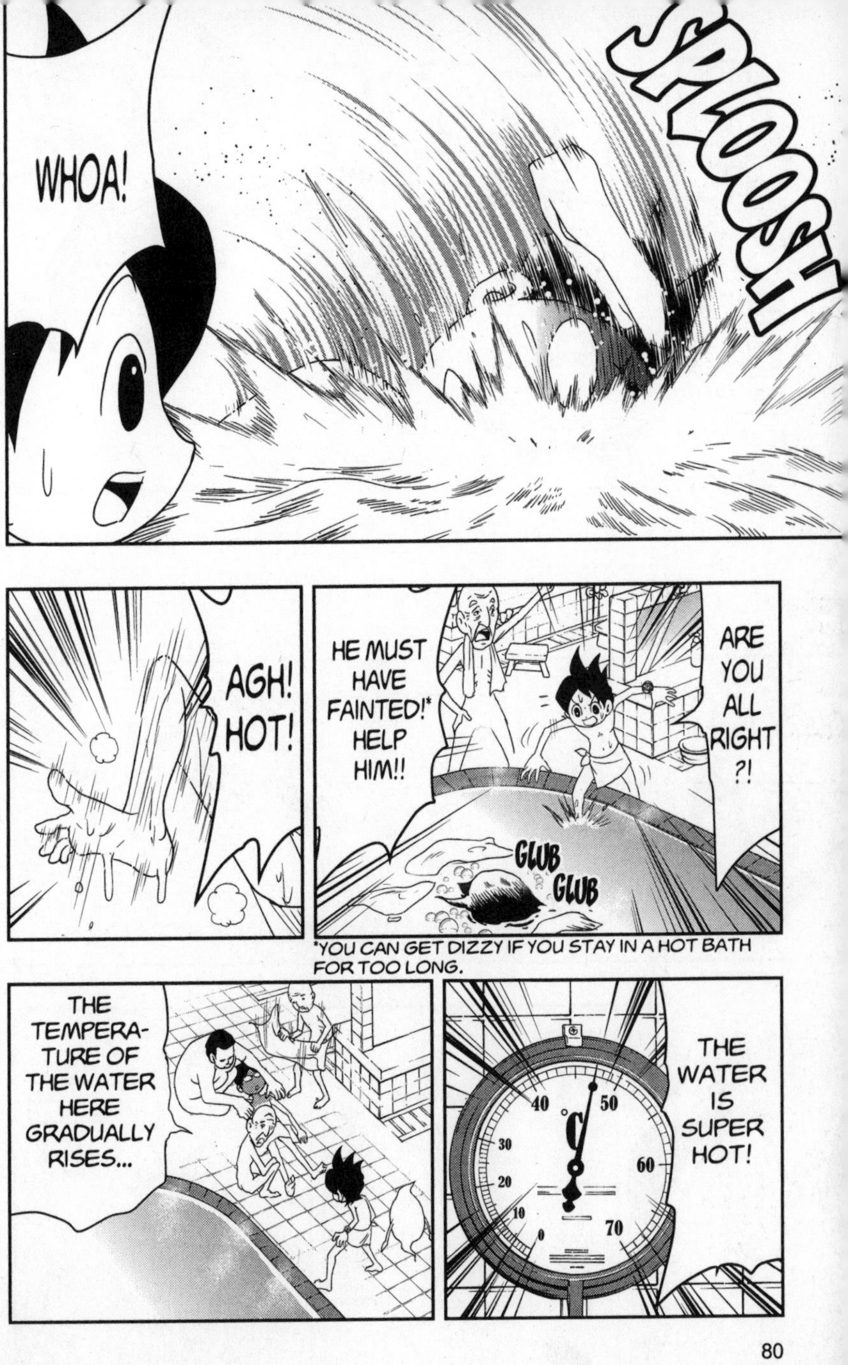
SPLOOSH!
WHOA!
ARE YOU ALL RIGHT?!
HE MUST HAVE FAINTED!* HELP HIM!!
GLUB GLUB
AGH! HOT!
THE WATER IS SUPER HOT!
THE TEMPERATURE OF THE WATER HERE GRADUALLY RISES...

*YOU CAN GET DIZZY IF YOU STAY IN A HOT BATH FOR TOO LONG.

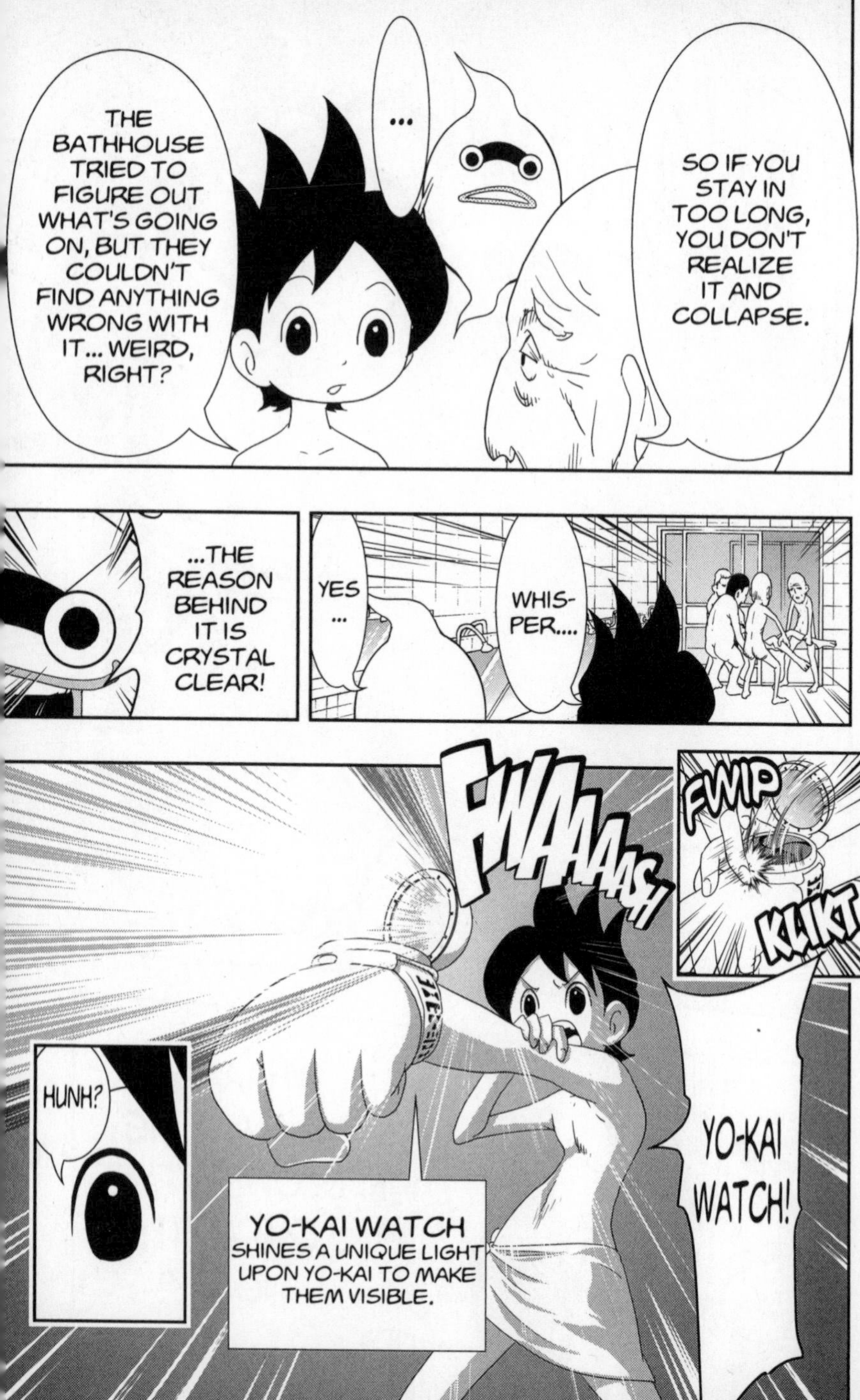
SO IF YOU STAY IN TOO LONG, YOU DON'T REALIZE IT AND COLLAPSE.
...
THE BATHHOUSE TRIED TO FIGURE OUT WHAT'S GOING ON, BUT THEY COULDN'T FIND ANYTHING WRONG WITH IT... WEIRD, RIGHT?
WHIS-PER....
YES...
...THE REASON BEHIND IT IS CRYSTAL CLEAR!
FWIP
KLIKT
FWAAAASH
YO-KAI WATCH!
YO-KAI WATCH SHINES A UNIQUE LIGHT UPON YO-KAI TO MAKE THEM VISIBLE.
HUNH?

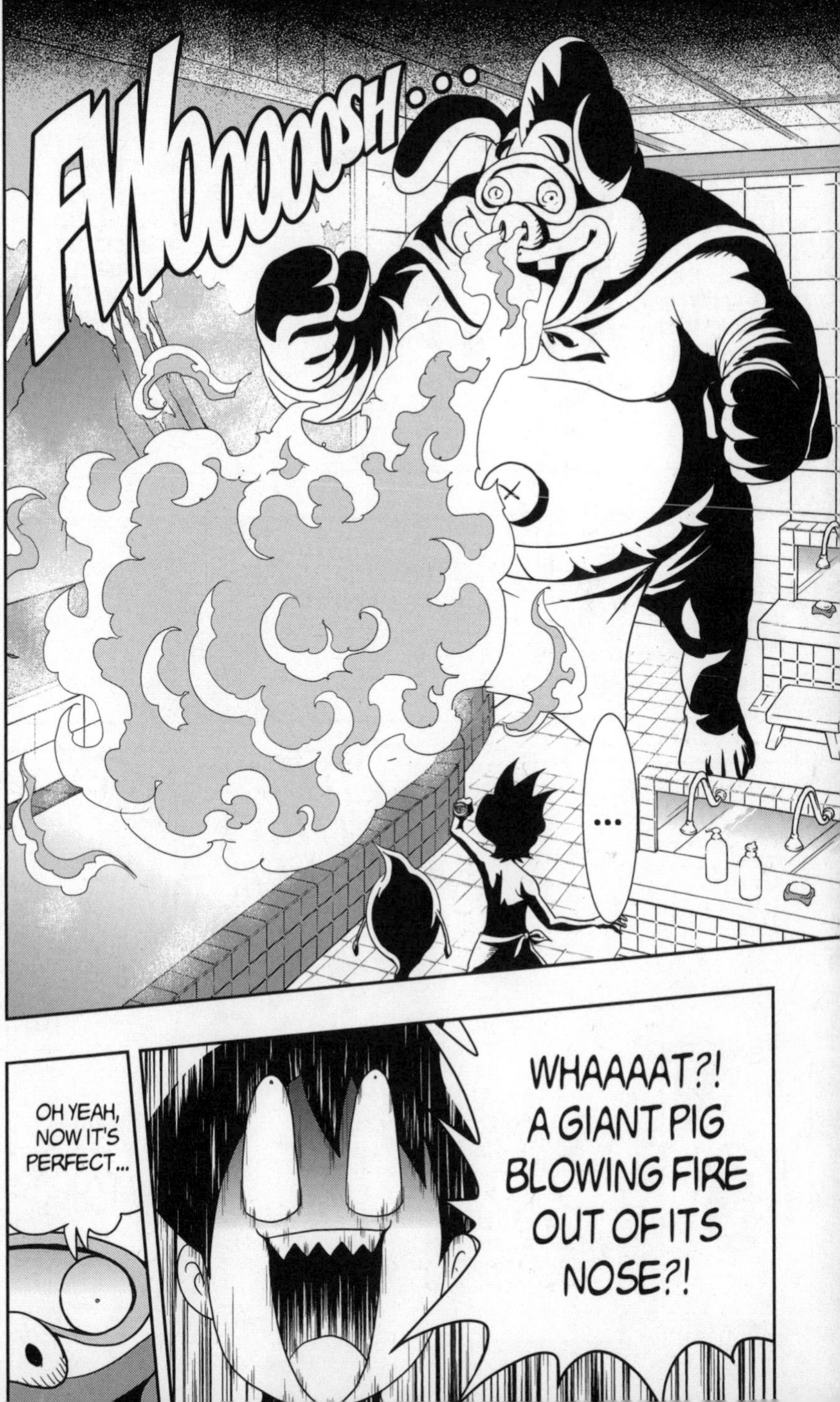
FWOOOOOSH...
...
WHAAAAT?! A GIANT PIG BLOWING FIRE OUT OF ITS NOSE?!
OH YEAH, NOW IT'S PERFECT...

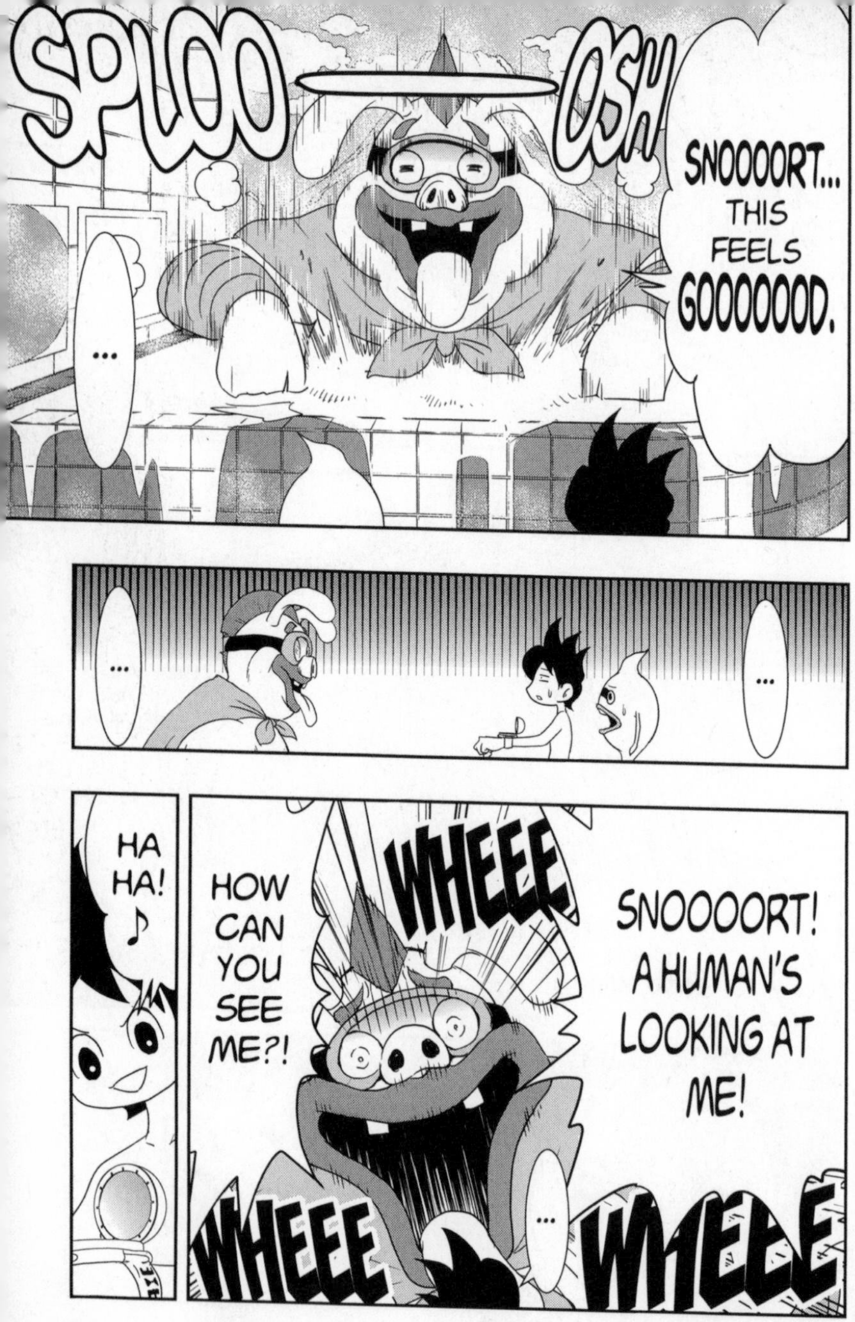
SPLOO—OSH
SNOOOORT... THIS FEELS GOOOOOOD.
...
...
...
SNOOOORT! A HUMAN'S LOOKING AT ME!
WHEEE
HOW CAN YOU SEE ME?!
...
WHEEE
WHEEE
HA HA! ♪

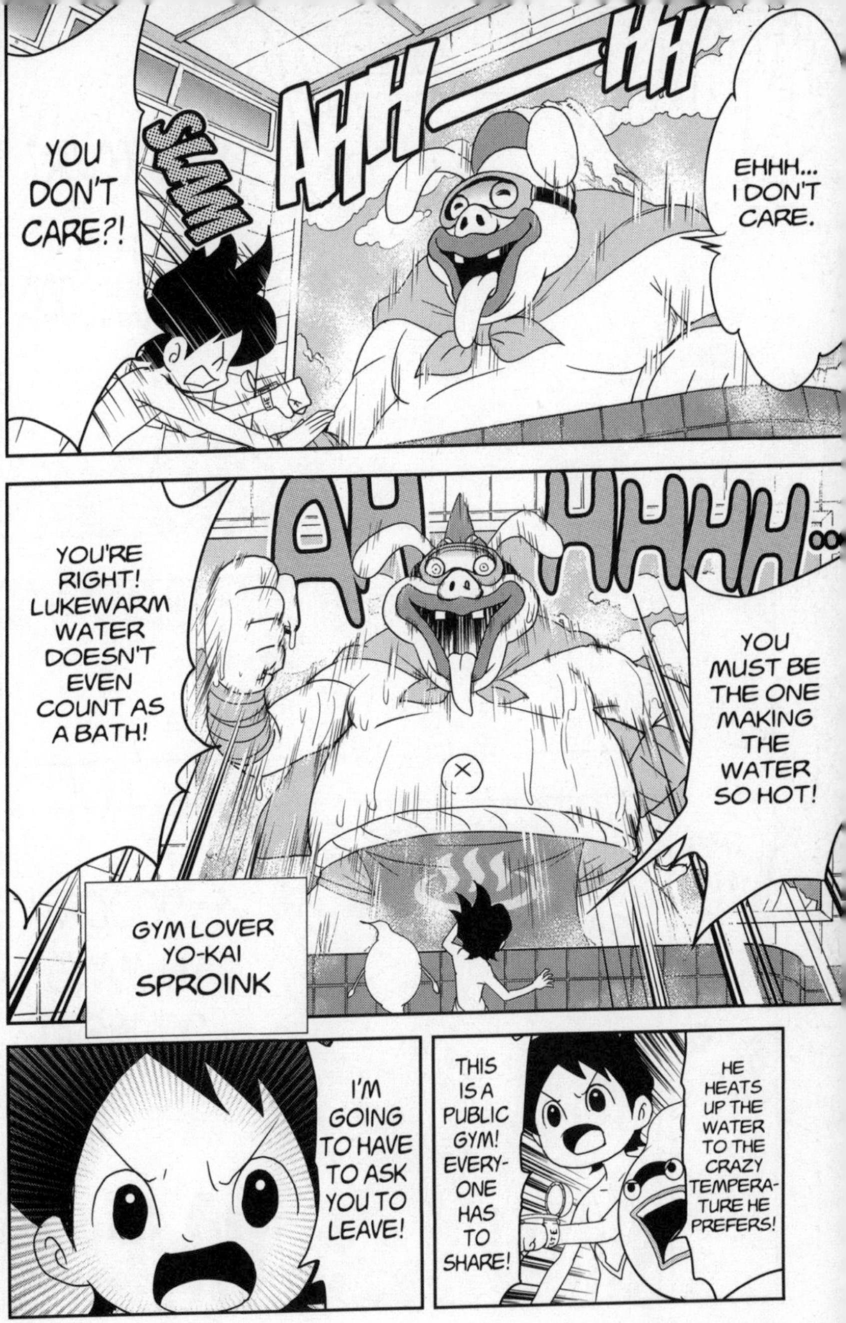
AHH——HH
EHHH... I DON'T CARE.
YOU DON'T CARE?!
AHHHHHH...
YOU MUST BE THE ONE MAKING THE WATER SO HOT!
YOU'RE RIGHT! LUKEWARM WATER DOESN'T EVEN COUNT AS A BATH!
GYM LOVER YO-KAI SPROINK
HE HEATS UP THE WATER TO THE CRAZY TEMPERA-TURE HE PREFERS!
THIS IS A PUBLIC GYM! EVERY-ONE HAS TO SHARE!
I'M GOING TO HAVE TO ASK YOU TO LEAVE!

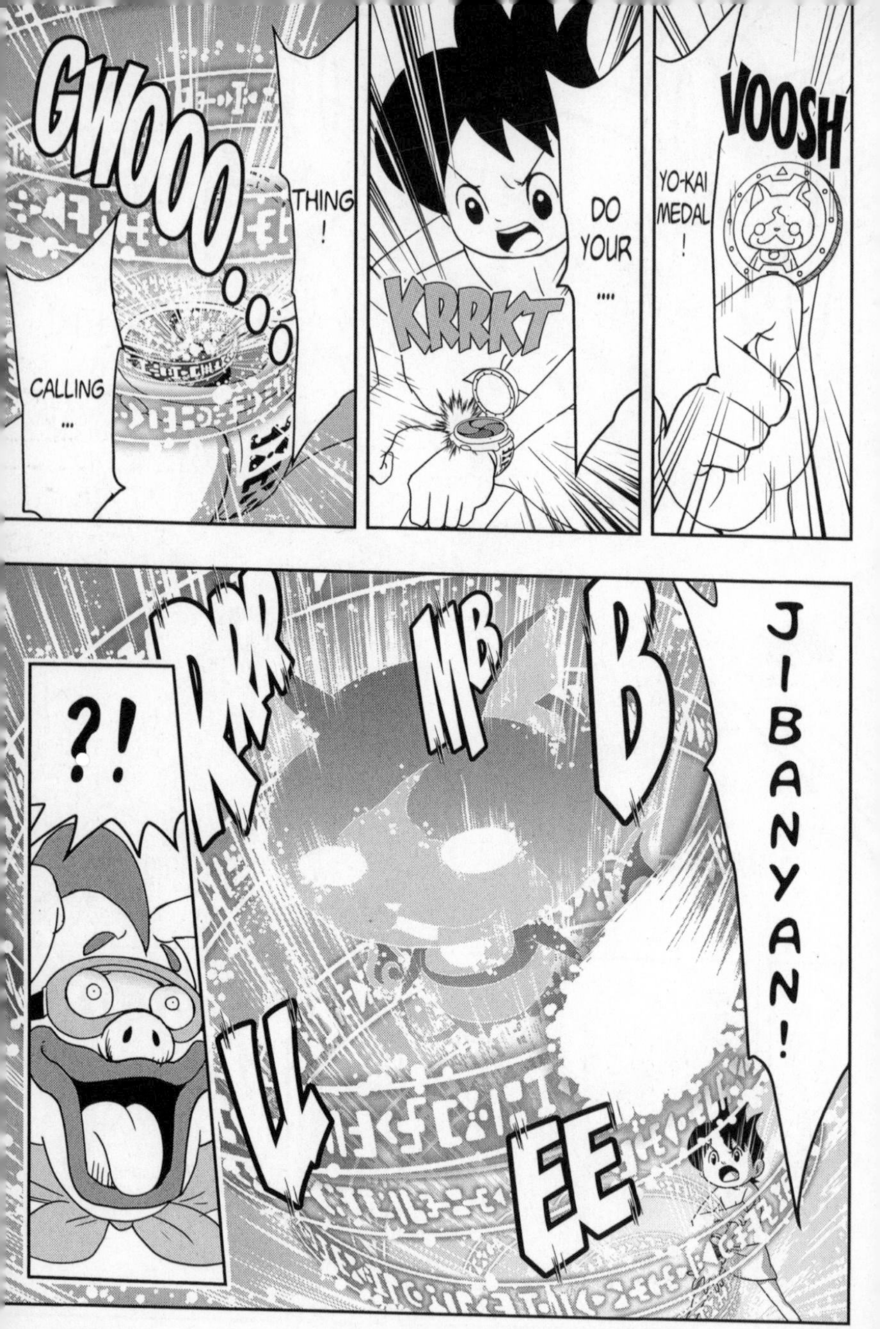
VOOSH
YO-KAI MEDAL!
DO YOUR ....
KRRKT
THING!
GWOOOO...
CALLING ...
JIBANYAN!
B
MB
RR
U
EE
?!

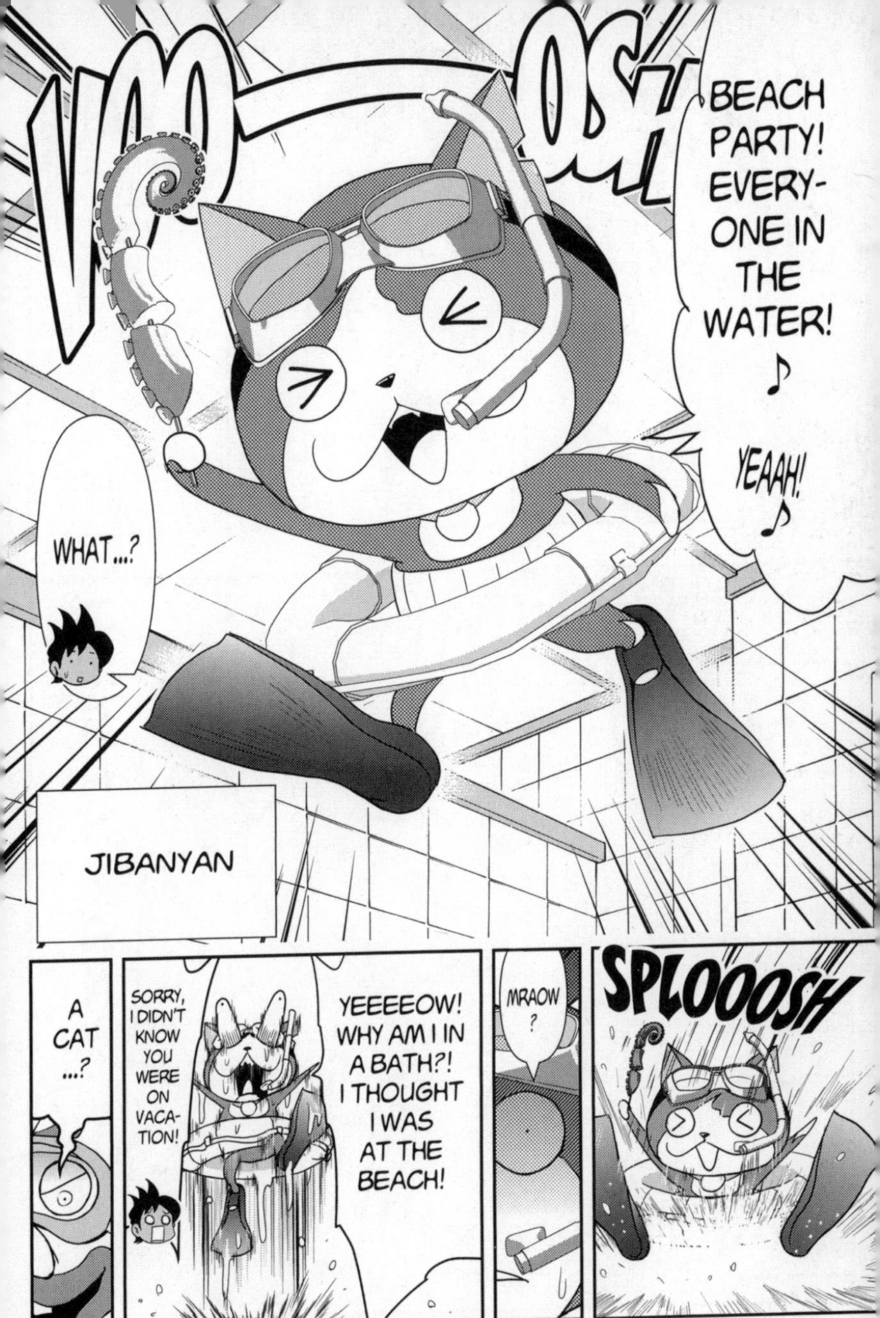
VOOOSH
BEACH PARTY! EVERY-ONE IN THE WATER! ♪
YEAAH! ♪
WHAT...?
JIBANYAN
SPLOOOSH
MRAOW ?
YEEEEOW! WHY AM I IN A BATH?! I THOUGHT I WAS AT THE BEACH!
SORRY, I DIDN'T KNOW YOU WERE ON VACA-TION!
A CAT ...?

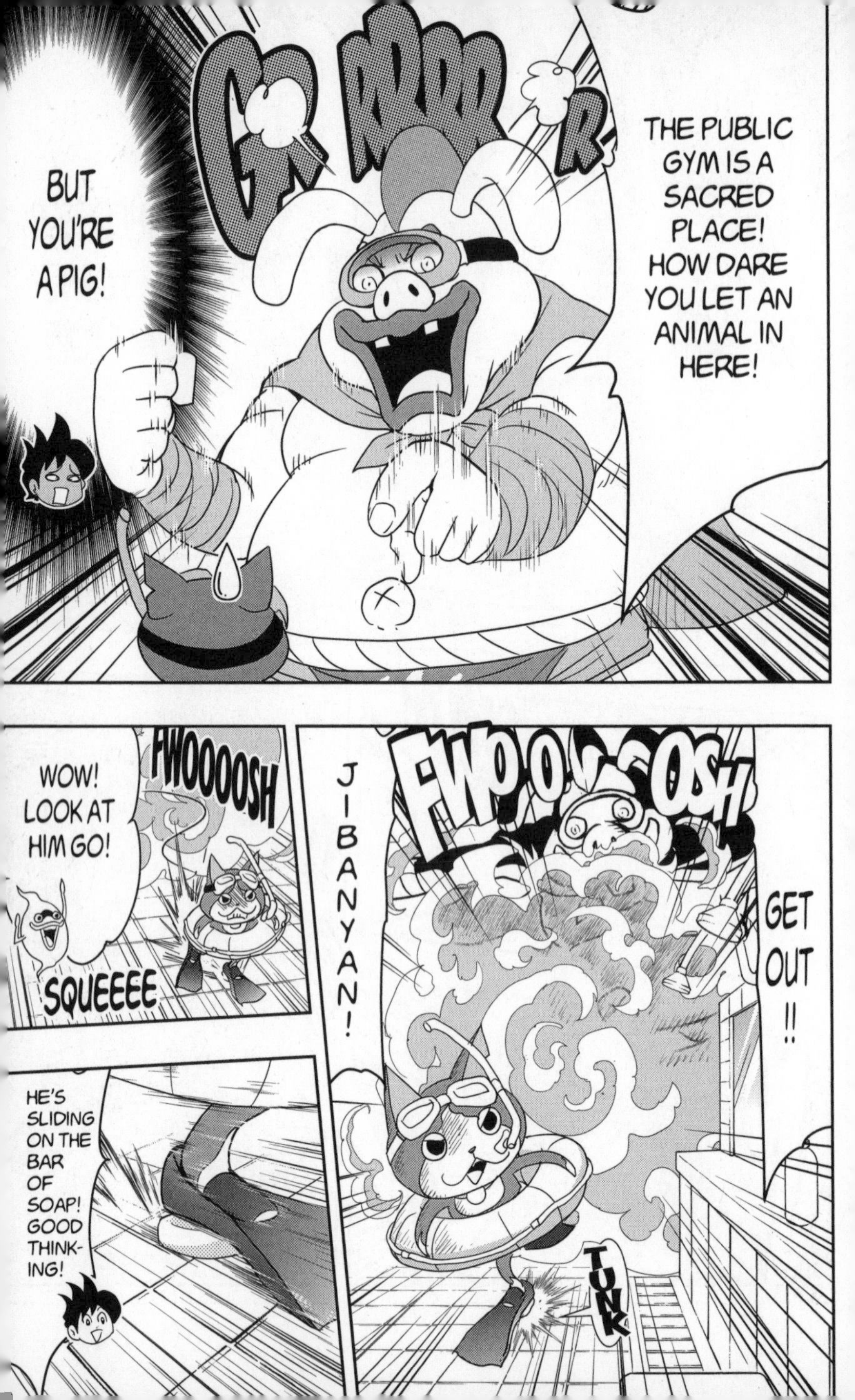
THE PUBLIC GYM IS A SACRED PLACE! HOW DARE YOU LET AN ANIMAL IN HERE!
BUT YOU'RE A PIG!
GET OUT !!
FWOOOSH
JIBANYAN!
TUNK
FWOOOOSH
WOW! LOOK AT HIM GO!
SQUEEEE
HE'S SLIDING ON THE BAR OF SOAP! GOOD THINK-ING!

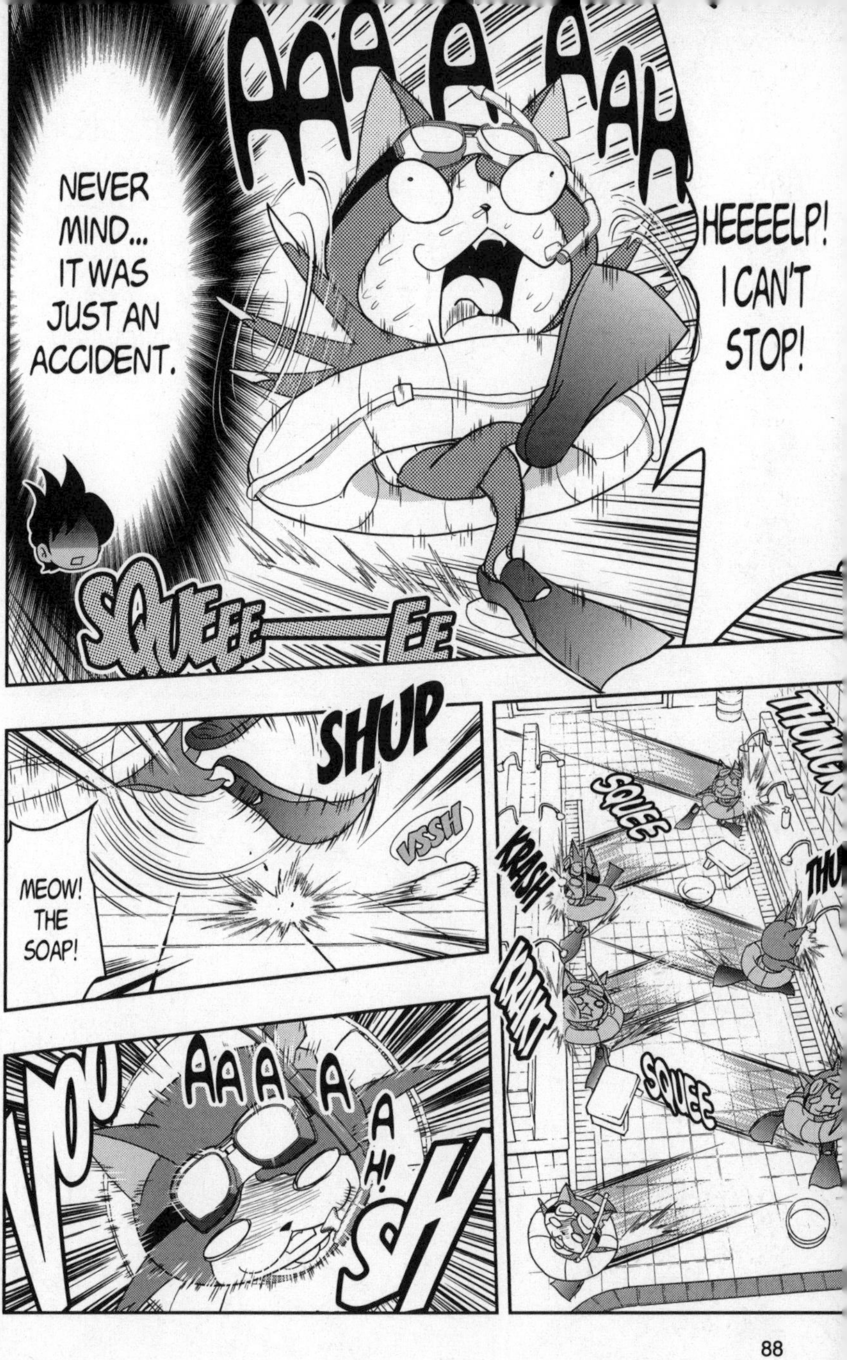
AAAAAAAH
HEEEEELP! I CAN'T STOP!
NEVER MIND... IT WAS JUST AN ACCIDENT.
SQUEEEE——EE
THUNK
SQUEE
KRASH
THU
KRAK
SQUEE
SHUP
VSSH
MEOW! THE SOAP!
AAAAAH!
SH
VOU

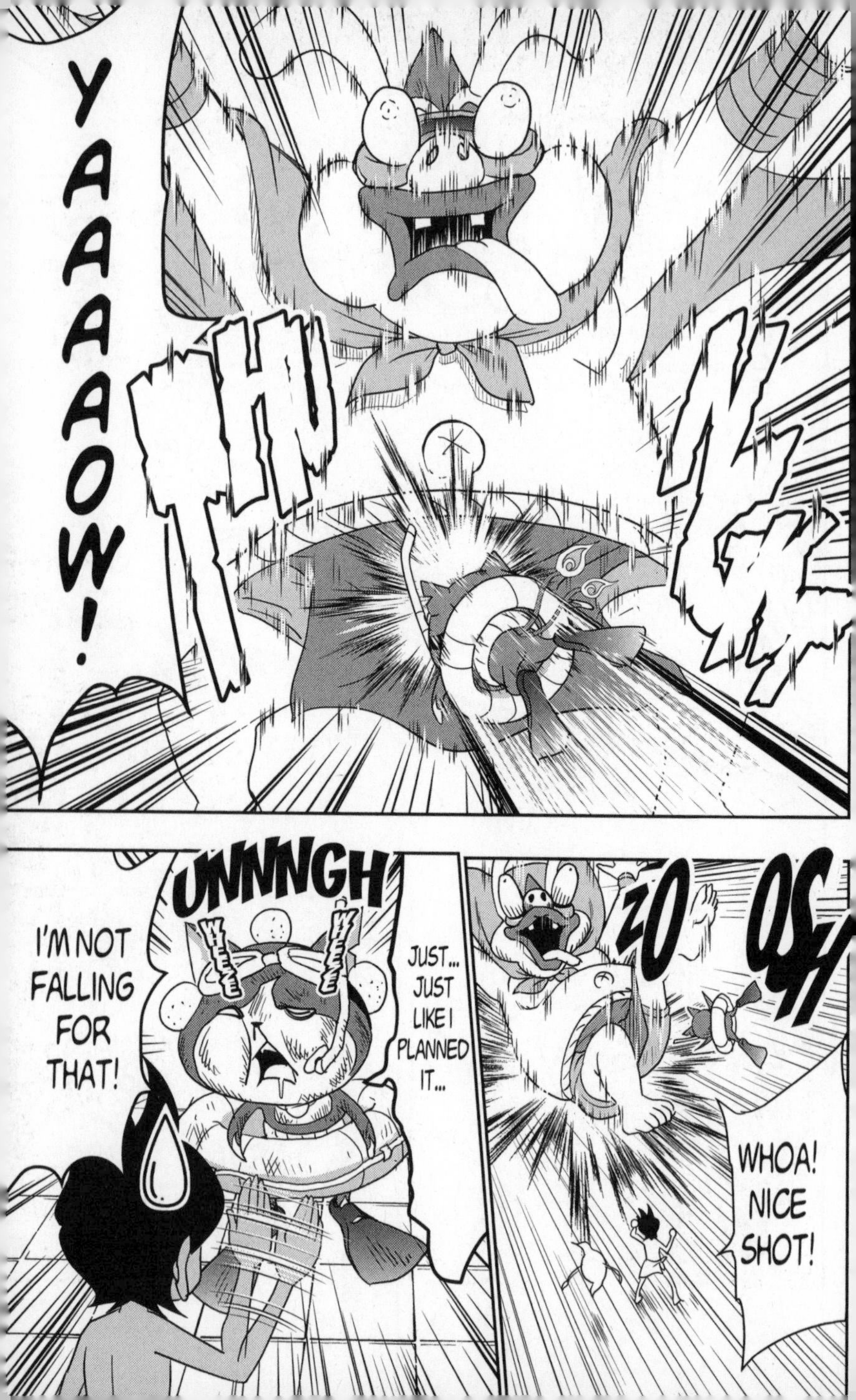
YAAAAAOW!
WHOA! NICE SHOT!
UNNNGH
WHEEZE
WHEEZE
JUST... JUST LIKE I PLANNED IT...
I'M NOT FALLING FOR THAT!

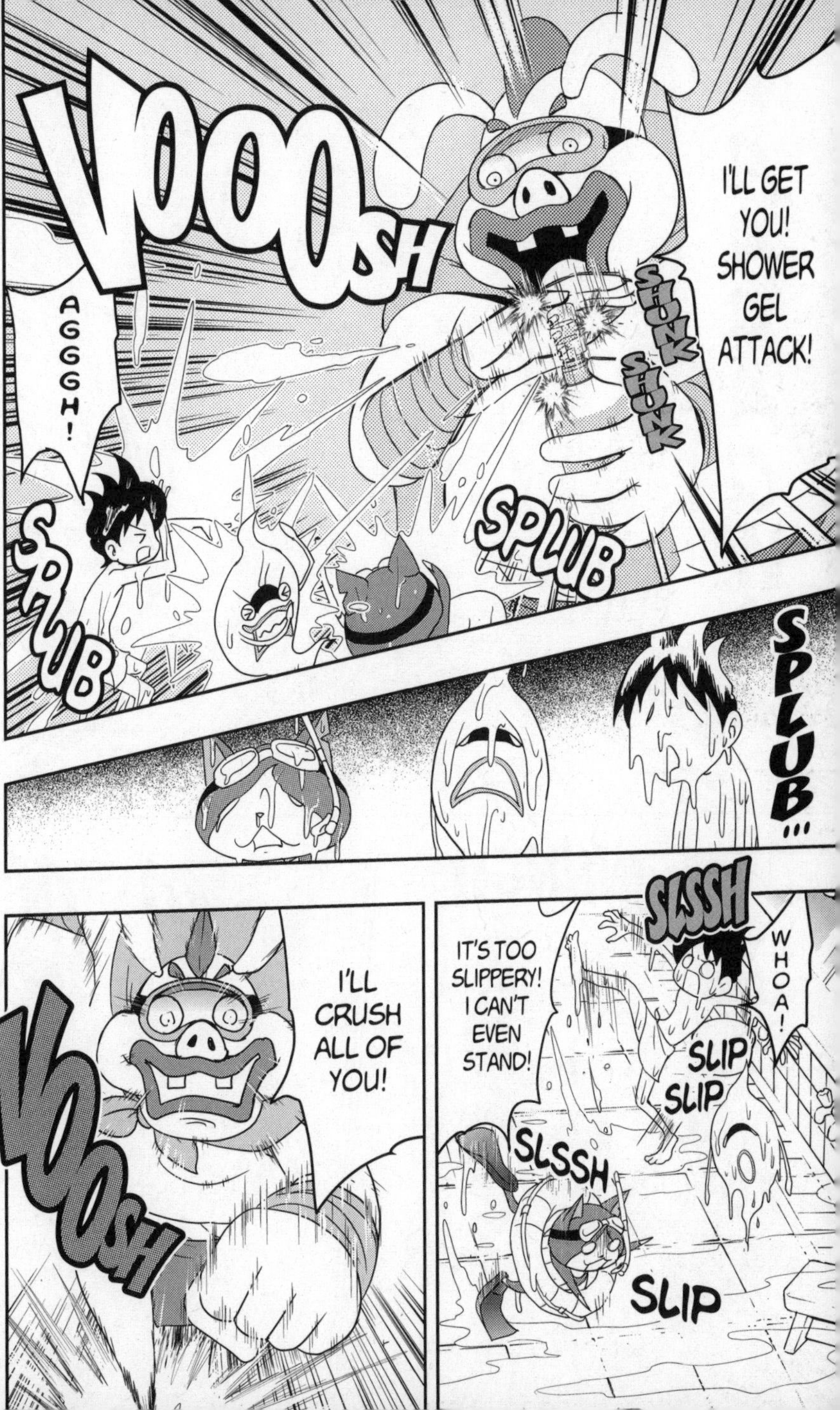
I'LL GET YOU! SHOWER GEL ATTACK!
SHUNK
SHUNK
VOOOOSH
SPLUB
AGGGGH!
SPLUB
SPLUB...
SLSSH
WHOA!
IT'S TOO SLIPPERY! I CAN'T EVEN STAND!
SLIP
SLIP
SLSSH
SLIP
I'LL CRUSH ALL OF YOU!
VOOOSH

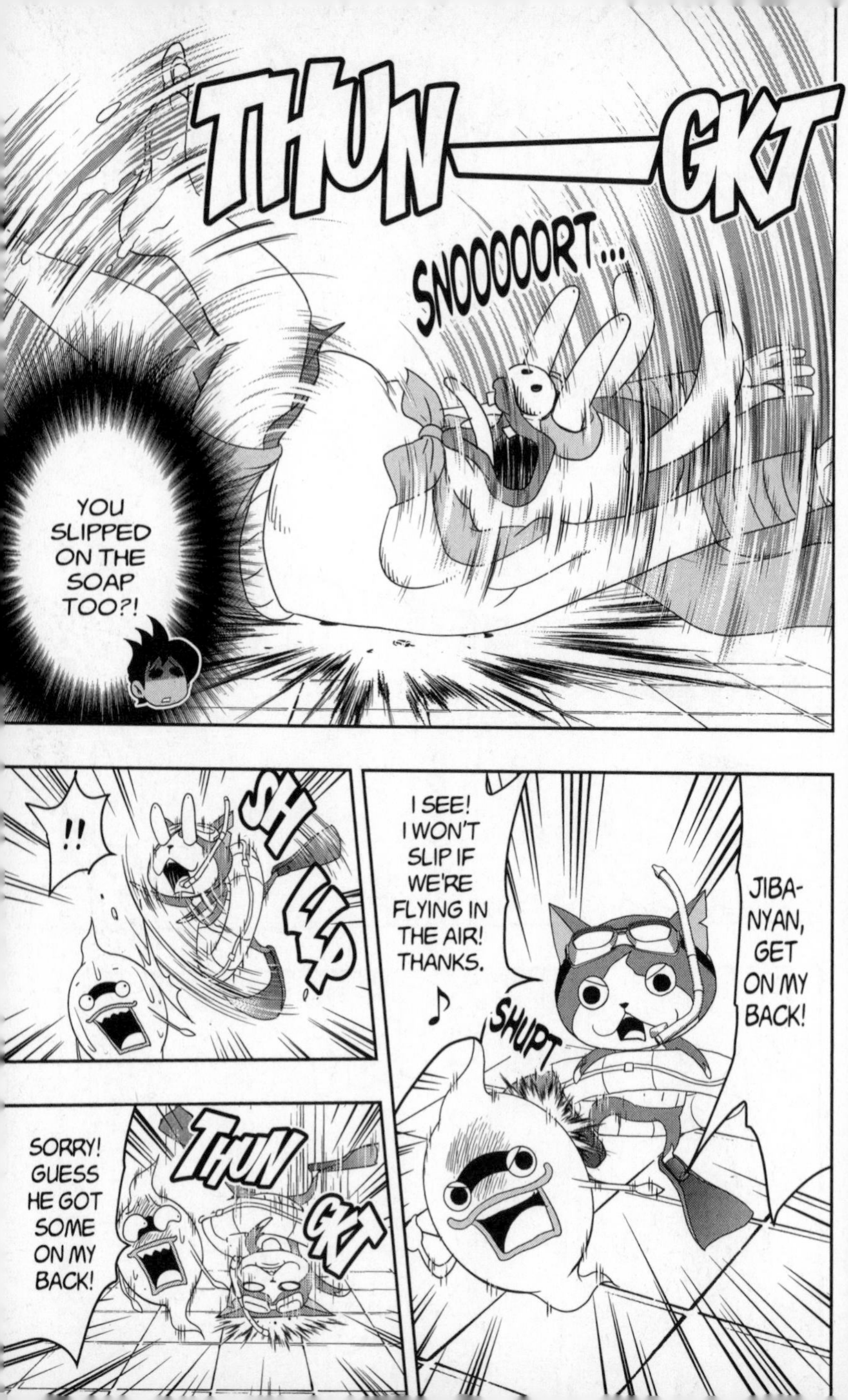
THUN—GKT
SNOOOORT...
YOU SLIPPED ON THE SOAP TOO?!
JIBA-NYAN, GET ON MY BACK!
I SEE! I WON'T SLIP IF WE'RE FLYING IN THE AIR! THANKS. ♪
SHUPT
SHLUP
!!
THUN GKT
SORRY! GUESS HE GOT SOME ON MY BACK!

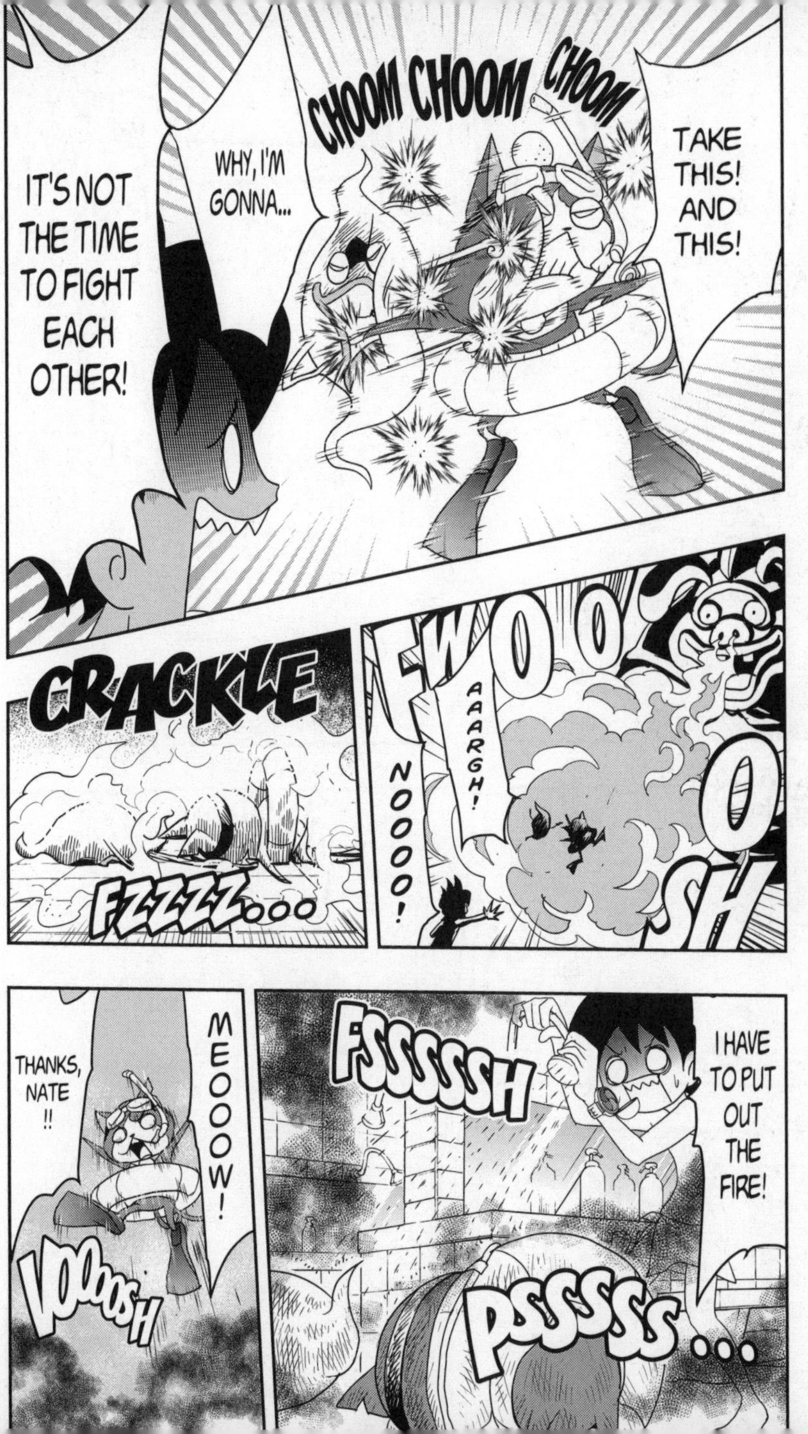
TAKE THIS! AND THIS!
CHOOM CHOOM CHOOM
WHY, I'M GONNA...
IT'S NOT THE TIME TO FIGHT EACH OTHER!
FWOOOOSH
AAAARGH!
NOOOOO!
CRACKLE
FZZZZZ...
I HAVE TO PUT OUT THE FIRE!
FSSSSSH
PSSSSS...
MEOOOOW!
THANKS, NATE !!
VOOOOSH

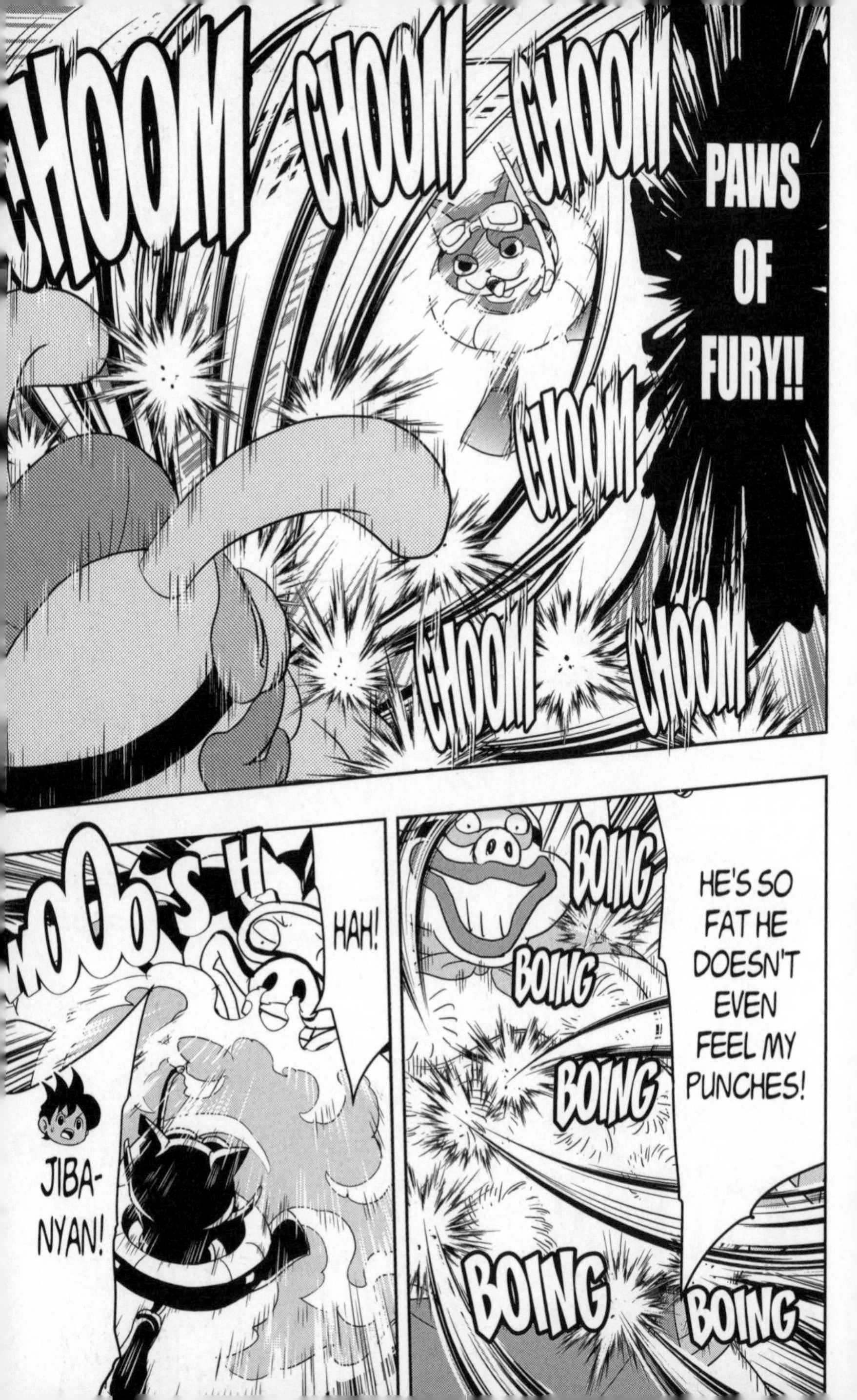
PAWS OF FURY!!
CHOOM
CHOOM
CHOOM
CHOOM
CHOOM
CHOOM
HE'S SO FAT HE DOESN'T EVEN FEEL MY PUNCHES!
BOING
BOING
BOING
BOING
BOING
HAH!
WHOOOSH
JIBA-NYAN!

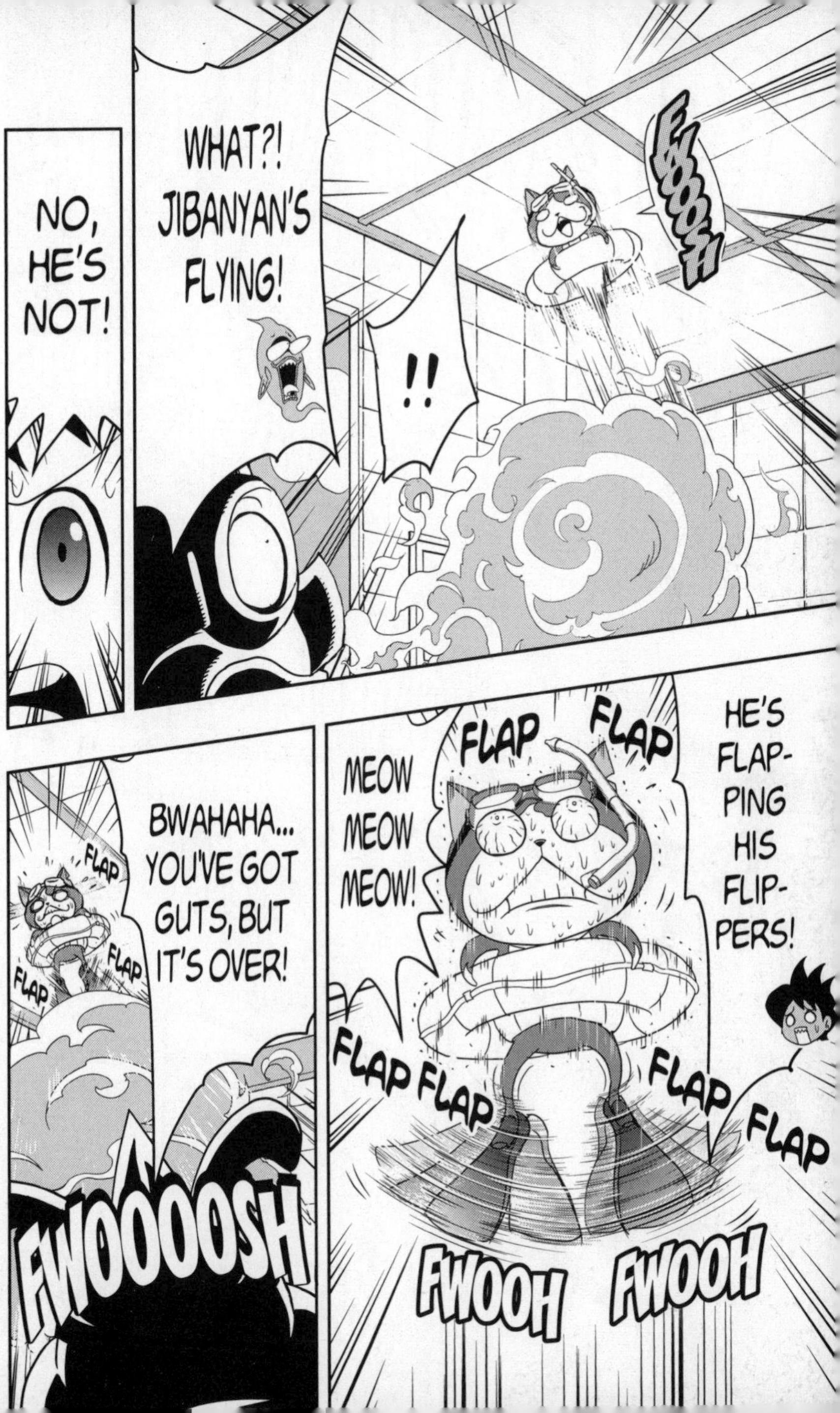

FWOOOSH!
WHAT?! JIBANYAN'S FLYING!
!!
NO, HE'S NOT!
FLAP FLAP
HE'S FLAP-PING HIS FLIP-PERS!
MEOW MEOW MEOW!
FLAP FLAP
FLAP FLAP
FWOOH FWOOH
FLAP
FLAP
FLAP
BWAHAHA... YOU'VE GOT GUTS, BUT IT'S OVER!
FWOOOOSH

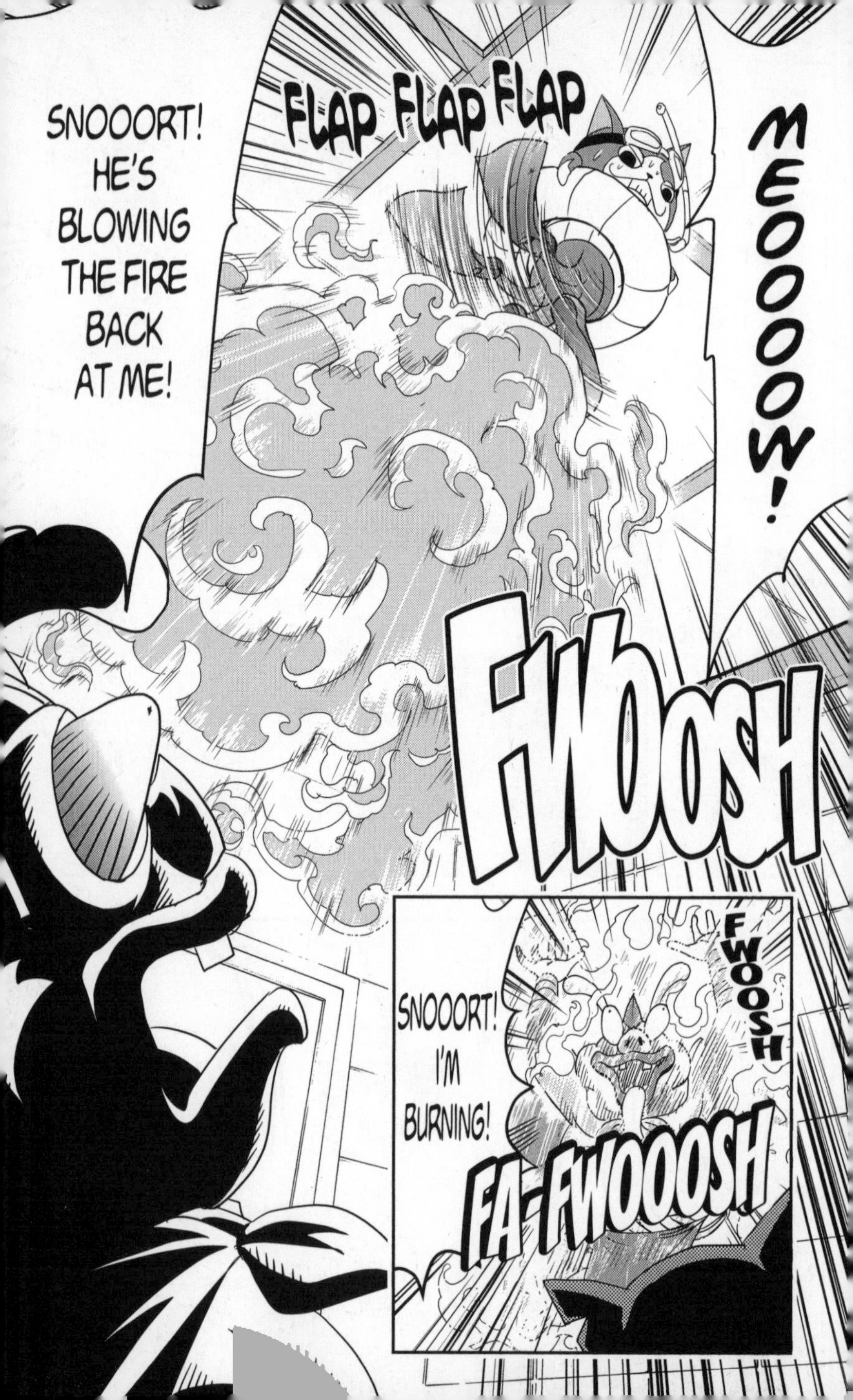
MEOOOOOW!
FLAP FLAP FLAP
SNOOORT! HE'S BLOWING THE FIRE BACK AT ME!
FWOOSH
FWOOSH
SNOOORT! I'M BURNING!
FA-FWOOOSH

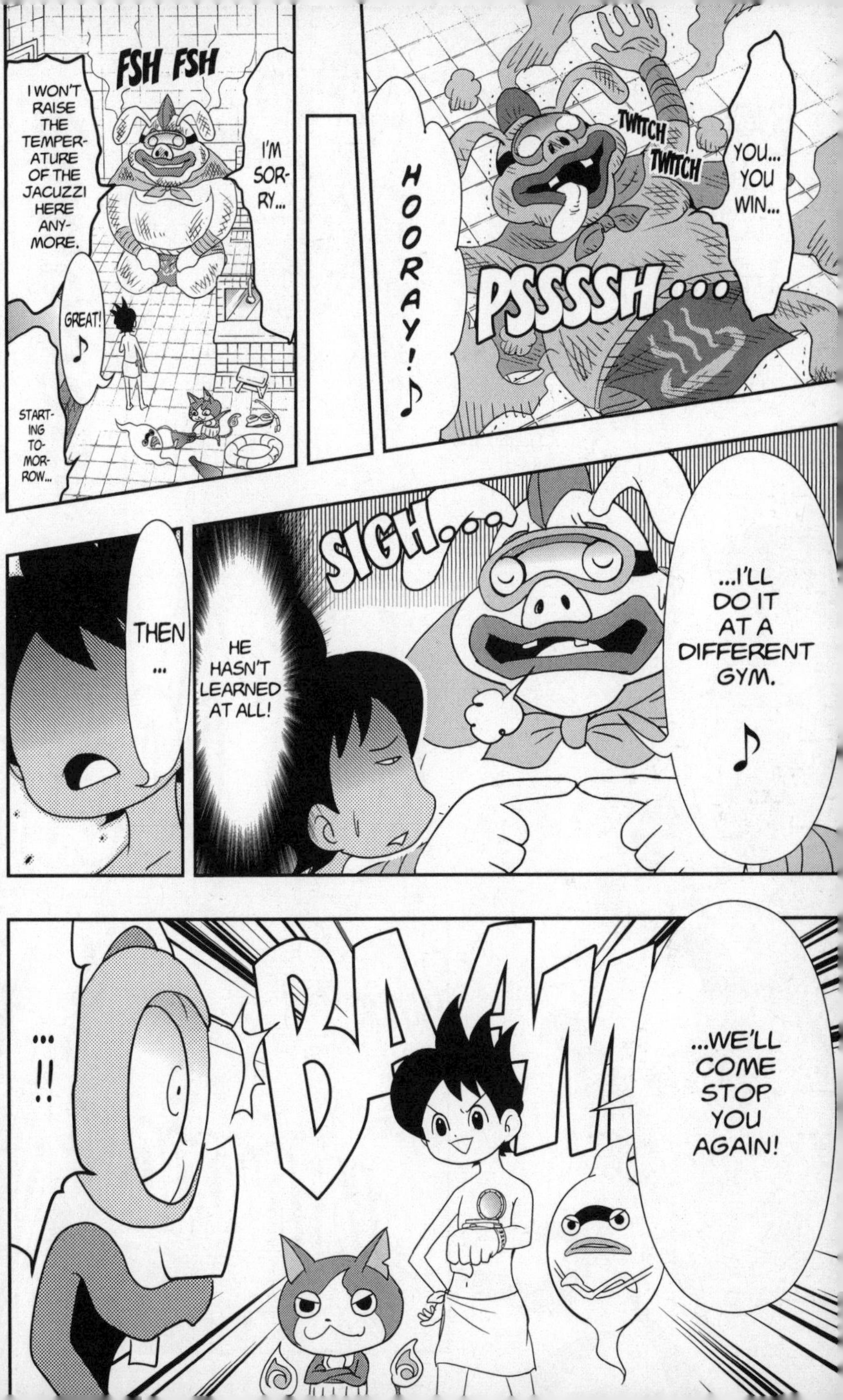

TWITCH TWITCH
YOU... YOU WIN...
PSSSSH...
HOORAY!♪
FSH FSH
I'M SORRY...
STARTING TOMORROW...
I WON'T RAISE THE TEMPERATURE OF THE JACUZZI HERE ANYMORE.
GREAT! ♪
SIGH...
...I'LL DO IT AT A DIFFERENT GYM. ♪
HE HASN'T LEARNED AT ALL!
THEN ...
...WE'LL COME STOP YOU AGAIN!
BAM
... !!

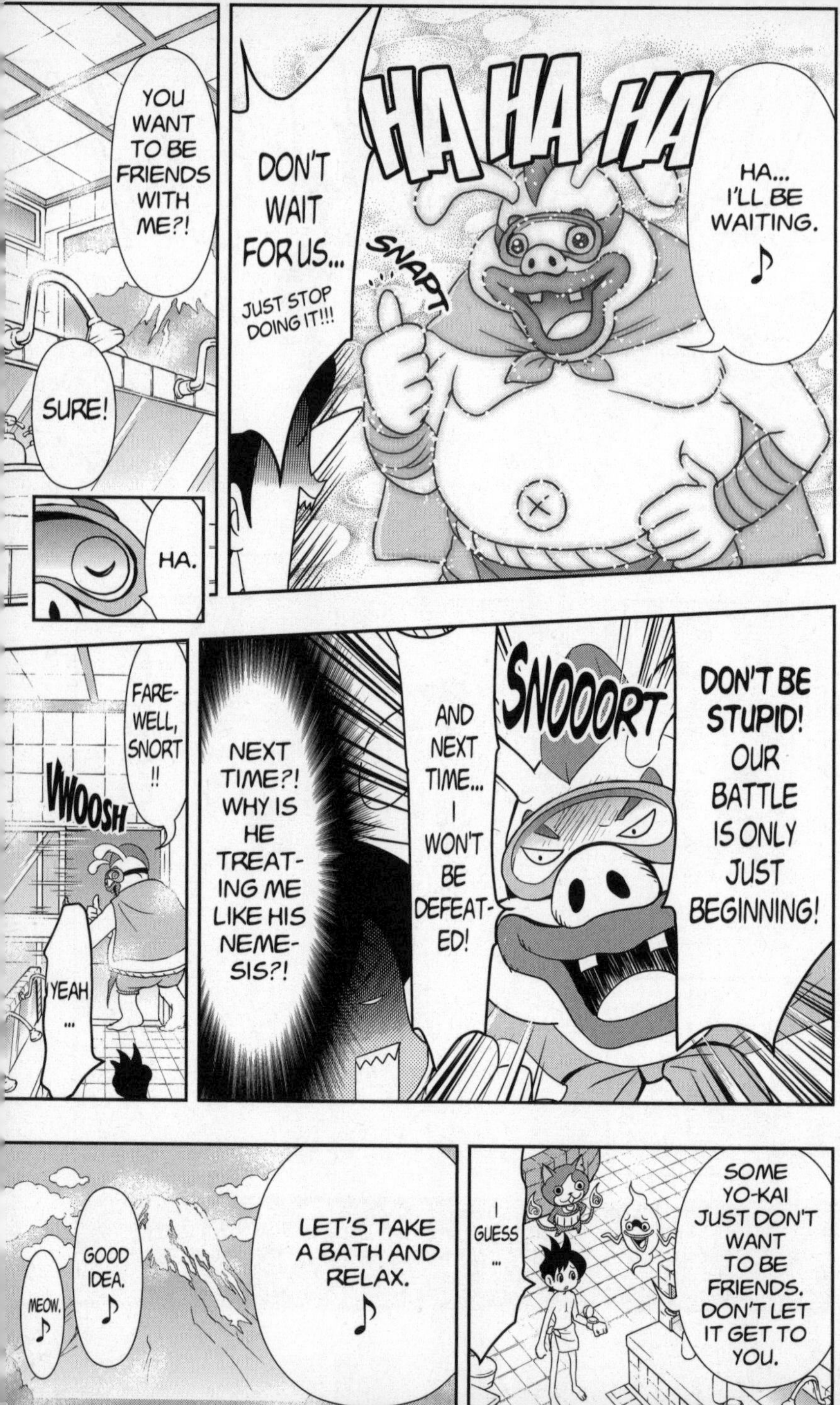
HA HA HA
HA... I'LL BE WAITING. ♪
SNAPT
DON'T WAIT FOR US...
JUST STOP DOING IT!!!
YOU WANT TO BE FRIENDS WITH ME?!
SURE!
HA.
DON'T BE STUPID! OUR BATTLE IS ONLY JUST BEGINNING!
SNOOORT
AND NEXT TIME... I WON'T BE DEFEATED!
NEXT TIME?! WHY IS HE TREATING ME LIKE HIS NEMESIS?!
FARE-WELL, SNORT!!
VWOOSH
YEAH...
SOME YO-KAI JUST DON'T WANT TO BE FRIENDS. DON'T LET IT GET TO YOU.
I GUESS...
LET'S TAKE A BATH AND RELAX. ♪
GOOD IDEA. ♪
MEOW. ♪

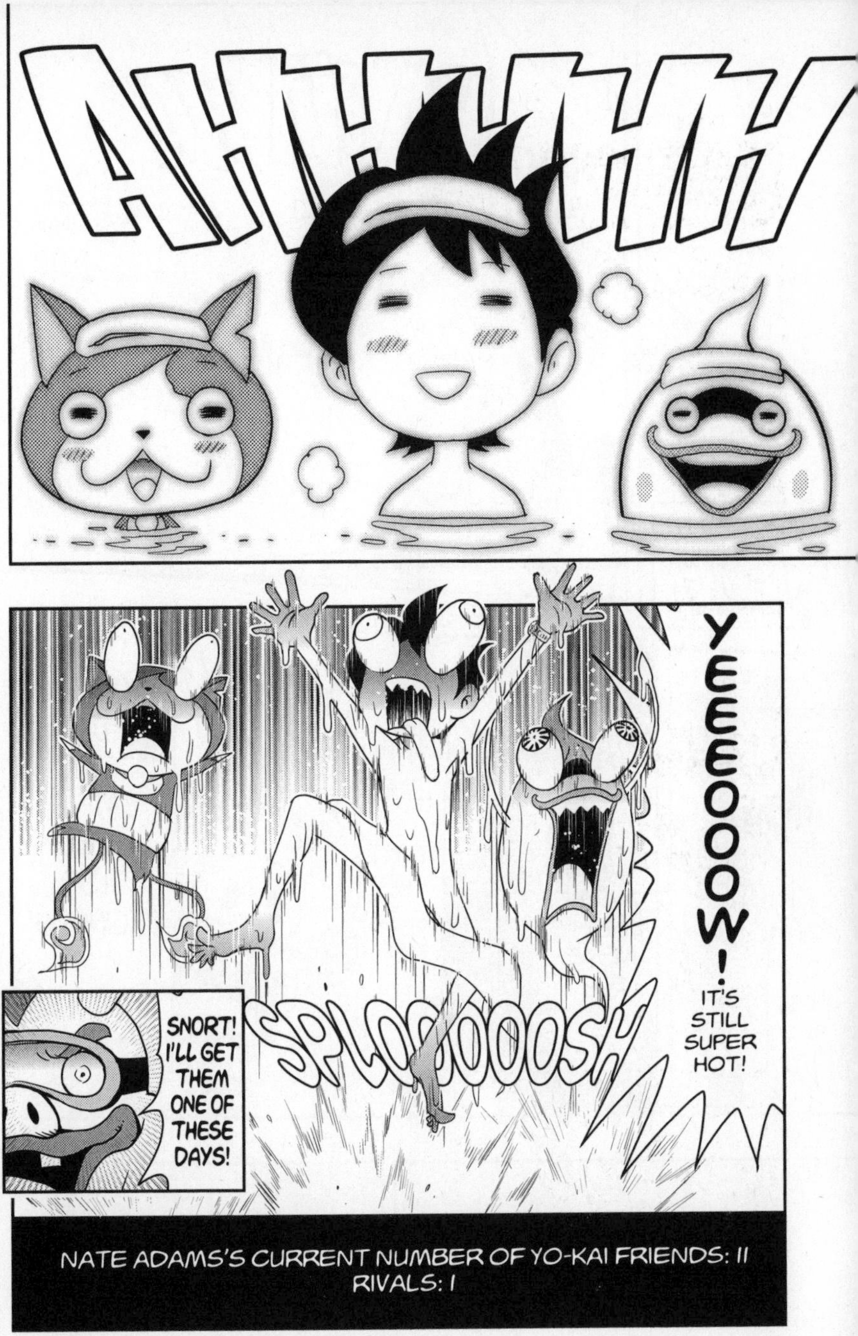
AHHHHH
YEEEOOOW!
IT'S STILL SUPER HOT!
SPLOOOOOSH
SNORT! I'LL GET THEM ONE OF THESE DAYS!
NATE ADAMS'S CURRENT NUMBER OF YO-KAI FRIENDS: 11
RIVALS: 1

THE EFFECT OF BOILING WATER

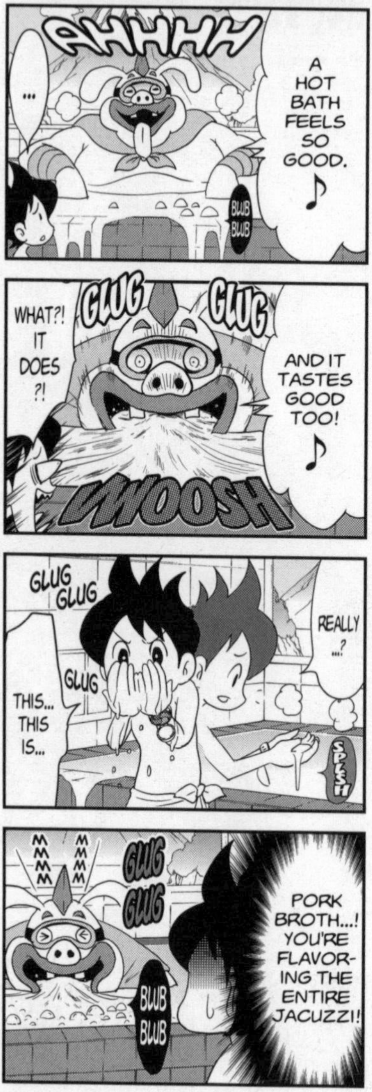
AHHHH
A HOT BATH FEELS SO GOOD. ♪
...
BLUB BLUB
GLUG GLUG
AND IT TASTES GOOD TOO! ♪
WHAT?! IT DOES?!
WOOSH
REALLY ...?
GLUG GLUG
GLUG
THIS... THIS IS...
SPLSH
PORK BROTH...! YOU'RE FLAVORING THE ENTIRE JACUZZI!
GLUG GLUG
MMMM MMMM
BLUB BLUB

CHAPTER 12: DON'T CATCH COLD!

FEATURING SORE THROAT YO-KAI COUGHKOFF

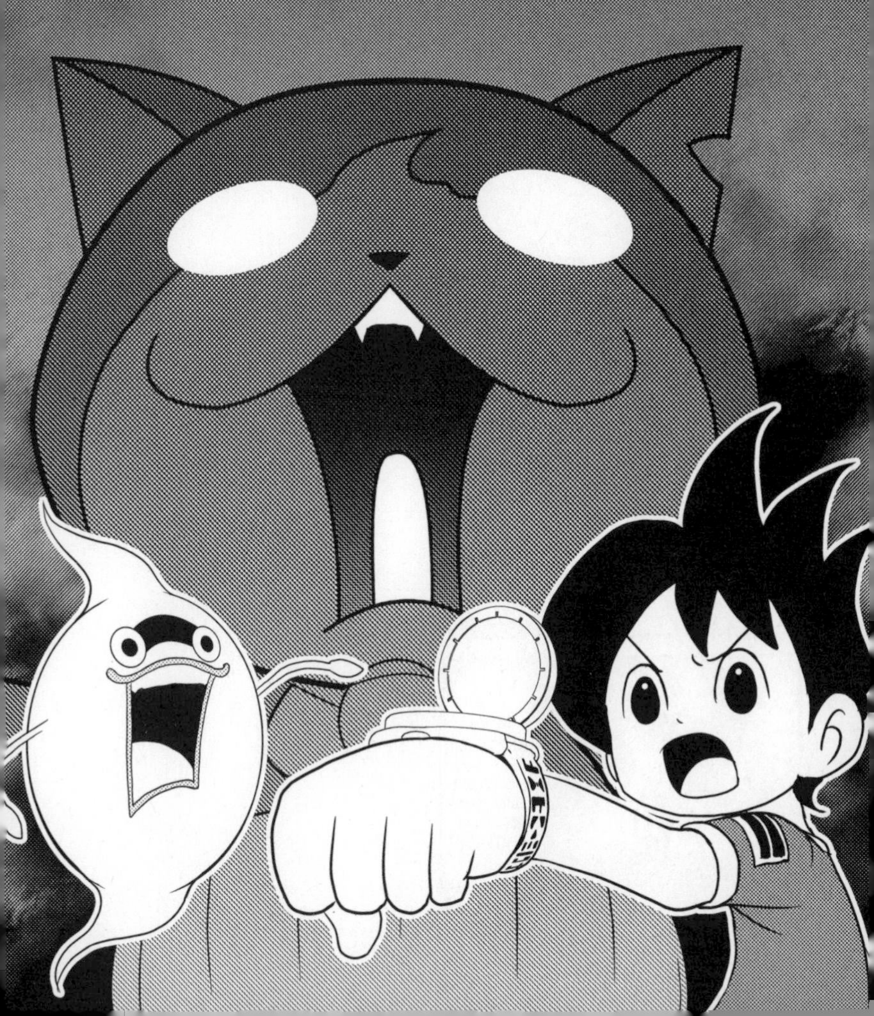

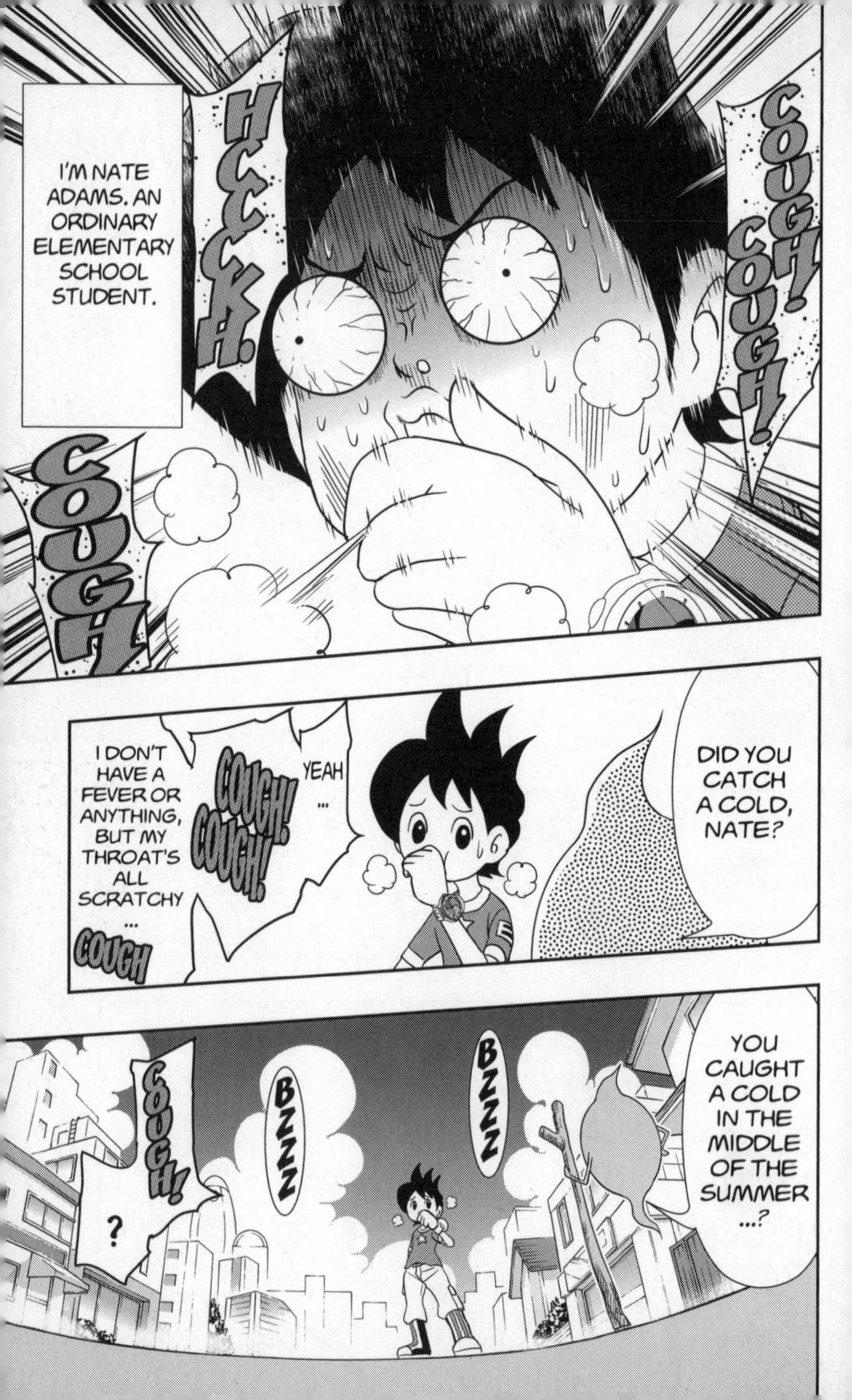
COUGH! COUGH!
HCCK.
I'M NATE ADAMS. AN ORDINARY ELEMENTARY SCHOOL STUDENT.
COUGH
DID YOU CATCH A COLD, NATE?
YEAH ...
COUGH! COUGH!
I DON'T HAVE A FEVER OR ANYTHING, BUT MY THROAT'S ALL SCRATCHY ...
COUGH
YOU CAUGHT A COLD IN THE MIDDLE OF THE SUMMER ...?
BZZZ
BZZZ
COUGH!
?

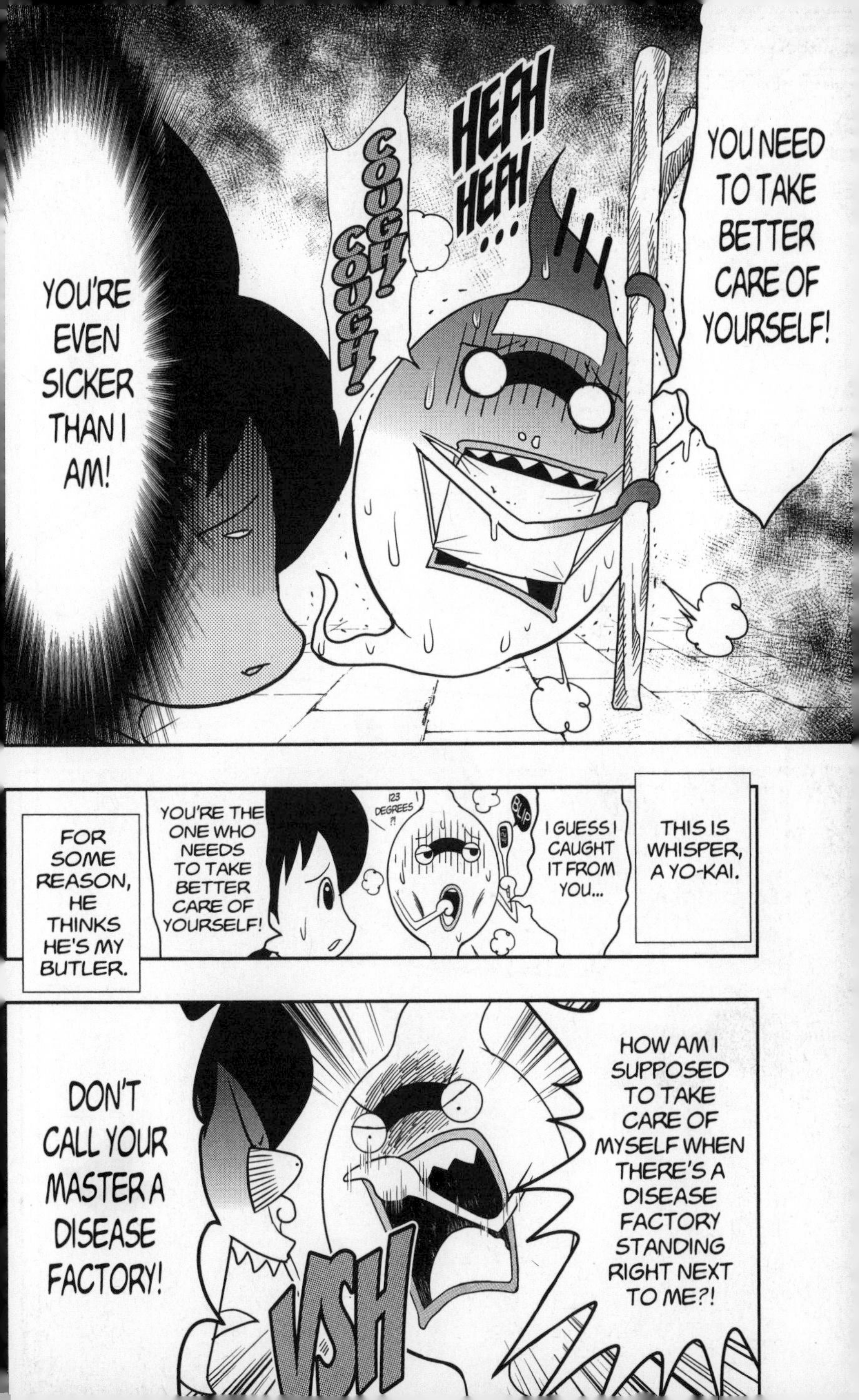
YOU NEED TO TAKE BETTER CARE OF YOURSELF!
HEFH HEFH...
COUGH! COUGH!
YOU'RE EVEN SICKER THAN I AM!
THIS IS WHISPER, A YO-KAI.
I GUESS I CAUGHT IT FROM YOU...
BLIP
123 DEGREES?!
YOU'RE THE ONE WHO NEEDS TO TAKE BETTER CARE OF YOURSELF!
FOR SOME REASON, HE THINKS HE'S MY BUTLER.
HOW AM I SUPPOSED TO TAKE CARE OF MYSELF WHEN THERE'S A DISEASE FACTORY STANDING RIGHT NEXT TO ME?!
DON'T CALL YOUR MASTER A DISEASE FACTORY!
VSH

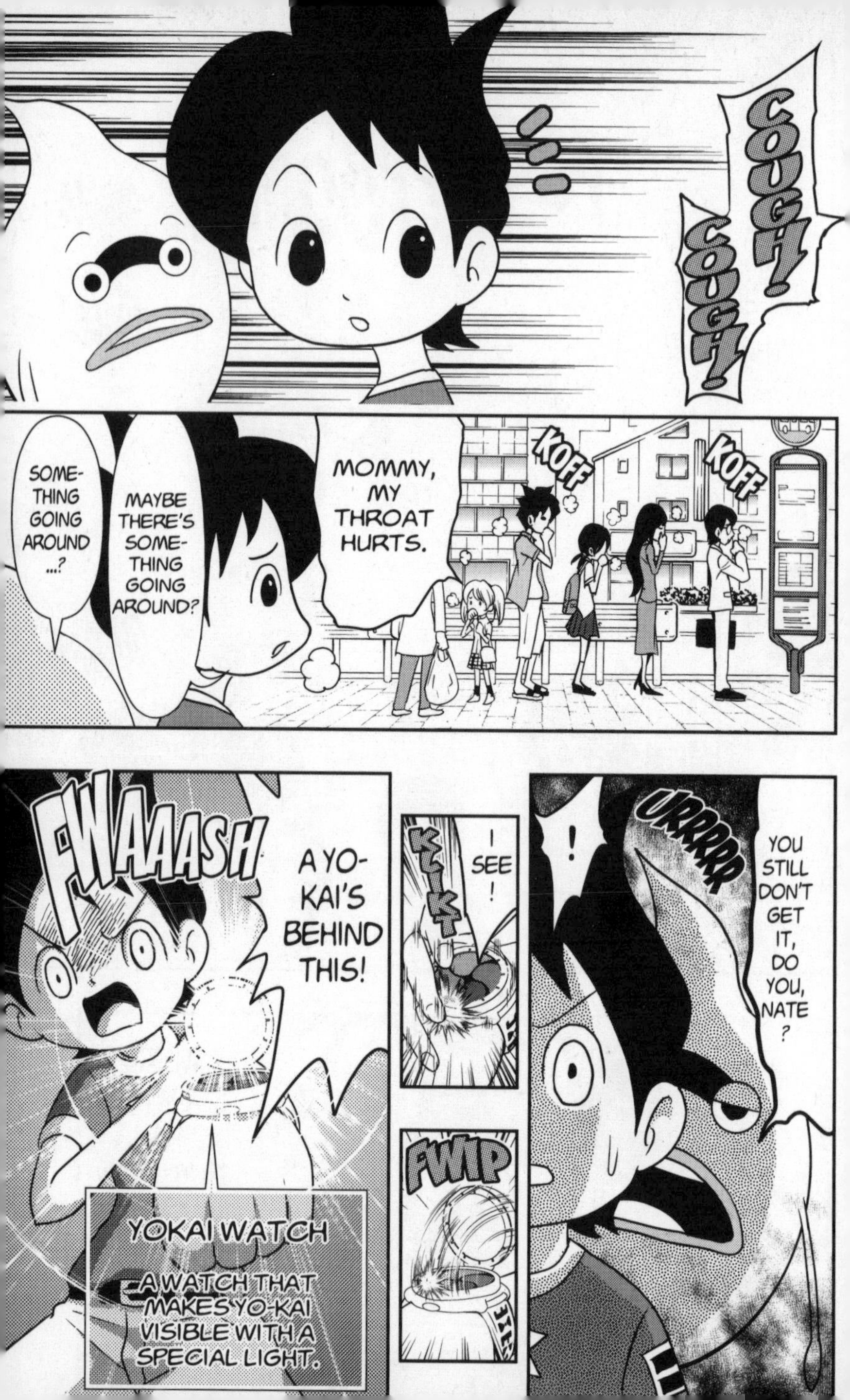
COUGH!
COUGH!
KOFF
MOMMY, MY THROAT HURTS.
KOFF
MAYBE THERE'S SOME-THING GOING AROUND?
SOME-THING GOING AROUND ...?
YOU STILL DON'T GET IT, DO YOU, NATE?
URRRRR
!
I SEE!
KLIK
FWIP
A YO-KAI'S BEHIND THIS!
FWAAASH
YOKAI WATCH
A WATCH THAT MAKES YO-KAI VISIBLE WITH A SPECIAL LIGHT.

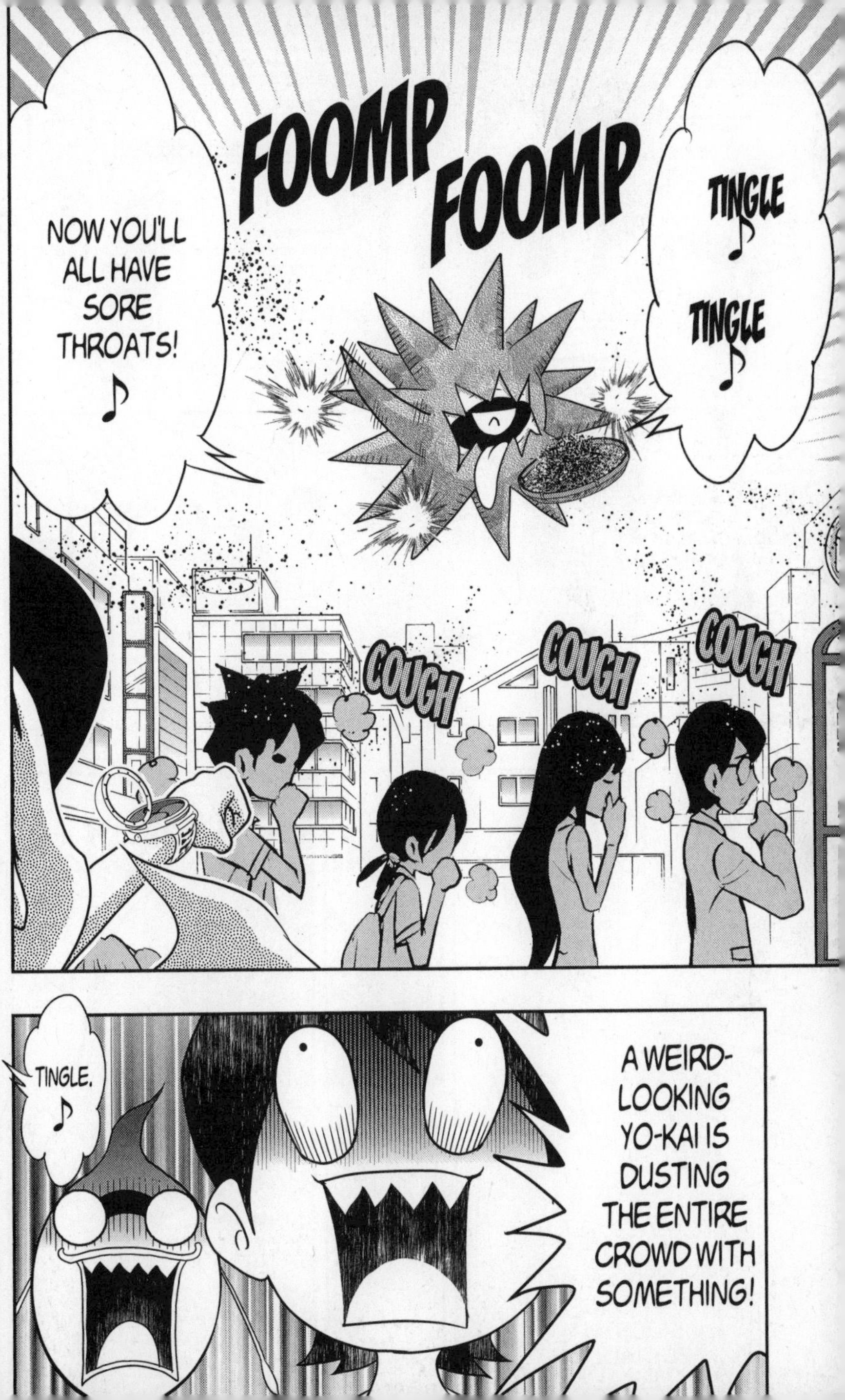
TINGLE ♪ TINGLE ♪
FOOMP FOOMP
NOW YOU'LL ALL HAVE SORE THROATS! ♪
COUGH
COUGH
COUGH
A WEIRD-LOOKING YO-KAI IS DUSTING THE ENTIRE CROWD WITH SOMETHING!
TINGLE. ♪

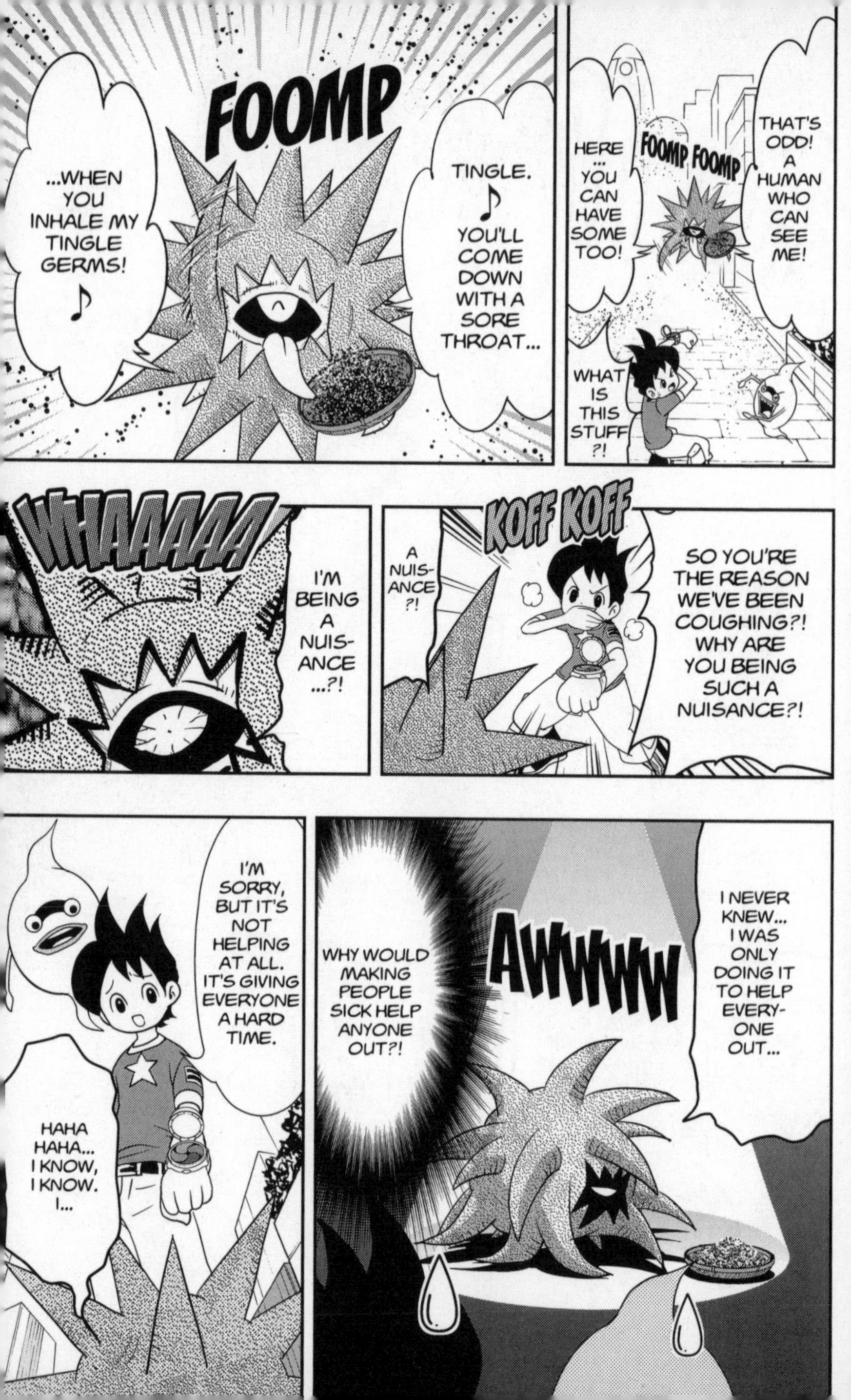
THAT'S ODD! A HUMAN WHO CAN SEE ME!
FOOMP FOOMP
HERE... YOU CAN HAVE SOME TOO!
WHAT IS THIS STUFF?!
FOOMP
TINGLE. ♪ YOU'LL COME DOWN WITH A SORE THROAT...
...WHEN YOU INHALE MY TINGLE GERMS! ♪
KOFF KOFF
SO YOU'RE THE REASON WE'VE BEEN COUGHING?! WHY ARE YOU BEING SUCH A NUISANCE?!
A NUISANCE?!
WHAAAAAA
I'M BEING A NUISANCE...?!
I NEVER KNEW... I WAS ONLY DOING IT TO HELP EVERYONE OUT...
AWWWW
WHY WOULD MAKING PEOPLE SICK HELP ANYONE OUT?!
I'M SORRY, BUT IT'S NOT HELPING AT ALL. IT'S GIVING EVERYONE A HARD TIME.
HAHA HAHA... I KNOW, I KNOW. I...

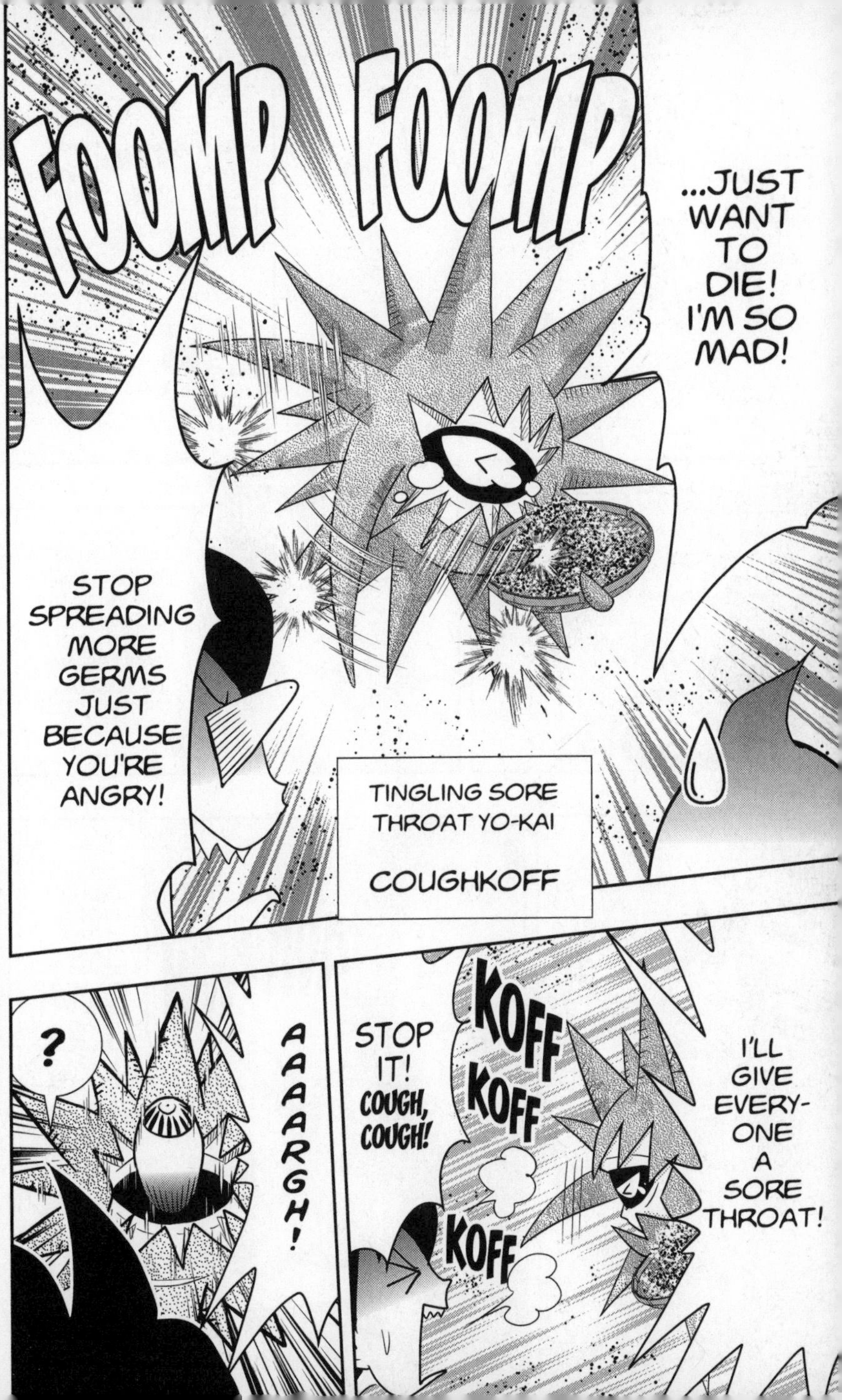
...JUST WANT TO DIE! I'M SO MAD!
FOOMP FOOMP
STOP SPREADING MORE GERMS JUST BECAUSE YOU'RE ANGRY!
TINGLING SORE THROAT YO-KAI
COUGHKOFF
I'LL GIVE EVERY-ONE A SORE THROAT!
KOFF KOFF
KOFF
STOP IT! COUGH, COUGH!
AAAARGH!
?

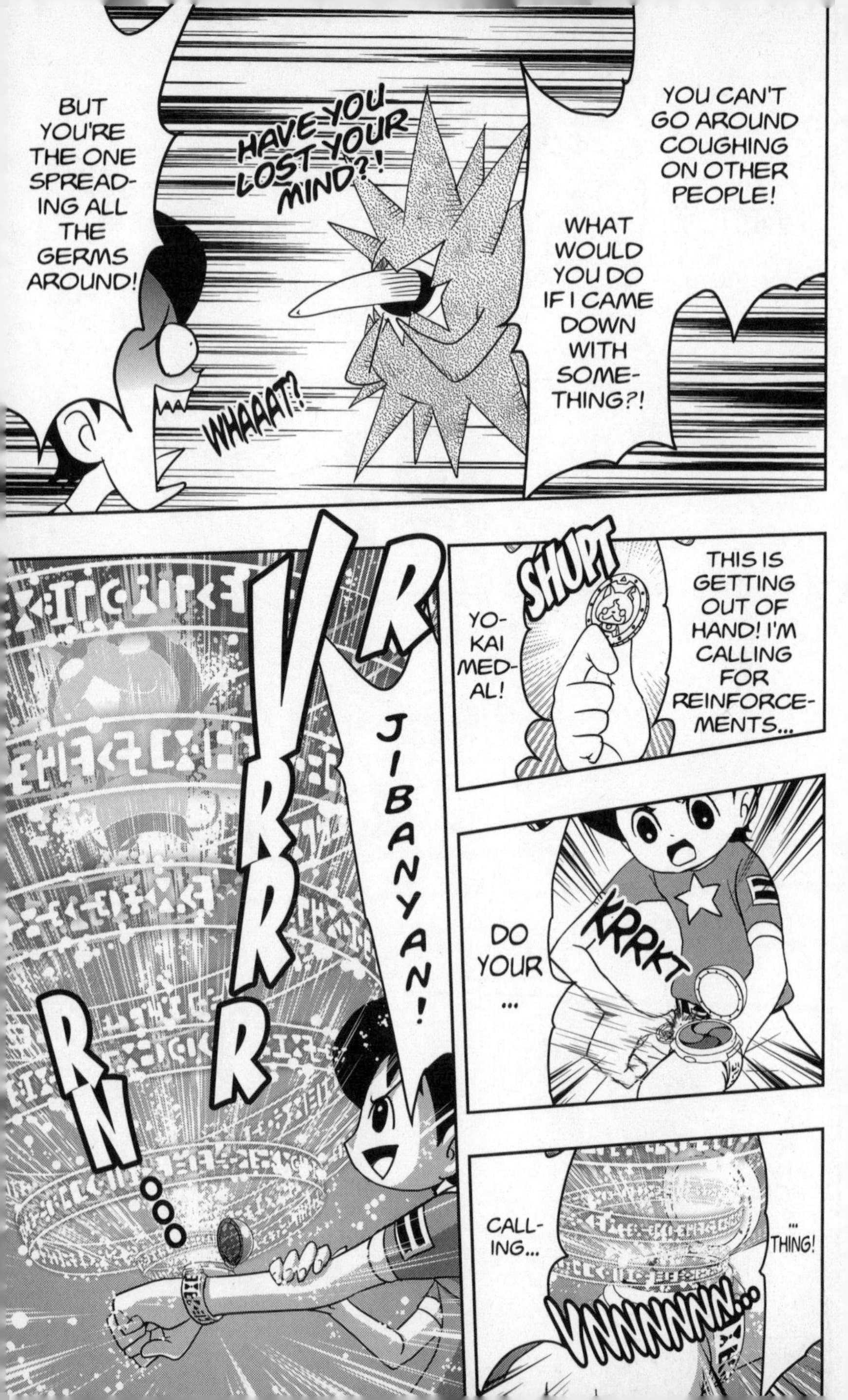
YOU CAN'T GO AROUND COUGHING ON OTHER PEOPLE!
WHAT WOULD YOU DO IF I CAME DOWN WITH SOME-THING?!
HAVE YOU LOST YOUR MIND?!
WHAAAT?
BUT YOU'RE THE ONE SPREAD-ING ALL THE GERMS AROUND!
THIS IS GETTING OUT OF HAND! I'M CALLING FOR REINFORCE-MENTS...
SHUPT
YO-KAI MED-AL!
KRRKT
DO YOUR ...
... THING!
CALL-ING...
VNNNNNN...
VRRRR
JIBANYAN!
RNOOO

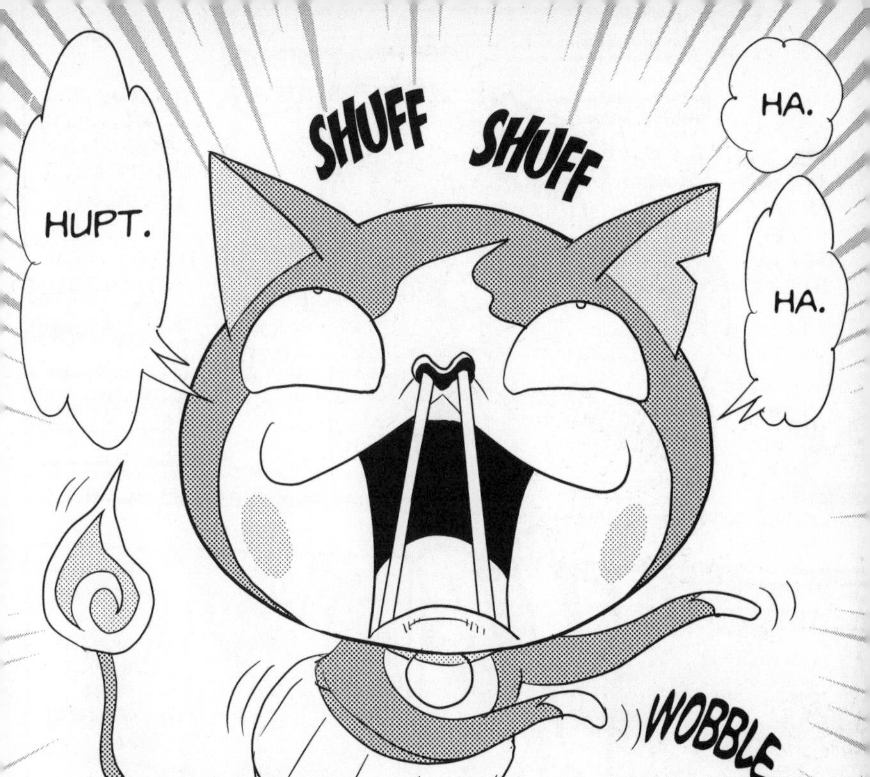
HA.
HA.
SHUFF
SHUFF
HUPT.
WOBBLE...
WOBBLE...
WOBBLE...
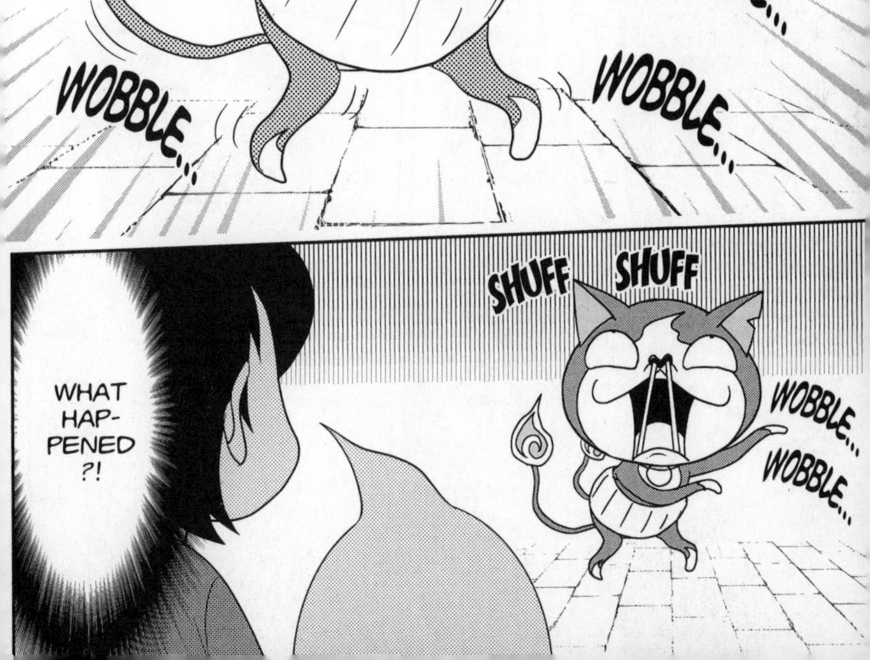
SHUFF
SHUFF
WOBBLE...
WOBBLE...
WHAT HAP-PENED?!

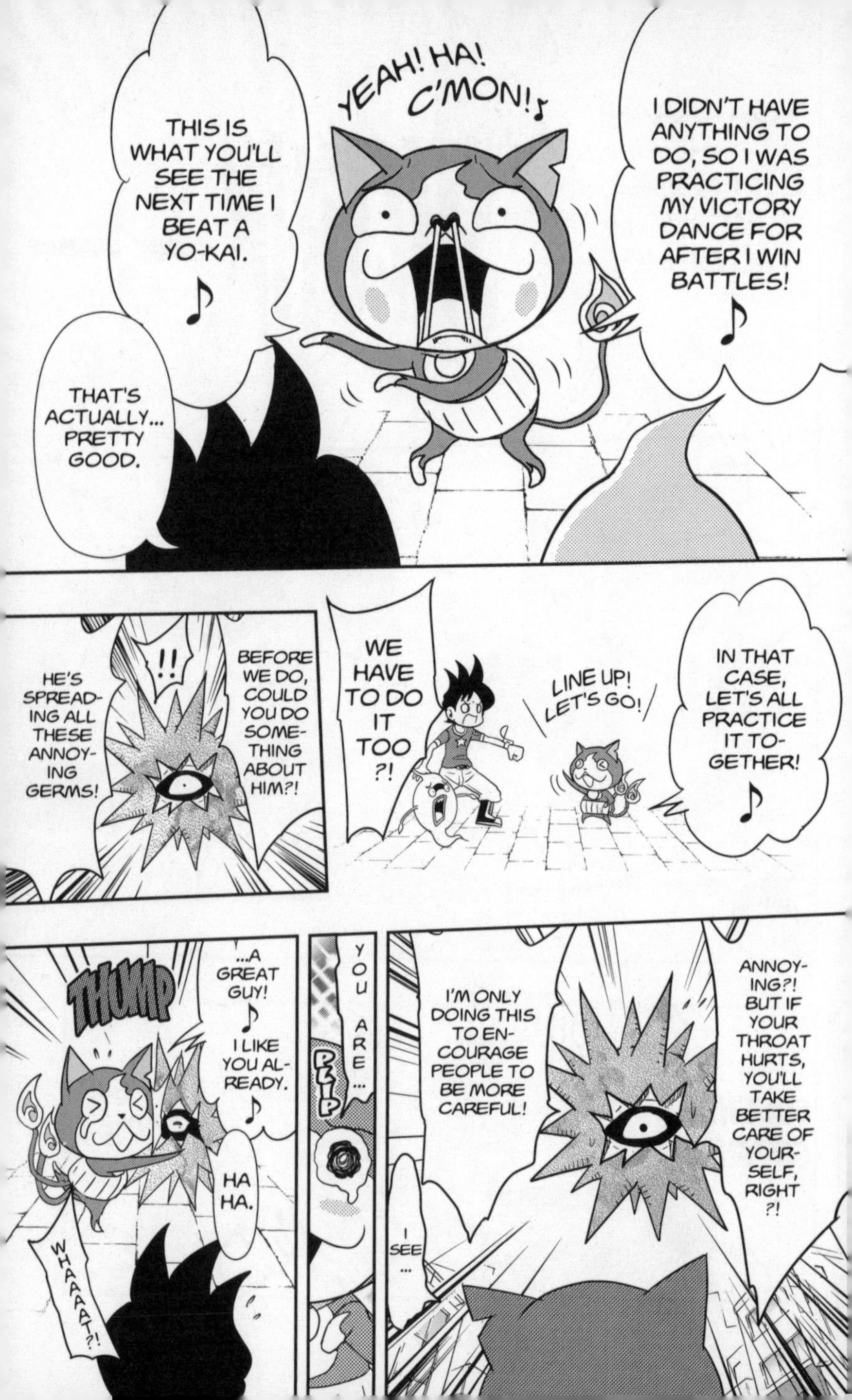
I DIDN'T HAVE ANYTHING TO DO, SO I WAS PRACTICING MY VICTORY DANCE FOR AFTER I WIN BATTLES! ♪
YEAH! HA! C'MON! ♪
THIS IS WHAT YOU'LL SEE THE NEXT TIME I BEAT A YO-KAI. ♪
THAT'S ACTUALLY... PRETTY GOOD.
IN THAT CASE, LET'S ALL PRACTICE IT TOGETHER! ♪
LINE UP! LET'S GO!
WE HAVE TO DO IT TOO?!
BEFORE WE DO, COULD YOU DO SOMETHING ABOUT HIM?!
!!
HE'S SPREADING ALL THESE ANNOYING GERMS!
ANNOYING?! BUT IF YOUR THROAT HURTS, YOU'LL TAKE BETTER CARE OF YOURSELF, RIGHT?!
I'M ONLY DOING THIS TO ENCOURAGE PEOPLE TO BE MORE CAREFUL!
YOU ARE...
BLIP
I SEE...
...A GREAT GUY! ♪
I LIKE YOU ALREADY. ♪
THUMP
HA HA.
WHAAAAT?!

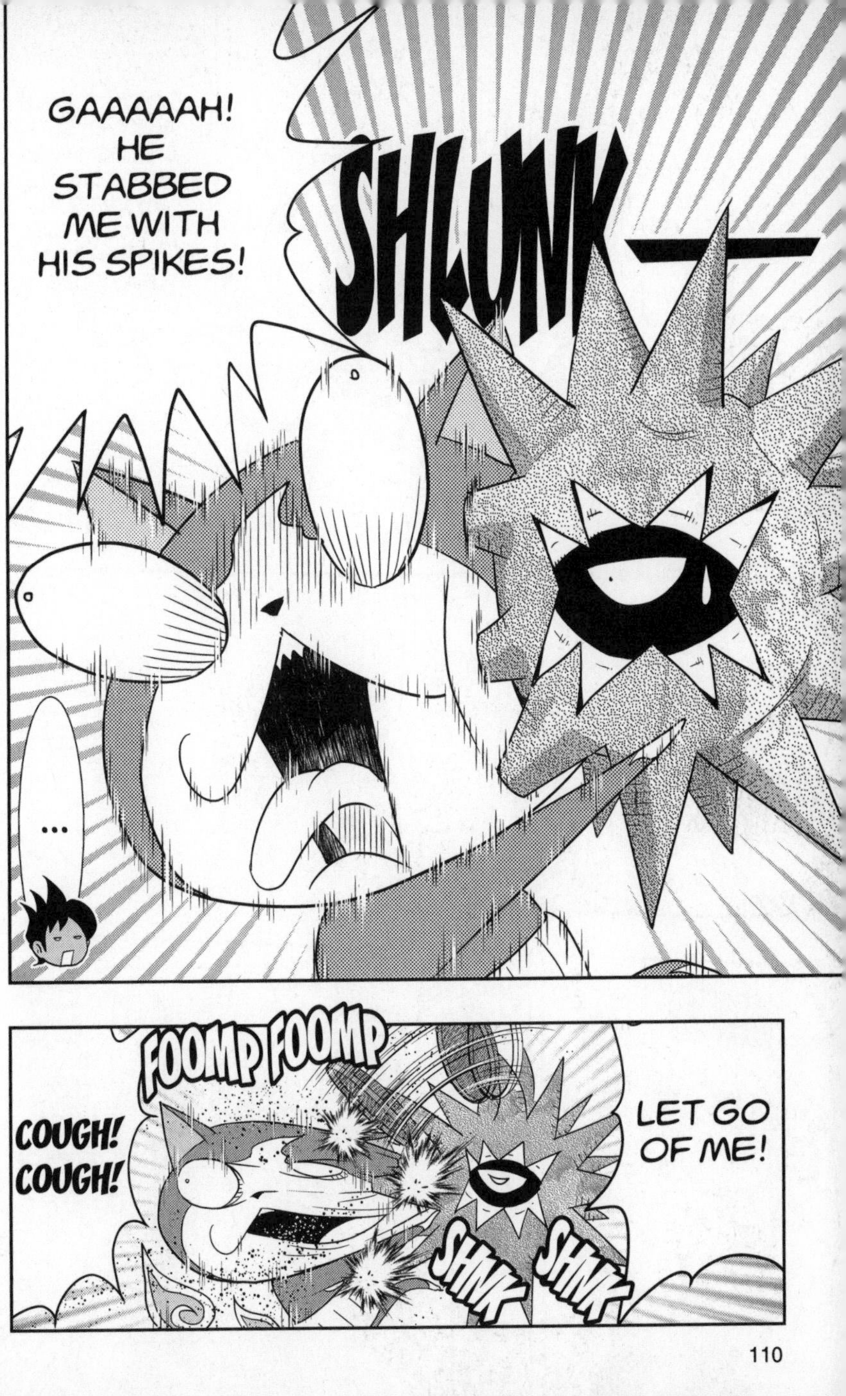
SHLUNK
GAAAAAH! HE STABBED ME WITH HIS SPIKES!
...
LET GO OF ME!
SHNK SHNK
FOOMP FOOMP
COUGH! COUGH!

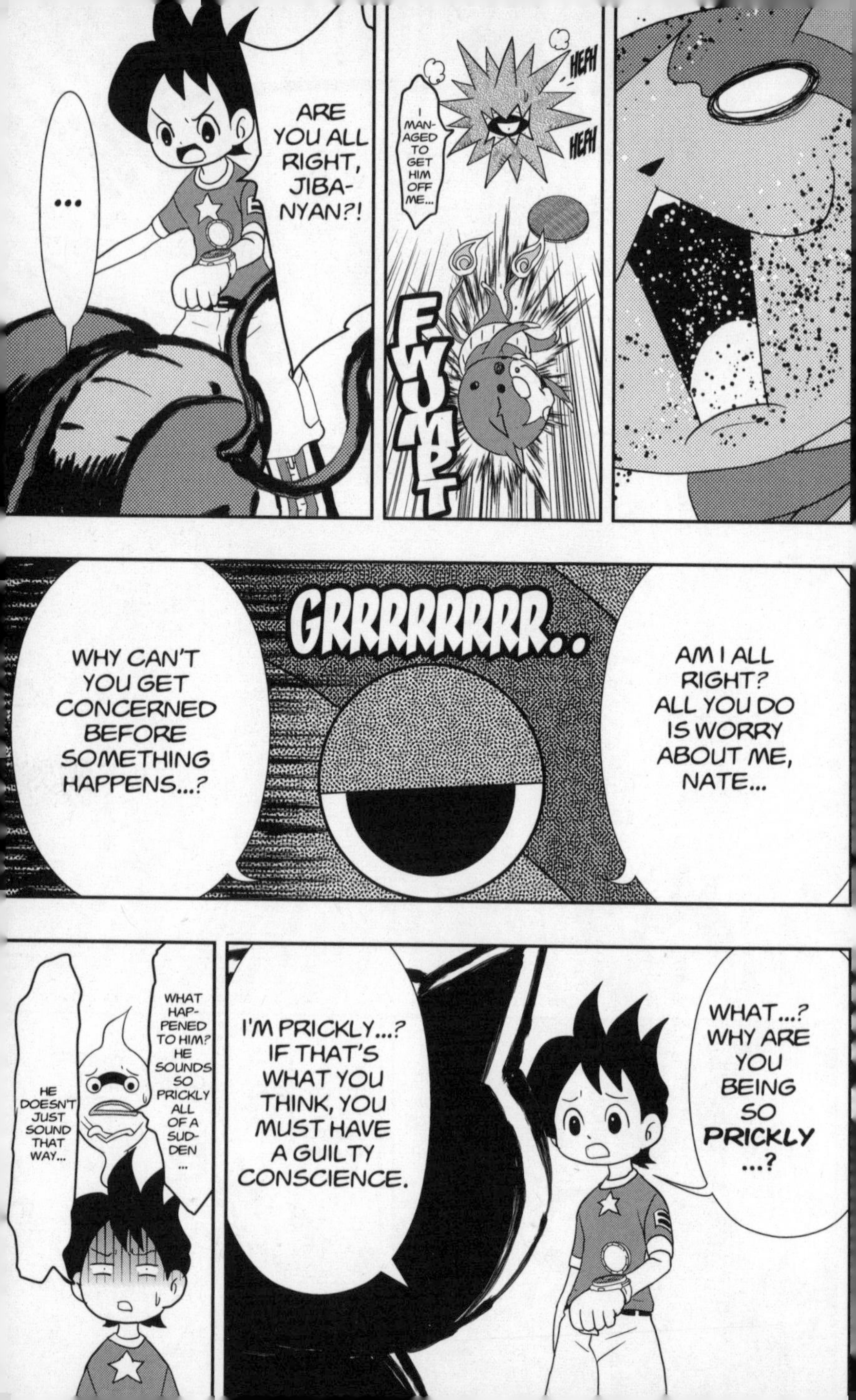
HEH
I MAN-AGED TO GET HIM OFF ME...
HEH
FWUMPT
ARE YOU ALL RIGHT, JIBA-NYAN?!
...
AM I ALL RIGHT? ALL YOU DO IS WORRY ABOUT ME, NATE...
GRRRRRRRR..
WHY CAN'T YOU GET CONCERNED BEFORE SOMETHING HAPPENS...?
WHAT...? WHY ARE YOU BEING SO PRICKLY...?
I'M PRICKLY...? IF THAT'S WHAT YOU THINK, YOU MUST HAVE A GUILTY CONSCIENCE.
WHAT HAP-PENED TO HIM? HE SOUNDS SO PRICKLY ALL OF A SUD-DEN...
HE DOESN'T JUST SOUND THAT WAY...

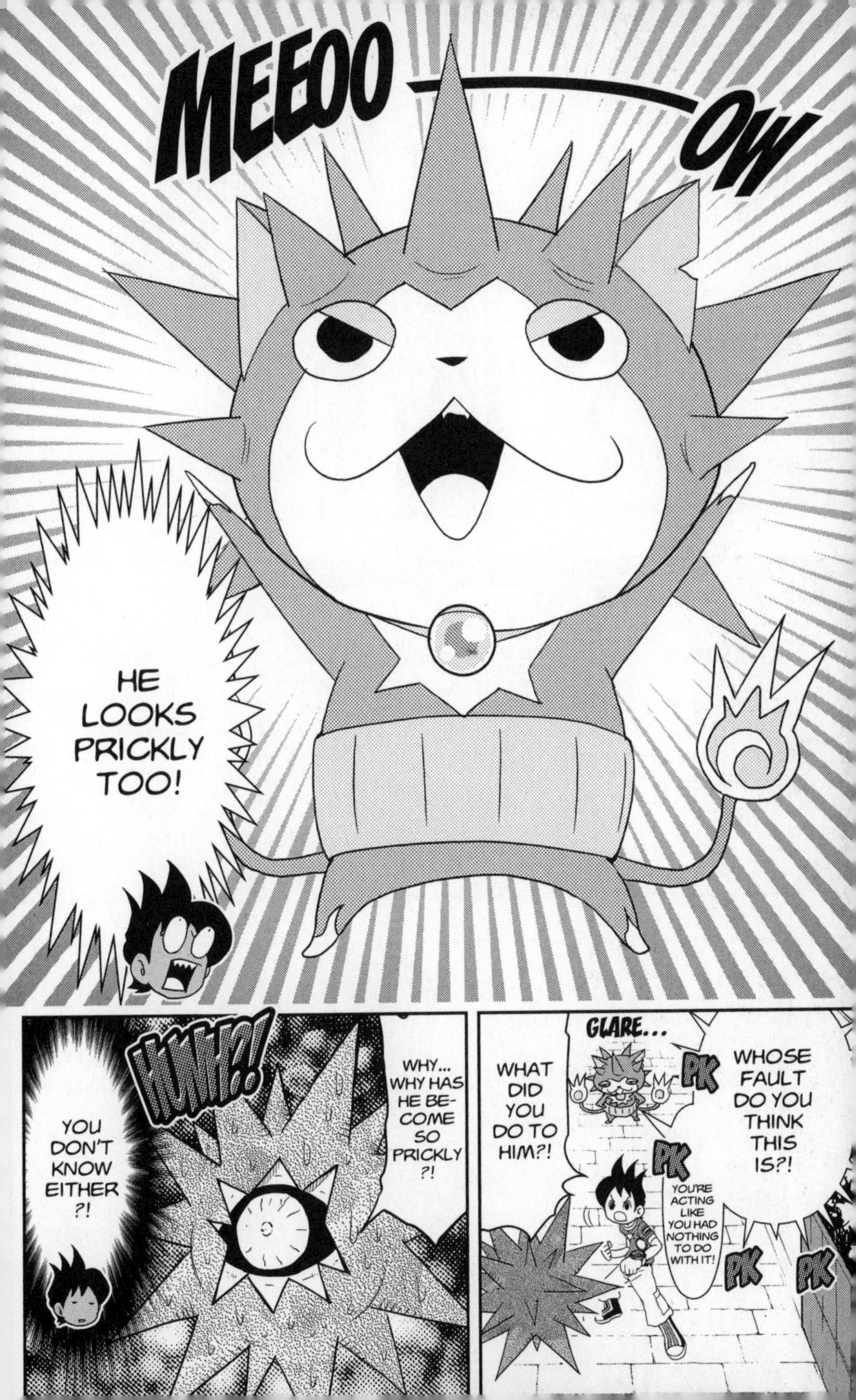
MEEOO—OW
HE LOOKS PRICKLY TOO!
GLARE...
WHOSE FAULT DO YOU THINK THIS IS?!
PK
WHAT DID YOU DO TO HIM?!
PK
YOU'RE ACTING LIKE YOU HAD NOTHING TO DO WITH IT!
PK
PK
WHY... WHY HAS HE BE-COME SO PRICKLY?!
HUHH?!
YOU DON'T KNOW EITHER?!

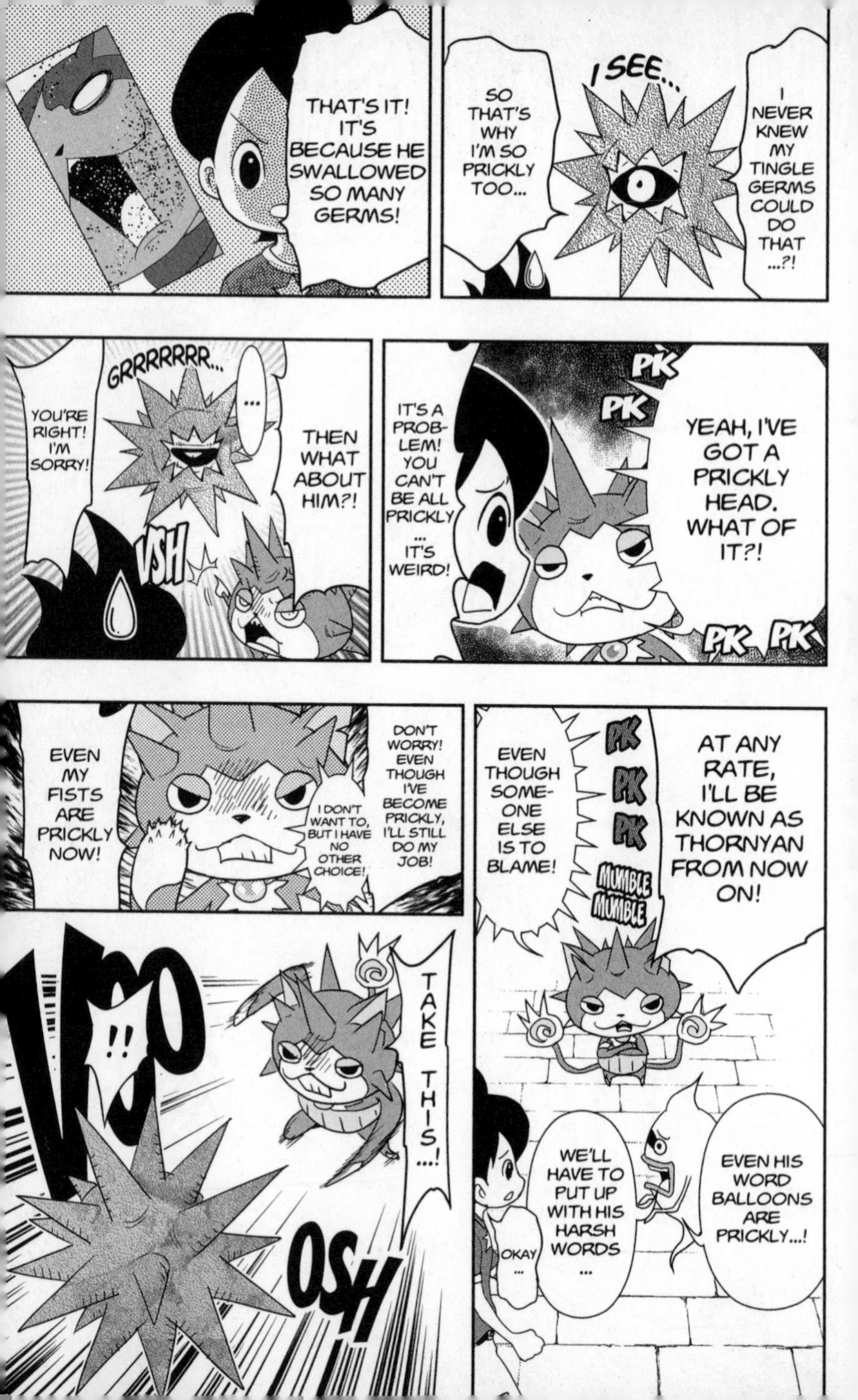
I SEE...
I NEVER KNEW MY TINGLE GERMS COULD DO THAT ...?!
SO THAT'S WHY I'M SO PRICKLY TOO...
THAT'S IT! IT'S BECAUSE HE SWALLOWED SO MANY GERMS!
PK
PK
YEAH, I'VE GOT A PRICKLY HEAD. WHAT OF IT?!
IT'S A PROBLEM! YOU CAN'T BE ALL PRICKLY ... IT'S WEIRD!
PK PK
...
THEN WHAT ABOUT HIM?!
GRRRRRRR...
YOU'RE RIGHT! I'M SORRY!
VSH
AT ANY RATE, I'LL BE KNOWN AS THORNYAN FROM NOW ON!
PK
PK
PK
MUMBLE MUMBLE
EVEN THOUGH SOMEONE ELSE IS TO BLAME!
EVEN HIS WORD BALLOONS ARE PRICKLY...!
WE'LL HAVE TO PUT UP WITH HIS HARSH WORDS ...
OKAY ...
DON'T WORRY! EVEN THOUGH I'VE BECOME PRICKLY, I'LL STILL DO MY JOB!
I DON'T WANT TO, BUT I HAVE NO OTHER CHOICE!
EVEN MY FISTS ARE PRICKLY NOW!
TAKE THIS...!
!!
WOO
OSH

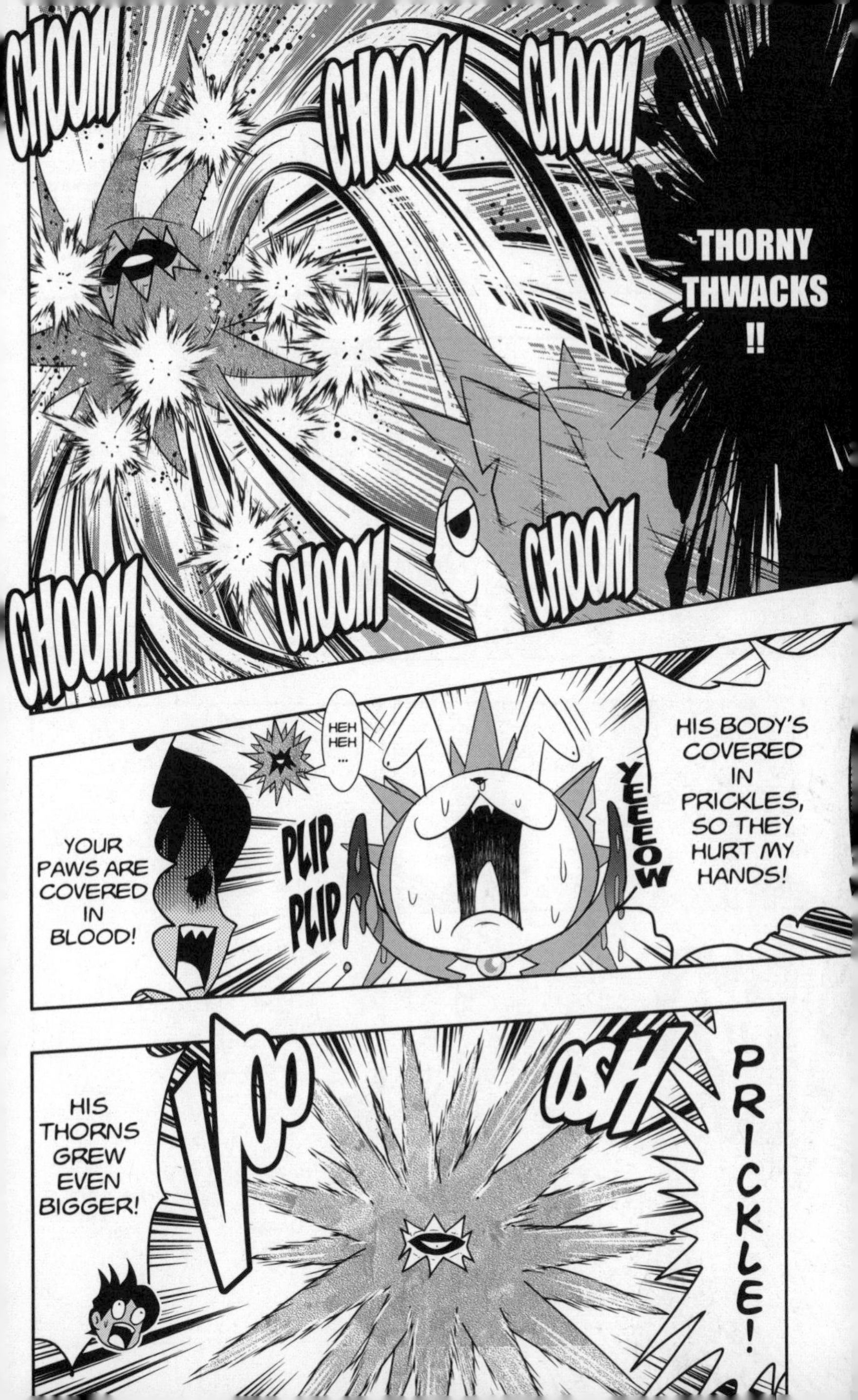
THORNY THWACKS !!
CHOOM
CHOOM
CHOOM
CHOOM
CHOOM
CHOOM
CHOOM
HIS BODY'S COVERED IN PRICKLES, SO THEY HURT MY HANDS!
YEEEOW
HEH HEH ...
PLIP PLIP
YOUR PAWS ARE COVERED IN BLOOD!
PRICKLE!
VOOOSH
HIS THORNS GREW EVEN BIGGER!

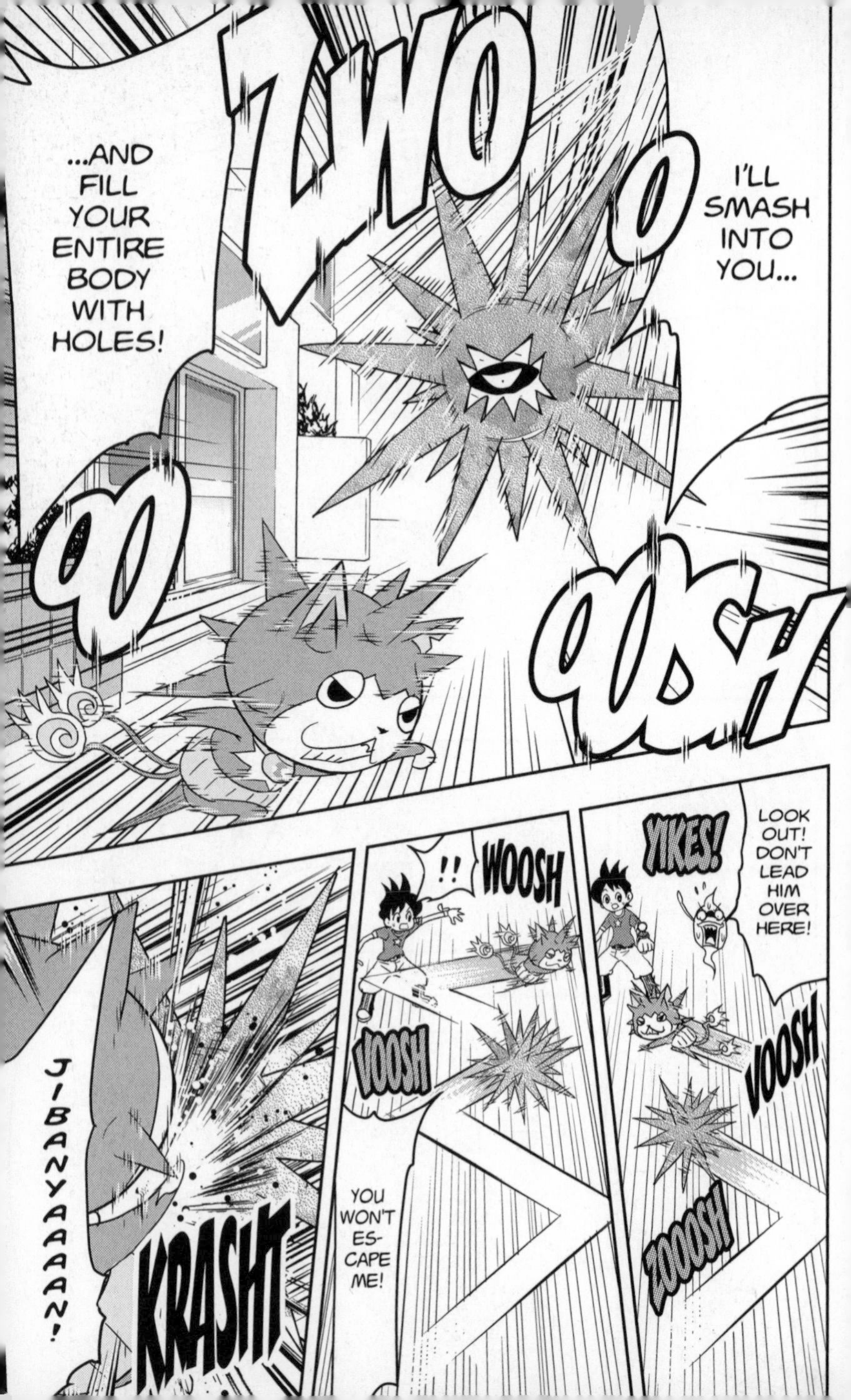
I'LL SMASH INTO YOU...
...AND FILL YOUR ENTIRE BODY WITH HOLES!
ZWOOOOOSH
YIKES!
LOOK OUT! DON'T LEAD HIM OVER HERE!
VOOSH
ZOOOSH
!!
WOOSH
VOOSH
YOU WON'T ES-CAPE ME!
JIBANYAAAAAN!
KRASHT

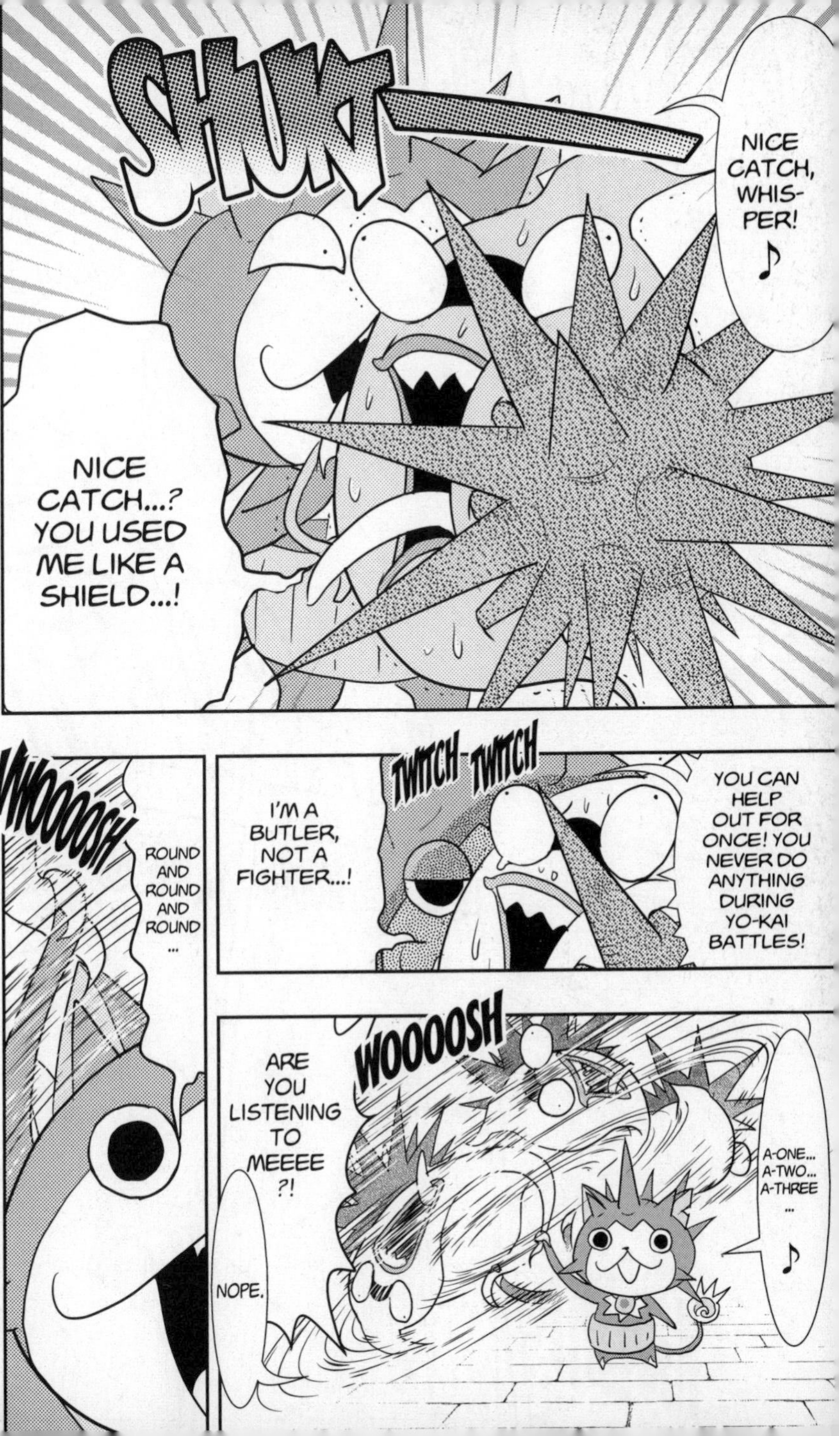
SHUNT
NICE CATCH, WHISPER! ♪
NICE CATCH...? YOU USED ME LIKE A SHIELD...!
TWITCH-TWITCH
YOU CAN HELP OUT FOR ONCE! YOU NEVER DO ANYTHING DURING YO-KAI BATTLES!
I'M A BUTLER, NOT A FIGHTER...!
WOOOOSH
A-ONE... A-TWO... A-THREE ... ♪
ARE YOU LISTENING TO MEEEE?!
NOPE.
VWOOOOOSH
ROUND AND ROUND AND ROUND ...

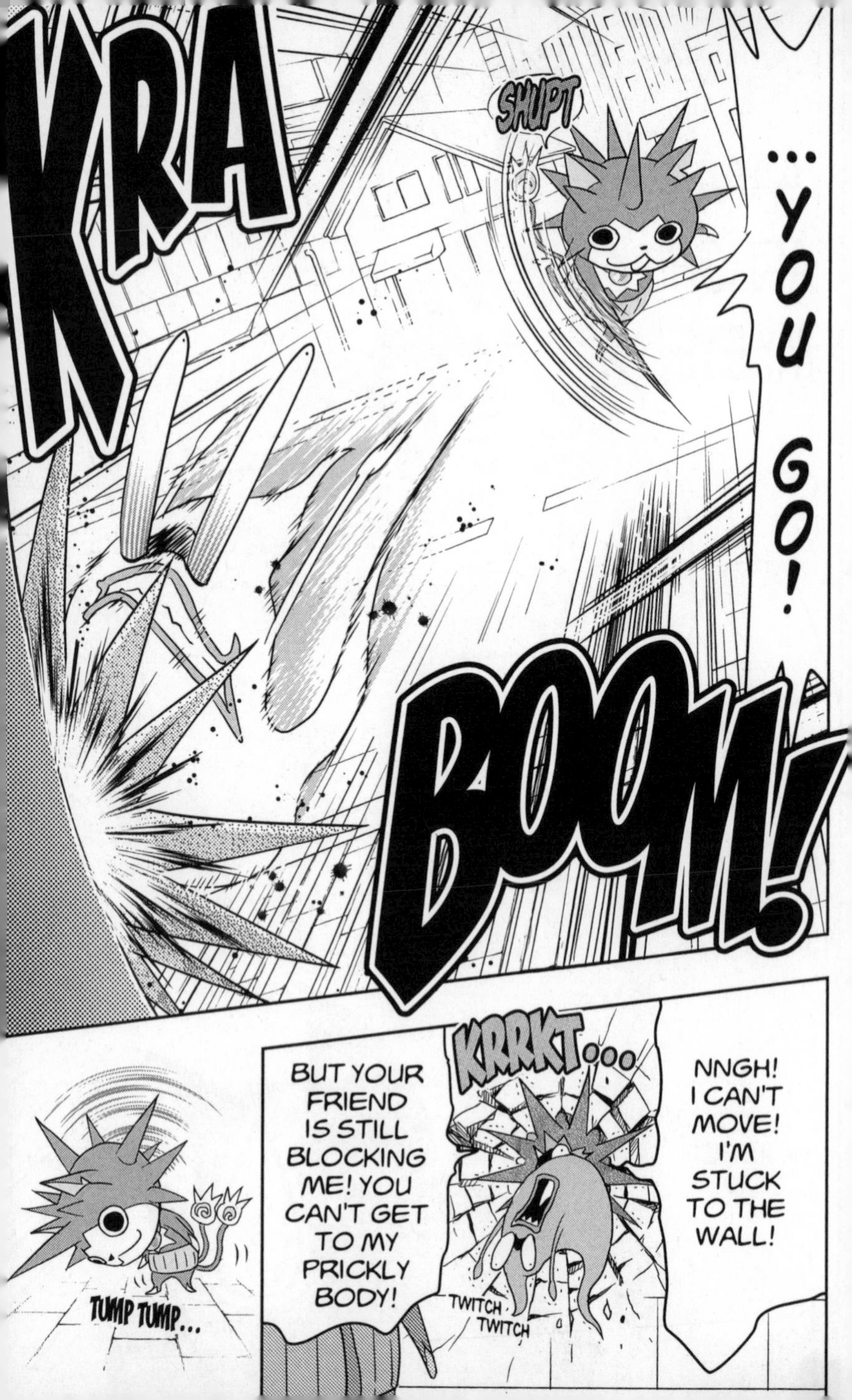
...YOU GO!
SHUPT
KRA
BOOM!
NNGH! I CAN'T MOVE! I'M STUCK TO THE WALL!
KRRKT...
BUT YOUR FRIEND IS STILL BLOCKING ME! YOU CAN'T GET TO MY PRICKLY BODY!
TWITCH TWITCH
TUMP TUMP...

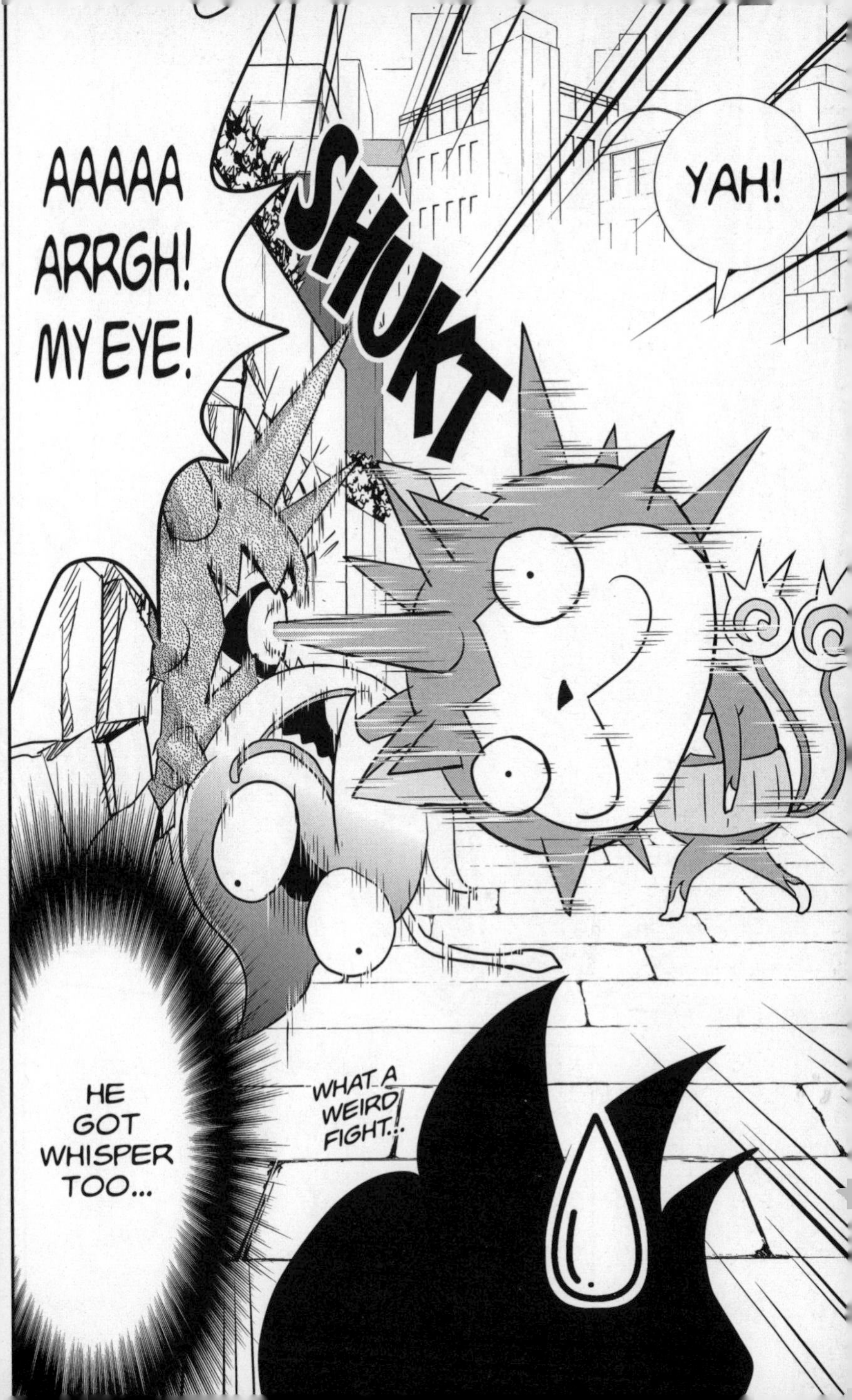
YAH!
SHUKT
AAAAA ARRGH! MY EYE!
WHAT A WEIRD FIGHT...
HE GOT WHISPER TOO...

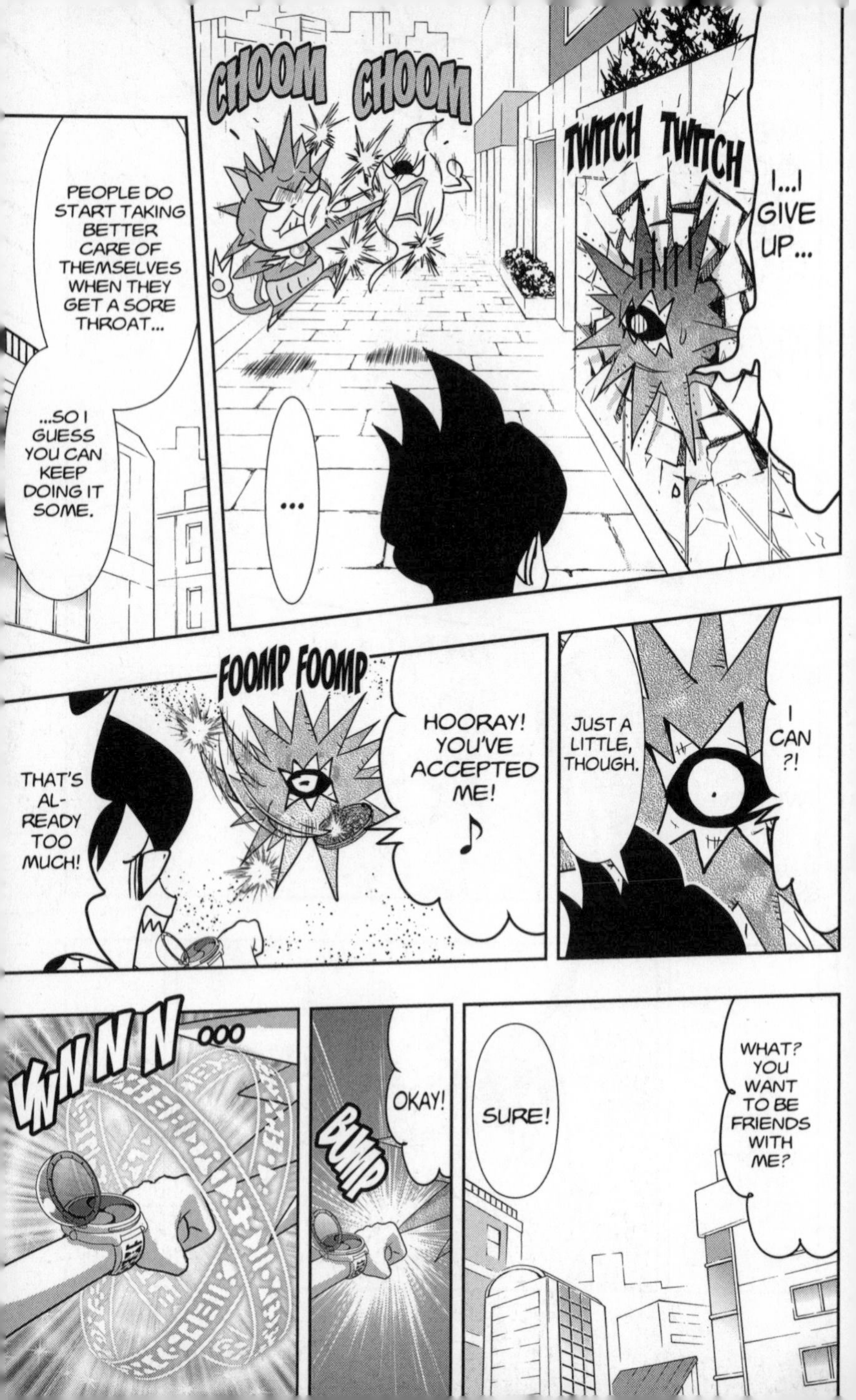
TWITCH TWITCH
I...I GIVE UP...
CHOOM CHOOM
...
PEOPLE DO START TAKING BETTER CARE OF THEMSELVES WHEN THEY GET A SORE THROAT...
...SO I GUESS YOU CAN KEEP DOING IT SOME.
I CAN ?!
JUST A LITTLE, THOUGH.
HOORAY! YOU'VE ACCEPTED ME! ♪
FOOMP FOOMP
THAT'S AL-READY TOO MUCH!
WHAT? YOU WANT TO BE FRIENDS WITH ME?
SURE!
OKAY!
BUMP
VWNNN OOO

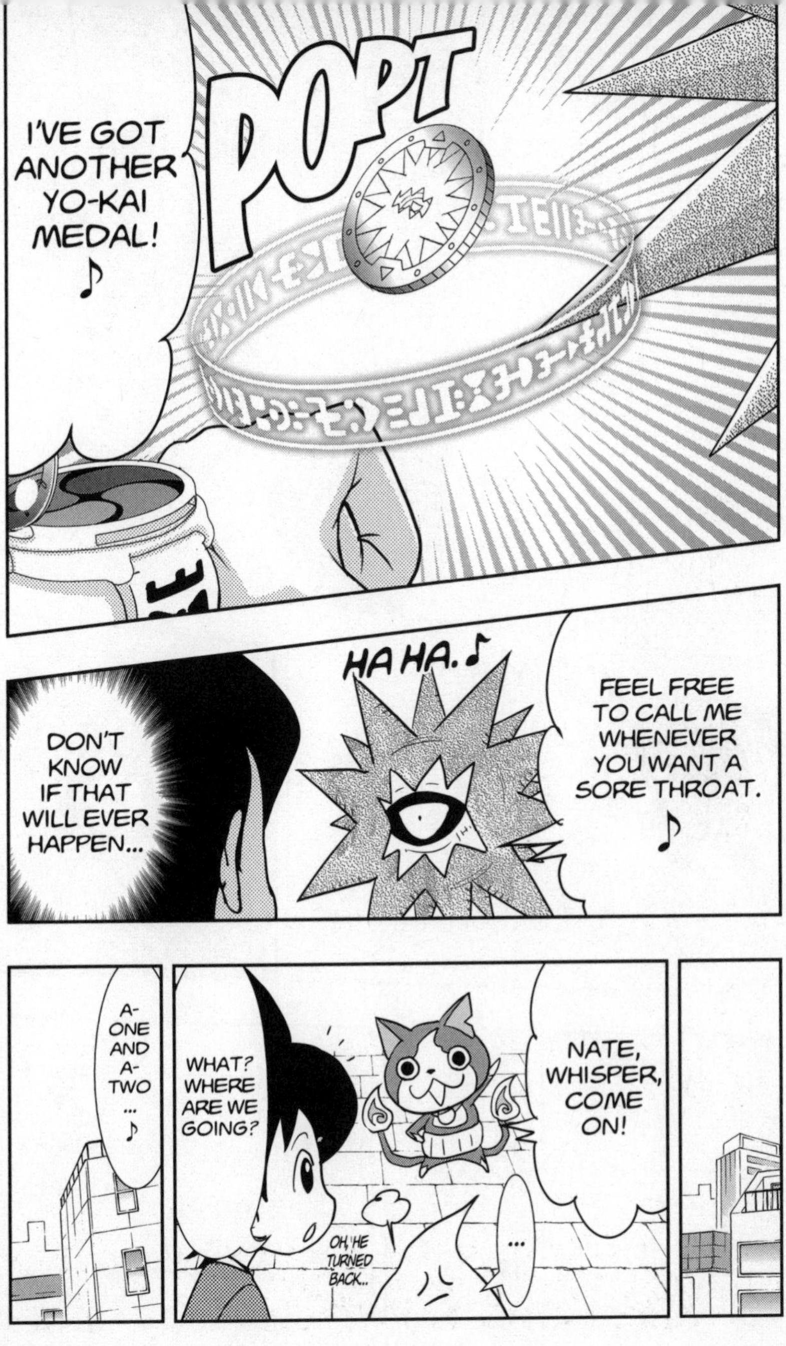
POPT
I'VE GOT ANOTHER YO-KAI MEDAL! ♪
HA HA. ♪
FEEL FREE TO CALL ME WHENEVER YOU WANT A SORE THROAT. ♪
DON'T KNOW IF THAT WILL EVER HAPPEN...
NATE, WHISPER, COME ON!
...
WHAT? WHERE ARE WE GOING?
OH, HE TURNED BACK...
A-ONE AND A-TWO ... ♪

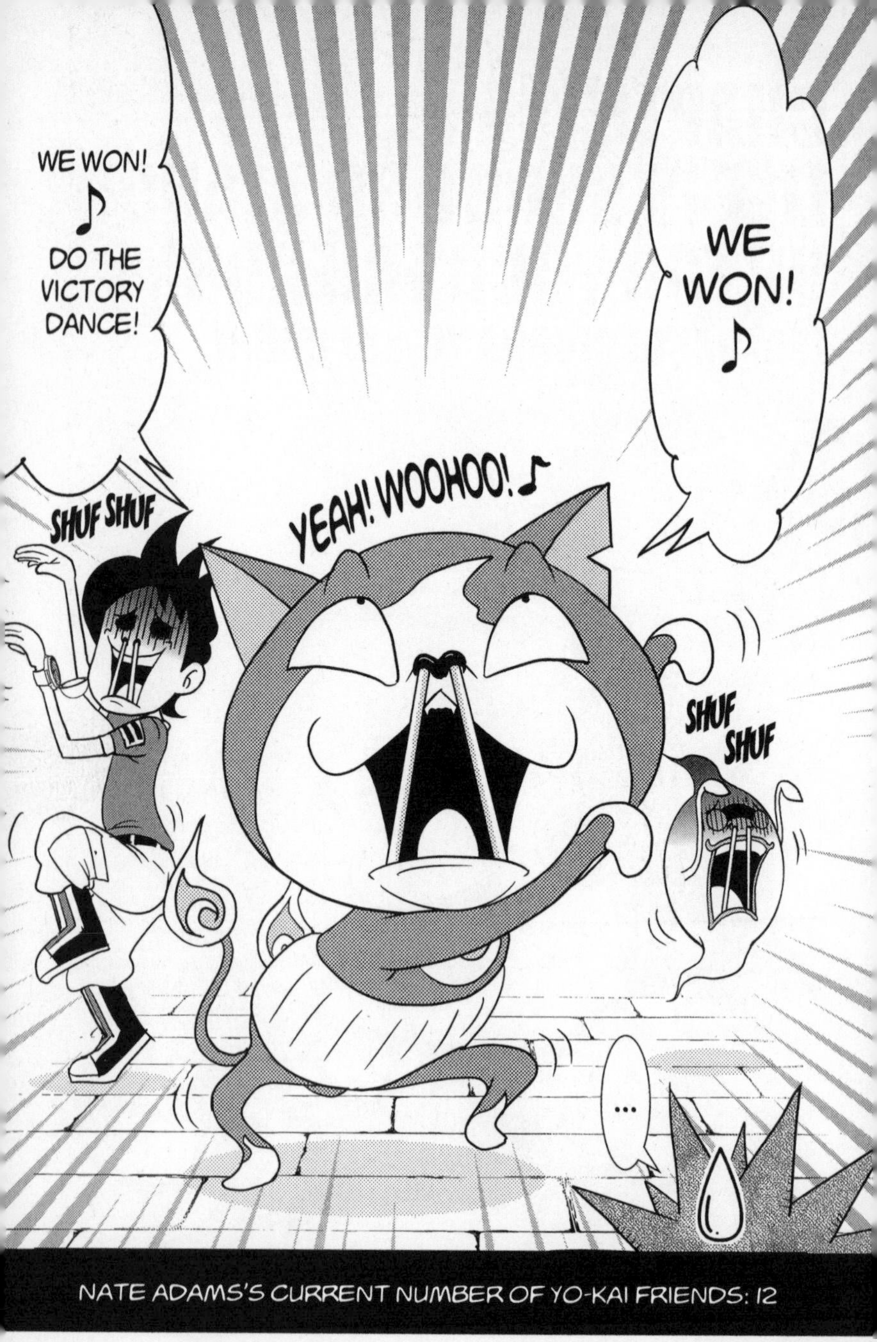
WE WON! ♪
WE WON! ♪ DO THE VICTORY DANCE!
YEAH! WOOHOO! ♪
SHUF SHUF
SHUF SHUF
...
NATE ADAMS'S CURRENT NUMBER OF YO-KAI FRIENDS: 12

CHAPTER 13: LIFE IS SHORT, SO STAND UP FOR YOUR FRIENDS!

FEATURING CICADA YO-KAI CADIN

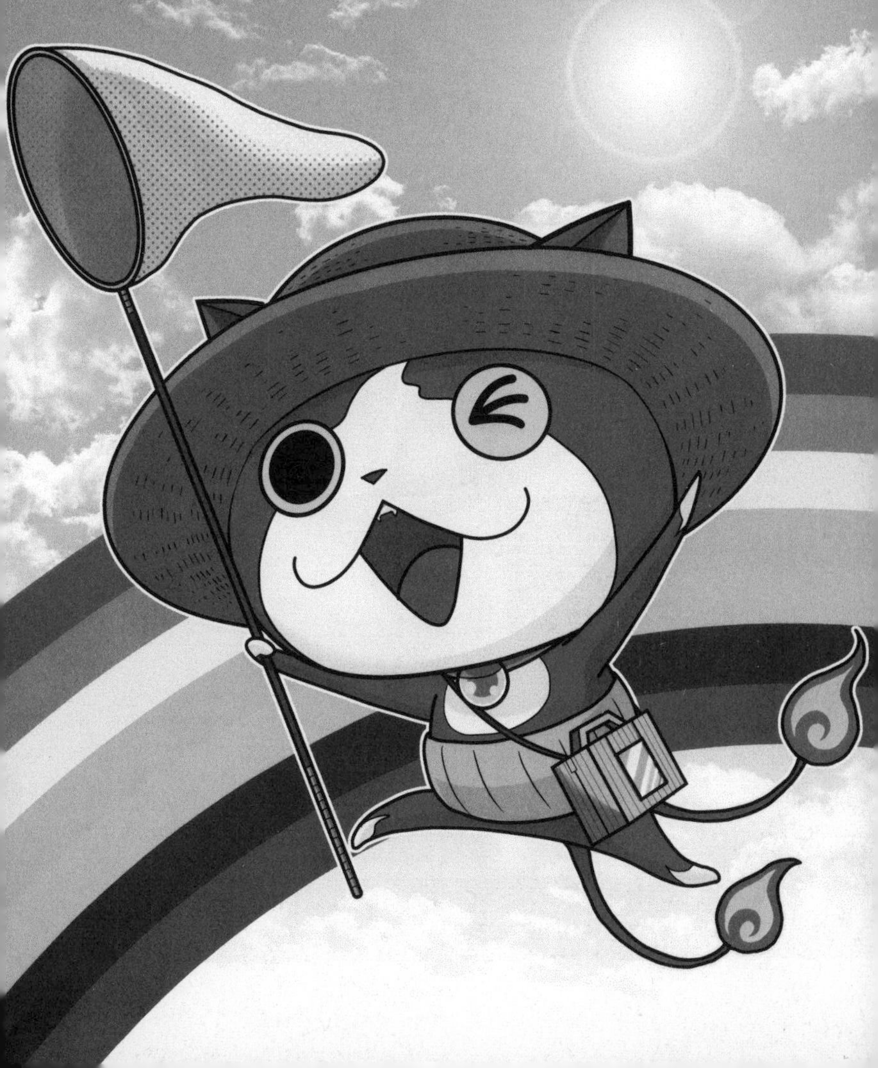

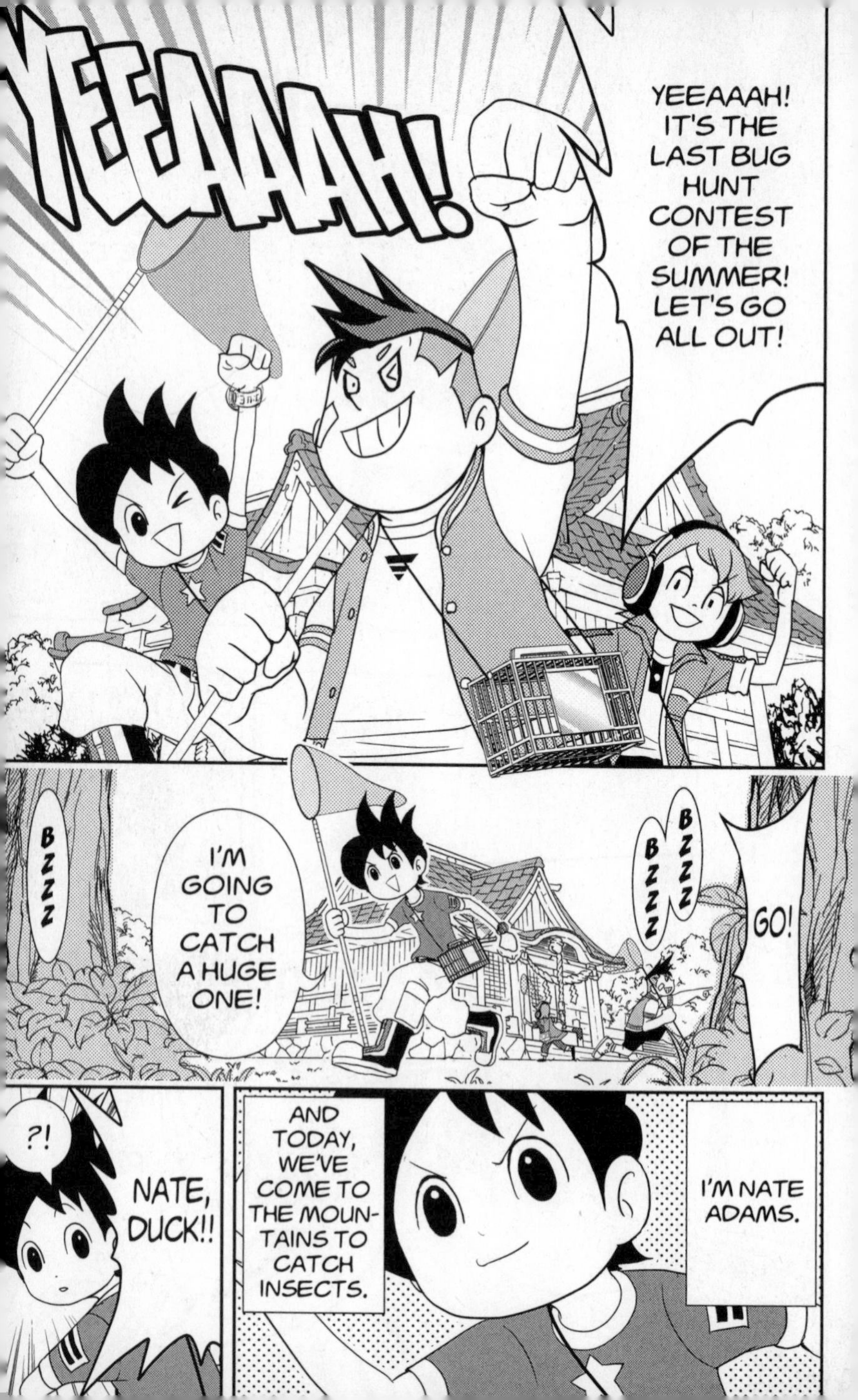
YEEAAAH! IT'S THE LAST BUG HUNT CONTEST OF THE SUMMER! LET'S GO ALL OUT!
YEEAAAH!
GO!
BZZZ
BZZZ
I'M GOING TO CATCH A HUGE ONE!
BZZZ
I'M NATE ADAMS.
AND TODAY, WE'VE COME TO THE MOUNTAINS TO CATCH INSECTS.
NATE, DUCK!!
?!

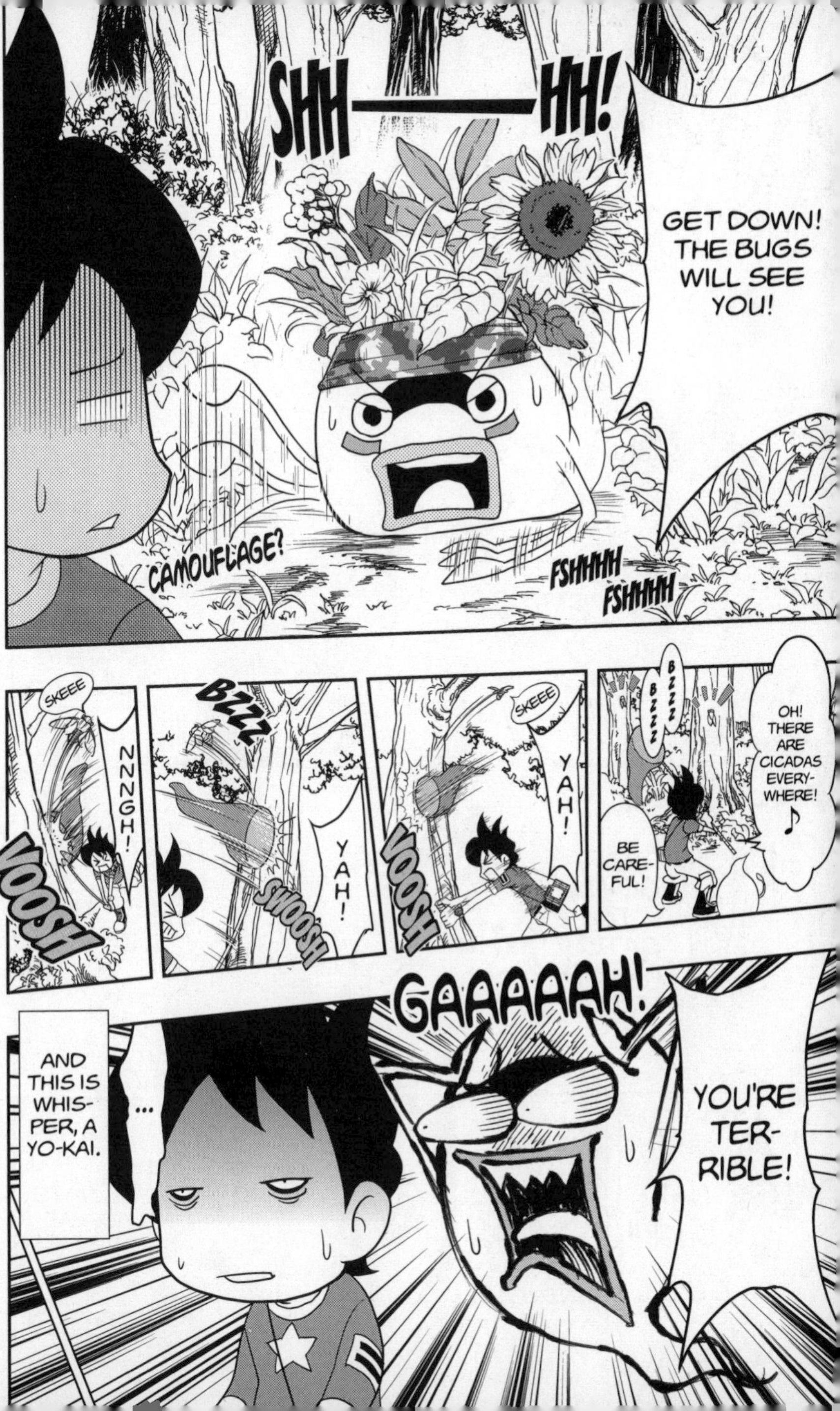
SHH——HH!
GET DOWN! THE BUGS WILL SEE YOU!
FSHHHH FSHHHH
CAMOUFLAGE?
OH! THERE ARE CICADAS EVERY-WHERE! ♪
BZZZ BZZZ
BE CARE-FUL!
SKEEE
YAH!
VOOSH
BZZZ
YAH!
SWOOSH
SKEEE
NNNGH!
VOOSH
GAAAAAH!
YOU'RE TER-RIBLE!
...
AND THIS IS WHIS-PER, A YO-KAI.

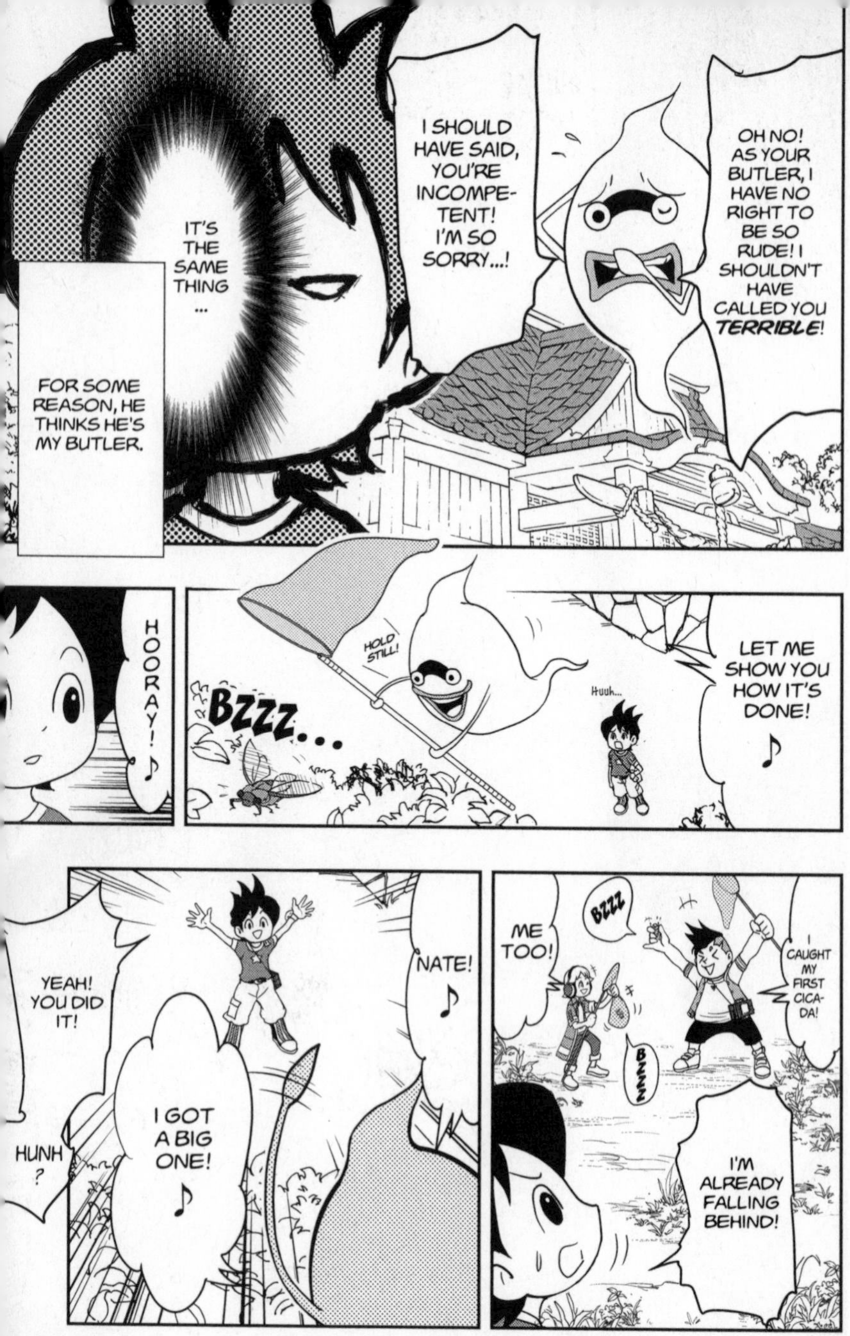
OH NO! AS YOUR BUTLER, I HAVE NO RIGHT TO BE SO RUDE! I SHOULDN'T HAVE CALLED YOU *TERRIBLE*!
I SHOULD HAVE SAID, YOU'RE INCOMPETENT! I'M SO SORRY...!
IT'S THE SAME THING...
FOR SOME REASON, HE THINKS HE'S MY BUTLER.
LET ME SHOW YOU HOW IT'S DONE! ♪
Huuh...
HOLD STILL!
BZZZ...
HOORAY! ♪
I CAUGHT MY FIRST CICADA!
BZZZ
ME TOO!
BZZZ
I'M ALREADY FALLING BEHIND!
NATE! ♪
I GOT A BIG ONE! ♪
YEAH! YOU DID IT!
HUNH?

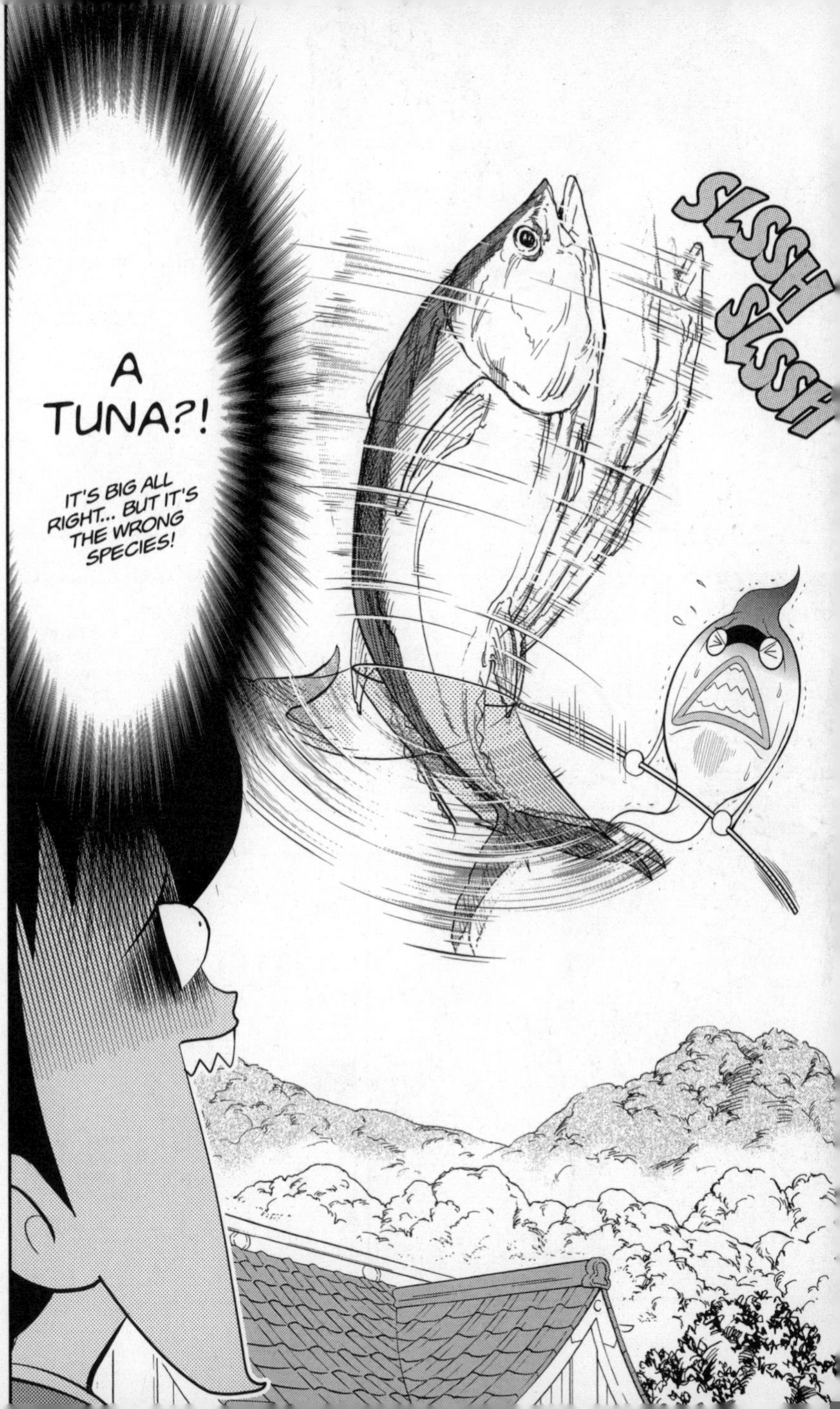
SLSSH SLSSH
A TUNA?!
IT'S BIG ALL RIGHT... BUT IT'S THE WRONG SPECIES!

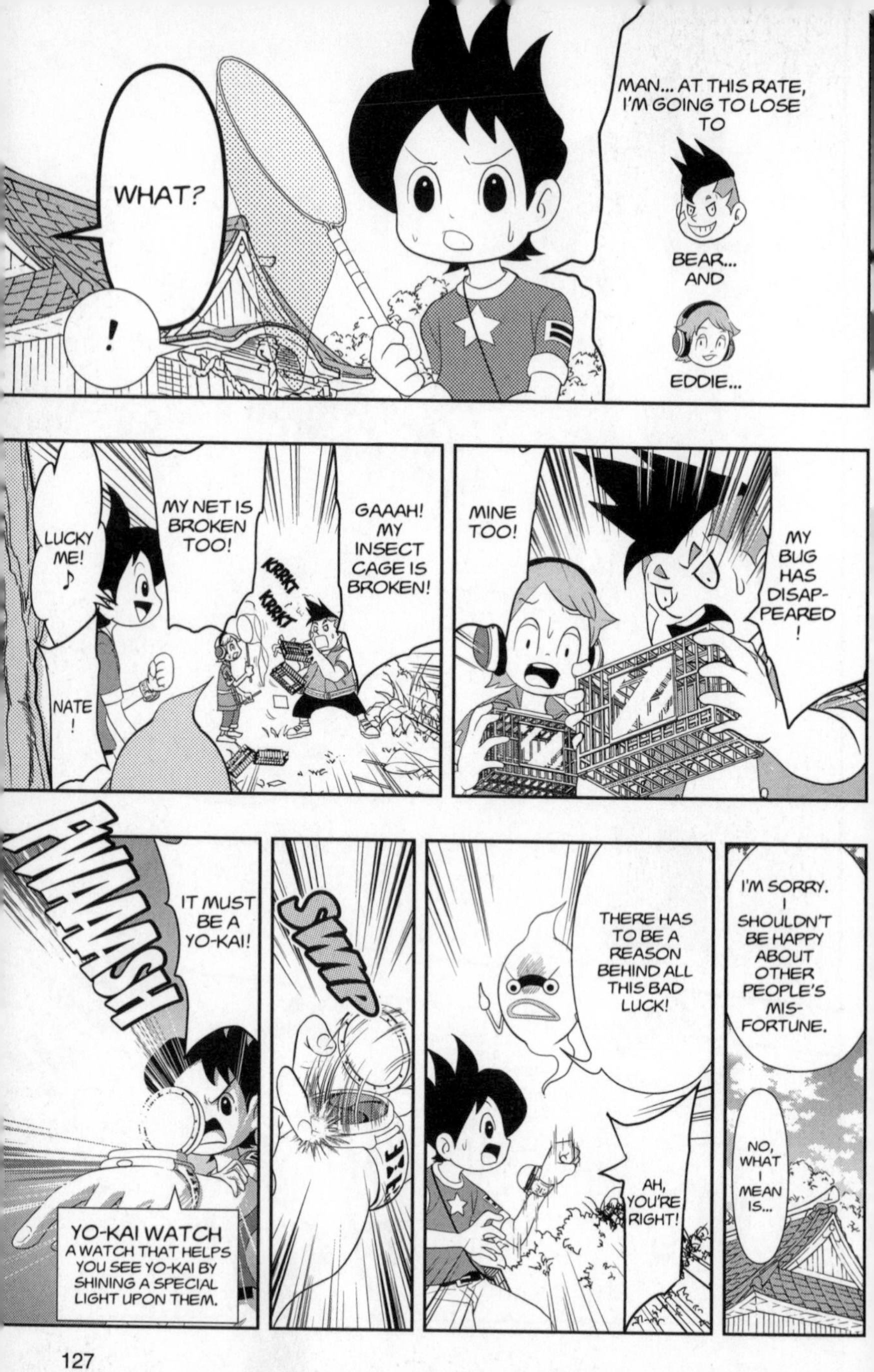
MAN... AT THIS RATE, I'M GOING TO LOSE TO
BEAR... AND
EDDIE...
WHAT?
!
MY BUG HAS DISAP-PEARED!
MINE TOO!
GAAAH! MY INSECT CAGE IS BROKEN!
KRRKT
KRRKT
MY NET IS BROKEN TOO!
LUCKY ME! ♪
NATE!
I'M SORRY. I SHOULDN'T BE HAPPY ABOUT OTHER PEOPLE'S MIS-FORTUNE.
NO, WHAT I MEAN IS...
THERE HAS TO BE A REASON BEHIND ALL THIS BAD LUCK!
AH, YOU'RE RIGHT!
SWIP
IT MUST BE A YO-KAI!
FWAASH
YO-KAI WATCH
A WATCH THAT HELPS YOU SEE YO-KAI BY SHINING A SPECIAL LIGHT UPON THEM.

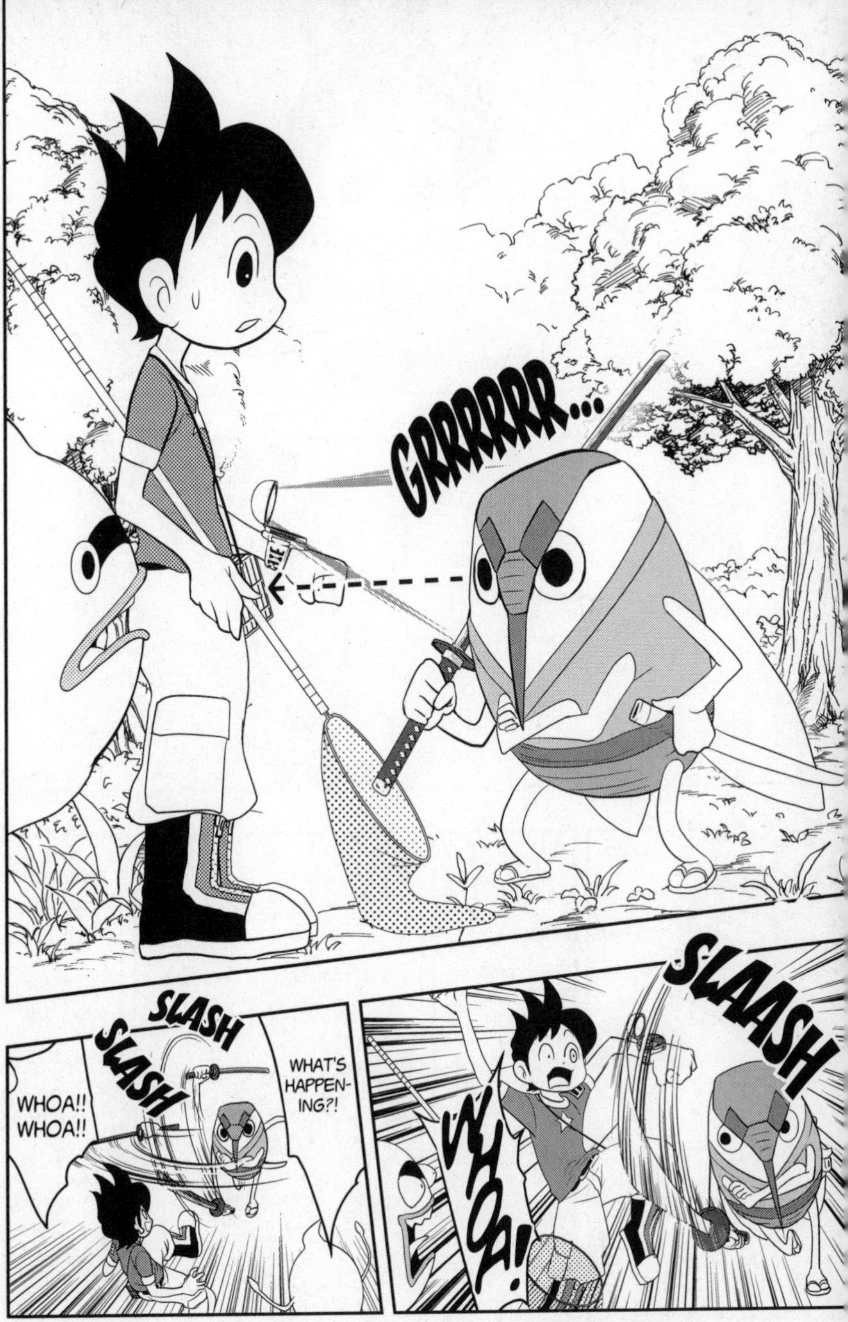
GRRRRRR...
SLAASH
WHOOA!
WHAT'S HAPPEN-ING?!
SLASH
SLASH
WHOA!! WHOA!!

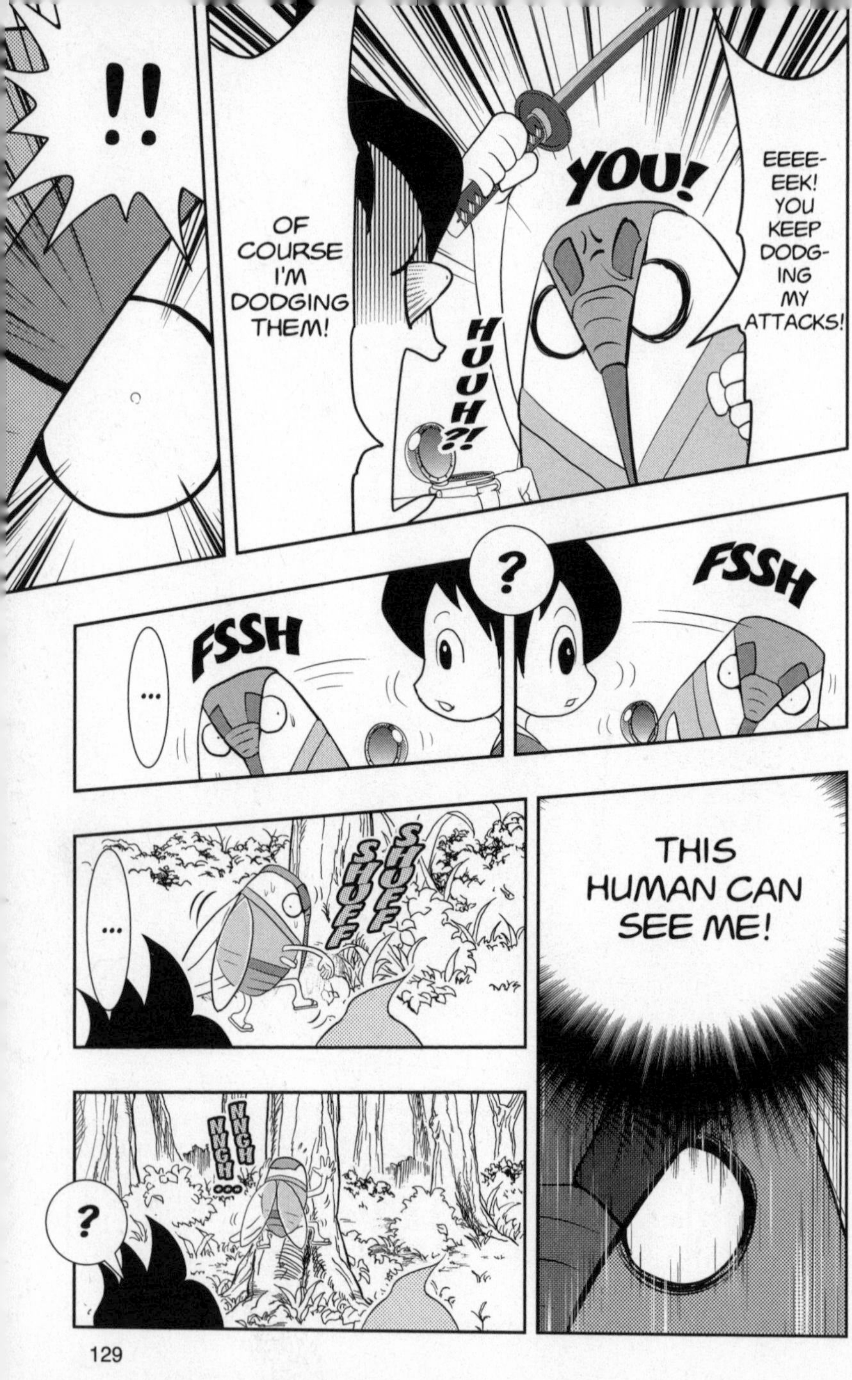
EEEE-EEK! YOU KEEP DODG-ING MY ATTACKS!
YOU!
HUUUH?!
OF COURSE I'M DODGING THEM!
!!
FSSH
?
FSSH
...
THIS HUMAN CAN SEE ME!
SHUFF SHUFF
...
NNGH NNGH...
?

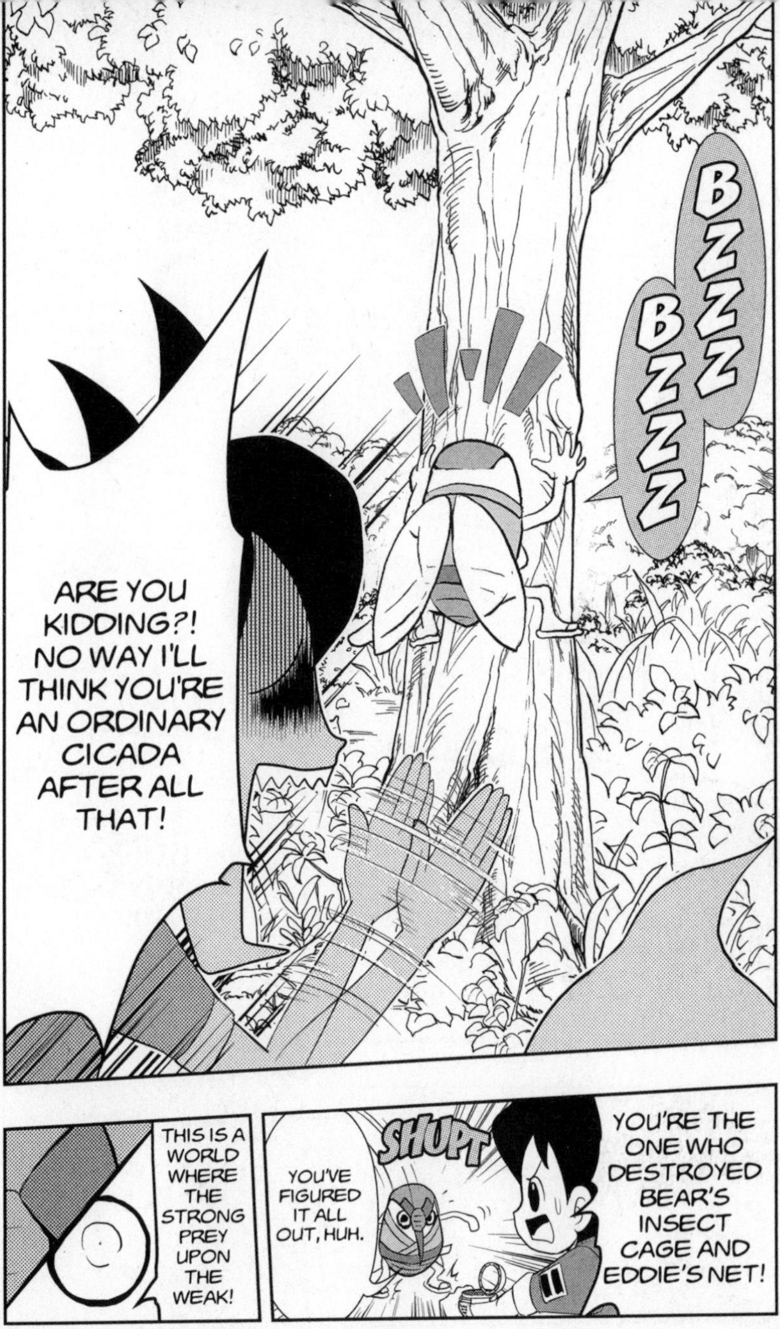
BZZZ
BZZZ
ARE YOU KIDDING?! NO WAY I'LL THINK YOU'RE AN ORDINARY CICADA AFTER ALL THAT!
YOU'RE THE ONE WHO DESTROYED BEAR'S INSECT CAGE AND EDDIE'S NET!
SHUPT
YOU'VE FIGURED IT ALL OUT, HUH.
THIS IS A WORLD WHERE THE STRONG PREY UPON THE WEAK!

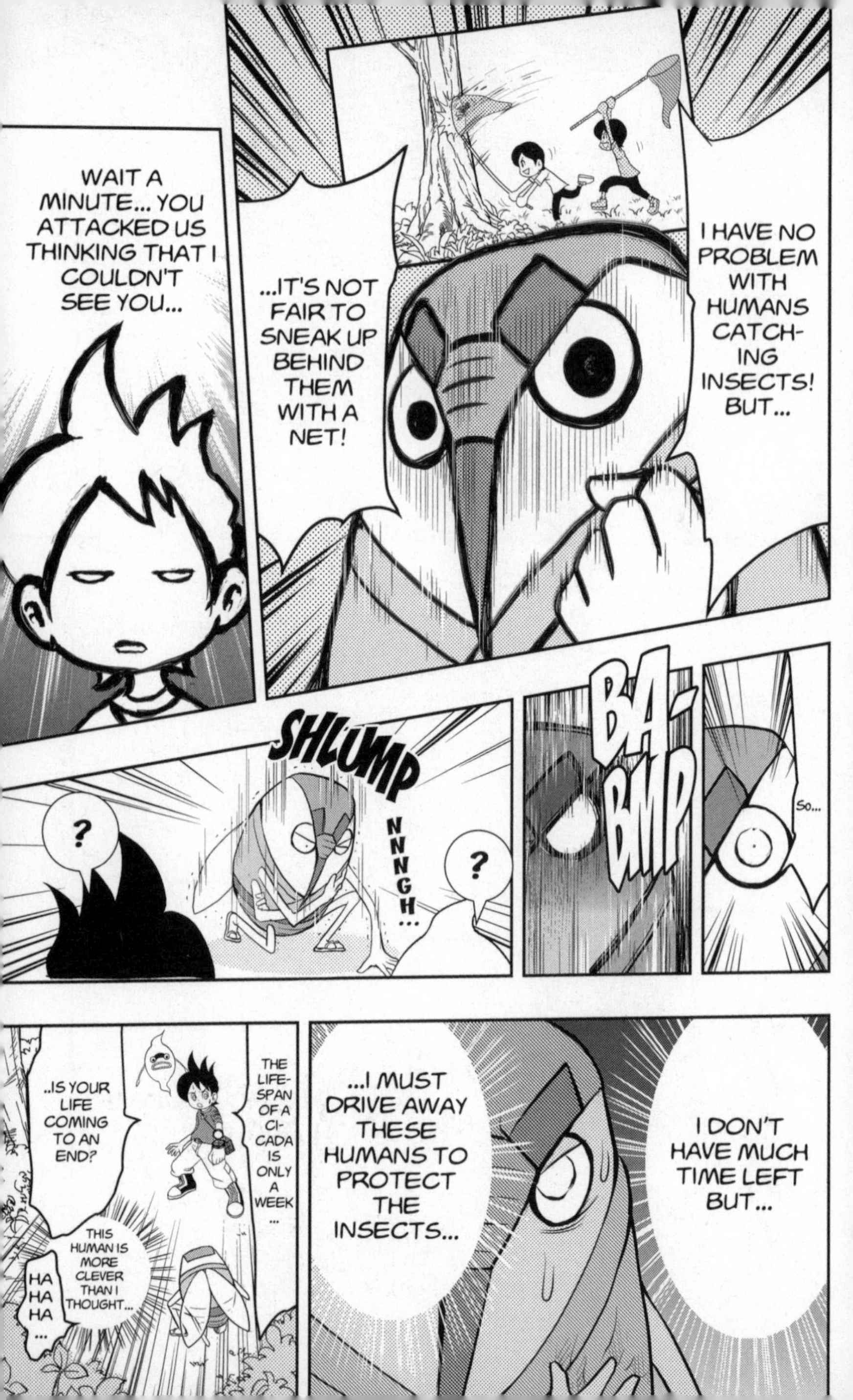
I HAVE NO PROBLEM WITH HUMANS CATCHING INSECTS! BUT...
...IT'S NOT FAIR TO SNEAK UP BEHIND THEM WITH A NET!
WAIT A MINUTE... YOU ATTACKED US THINKING THAT I COULDN'T SEE YOU...
SO...
BA-BMP
SHLUMP
NNNGH...
?
?
I DON'T HAVE MUCH TIME LEFT BUT...
...I MUST DRIVE AWAY THESE HUMANS TO PROTECT THE INSECTS...
THE LIFE-SPAN OF A CI-CADA IS ONLY A WEEK...
..IS YOUR LIFE COMING TO AN END?
THIS HUMAN IS MORE CLEVER THAN I THOUGHT...
HA HA HA...

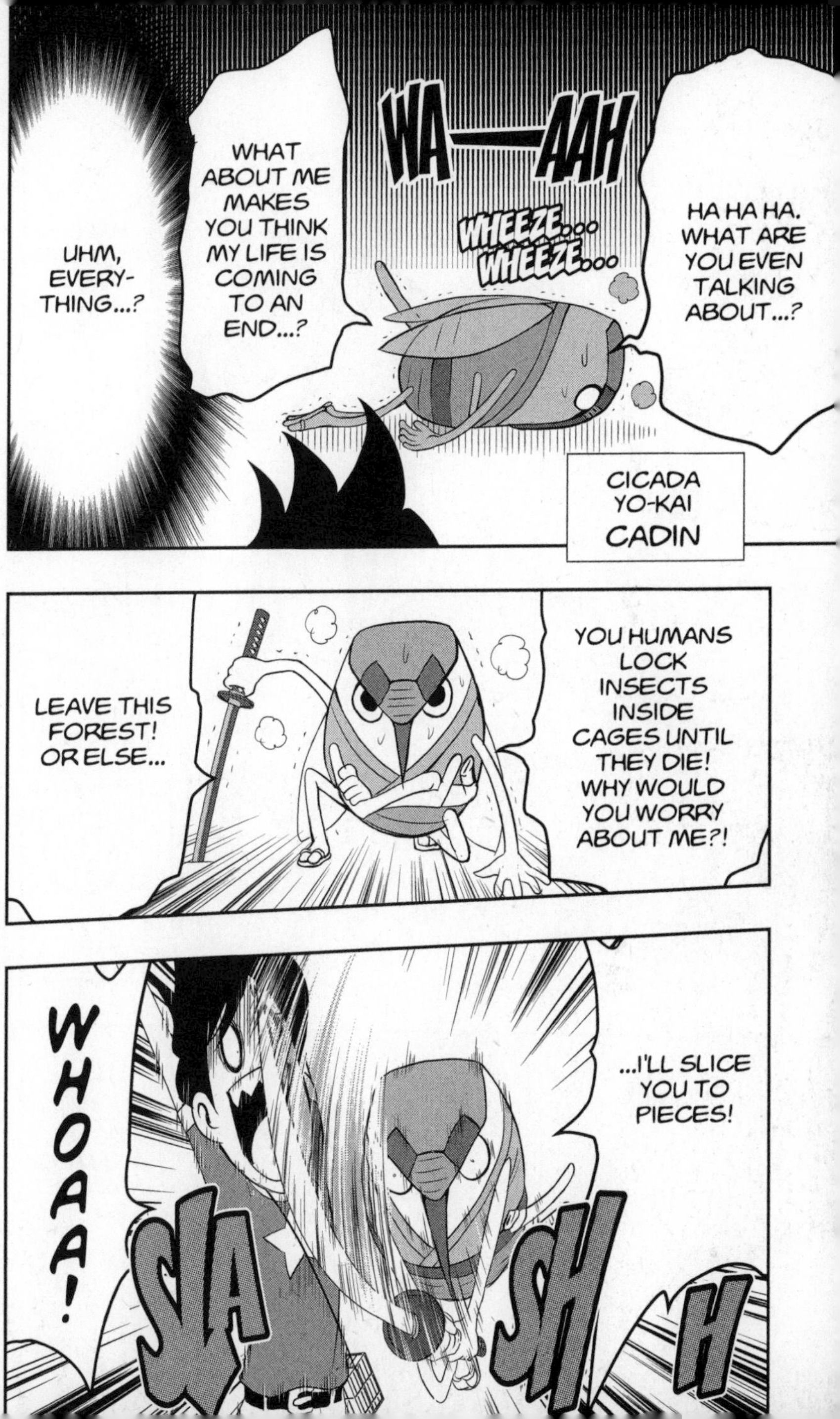
HA HA HA. WHAT ARE YOU EVEN TALKING ABOUT...?
CICADA YO-KAI CADIN
WA—AAH
WHEEZE... WHEEZE...
WHAT ABOUT ME MAKES YOU THINK MY LIFE IS COMING TO AN END...?
UHM, EVERY-THING...?
YOU HUMANS LOCK INSECTS INSIDE CAGES UNTIL THEY DIE! WHY WOULD YOU WORRY ABOUT ME?!
LEAVE THIS FOREST! OR ELSE...
...I'LL SLICE YOU TO PIECES!
SLASH
WHOAAA!

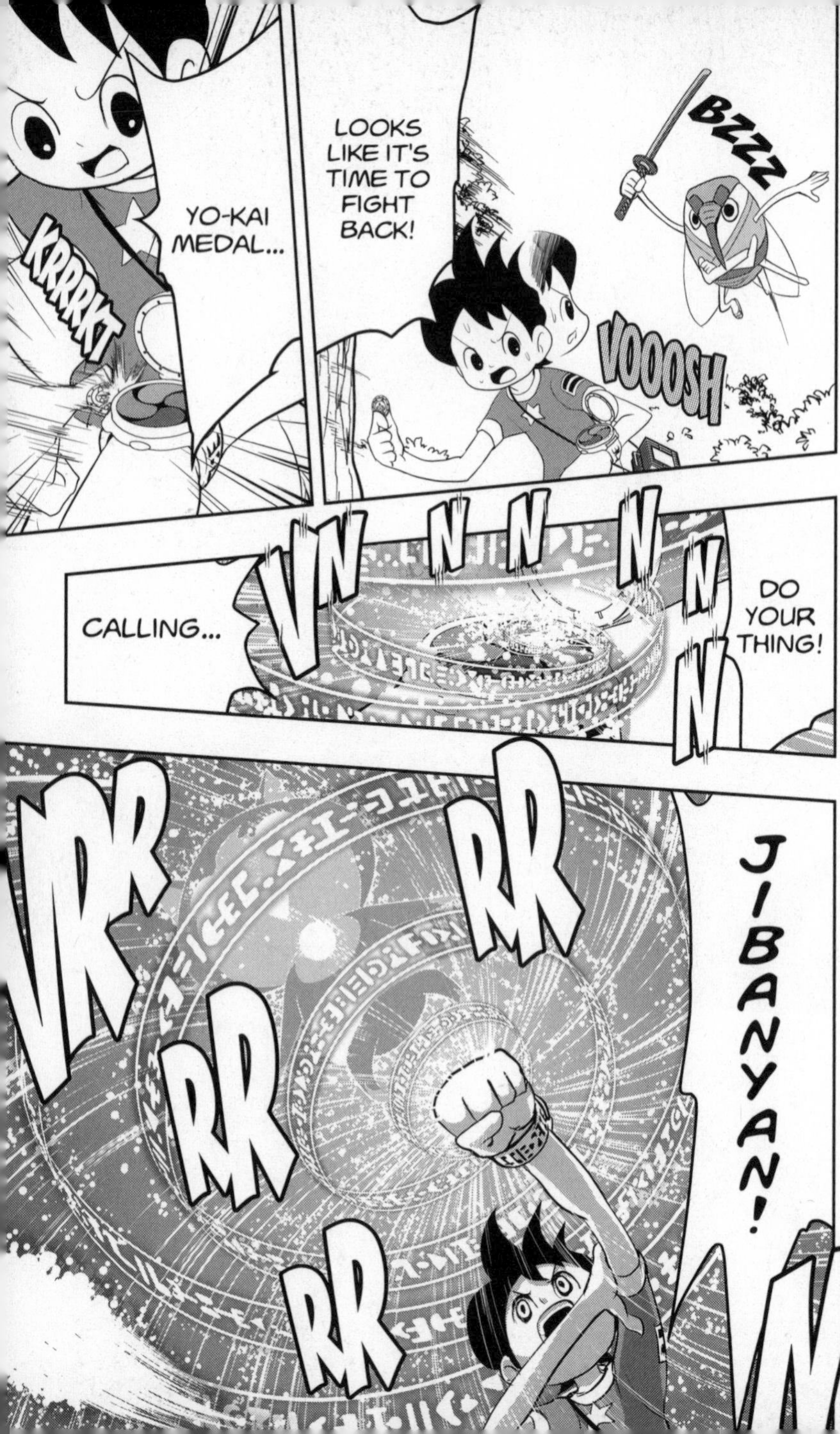
BZZZ
VOOOSH
LOOKS LIKE IT'S TIME TO FIGHT BACK!
YO-KAI MEDAL...
KRRRKT
DO YOUR THING!
VNNNNNNN
CALLING...
JIBANYAN!
VN
RR
RR
RR
VR

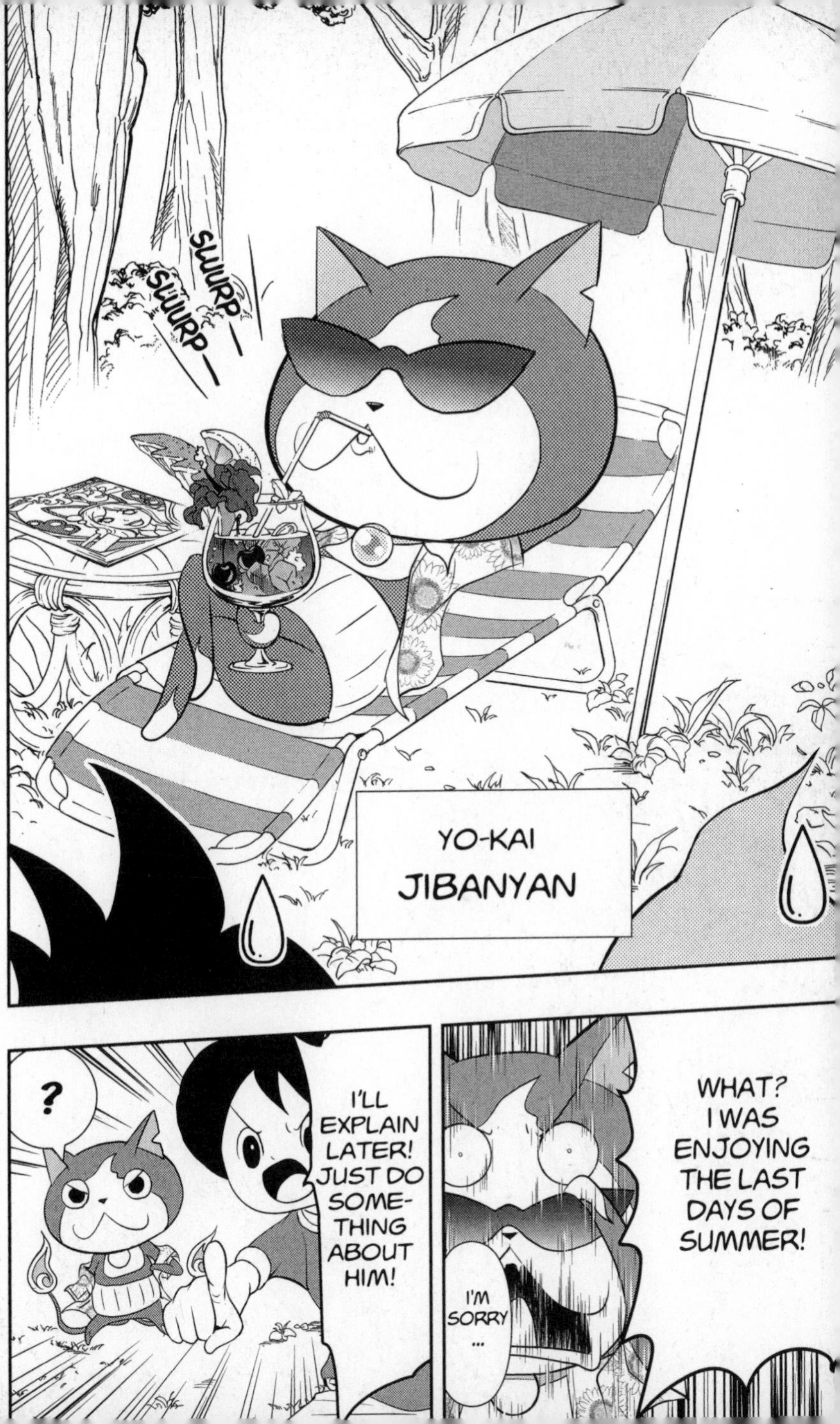
SLUURP
SLUURP
YO-KAI JIBANYAN
WHAT? I WAS ENJOYING THE LAST DAYS OF SUMMER!
I'M SORRY ...
I'LL EXPLAIN LATER! JUST DO SOME-THING ABOUT HIM!
?

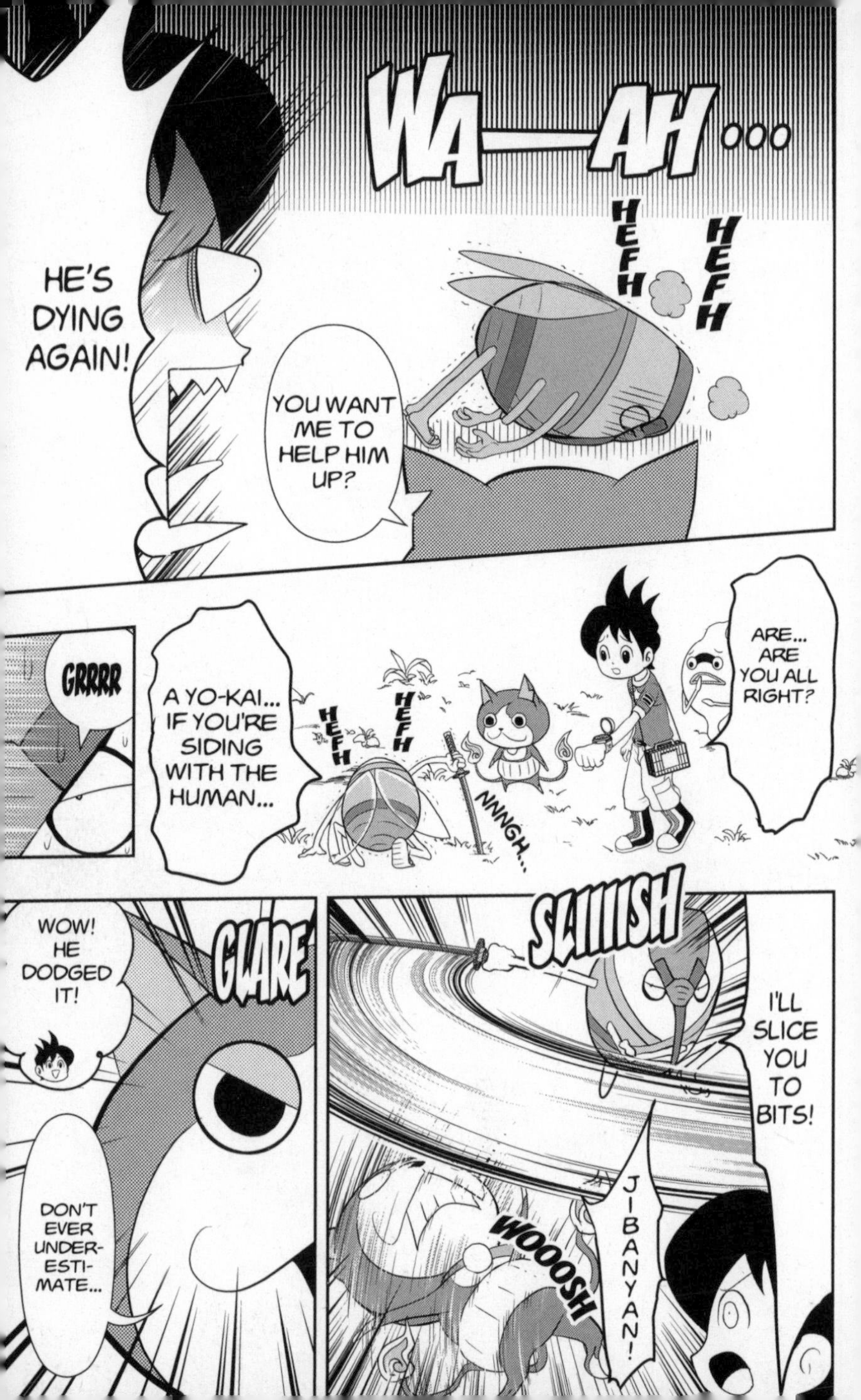
WA—AH...
HEFH HEFH
YOU WANT ME TO HELP HIM UP?
HE'S DYING AGAIN!
ARE... ARE YOU ALL RIGHT?
HEFH HEFH
A YO-KAI... IF YOU'RE SIDING WITH THE HUMAN...
NNNGH...
GRRRR
SLIIIISH
I'LL SLICE YOU TO BITS!
JIBANYAN!
WOOOSH
GLARE
WOW! HE DODGED IT!
DON'T EVER UNDER-ESTI-MATE...

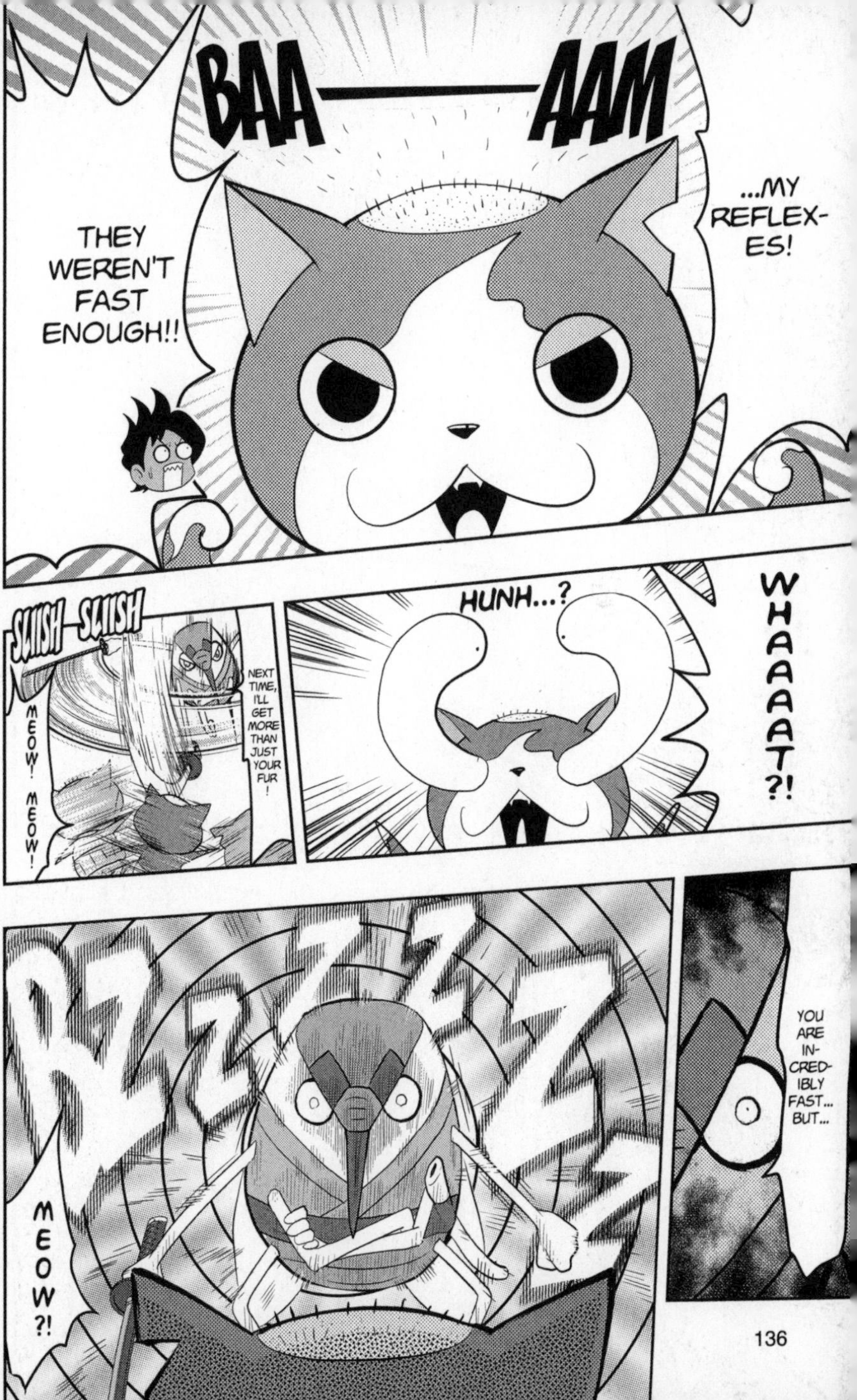
BAA——AAM
...MY REFLEXES!
THEY WEREN'T FAST ENOUGH!!
HUNH...?
WHAAAAAT?!
SLIISH SLIISH
NEXT TIME, I'LL GET MORE THAN JUST YOUR FUR!
MEOW! MEOW! MEOW!
YOU ARE INCREDIBLY FAST... BUT...
MEOW?!

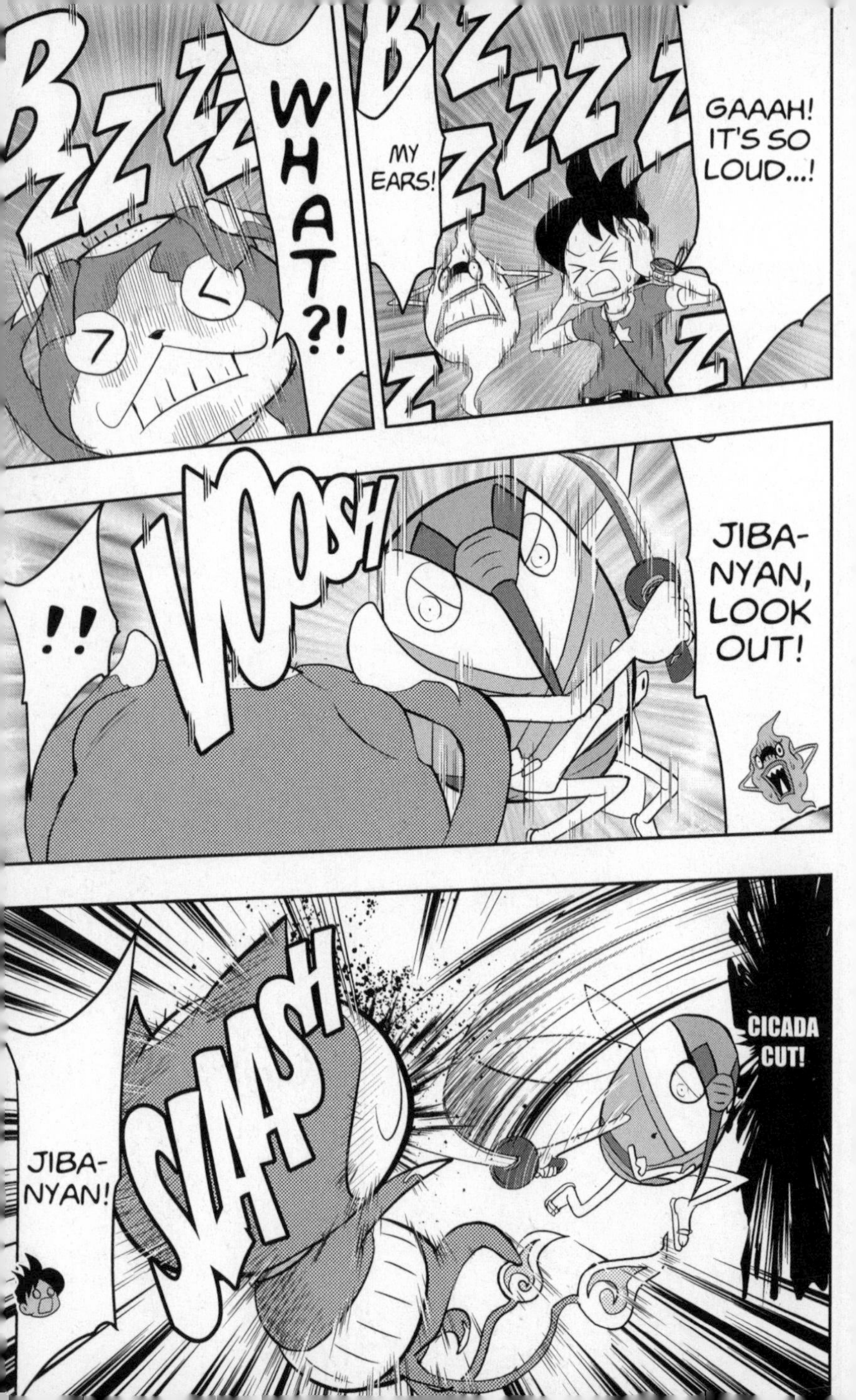
GAAAH! IT'S SO LOUD...!
MY EARS!
BZZZZZZ
BZZZZ
WHAT?!
JIBA-NYAN, LOOK OUT!
WOOSH
!!
CICADA CUT!
SLASH
JIBA-NYAN!

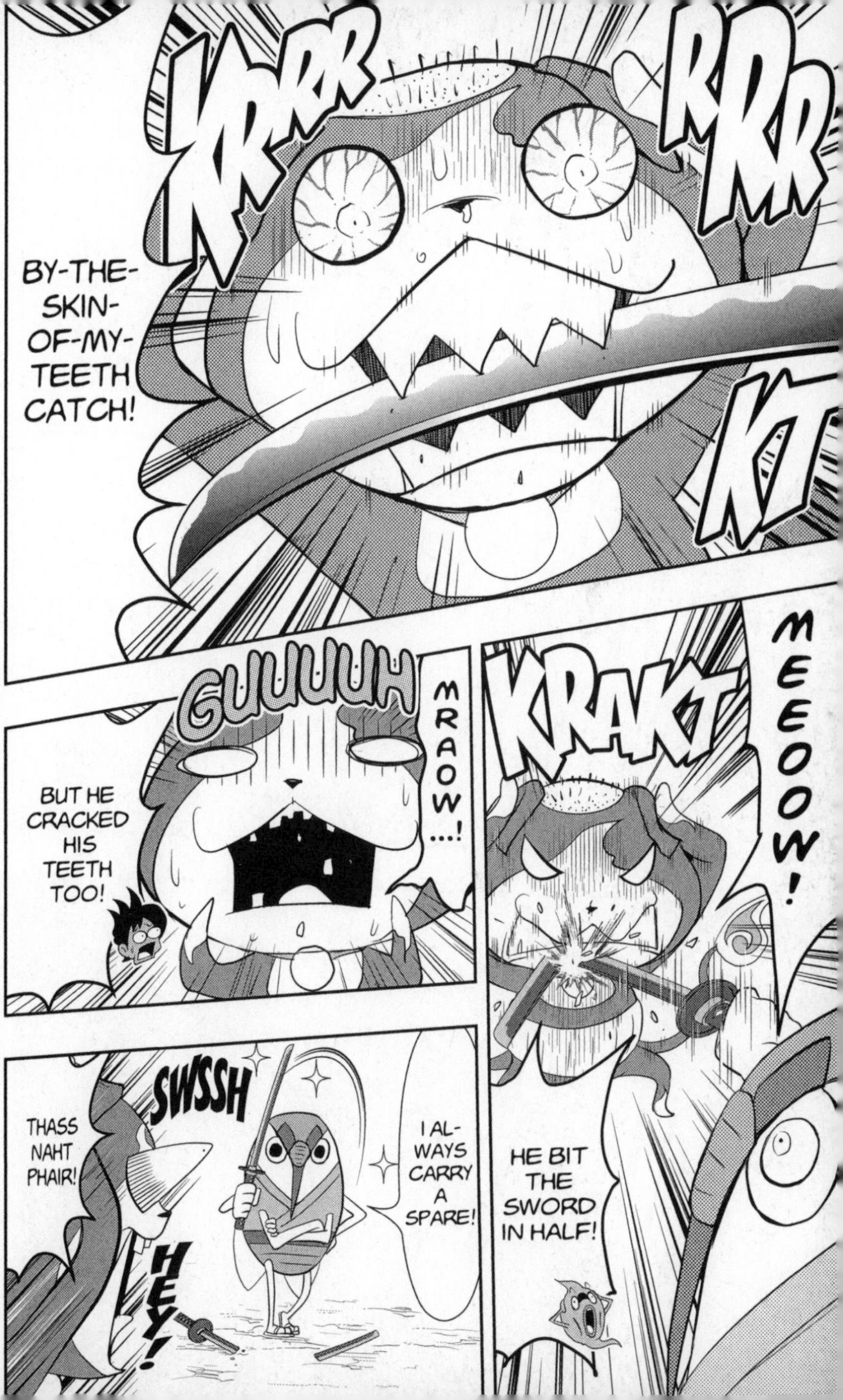
KRRRR
RRRR
KT
BY-THE-SKIN-OF-MY-TEETH CATCH!
KRAKT!
MEEOOOW!
HE BIT THE SWORD IN HALF!
GUUUUH
MRAOW...!
BUT HE CRACKED HIS TEETH TOO!
I AL-WAYS CARRY A SPARE!
SWSSH
THASS NAHT PHAIR!
HEY!

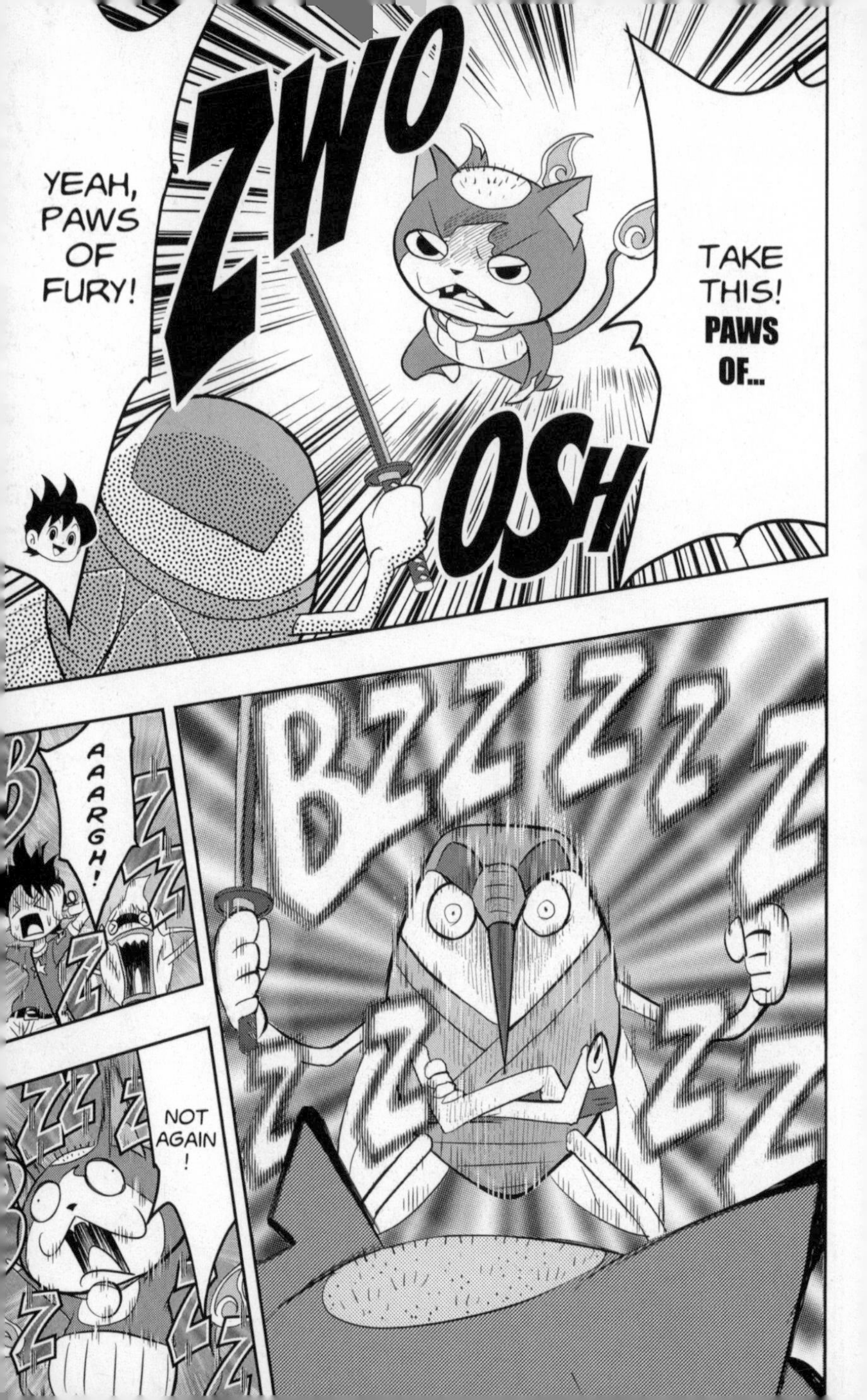
TAKE THIS! **PAWS OF...**
ZWOOSH
YEAH, PAWS OF FURY!
BZZZZZ
AAAARGH!
NOT AGAIN!

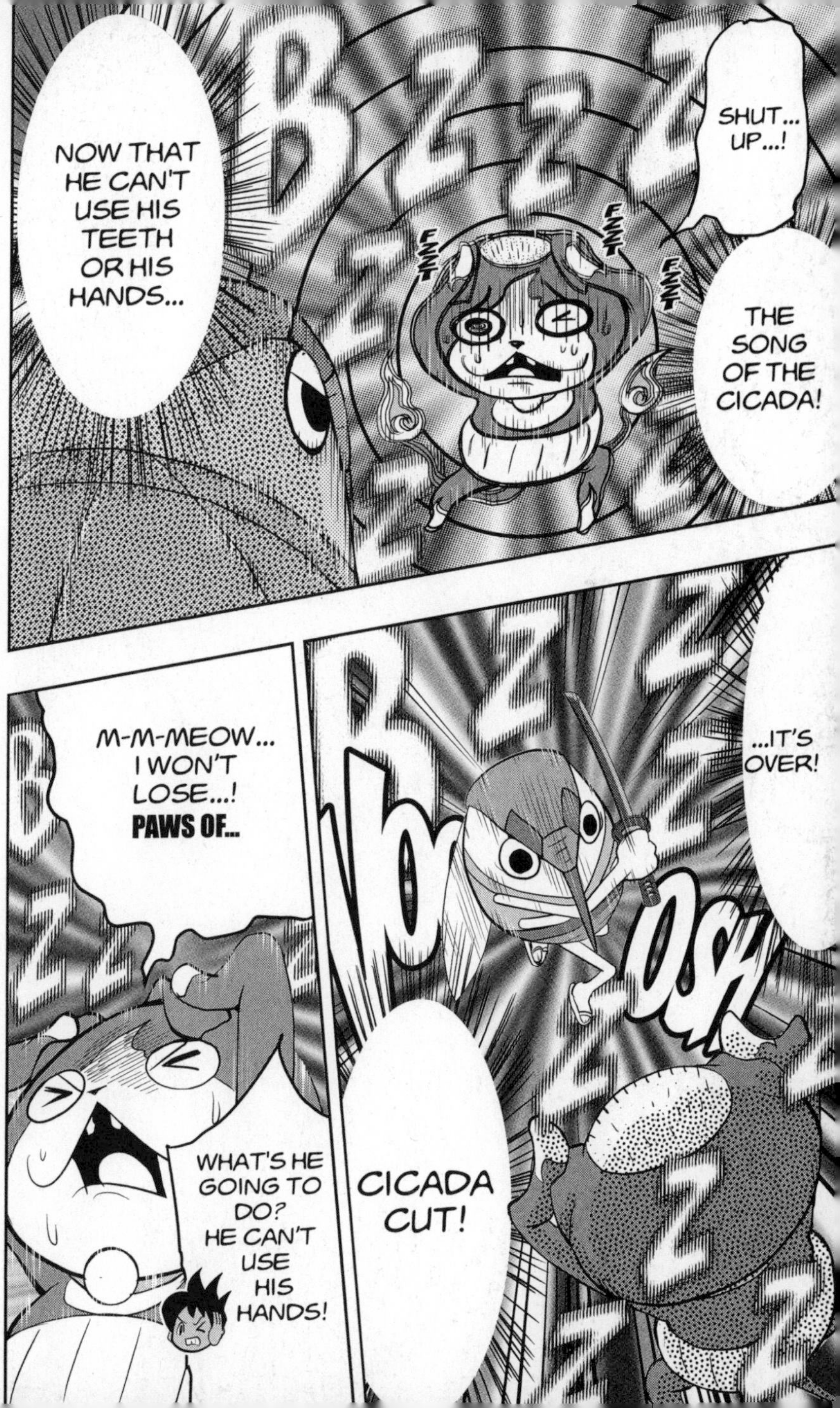
SHUT... UP...!
BZZZZ
FZZT
FZZT
FZZT
THE SONG OF THE CICADA!
NOW THAT HE CAN'T USE HIS TEETH OR HIS HANDS...
...IT'S OVER!
BZZZZ
CICADA CUT!
M-M-MEOW... I WON'T LOSE...! **PAWS OF...**
WHAT'S HE GOING TO DO? HE CAN'T USE HIS HANDS!

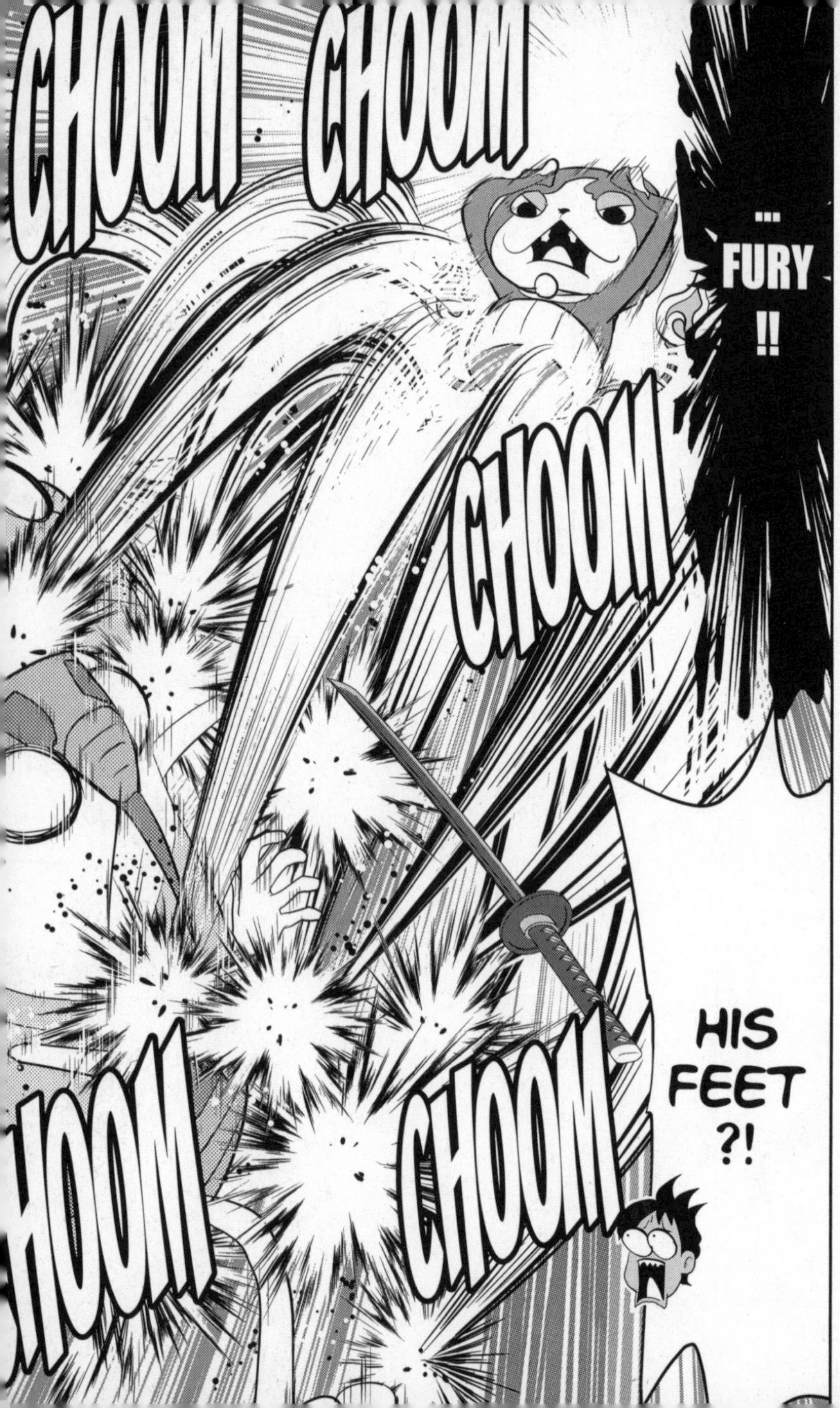
... FURY !!
CHOOM CHOOM
CHOOM
HIS FEET ?!
CHOOM
HOOM

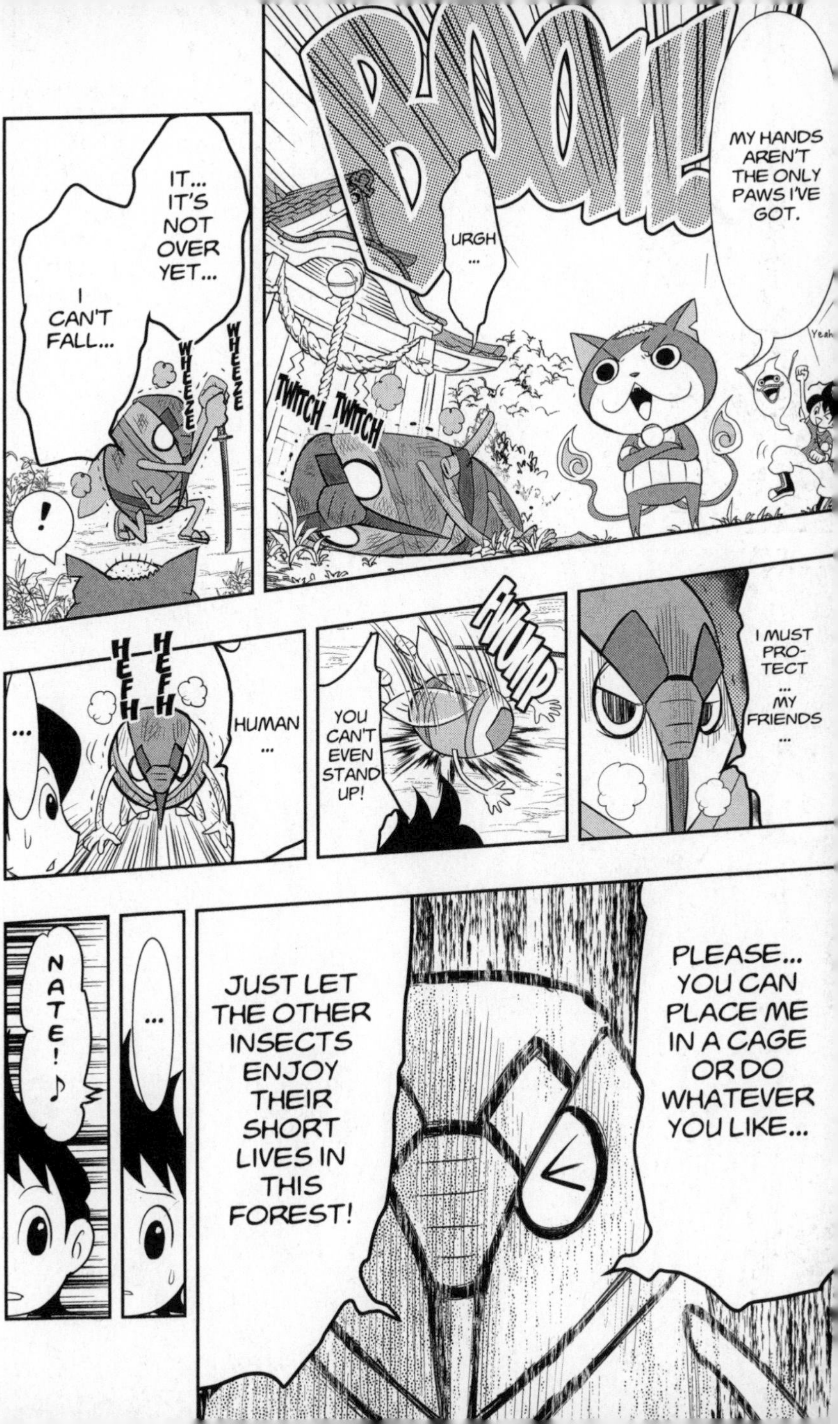
BOOM!
MY HANDS AREN'T THE ONLY PAWS I'VE GOT.
Yeah
URGH...
TWITCH TWITCH
IT... IT'S NOT OVER YET...
I CAN'T FALL...
WHEEZE WHEEZE
!
I MUST PROTECT... MY FRIENDS...
FWUMP
YOU CAN'T EVEN STAND UP!
HUMAN...
HEFH HEFH
...
PLEASE... YOU CAN PLACE ME IN A CAGE OR DO WHATEVER YOU LIKE...
JUST LET THE OTHER INSECTS ENJOY THEIR SHORT LIVES IN THIS FOREST!
...
NATE! ♪

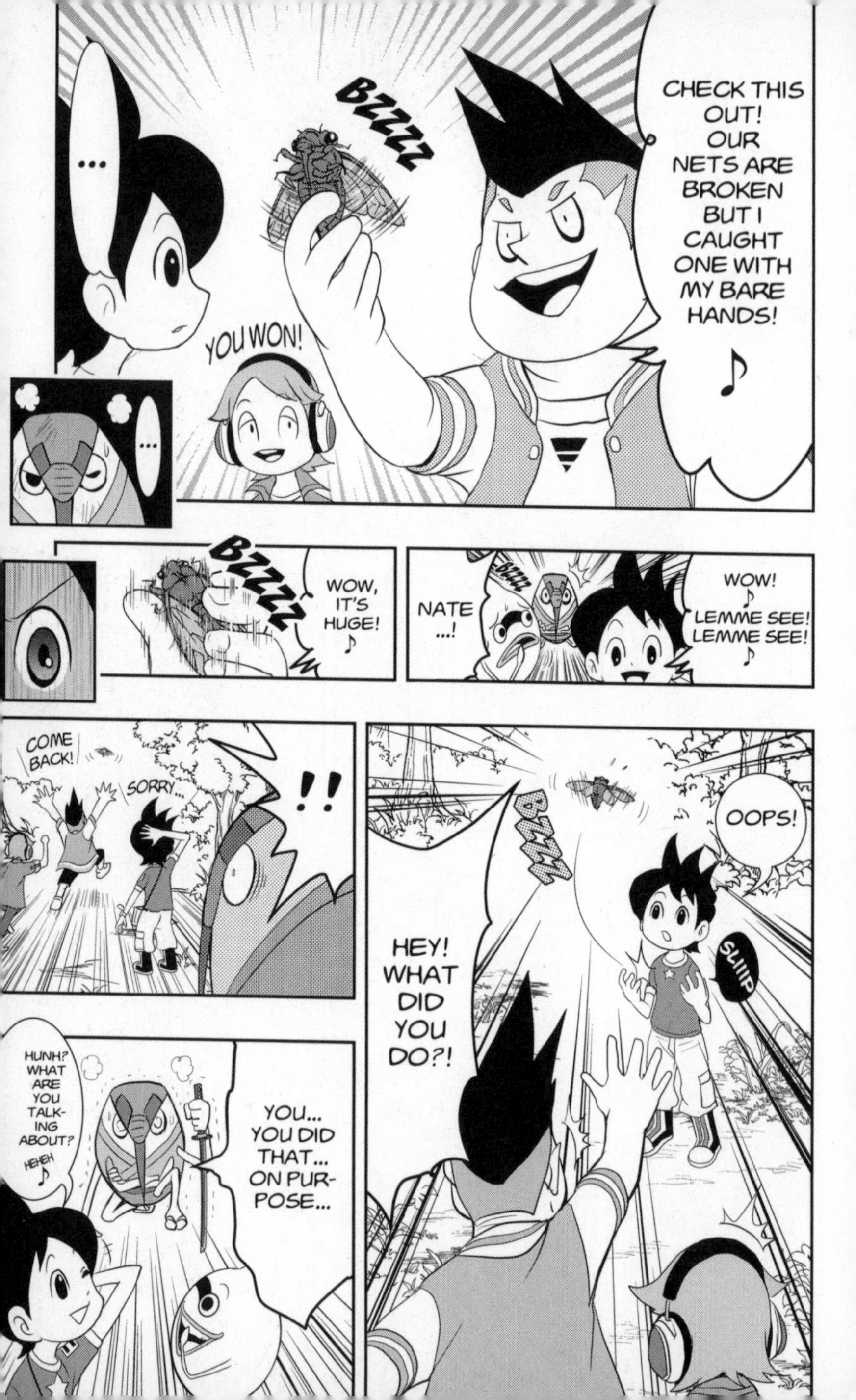
CHECK THIS OUT! OUR NETS ARE BROKEN BUT I CAUGHT ONE WITH MY BARE HANDS! ♪
BZZZZ
YOU WON!
...
...
WOW! ♪ LEMME SEE! LEMME SEE! ♪
BZZZZ
NATE ...!
WOW, IT'S HUGE! ♪
BZZZZ
OOPS!
SLIIIP
HEY! WHAT DID YOU DO?!
!!
SORRY...
COME BACK!
YOU... YOU DID THAT... ON PURPOSE...
HUNH? WHAT ARE YOU TALKING ABOUT?
HEHEH ♪

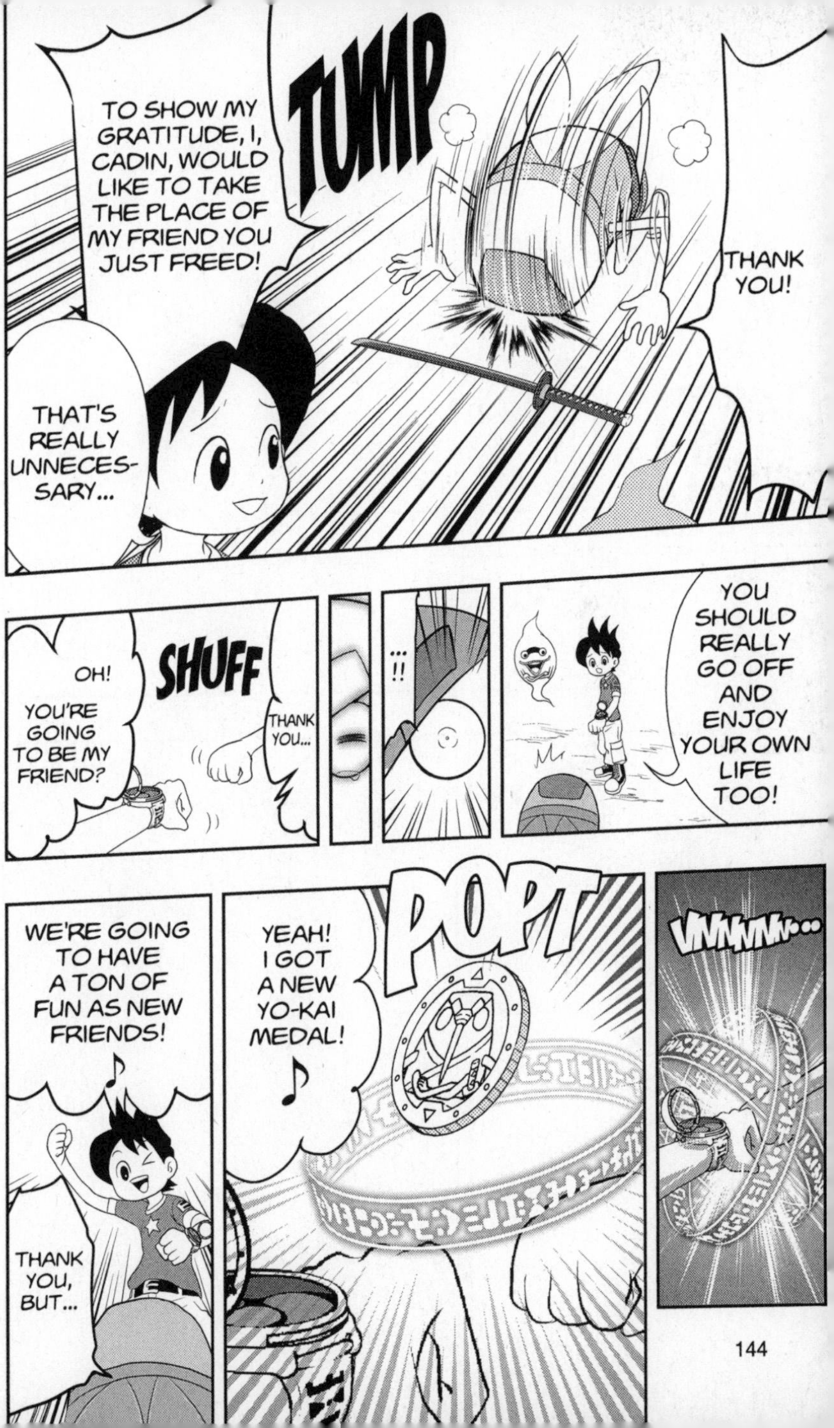
THANK YOU!
TUMP
TO SHOW MY GRATITUDE, I, CADIN, WOULD LIKE TO TAKE THE PLACE OF MY FRIEND YOU JUST FREED!
THAT'S REALLY UNNECES-SARY...
YOU SHOULD REALLY GO OFF AND ENJOY YOUR OWN LIFE TOO!
...!!
THANK YOU...
SHUFF
OH! YOU'RE GOING TO BE MY FRIEND?
POPT
YEAH! I GOT A NEW YO-KAI MEDAL! ♪
WE'RE GOING TO HAVE A TON OF FUN AS NEW FRIENDS! ♪
THANK YOU, BUT...

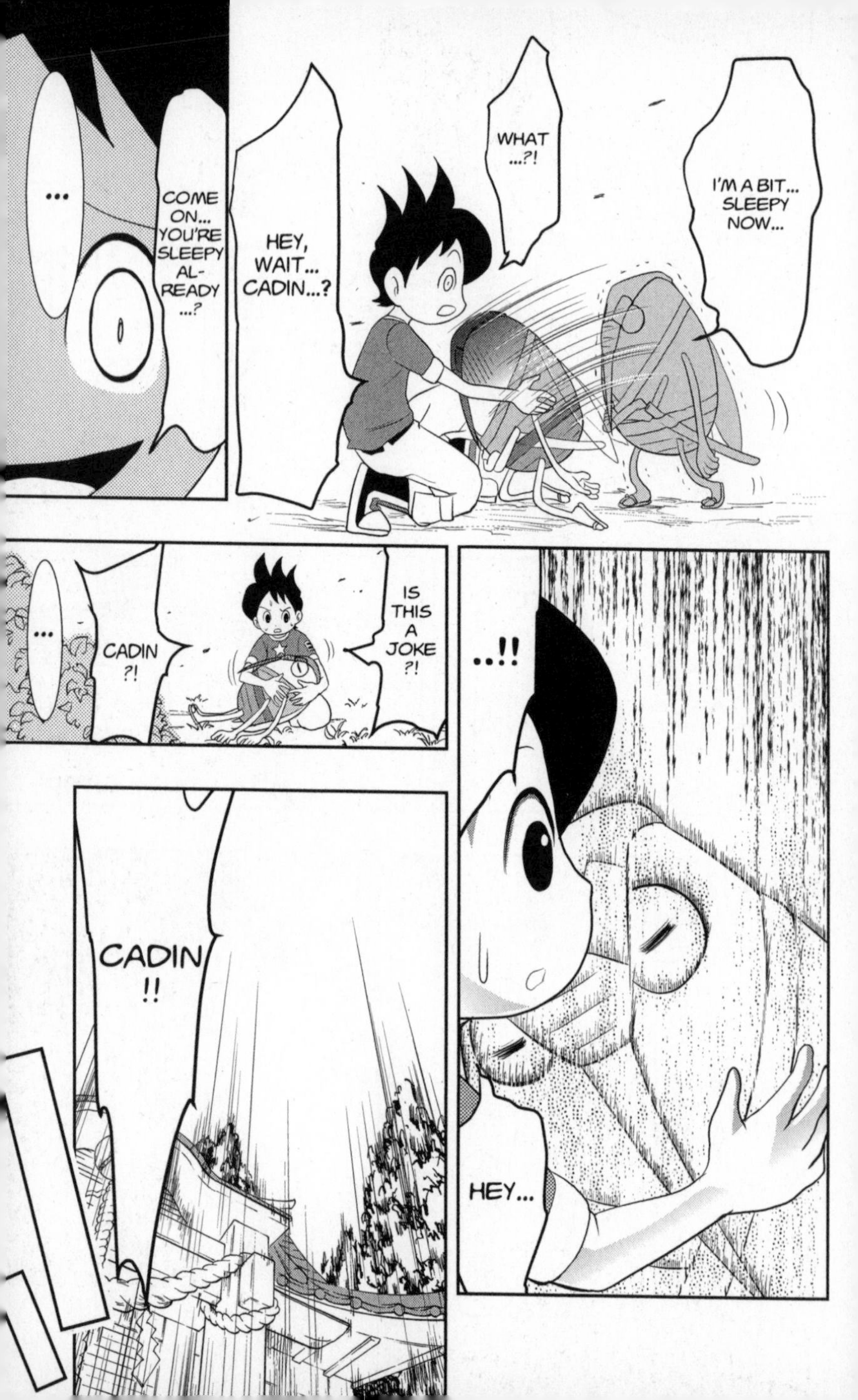
I'M A BIT... SLEEPY NOW...
WHAT...?!
HEY, WAIT... CADIN...?
COME ON... YOU'RE SLEEPY AL-READY...?
...
..!!
HEY...
IS THIS A JOKE?!
CADIN?!
...
CADIN!!

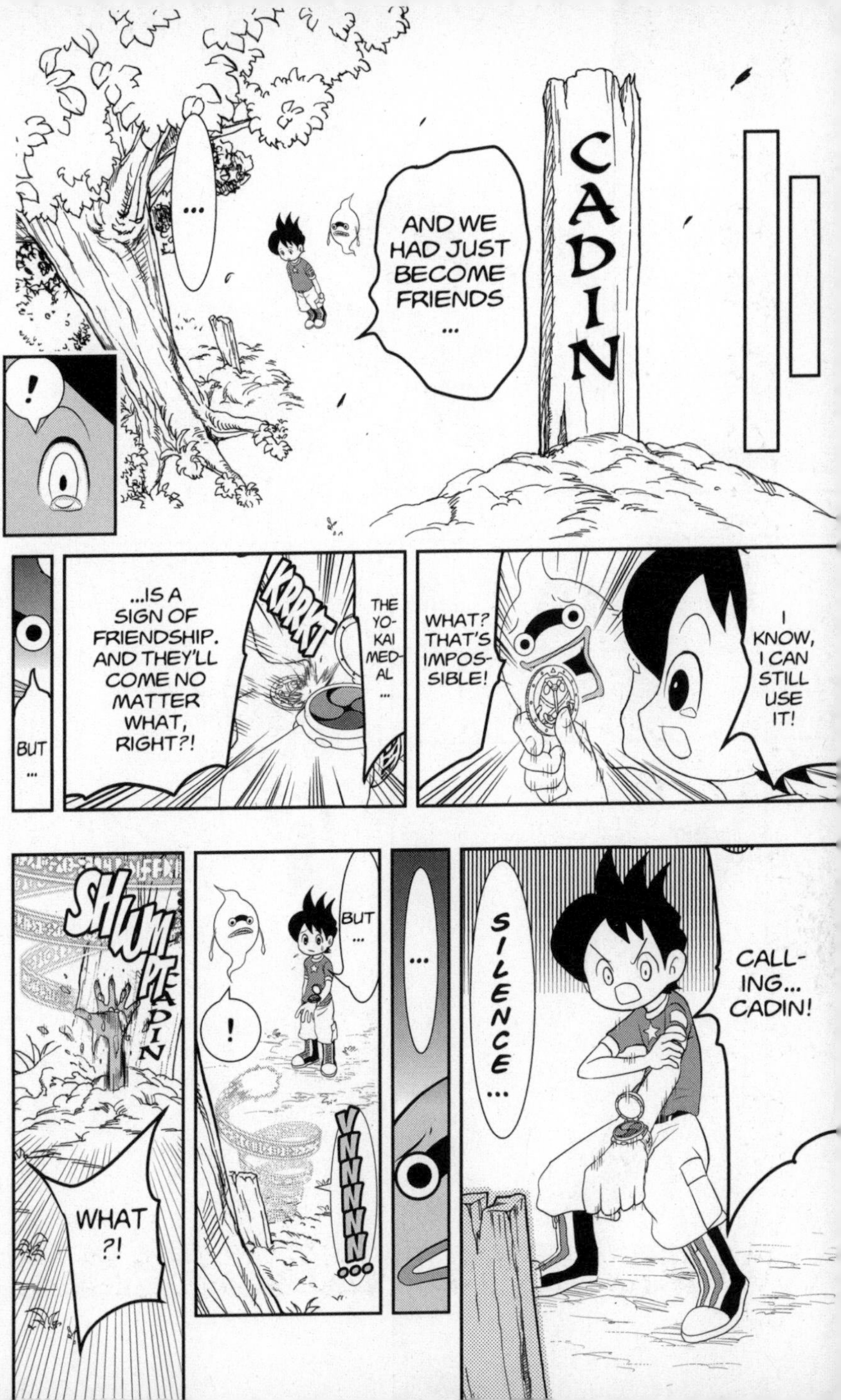

CADIN
AND WE HAD JUST BECOME FRIENDS ...
...
!
I KNOW, I CAN STILL USE IT!
WHAT? THAT'S IMPOSSIBLE!
THE YO-KAI MEDAL ...
KRRKT
...IS A SIGN OF FRIENDSHIP. AND THEY'LL COME NO MATTER WHAT, RIGHT?!
BUT ...
CALLING... CADIN!
SILENCE ...
...
BUT ...
!
VNNNNN
SHUMPT
CADIN
WHAT ?!

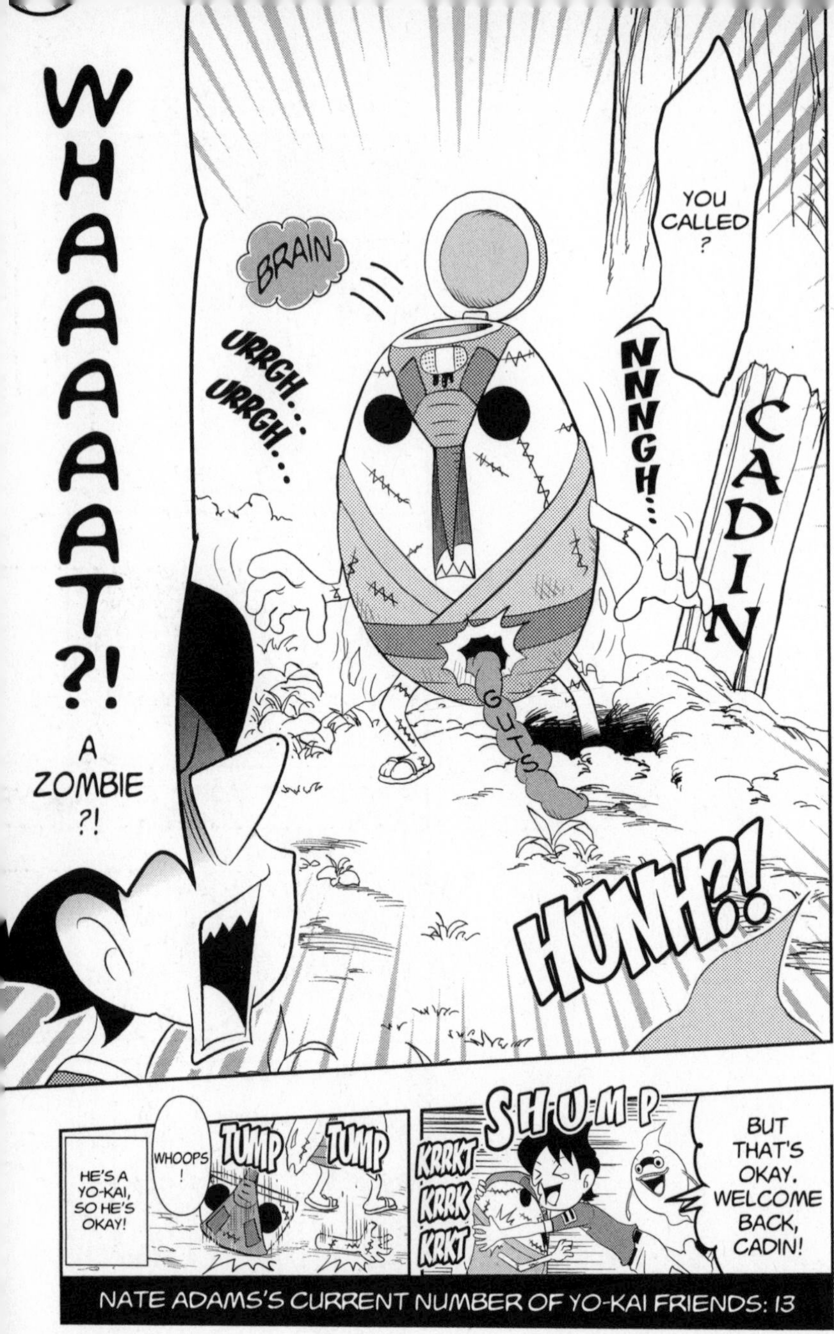
YOU CALLED?
CADIN
NNNGH...
BRAIN
URRGH... URRGH...
WHAAAAAT?!
A ZOMBIE?!
HUNH?!
BUT THAT'S OKAY. WELCOME BACK, CADIN!
SHUMP
KRRKT KRRK KRKT
TUMP TUMP
WHOOPS!
HE'S A YO-KAI, SO HE'S OKAY!

NATE ADAMS'S CURRENT NUMBER OF YO-KAI FRIENDS: 13

SOON AFTERWARD...
WHAAM
I'M SORRY! ARE YOU ALL RIGHT ?!
I JUST NEED TO PUT MYSELF BACK TOGETHER AND I'LL BE AS GOOD AS NEW. ♪
THAT'S GREAT TO HEAR!
HEY, BODY! PICK UP MY HEAD AND PUT IT BACK ON!
WHOA
OVER HERE!
CLO-SER!
CLO-
KRUNCH
HE STEP-PED ON HIM-SELF!
WHAAAA?!
OOPS.

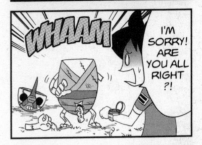

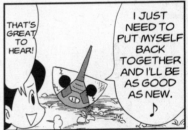

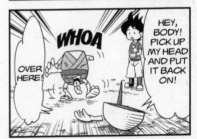

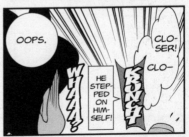

CHAPTER 14: THE ANCESTOR'S WISH

FEATURING ANCESTOR YO-KAI SHOGUNYAN AND REJECTION YO-KAI NOWAY

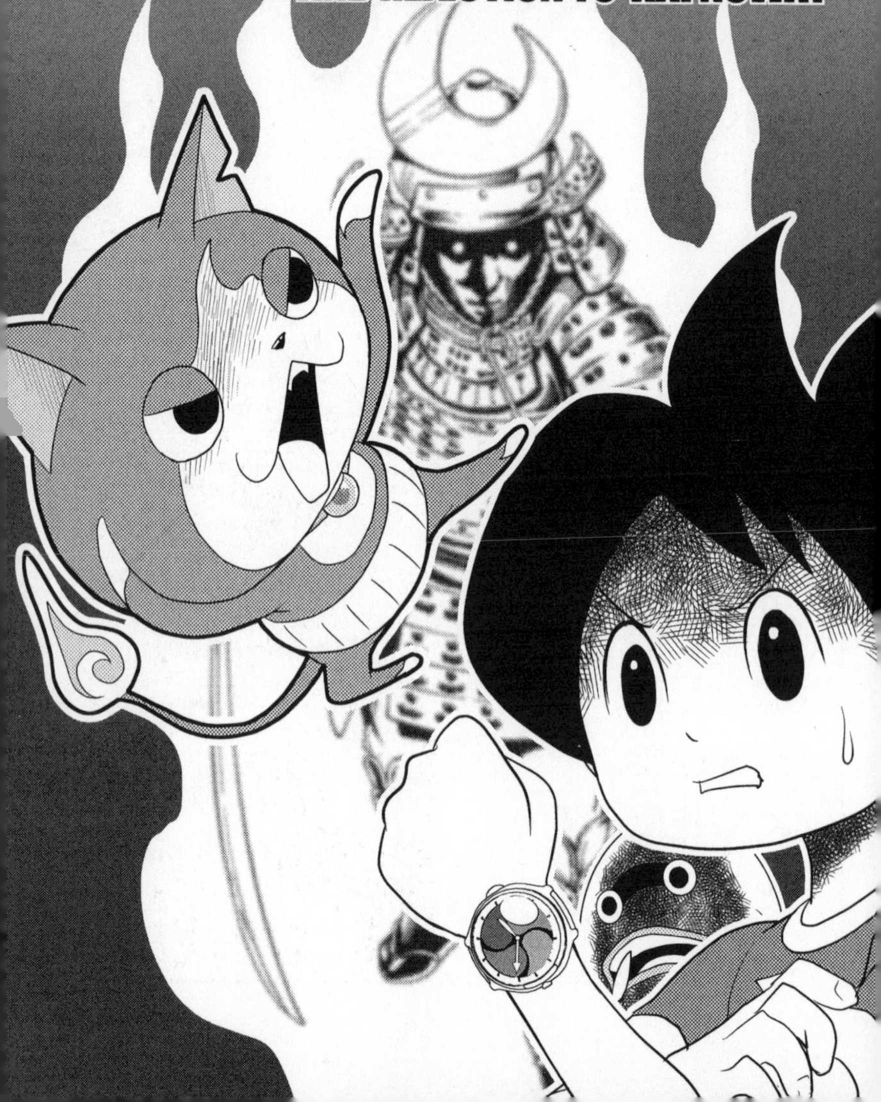

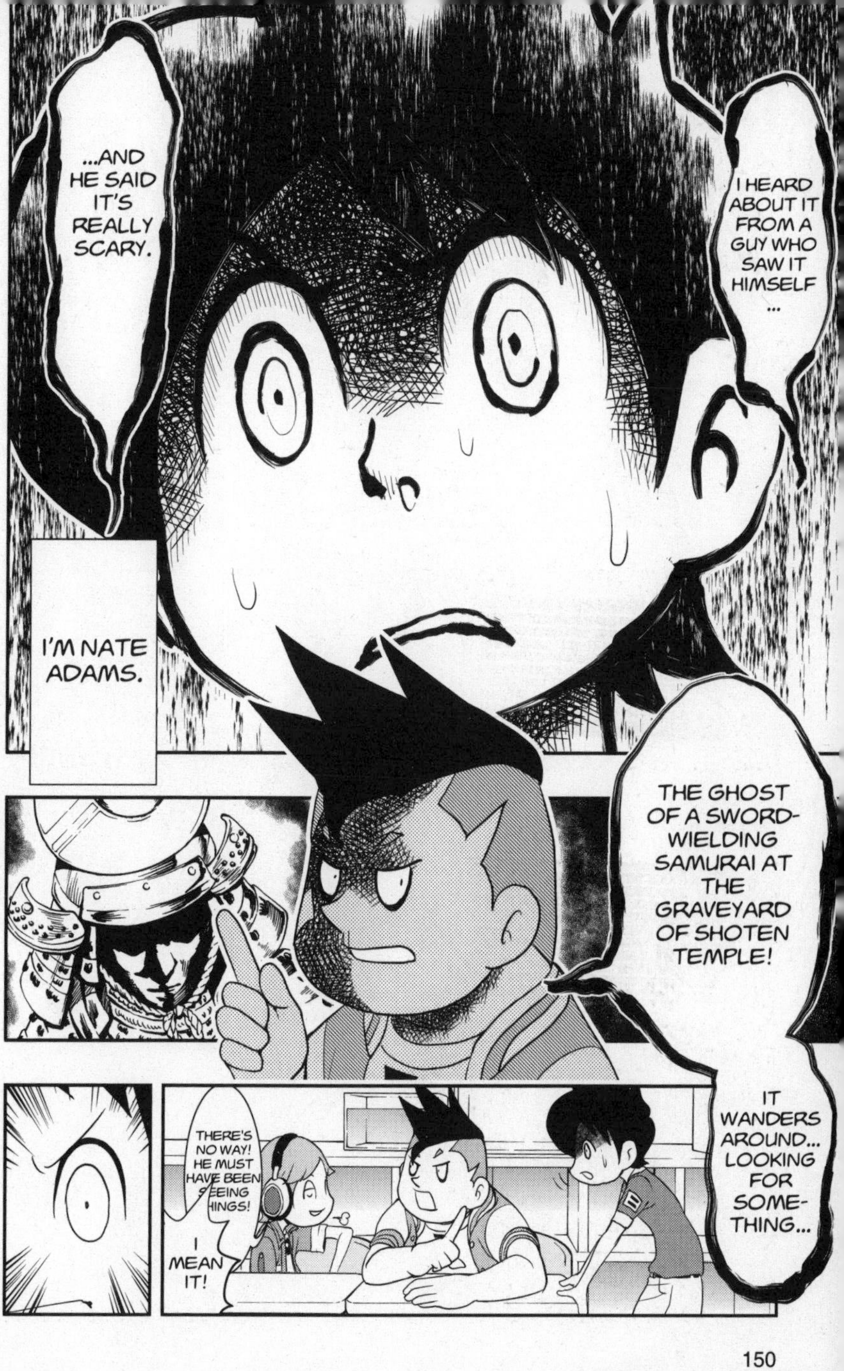
I HEARD ABOUT IT FROM A GUY WHO SAW IT HIMSELF ...
...AND HE SAID IT'S REALLY SCARY.
I'M NATE ADAMS.
THE GHOST OF A SWORD-WIELDING SAMURAI AT THE GRAVEYARD OF SHOTEN TEMPLE!
IT WANDERS AROUND... LOOKING FOR SOME-THING...
THERE'S NO WAY! HE MUST HAVE BEEN SEEING THINGS!
I MEAN IT!

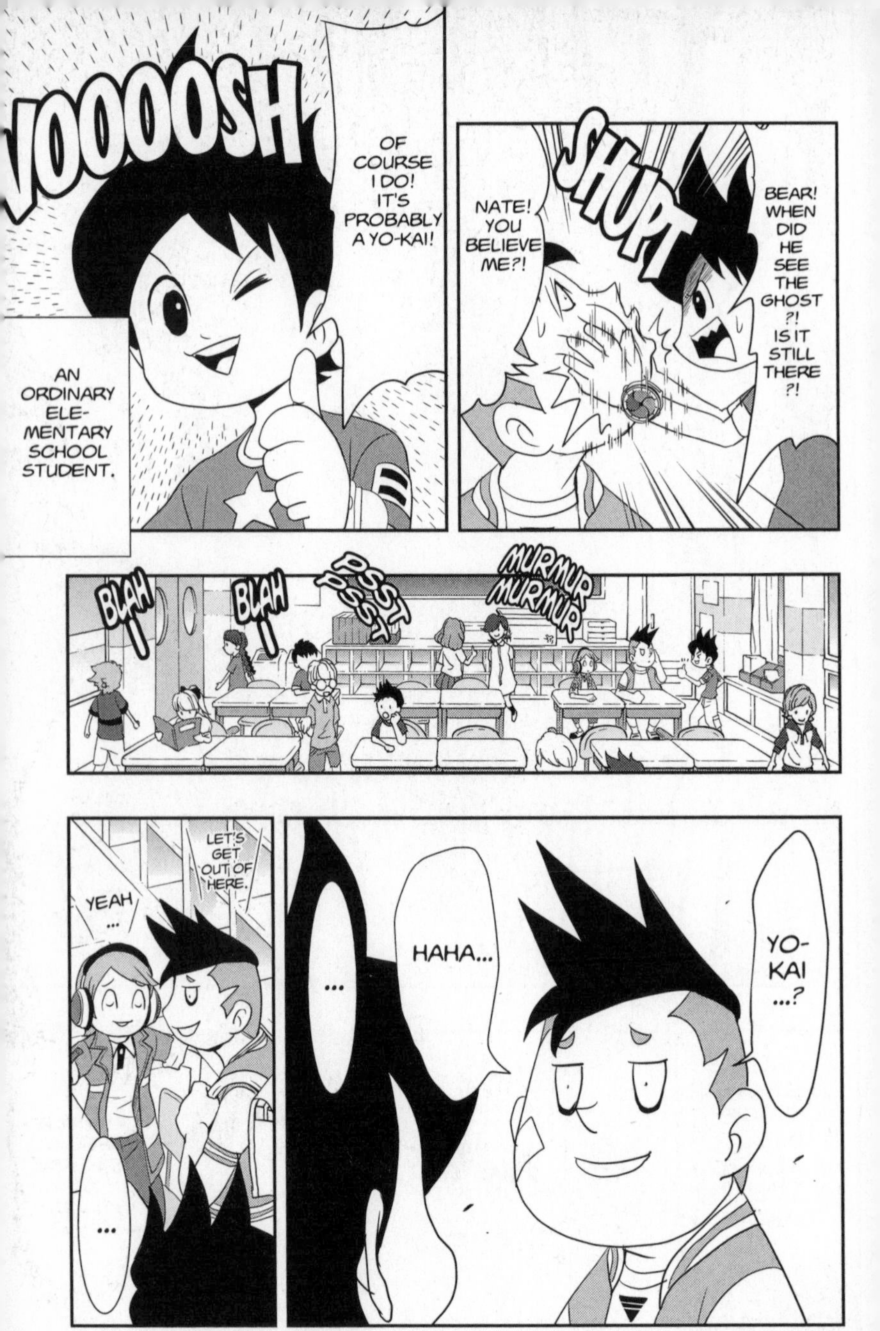
SHUPT
BEAR! WHEN DID HE SEE THE GHOST?! IS IT STILL THERE?!
NATE! YOU BELIEVE ME?!
VOOOOSH
OF COURSE I DO! IT'S PROBABLY A YO-KAI!
AN ORDINARY ELE-MENTARY SCHOOL STUDENT.
MURMUR MURMUR
PSST PSST
BLAH
BLAH
YO-KAI ...?
HAHA...
...
LET'S GET OUT OF HERE.
YEAH ...
...

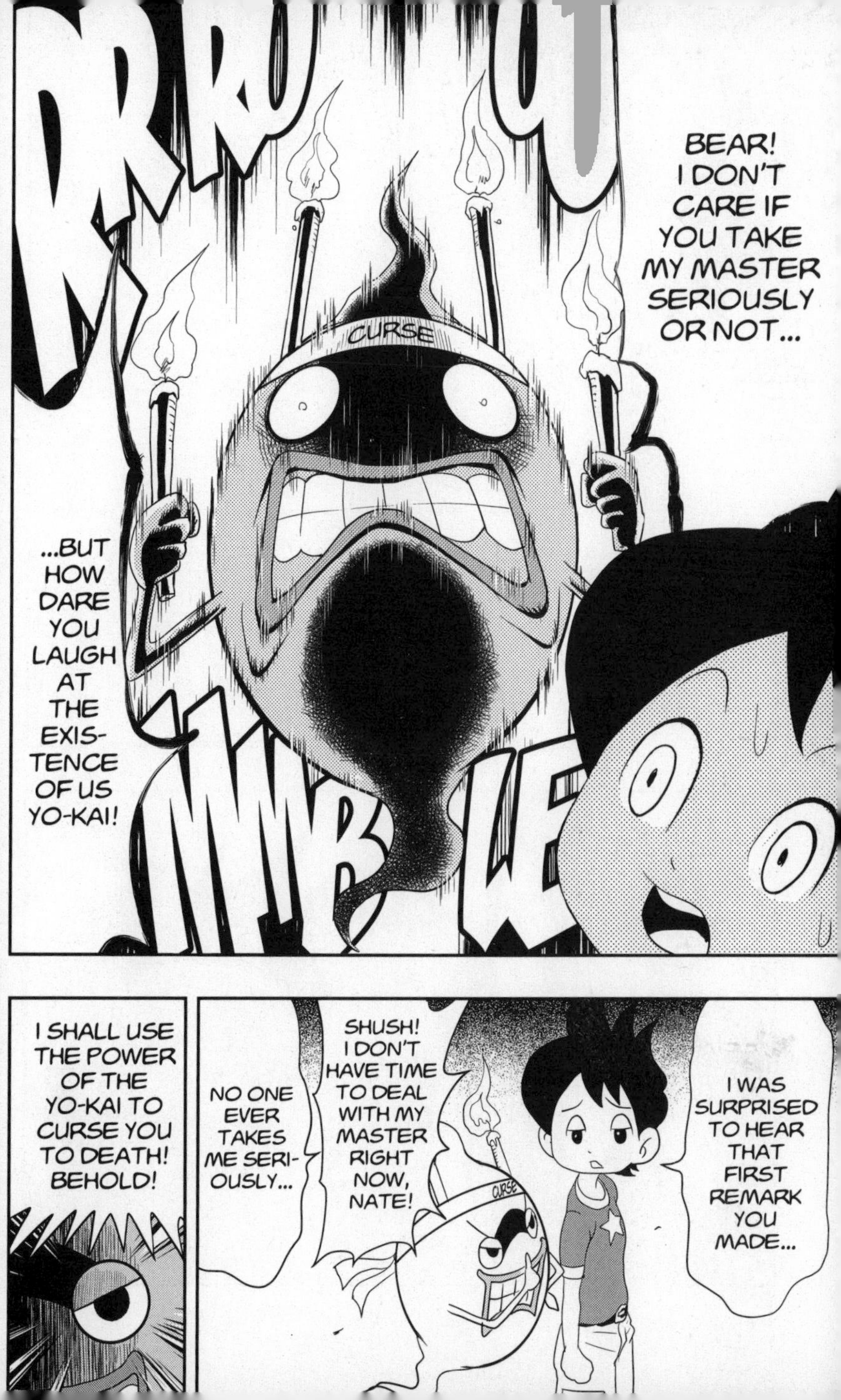
BEAR! I DON'T CARE IF YOU TAKE MY MASTER SERIOUSLY OR NOT...
CURSE
...BUT HOW DARE YOU LAUGH AT THE EXISTENCE OF US YO-KAI!
I WAS SURPRISED TO HEAR THAT FIRST REMARK YOU MADE...
SHUSH! I DON'T HAVE TIME TO DEAL WITH MY MASTER RIGHT NOW, NATE!
NO ONE EVER TAKES ME SERIOUSLY...
CURSE
I SHALL USE THE POWER OF THE YO-KAI TO CURSE YOU TO DEATH! BEHOLD!

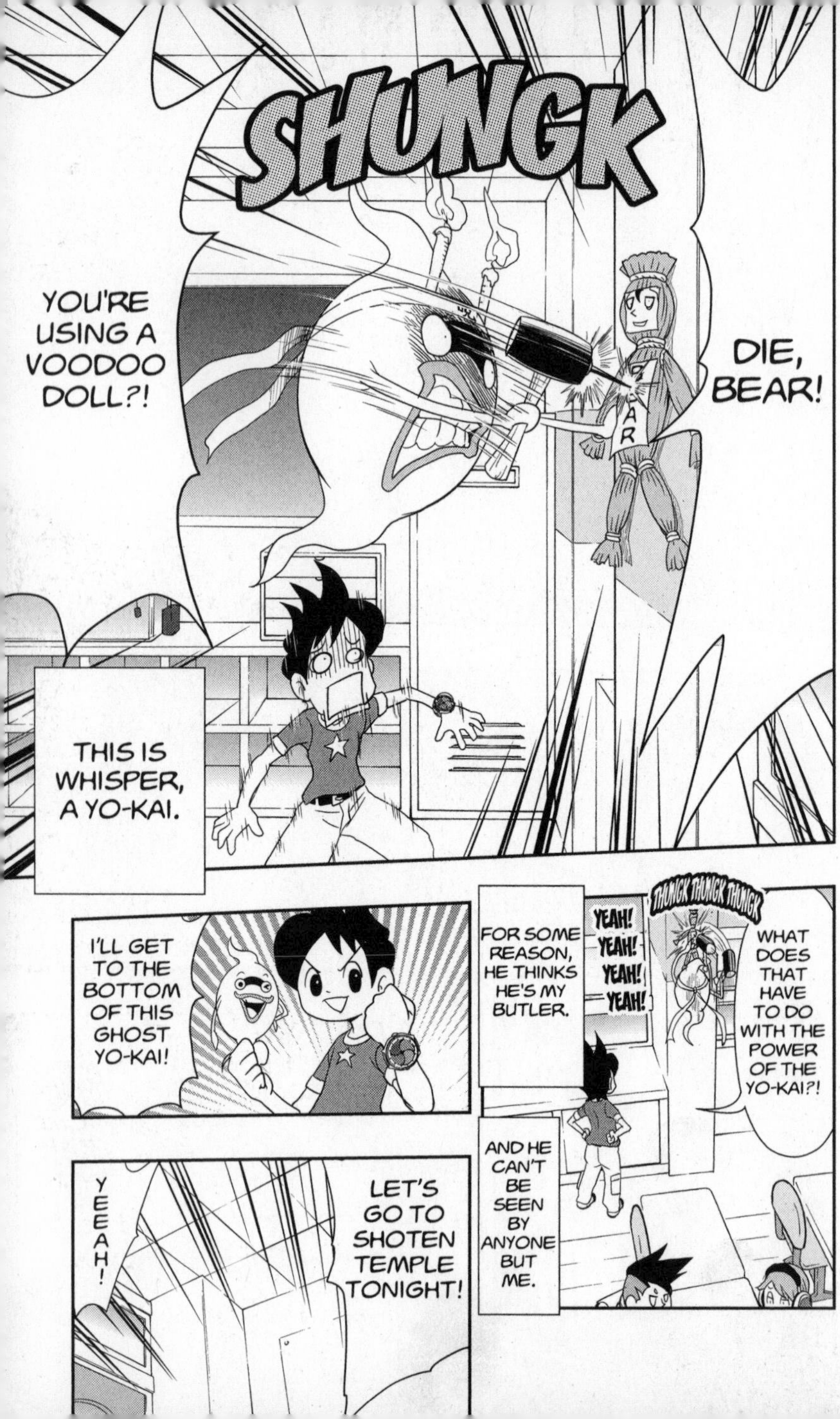
SHUNGK
DIE, BEAR!
YOU'RE USING A VOODOO DOLL?!
THIS IS WHISPER, A YO-KAI.
THUNCK THUNCK THUNCK
WHAT DOES THAT HAVE TO DO WITH THE POWER OF THE YO-KAI?!
YEAH! YEAH! YEAH! YEAH!
FOR SOME REASON, HE THINKS HE'S MY BUTLER.
AND HE CAN'T BE SEEN BY ANYONE BUT ME.
I'LL GET TO THE BOTTOM OF THIS GHOST YO-KAI!
LET'S GO TO SHOTEN TEMPLE TONIGHT!
YEEAH!

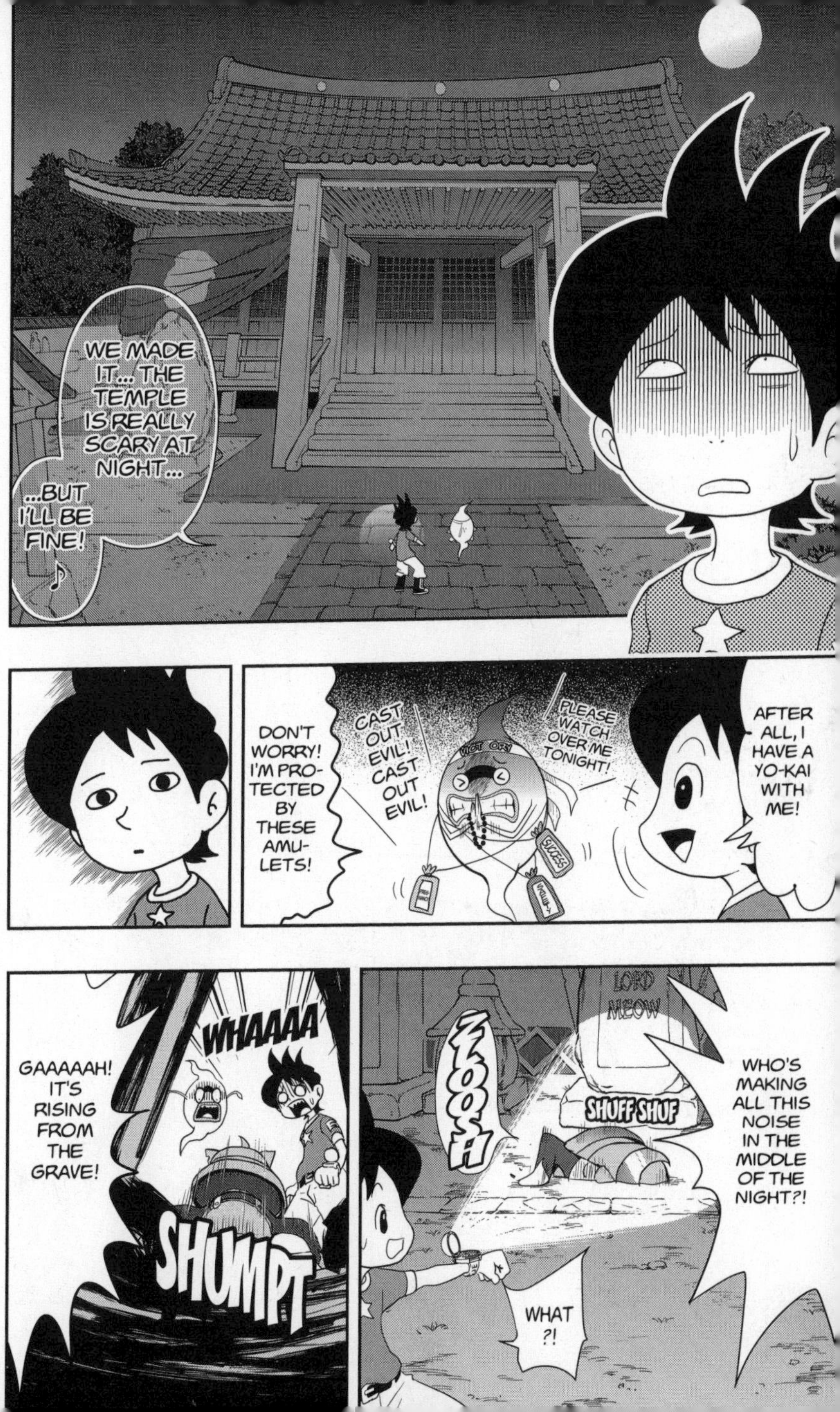
WE MADE IT... THE TEMPLE IS REALLY SCARY AT NIGHT...
...BUT I'LL BE FINE! ♪
AFTER ALL, I HAVE A YO-KAI WITH ME!
PLEASE WATCH OVER ME TONIGHT!
VICTORY
SUCCESS
CAST OUT EVIL! CAST OUT EVIL!
DON'T WORRY! I'M PROTECTED BY THESE AMULETS!
LORD MEOW
WHO'S MAKING ALL THIS NOISE IN THE MIDDLE OF THE NIGHT?!
ZOOSH
SHUFF SHUF
WHAT?!
WHAAAAA
GAAAAAH! IT'S RISING FROM THE GRAVE!
SHUMPT

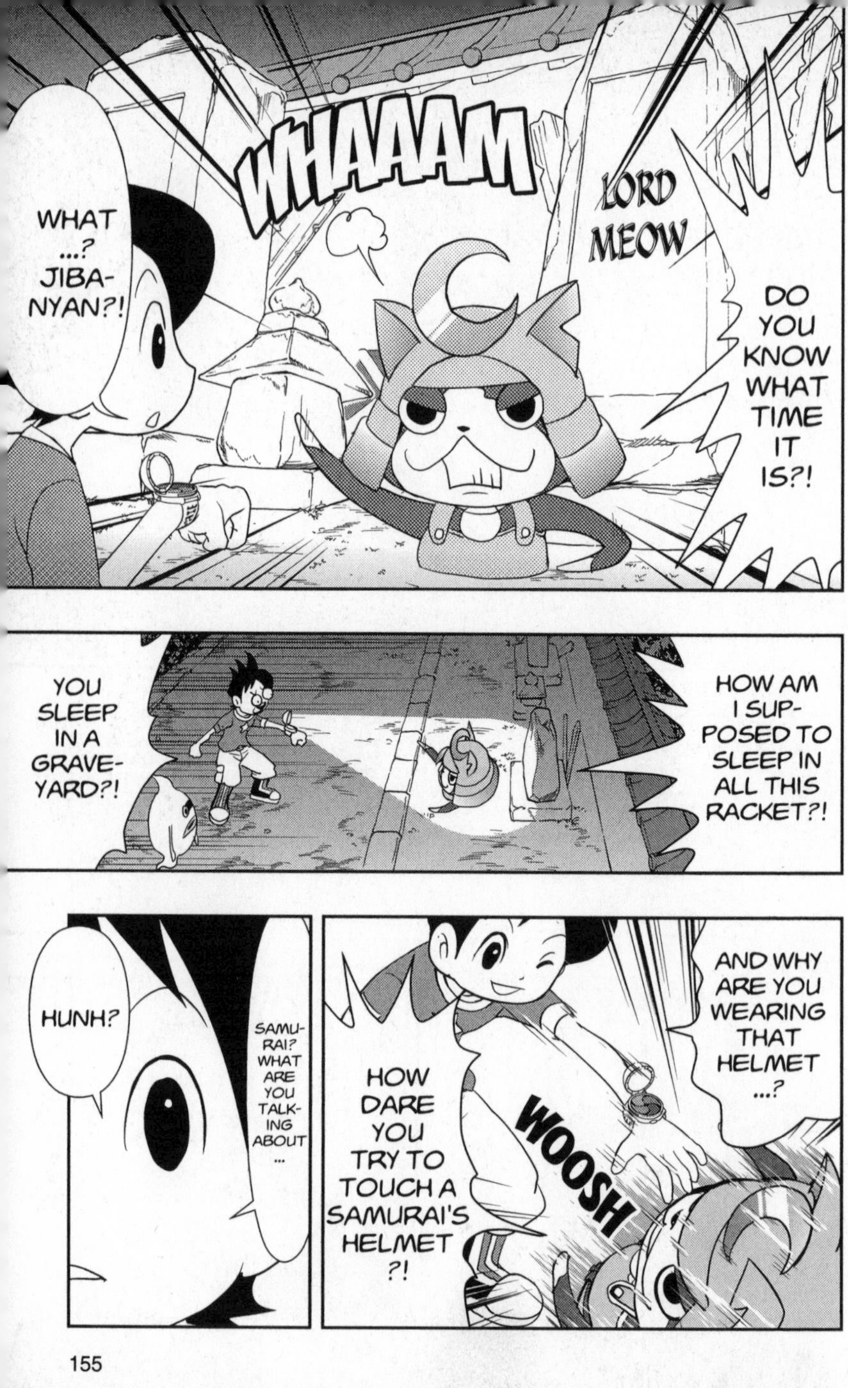
LORD MEOW
DO YOU KNOW WHAT TIME IT IS?!
WHAAAAM
WHAT ...? JIBANYAN?!
HOW AM I SUPPOSED TO SLEEP IN ALL THIS RACKET?!
YOU SLEEP IN A GRAVEYARD?!
AND WHY ARE YOU WEARING THAT HELMET ...?
WOOSH
HOW DARE YOU TRY TO TOUCH A SAMURAI'S HELMET ?!
SAMURAI? WHAT ARE YOU TALKING ABOUT ...
HUNH?

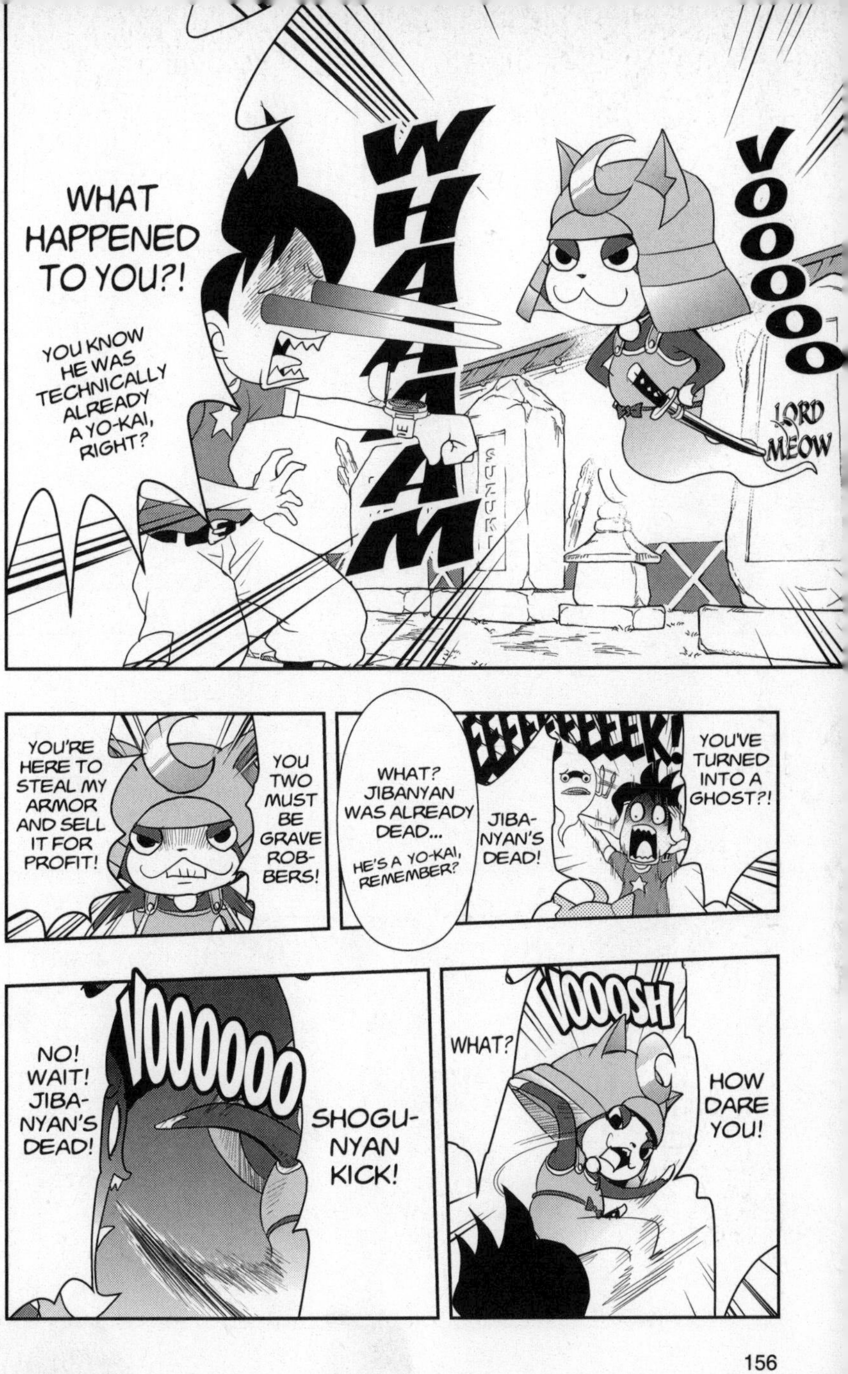
VOOOOO
LORD MEOW
WHAM
WHAT HAPPENED TO YOU?!
YOU KNOW HE WAS TECHNICALLY ALREADY A YO-KAI, RIGHT?
YOU'VE TURNED INTO A GHOST?!
EEEEEEEK!
JIBA-NYAN'S DEAD!
WHAT? JIBANYAN WAS ALREADY DEAD...
HE'S A YO-KAI, REMEMBER?
YOU TWO MUST BE GRAVE ROB-BERS!
YOU'RE HERE TO STEAL MY ARMOR AND SELL IT FOR PROFIT!
VOOOSH
HOW DARE YOU!
WHAT?
VOOOOOO
SHOGU-NYAN KICK!
NO! WAIT! JIBA-NYAN'S DEAD!

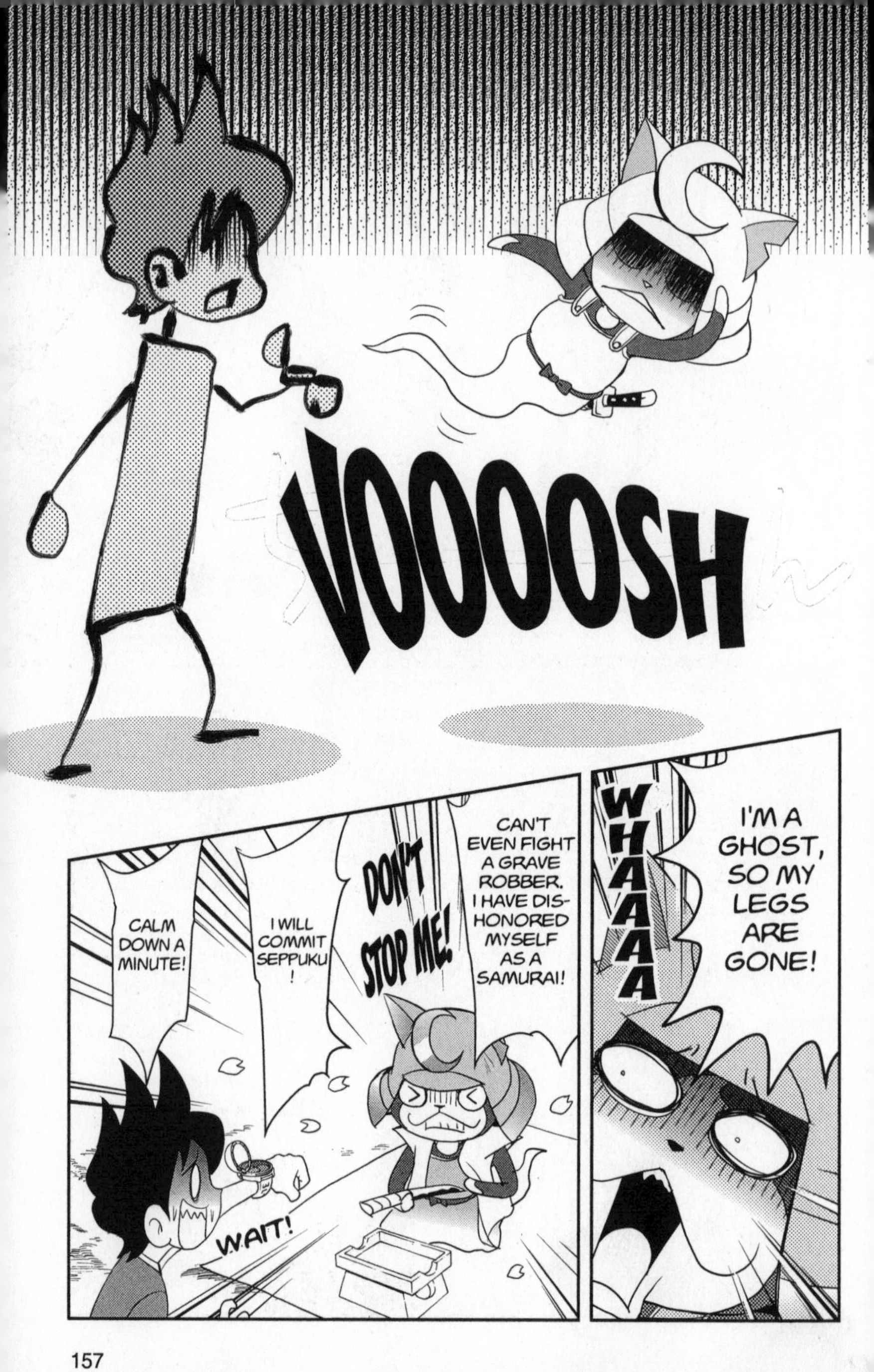
VOOOOSH
WHAAAA
I'M A GHOST, SO MY LEGS ARE GONE!
CAN'T EVEN FIGHT A GRAVE ROBBER. I HAVE DISHONORED MYSELF AS A SAMURAI!
DON'T STOP ME!
I WILL COMMIT SEPPUKU!
CALM DOWN A MINUTE!
WAIT!

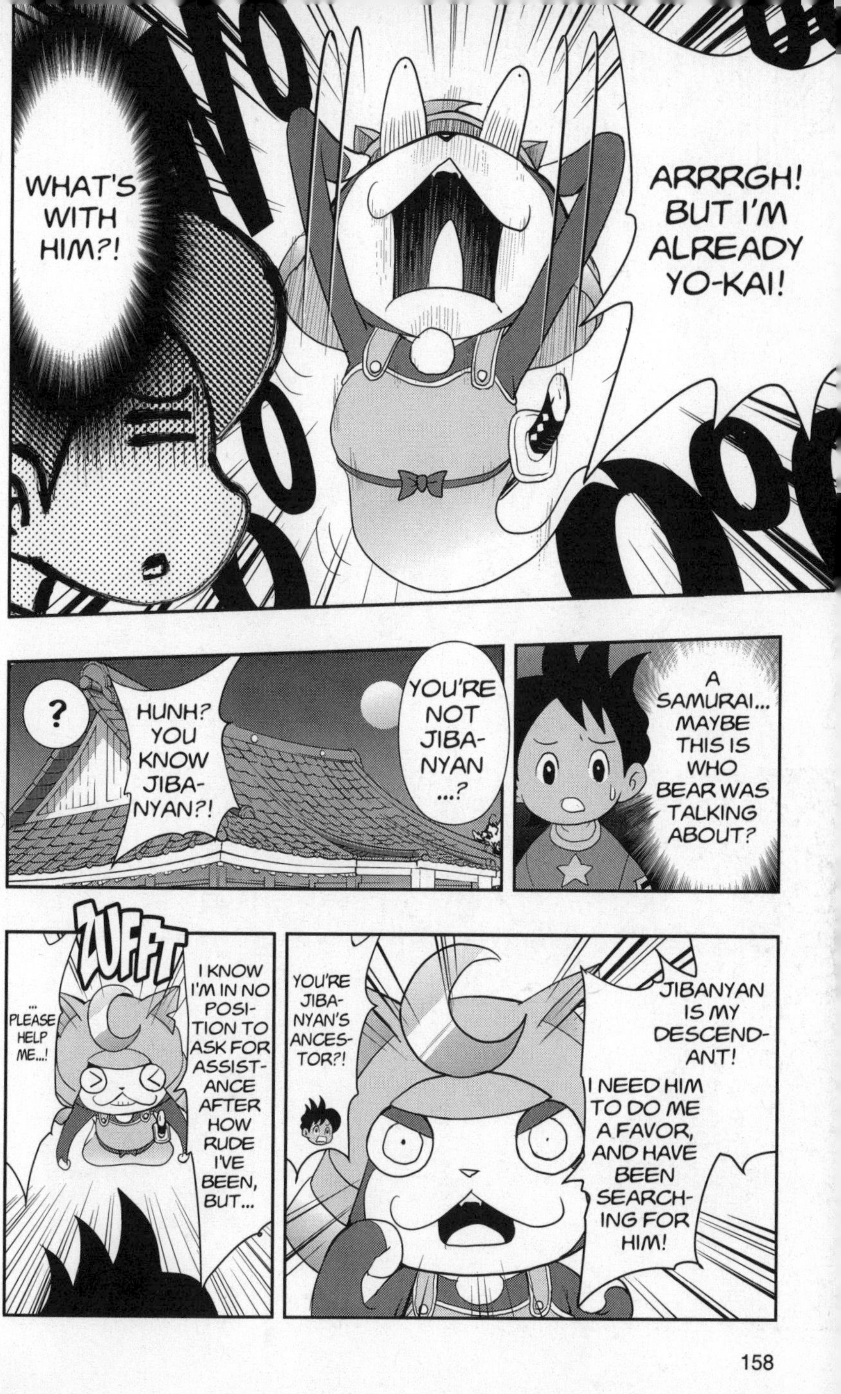
ARRRGH! BUT I'M ALREADY YO-KAI!
WHAT'S WITH HIM?!
A SAMURAI... MAYBE THIS IS WHO BEAR WAS TALKING ABOUT?
YOU'RE NOT JIBA-NYAN ...?
HUNH? YOU KNOW JIBA-NYAN?!
?
JIBANYAN IS MY DESCEND-ANT!
I NEED HIM TO DO ME A FAVOR, AND HAVE BEEN SEARCH-ING FOR HIM!
YOU'RE JIBA-NYAN'S ANCES-TOR?!
ZUFFT
I KNOW I'M IN NO POSI-TION TO ASK FOR ASSIST-ANCE AFTER HOW RUDE I'VE BEEN, BUT...
...PLEASE HELP ME...!

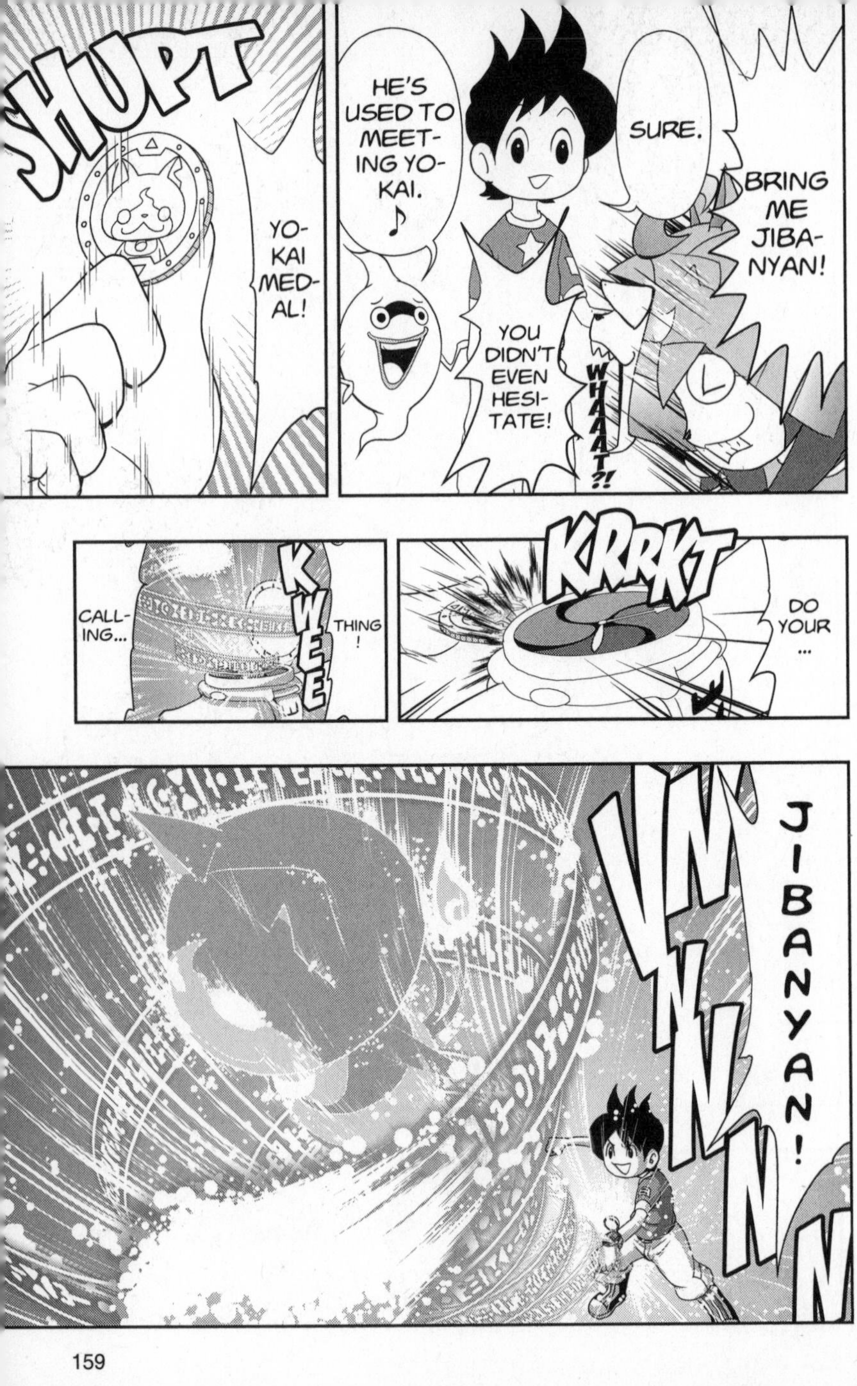
SURE.
BRING ME JIBA-NYAN!
HE'S USED TO MEET-ING YO-KAI. ♪
WHAAAAT?!
YOU DIDN'T EVEN HESI-TATE!
SHUPT
YO-KAI MED-AL!
KRRKT
DO YOUR ...
THING !
KWEE
CALL-ING...
VMNNNN
JIBANYAN!

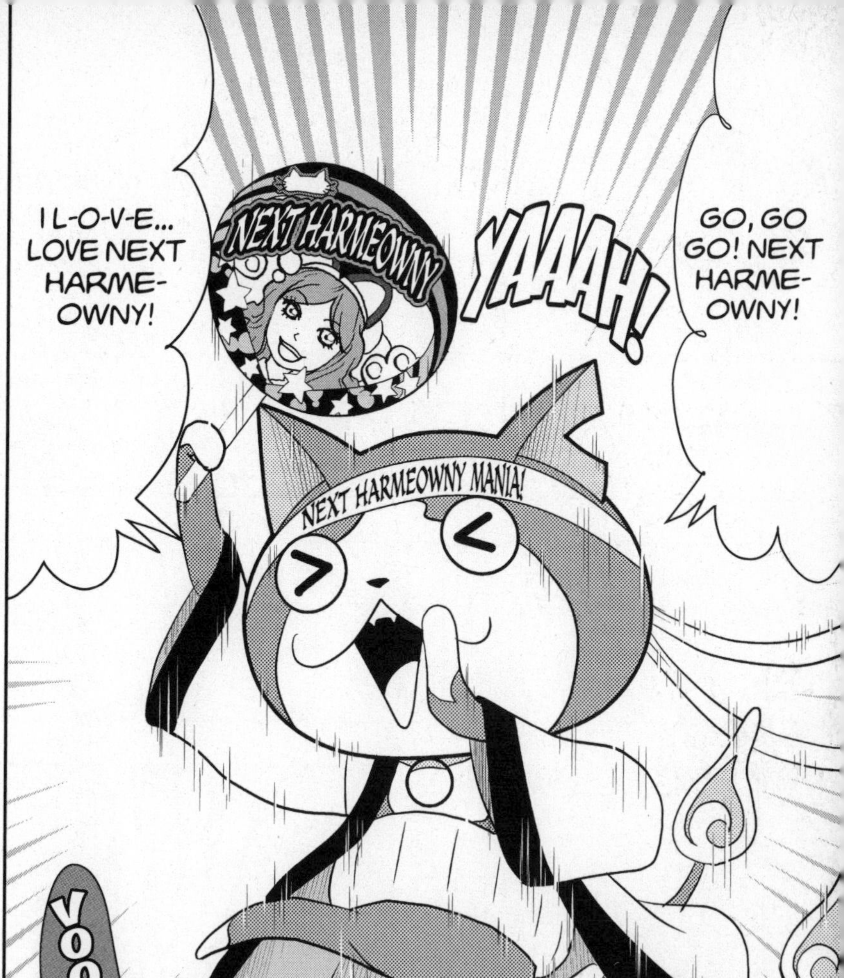
GO, GO GO! NEXT HARME-OWNY!
YAAAAH!
I L-O-V-E... LOVE NEXT HARME-OWNY!
NEXT HARMEOWNY
NEXT HARMEOWNY MANIA!
VOOOSH

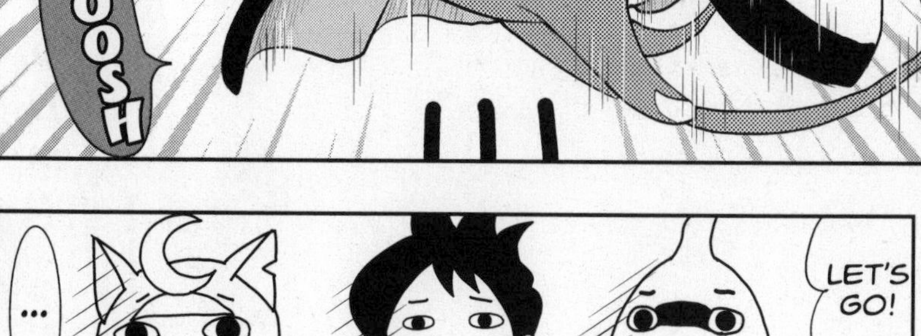
LET'S GO!
...

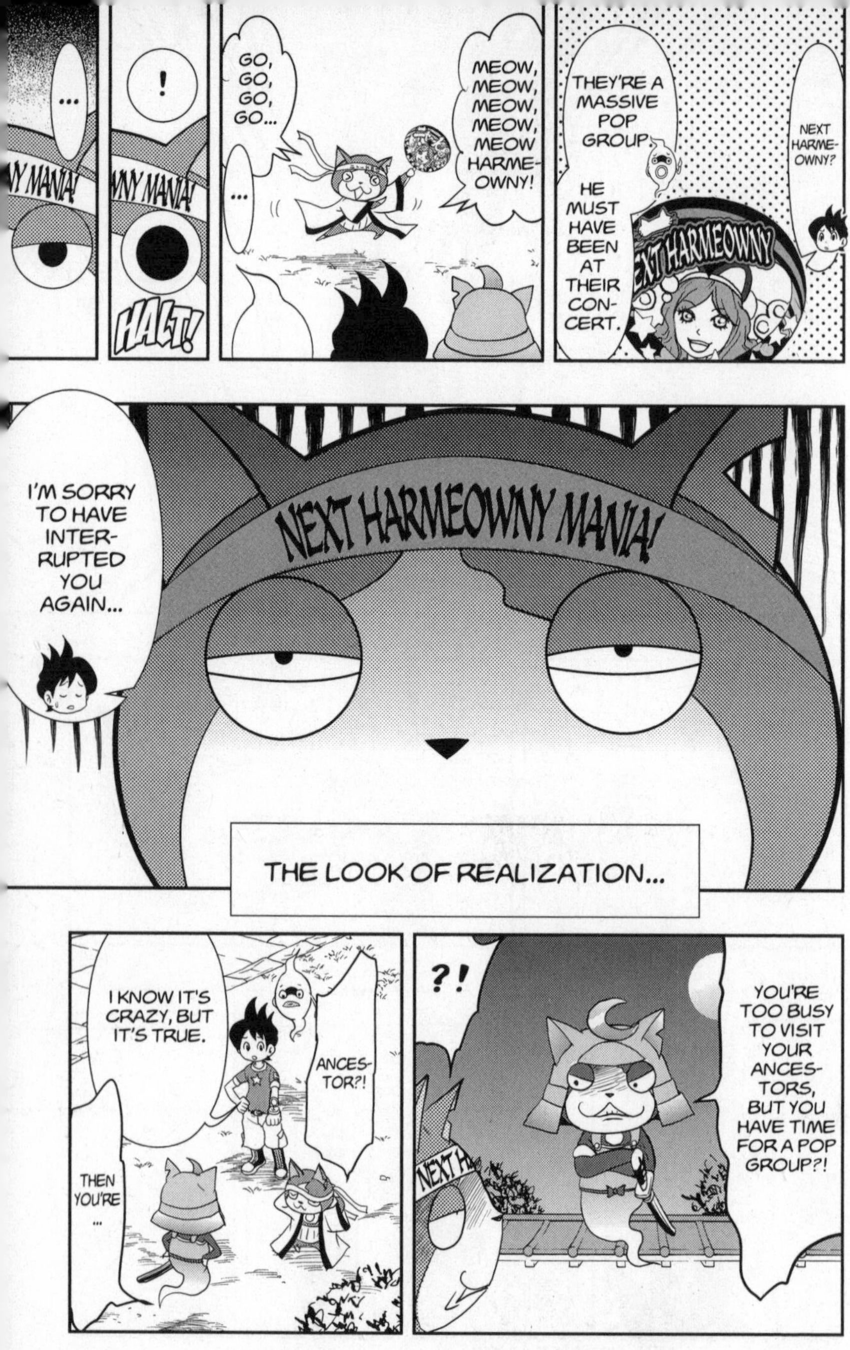
NEXT HARMEOWNY?
THEY'RE A MASSIVE POP GROUP.
HE MUST HAVE BEEN AT THEIR CONCERT.
NEXT HARMEOWNY
MEOW, MEOW, MEOW, MEOW, MEOW HARMEOWNY!
GO, GO, GO, GO...
...
!
WNY MANIA!
HALT!
...
NY MANIA!
NEXT HARMEOWNY MANIA!
I'M SORRY TO HAVE INTERRUPTED YOU AGAIN...
THE LOOK OF REALIZATION...
?!
YOU'RE TOO BUSY TO VISIT YOUR ANCESTORS, BUT YOU HAVE TIME FOR A POP GROUP?!
I KNOW IT'S CRAZY, BUT IT'S TRUE.
ANCESTOR?!
THEN YOU'RE ...

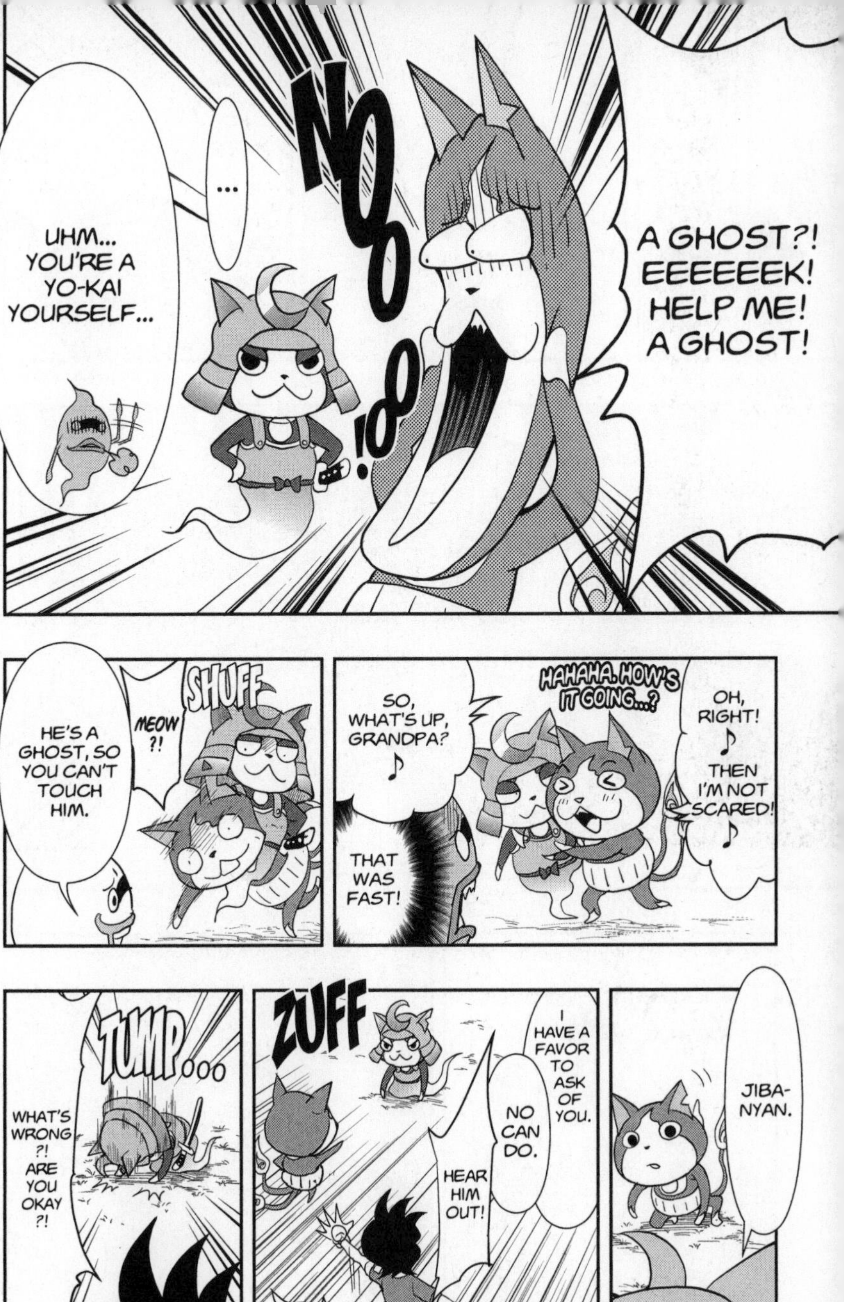
A GHOST?! EEEEEEK! HELP ME! A GHOST!
NOOOOO!
...
UHM... YOU'RE A YO-KAI YOURSELF...
OH, RIGHT! ♪ THEN I'M NOT SCARED! ♪
HAHAHA. HOW'S IT GOING...?
SO, WHAT'S UP, GRANDPA? ♪
THAT WAS FAST!
SHUFF
MEOW?!
HE'S A GHOST, SO YOU CAN'T TOUCH HIM.
JIBA-NYAN.
I HAVE A FAVOR TO ASK OF YOU.
NO CAN DO.
ZUFF
HEAR HIM OUT!
TUMP
WHAT'S WRONG?! ARE YOU OKAY?!

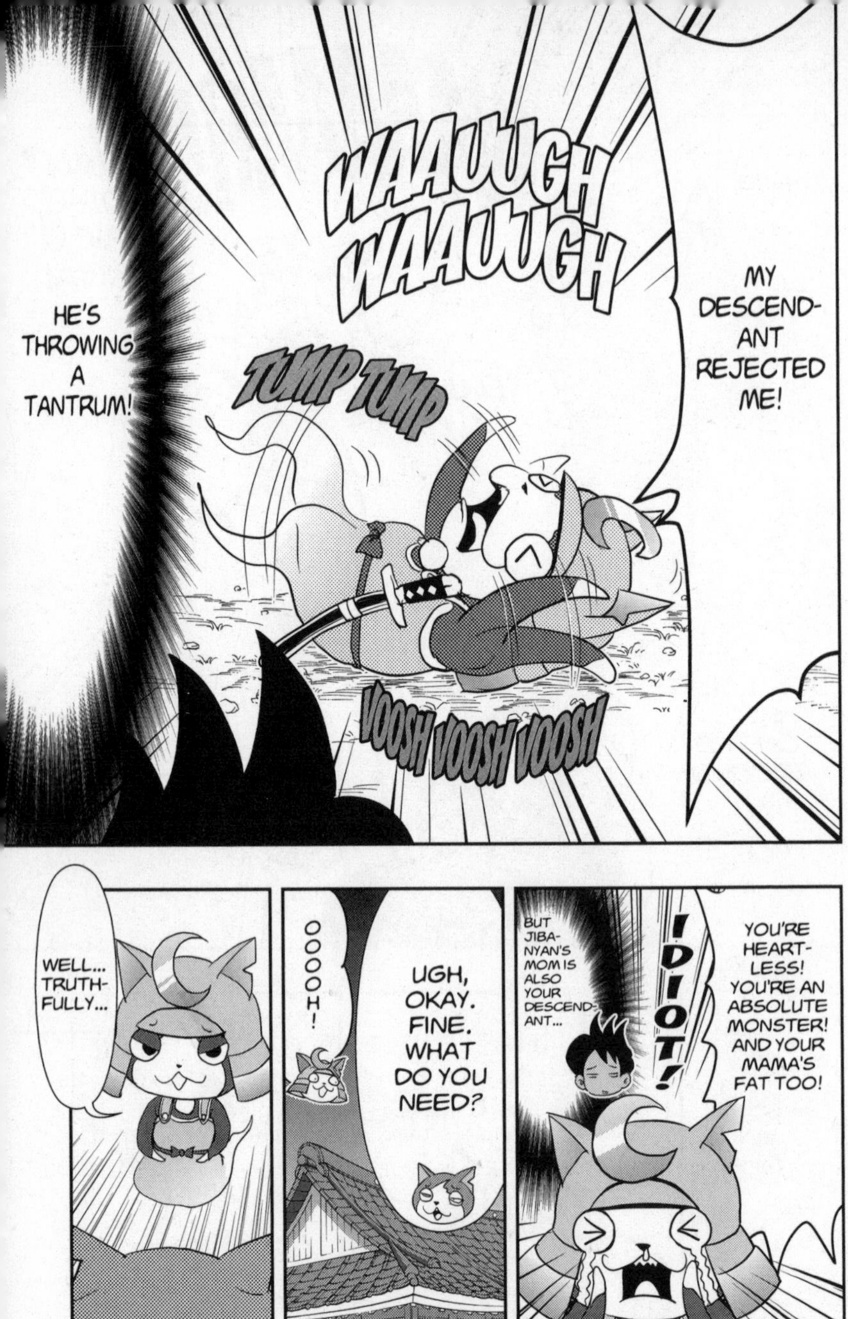
MY DESCEND-ANT REJECTED ME!
WAAUUGH WAAUUGH
TUMP TUMP
VOOSH VOOSH VOOSH
HE'S THROWING A TANTRUM!
YOU'RE HEART-LESS! YOU'RE AN ABSOLUTE MONSTER! AND YOUR MAMA'S FAT TOO!
IDIOT!
BUT JIBA-NYAN'S MOM IS ALSO YOUR DESCEND-ANT...
UGH, OKAY. FINE. WHAT DO YOU NEED?
OOOOH!
WELL... TRUTH-FULLY...

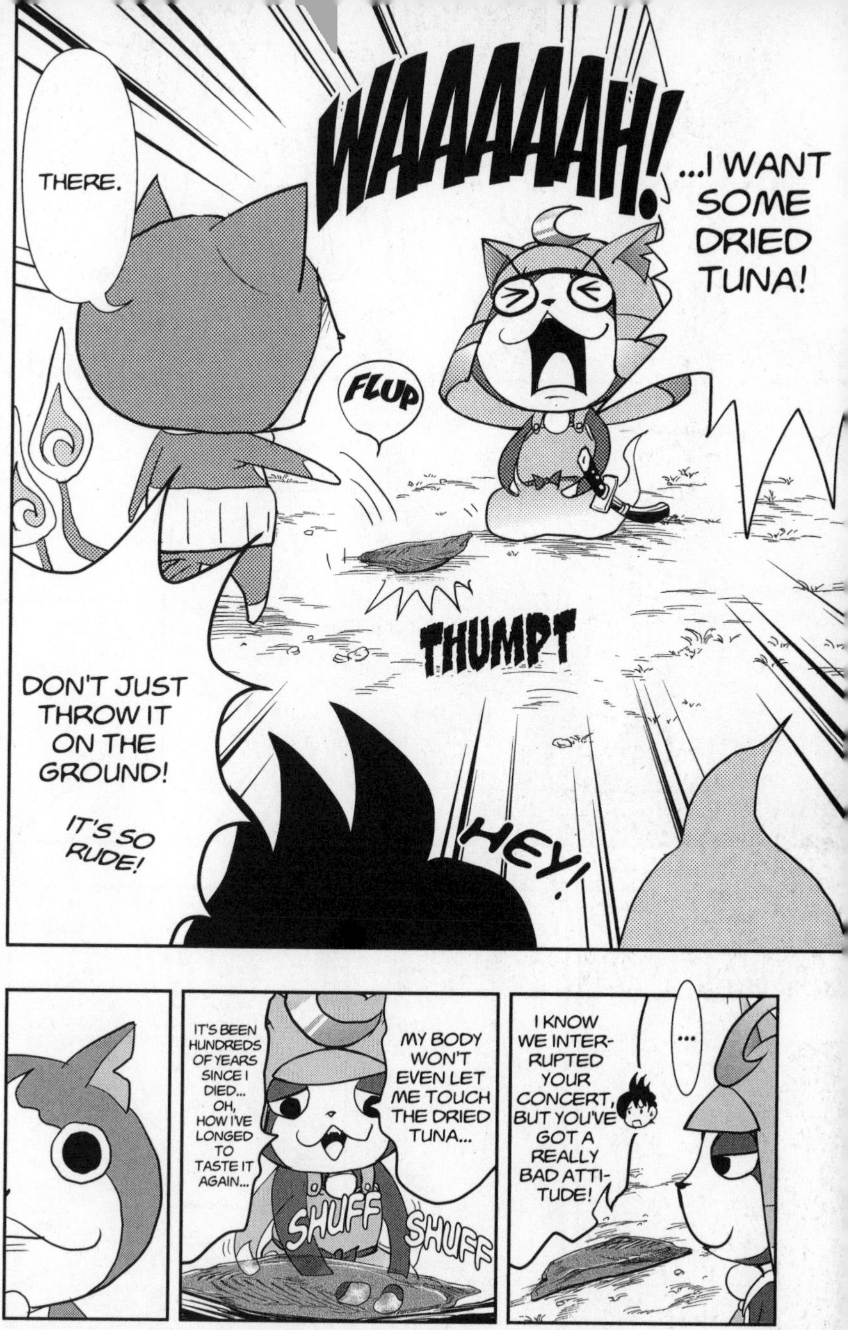
WAAAAAH!
...I WANT SOME DRIED TUNA!
THERE.
FLUP
THUMPT
HEY!
DON'T JUST THROW IT ON THE GROUND!
IT'S SO RUDE!
...
I KNOW WE INTERRUPTED YOUR CONCERT, BUT YOU'VE GOT A REALLY BAD ATTITUDE!
MY BODY WON'T EVEN LET ME TOUCH THE DRIED TUNA...
IT'S BEEN HUNDREDS OF YEARS SINCE I DIED... OH, HOW I'VE LONGED TO TASTE IT AGAIN...
SHUFF
SHUFF

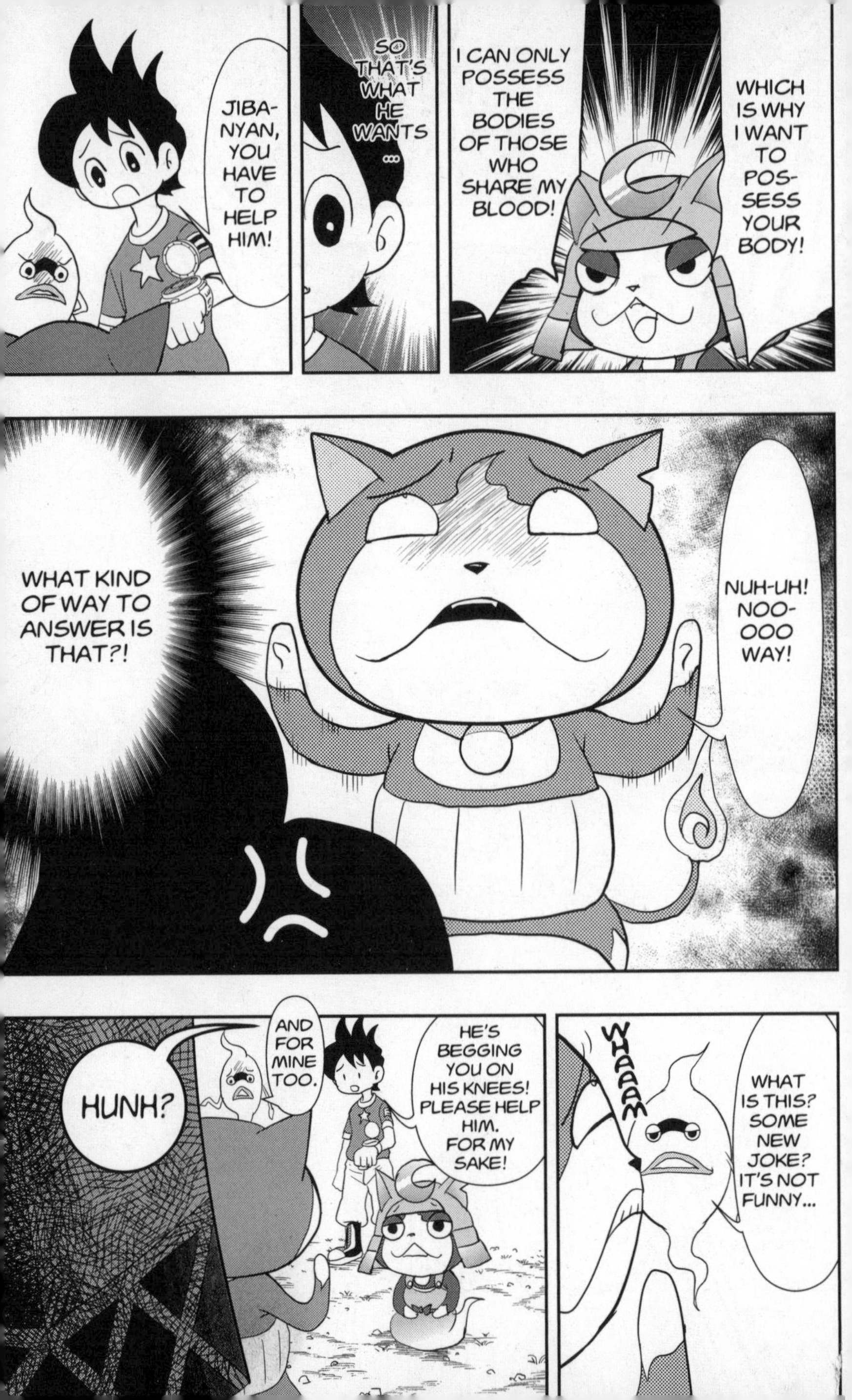
WHICH IS WHY I WANT TO POS-SESS YOUR BODY!
I CAN ONLY POSSESS THE BODIES OF THOSE WHO SHARE MY BLOOD!
SO THAT'S WHAT HE WANTS...
JIBA-NYAN, YOU HAVE TO HELP HIM!
NUH-UH! NOO-OOO WAY!
WHAT KIND OF WAY TO ANSWER IS THAT?!
WHAT IS THIS? SOME NEW JOKE? IT'S NOT FUNNY...
WHAAAM
HE'S BEGGING YOU ON HIS KNEES! PLEASE HELP HIM. FOR MY SAKE!
AND FOR MINE TOO.
HUNH?

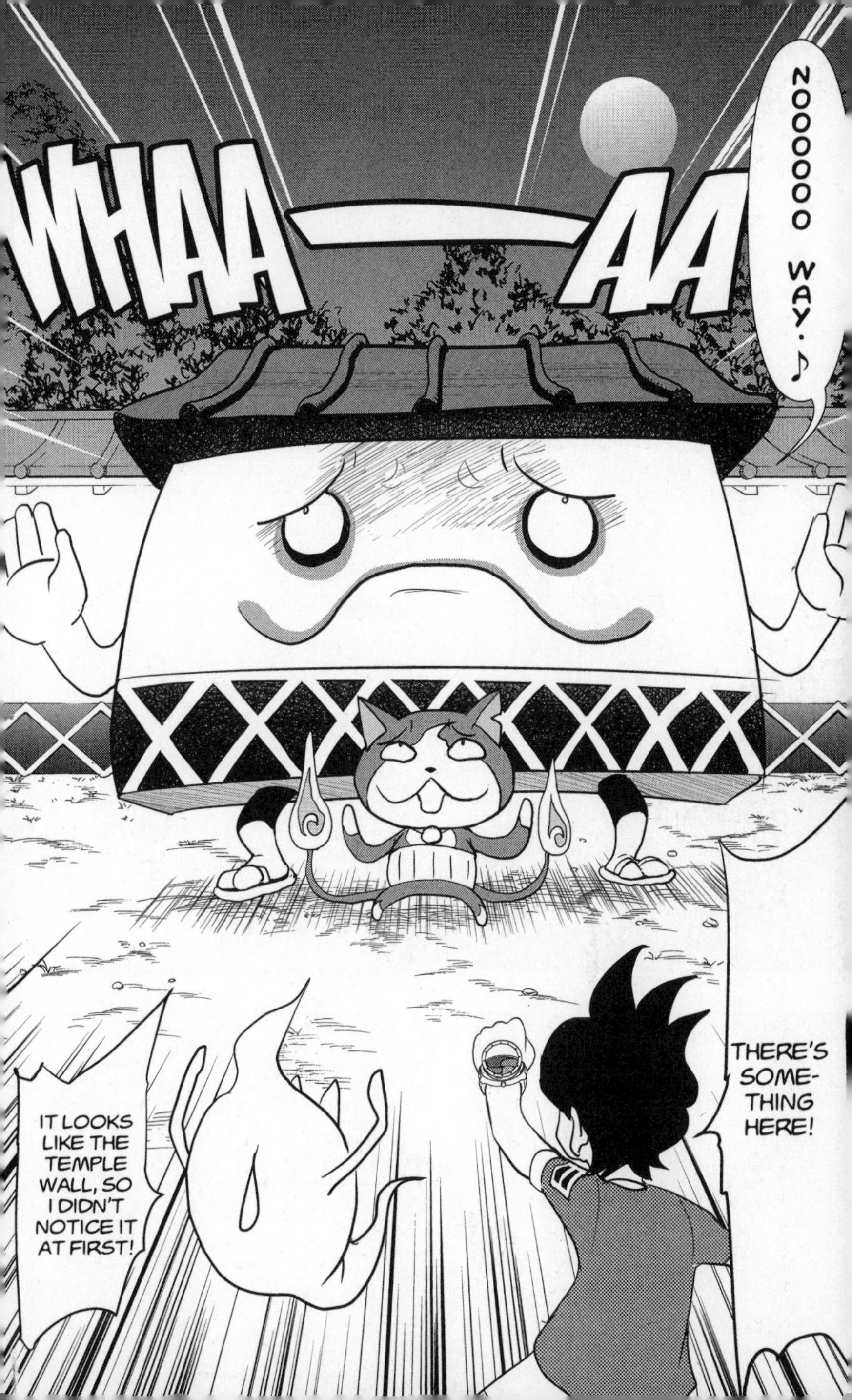
NOOOOOO WAY.♪
WHAA—AA
THERE'S SOME-THING HERE!
IT LOOKS LIKE THE TEMPLE WALL, SO I DIDN'T NOTICE IT AT FIRST!

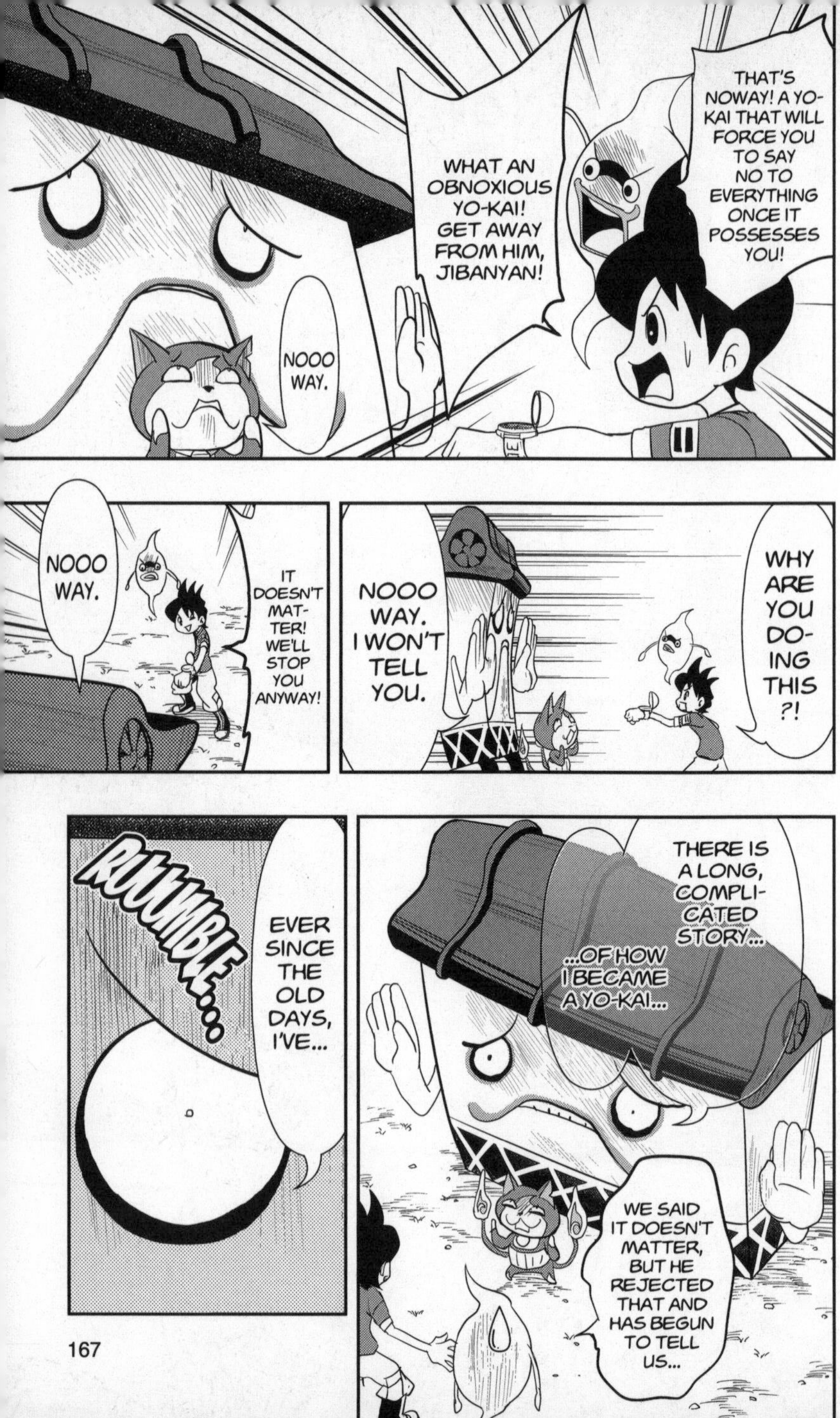
THAT'S NOWAY! A YO-KAI THAT WILL FORCE YOU TO SAY NO TO EVERYTHING ONCE IT POSSESSES YOU!
WHAT AN OBNOXIOUS YO-KAI! GET AWAY FROM HIM, JIBANYAN!
NOOO WAY.
WHY ARE YOU DOING THIS?!
NOOO WAY. I WON'T TELL YOU.
IT DOESN'T MATTER! WE'LL STOP YOU ANYWAY!
NOOO WAY.
THERE IS A LONG, COMPLICATED STORY...
...OF HOW I BECAME A YO-KAI...
WE SAID IT DOESN'T MATTER, BUT HE REJECTED THAT AND HAS BEGUN TO TELL US...
EVER SINCE THE OLD DAYS, I'VE...
RUUUMBLE...

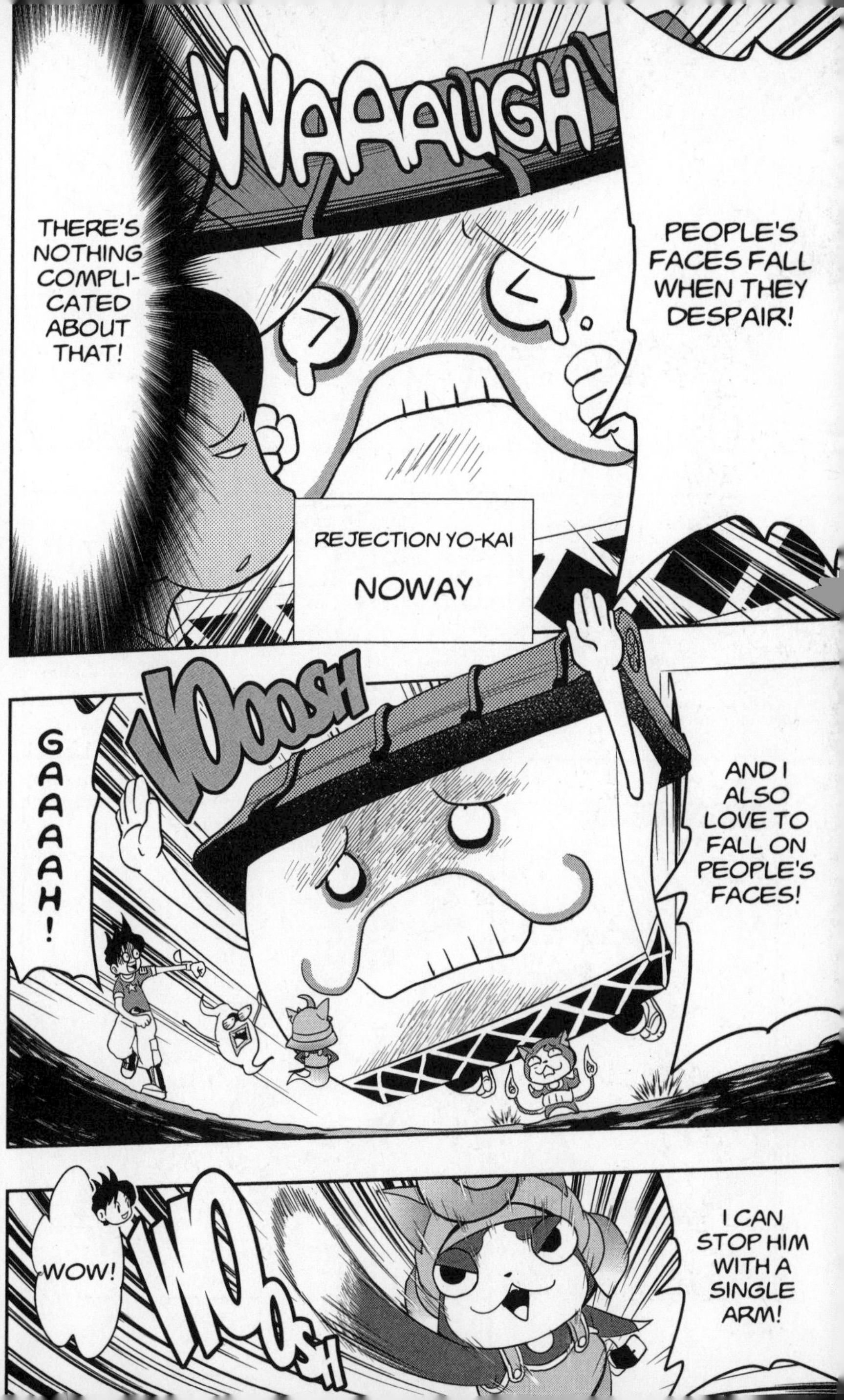
WAAAUGH
PEOPLE'S FACES FALL WHEN THEY DESPAIR!
THERE'S NOTHING COMPLI-CATED ABOUT THAT!
REJECTION YO-KAI
NOWAY
AND I ALSO LOVE TO FALL ON PEOPLE'S FACES!
WOOSH
GAAAAAH!
I CAN STOP HIM WITH A SINGLE ARM!
WOOSH
WOW!

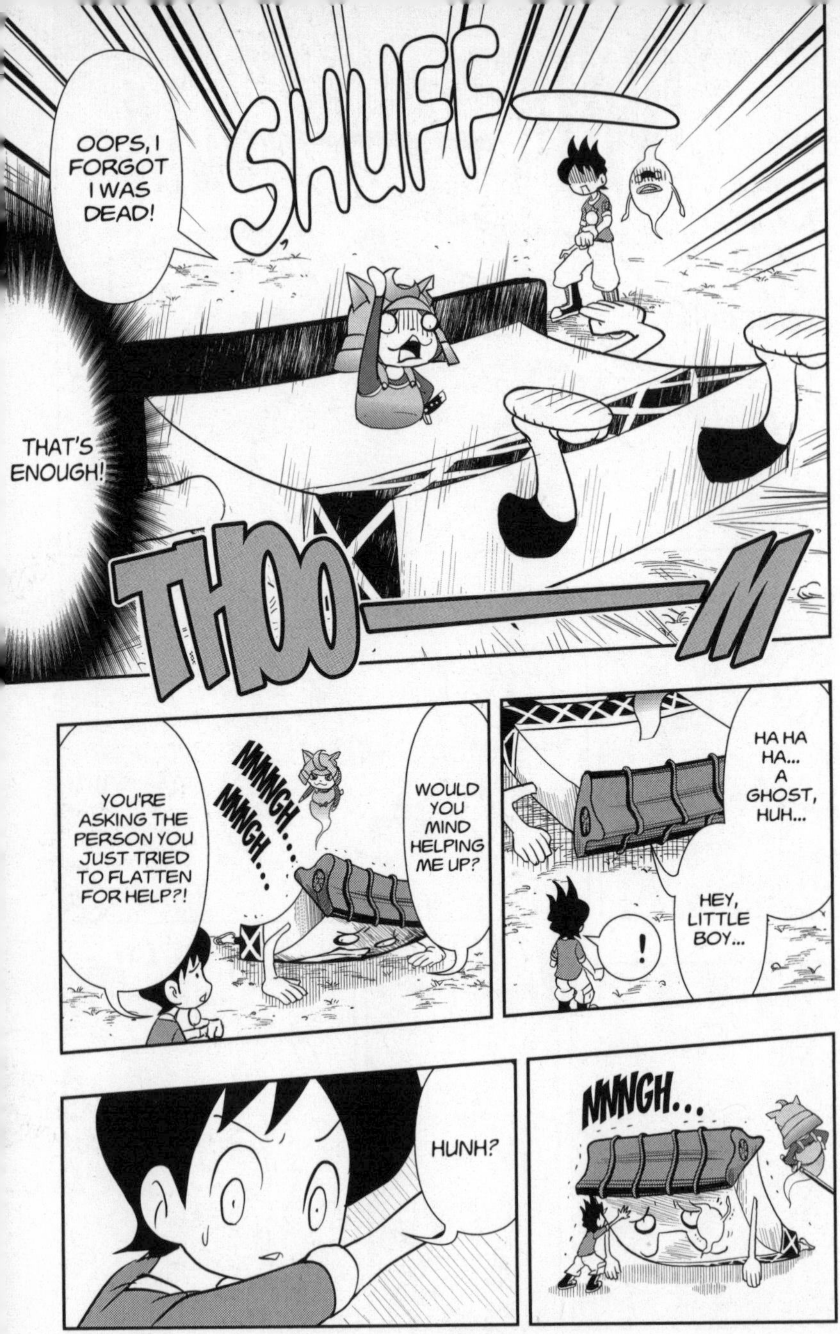
SHUFF—
OOPS, I FORGOT I WAS DEAD!
THAT'S ENOUGH!
THOO—M
HA HA HA... A GHOST, HUH...
HEY, LITTLE BOY...
!
WOULD YOU MIND HELPING ME UP?
MMMNGH... MMNGH...
YOU'RE ASKING THE PERSON YOU JUST TRIED TO FLATTEN FOR HELP?!
MMNGH...
HUNH?

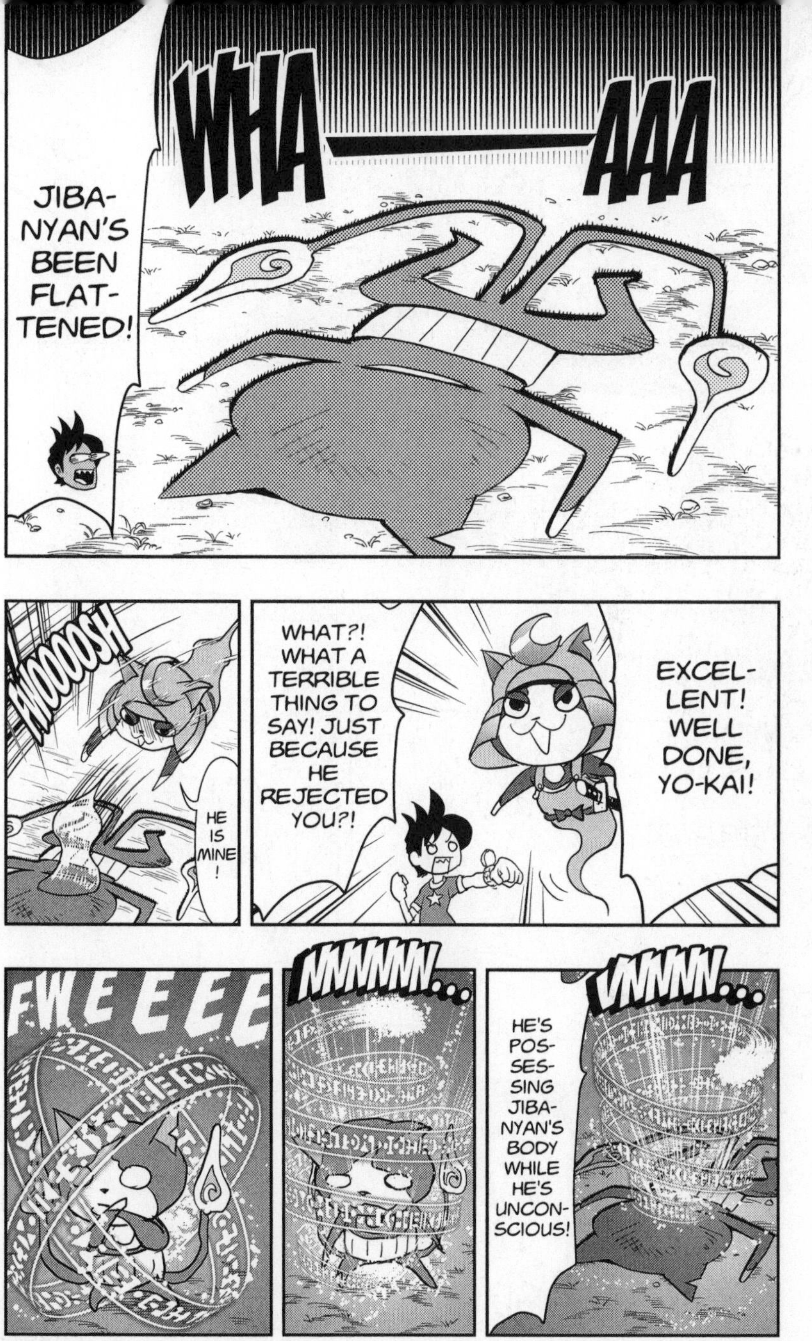
WHA—AAA
JIBANYAN'S BEEN FLATTENED!
EXCELLENT! WELL DONE, YO-KAI!
WHAT?! WHAT A TERRIBLE THING TO SAY! JUST BECAUSE HE REJECTED YOU?!
WOOOOSH
HE IS MINE!
VNNNN...
HE'S POSSESSING JIBANYAN'S BODY WHILE HE'S UNCONSCIOUS!
NNNNNN...
FWEEEE

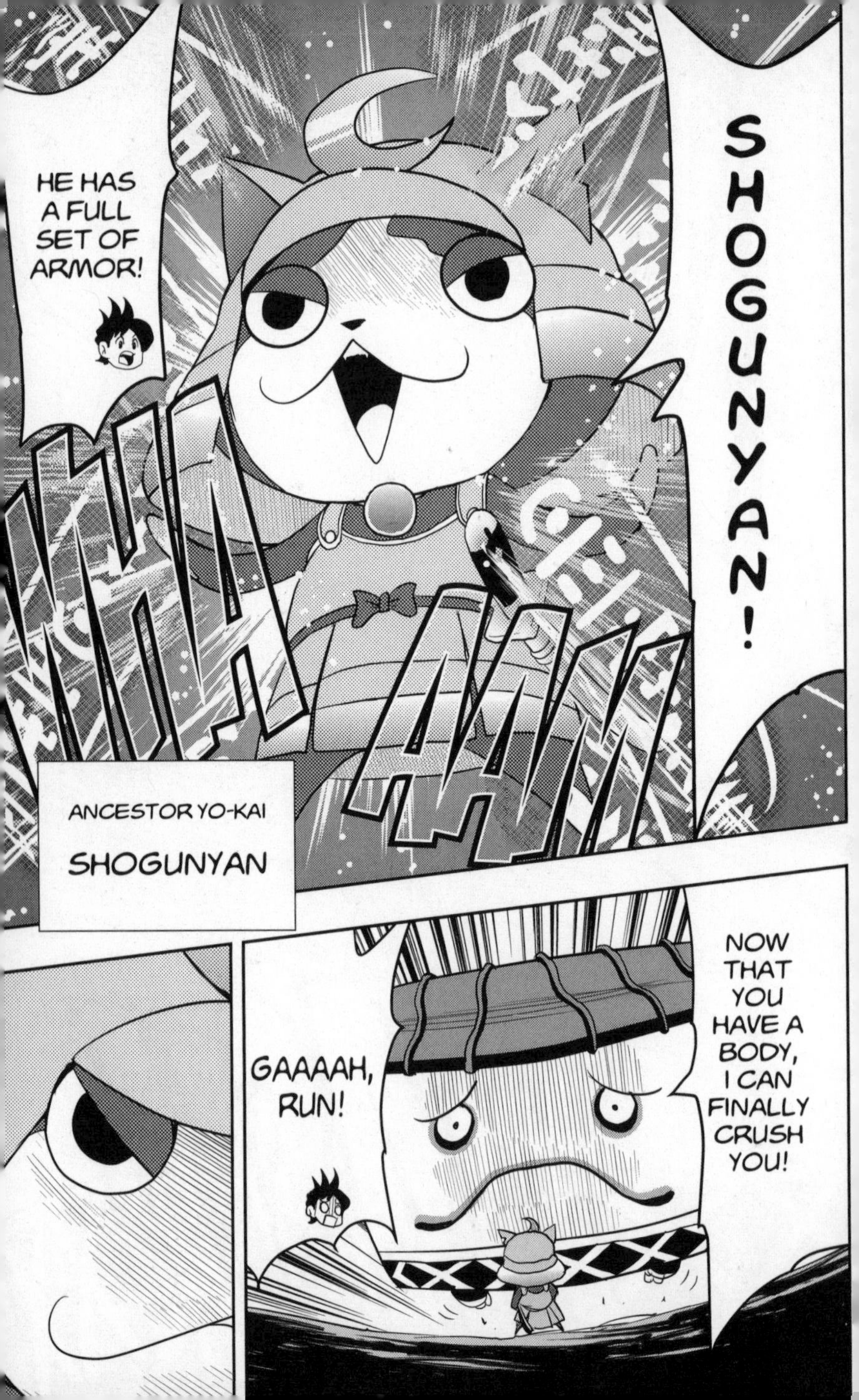
SHOGUNYAN!
WHAAAM
HE HAS A FULL SET OF ARMOR!
ANCESTOR YO-KAI
SHOGUNYAN
NOW THAT YOU HAVE A BODY, I CAN FINALLY CRUSH YOU!
GAAAAH, RUN!

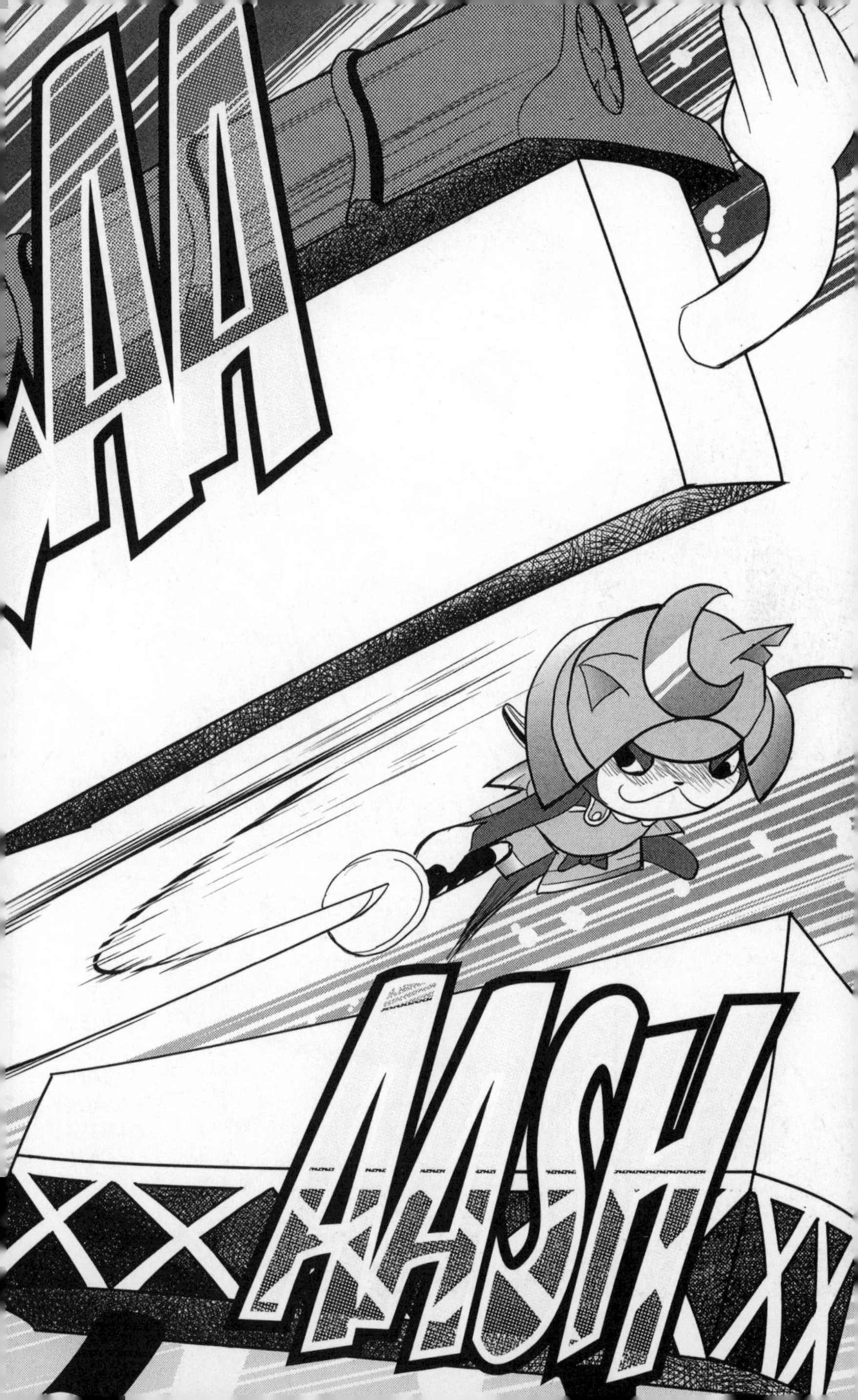
AA
MASH

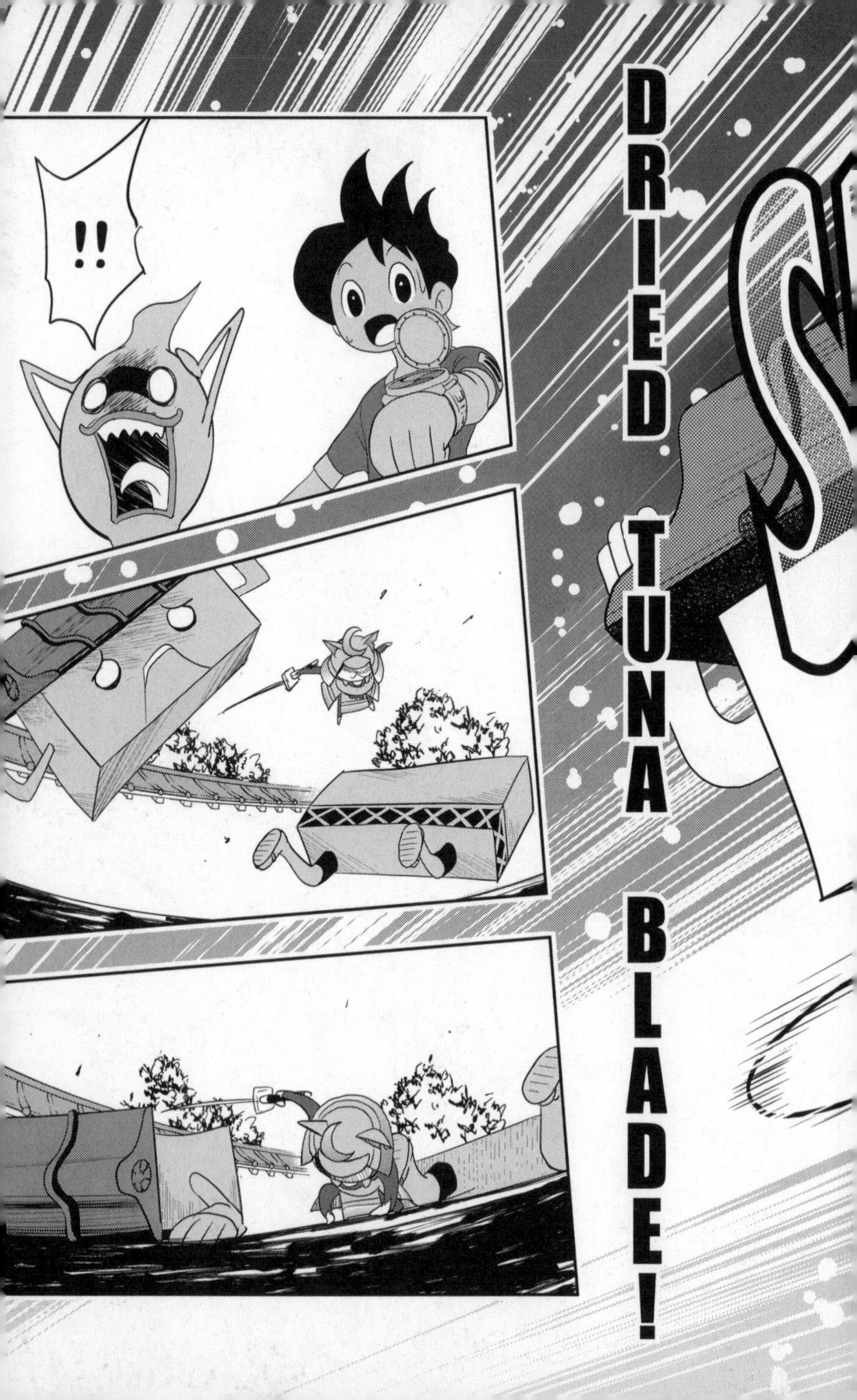
DRIED TUNA BLADE!
!!

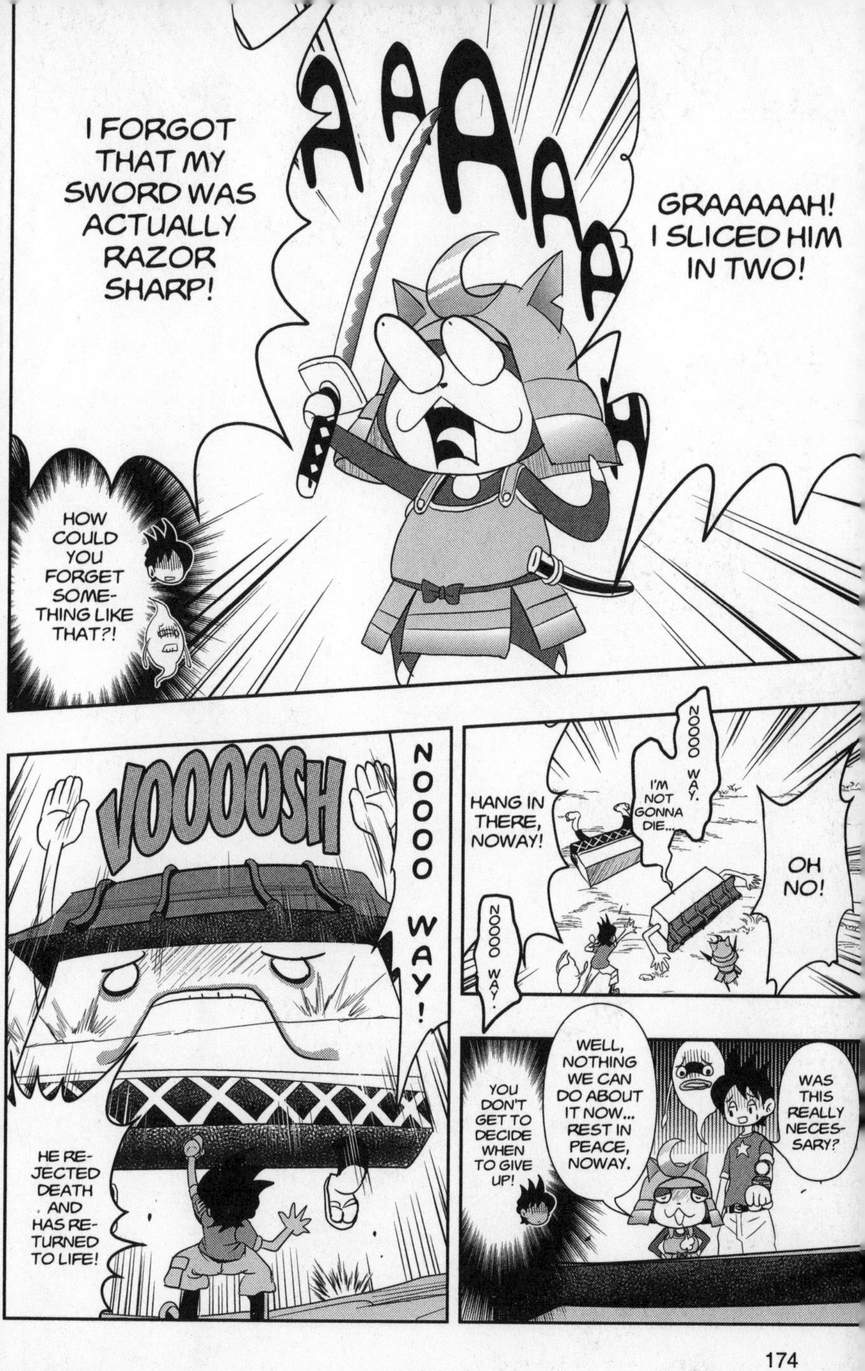
GRAAAAAH! I SLICED HIM IN TWO!
AAAAAAH
I FORGOT THAT MY SWORD WAS ACTUALLY RAZOR SHARP!
HOW COULD YOU FORGET SOME-THING LIKE THAT?!
NOOOO WAY.
I'M NOT GONNA DIE...
OH NO!
HANG IN THERE, NOWAY!
NOOOO WAY.
WAS THIS REALLY NECES-SARY?
WELL, NOTHING WE CAN DO ABOUT IT NOW... REST IN PEACE, NOWAY.
YOU DON'T GET TO DECIDE WHEN TO GIVE UP!
NOOOO WAY!
VOOOOSH
HE RE-JECTED DEATH AND HAS RE-TURNED TO LIFE!

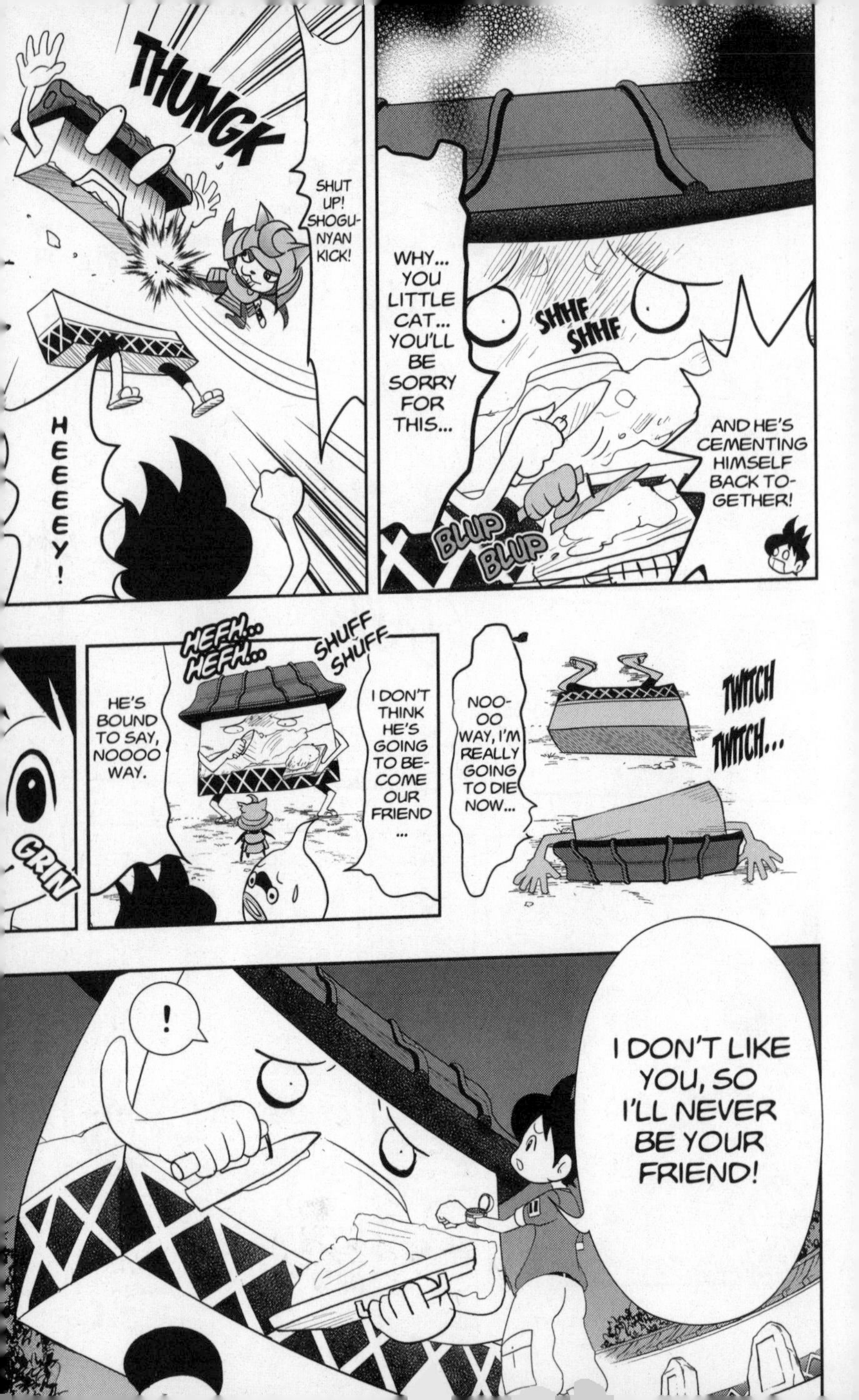
WHY... YOU LITTLE CAT... YOU'LL BE SORRY FOR THIS...
SHHF SHHF
AND HE'S CEMENTING HIMSELF BACK TO-GETHER!
BLUP BLUP
THUNGK
SHUT UP! SHOGU-NYAN KICK!
HEEEEEY!
TWITCH TWITCH...
NOO-OO WAY, I'M REALLY GOING TO DIE NOW...
SHUFF SHUFF
HEFH... HEFH...
I DON'T THINK HE'S GOING TO BE-COME OUR FRIEND ...
HE'S BOUND TO SAY, NOOOO WAY.
GRIN
I DON'T LIKE YOU, SO I'LL NEVER BE YOUR FRIEND!
!

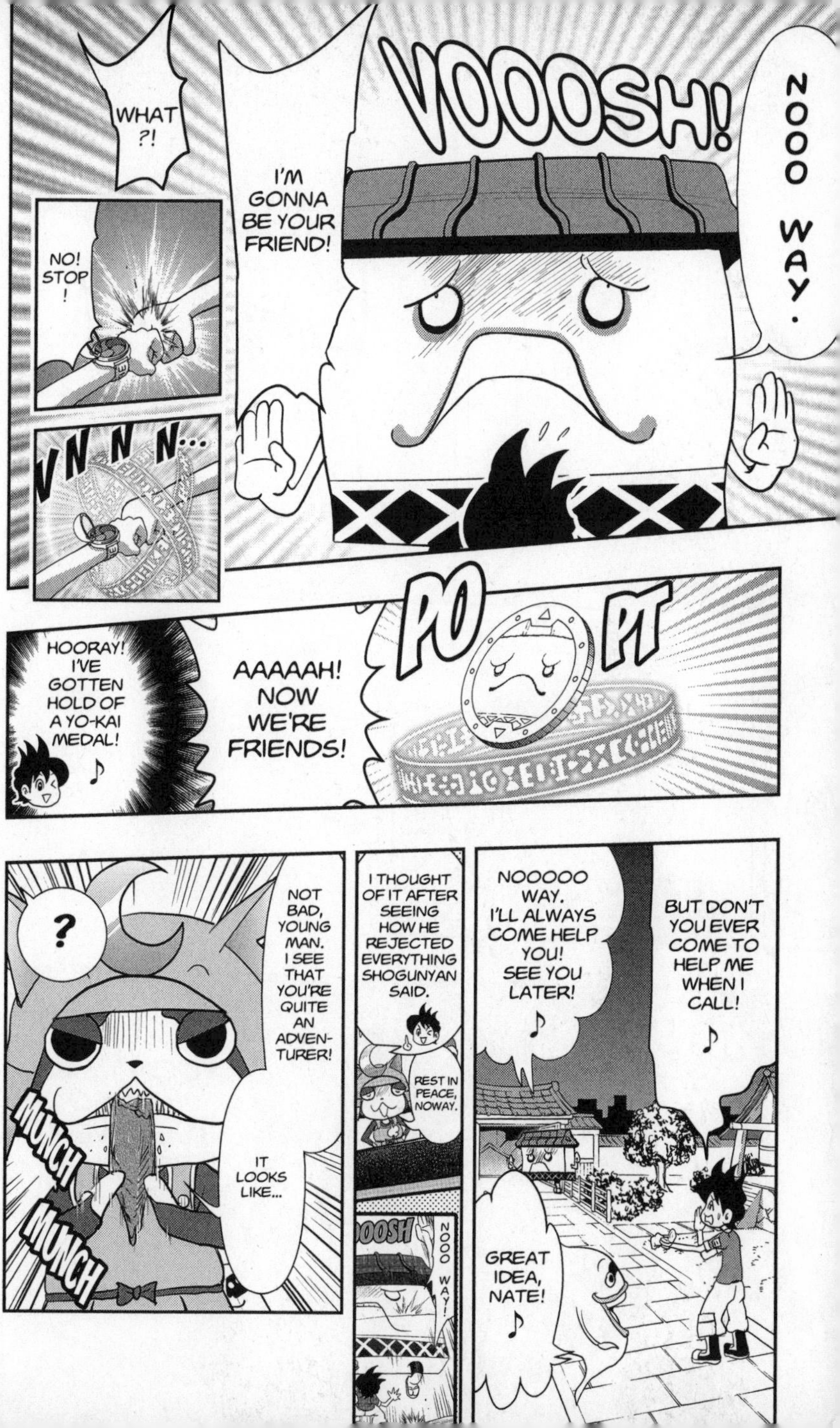
NOOO WAY.
VOOOSH!
I'M GONNA BE YOUR FRIEND!
WHAT?!
NO! STOP!
VNNN...
POPT
AAAAAH! NOW WE'RE FRIENDS!
HOORAY! I'VE GOTTEN HOLD OF A YO-KAI MEDAL! ♪
BUT DON'T YOU EVER COME TO HELP ME WHEN I CALL! ♪
NOOOOO WAY. I'LL ALWAYS COME HELP YOU! SEE YOU LATER! ♪
GREAT IDEA, NATE! ♪
I THOUGHT OF IT AFTER SEEING HOW HE REJECTED EVERYTHING SHOGUNYAN SAID.
REST IN PEACE, NOWAY.
OOOSH
NOOO WAY!
NOT BAD, YOUNG MAN. I SEE THAT YOU'RE QUITE AN ADVEN-TURER!
?
IT LOOKS LIKE...
MUNCH
MUNCH

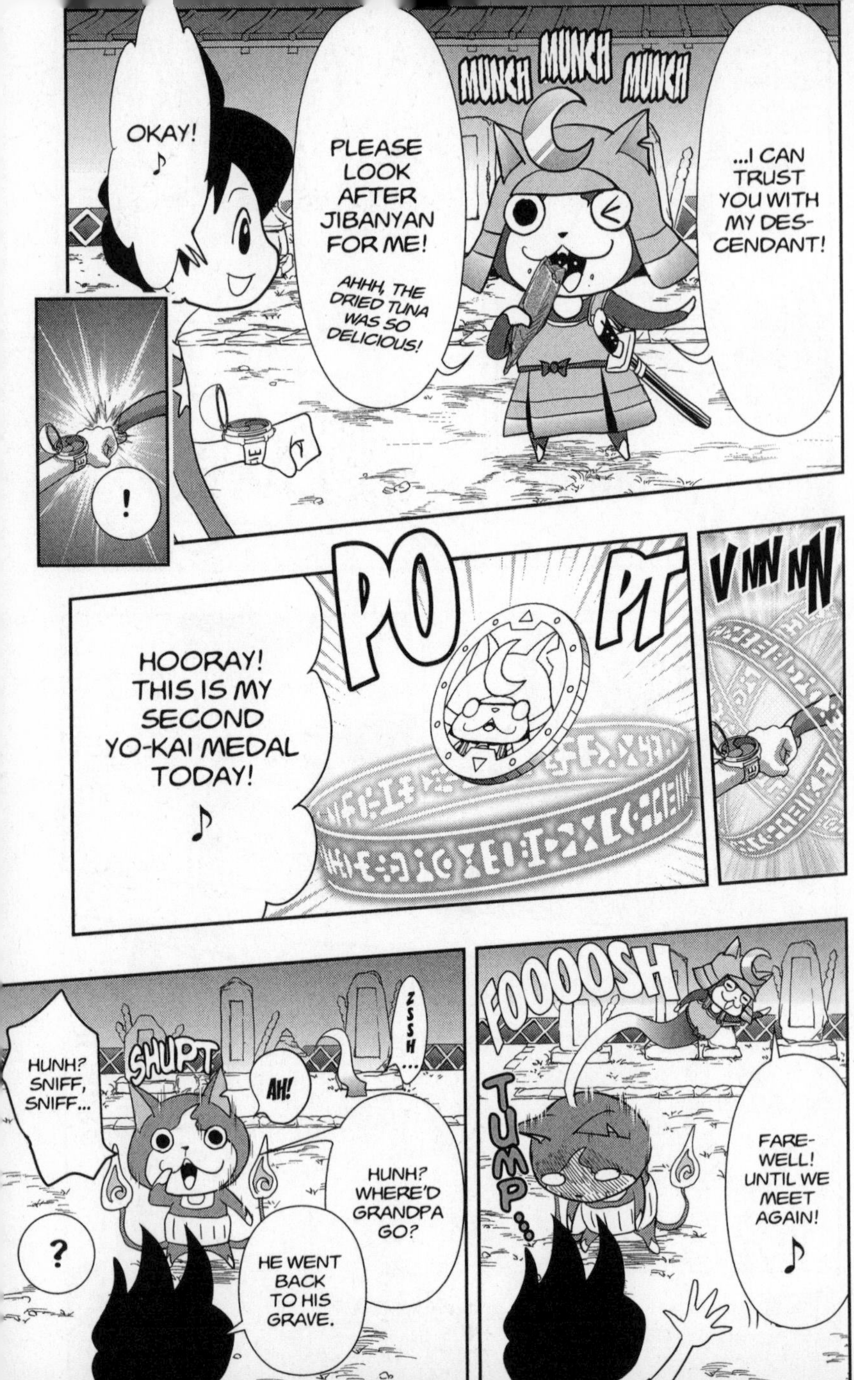
...I CAN TRUST YOU WITH MY DES-CENDANT!
MUNCH MUNCH MUNCH
PLEASE LOOK AFTER JIBANYAN FOR ME!
AHHH, THE DRIED TUNA WAS SO DELICIOUS!
OKAY! ♪
!
V MN MN
PO PT
HOORAY! THIS IS MY SECOND YO-KAI MEDAL TODAY! ♪
FOOOOSH
FARE-WELL! UNTIL WE MEET AGAIN! ♪
JUMP...
ZSSSH...
AH!
SHUPT
HUNH? SNIFF, SNIFF...
HUNH? WHERE'D GRANDPA GO?
HE WENT BACK TO HIS GRAVE.
?

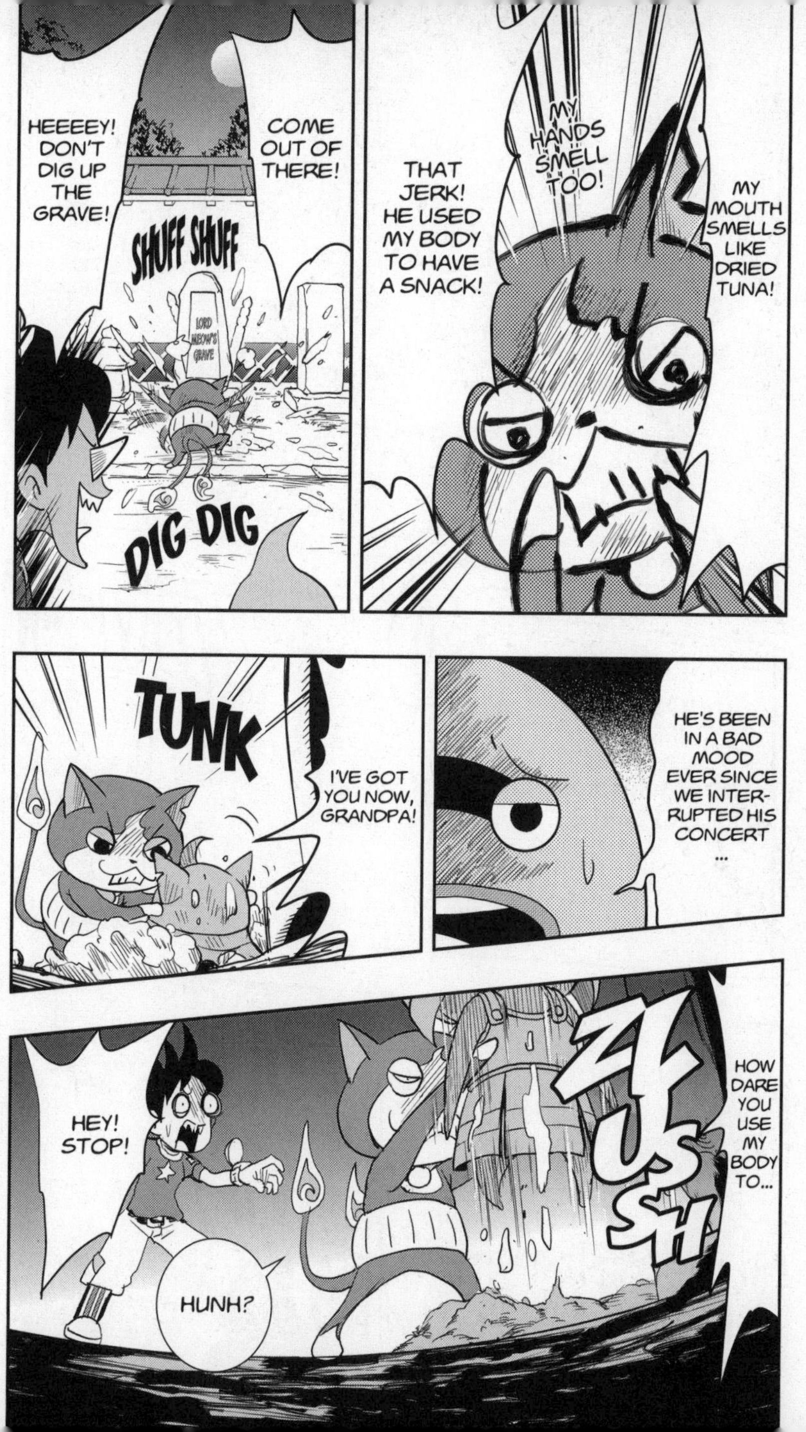
MY MOUTH SMELLS LIKE DRIED TUNA!
MY HANDS SMELL TOO!
THAT JERK! HE USED MY BODY TO HAVE A SNACK!
COME OUT OF THERE!
HEEEEY! DON'T DIG UP THE GRAVE!
SHUFF SHUFF
LORD MEOW'S GRAVE
DIG DIG
HE'S BEEN IN A BAD MOOD EVER SINCE WE INTER-RUPTED HIS CONCERT ...
TUNK
I'VE GOT YOU NOW, GRANDPA!
HOW DARE YOU USE MY BODY TO...
ZUSH
HEY! STOP!
HUNH?

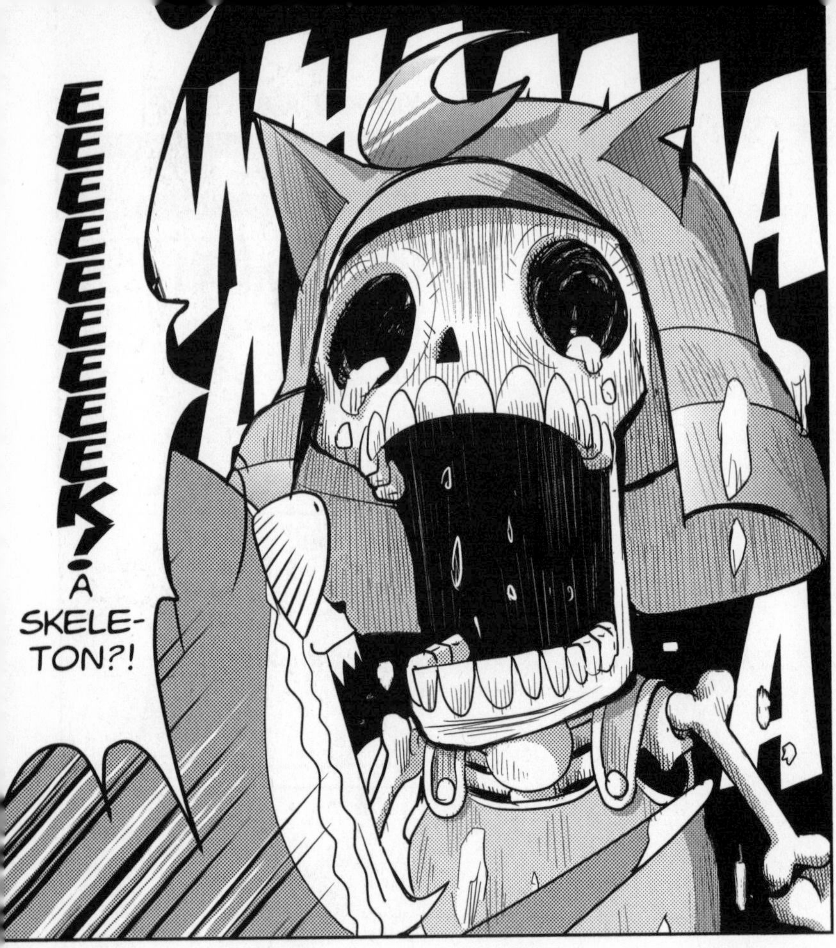
EEEEEEEEEEEEK!
A SKELE-TON?!

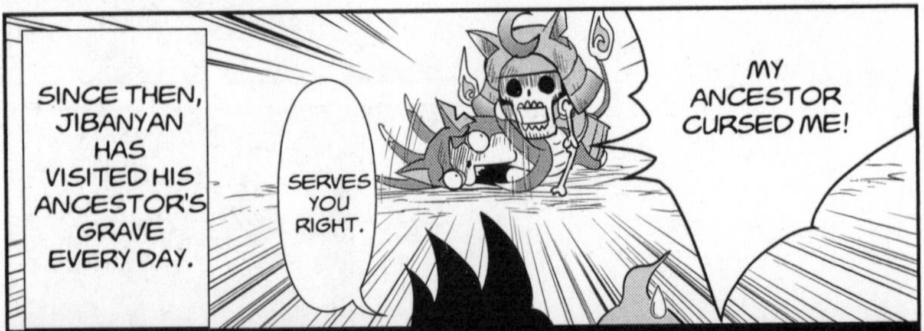
MY ANCESTOR CURSED ME!
SERVES YOU RIGHT.
SINCE THEN, JIBANYAN HAS VISITED HIS ANCESTOR'S GRAVE EVERY DAY.
NATE ADAMS'S CURRENT NUMBER OF YO-KAI FRIENDS: 15

YO-KAI WATCH 2

WHAT HAPPENED IN BETWEEN PANELS 1 AND 2 ON PAGE 177.

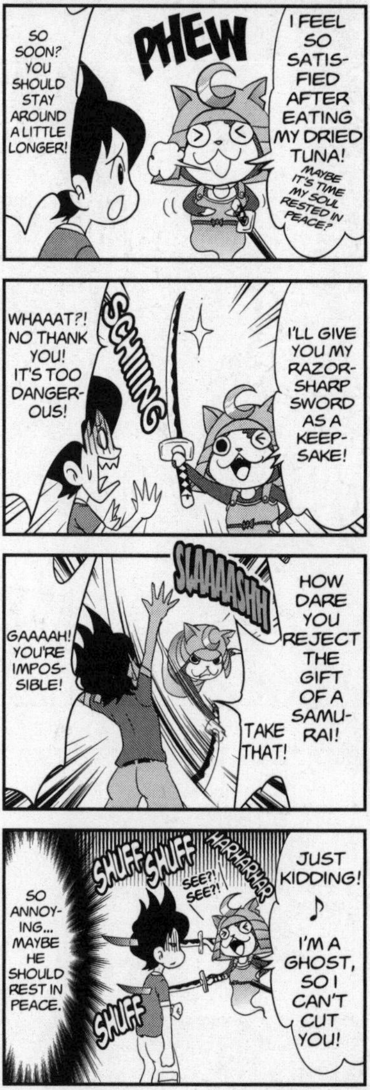
I FEEL SO SATISFIED AFTER EATING MY DRIED TUNA!
MAYBE IT'S TIME MY SOUL RESTED IN PEACE?
PHEW
SO SOON? YOU SHOULD STAY AROUND A LITTLE LONGER!
I'LL GIVE YOU MY RAZOR-SHARP SWORD AS A KEEPSAKE!
SCHIIING
WHAAAT?! NO THANK YOU! IT'S TOO DANGEROUS!
HOW DARE YOU REJECT THE GIFT OF A SAMURAI!
SLAAAASHH
TAKE THAT!
GAAAAH! YOU'RE IMPOSSIBLE!
JUST KIDDING! ♪
I'M A GHOST, SO I CAN'T CUT YOU!
HARHARHAR
SEE?! SEE?!
SHUFF SHUFF
SHUFF
SO ANNOYING... MAYBE HE SHOULD REST IN PEACE.

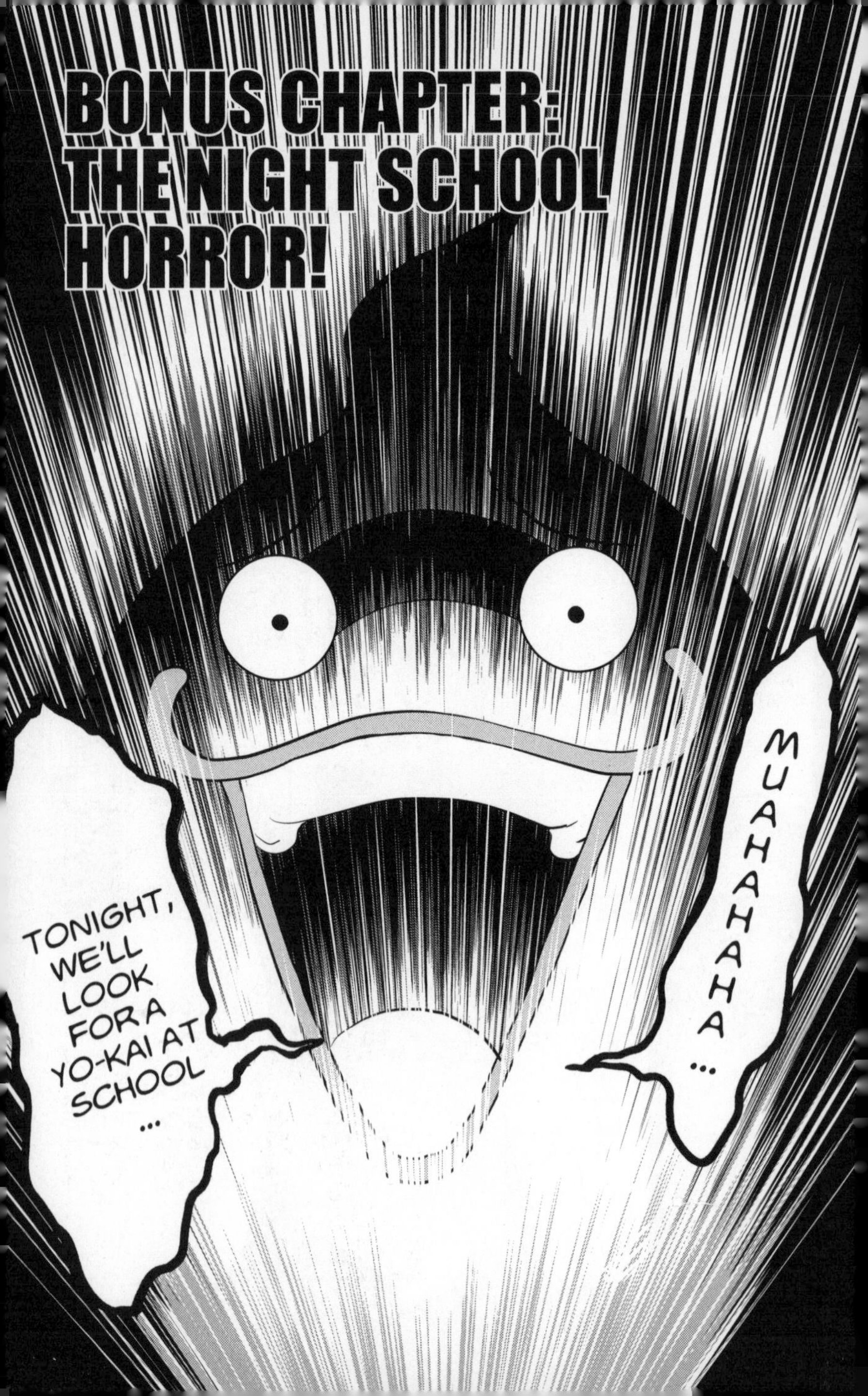
BONUS CHAPTER: THE NIGHT SCHOOL HORROR!
MUAHAHAHA...
TONIGHT, WE'LL LOOK FOR A YO-KAI AT SCHOOL...

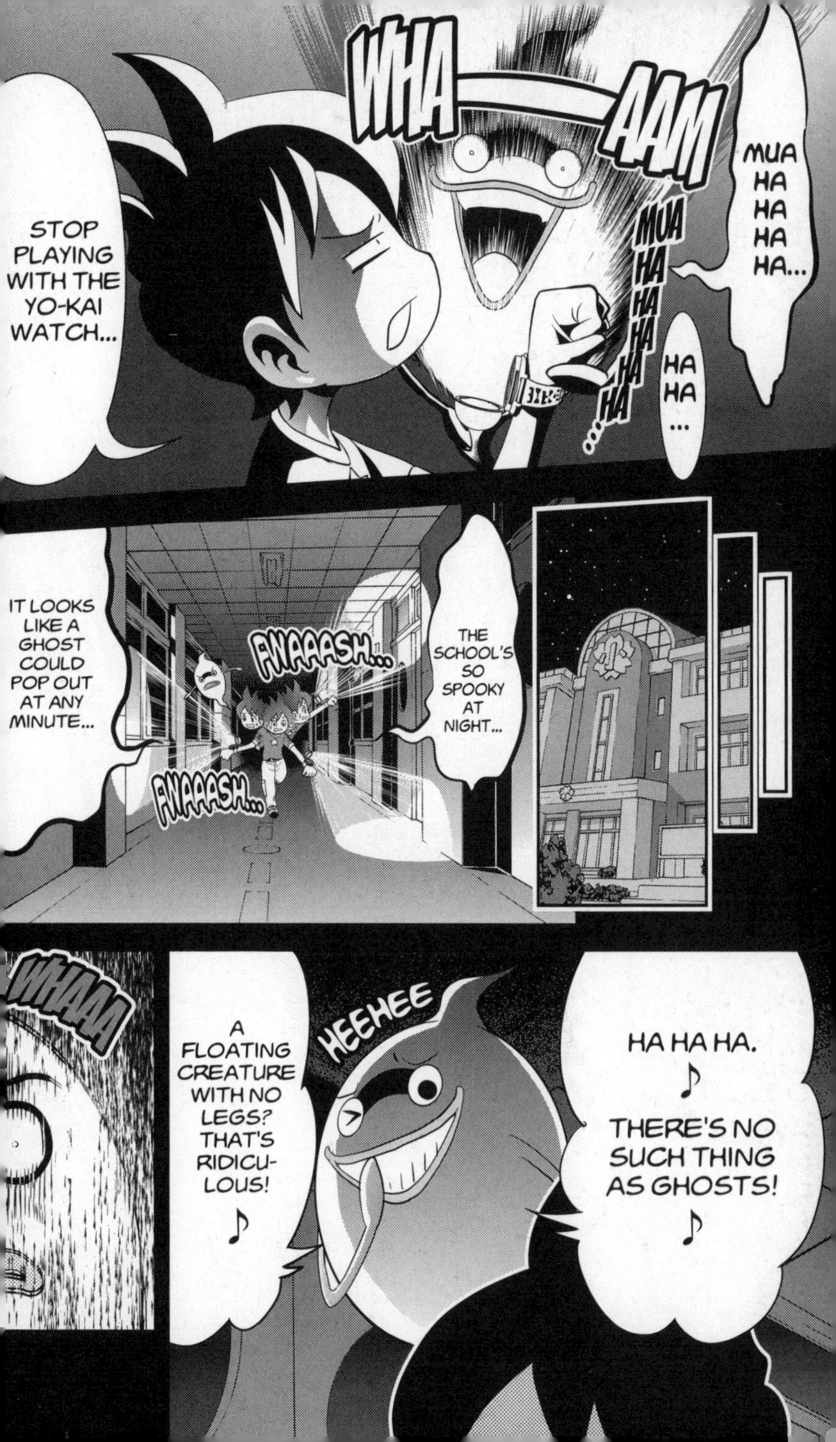
MUA HA HA HA HA...
WHAAAM
MUA HA HA HA HA HA...
HA HA ...
STOP PLAYING WITH THE YO-KAI WATCH...
THE SCHOOL'S SO SPOOKY AT NIGHT...
FWAAASH...
FWAAASH...
IT LOOKS LIKE A GHOST COULD POP OUT AT ANY MINUTE...
HA HA HA. ♪ THERE'S NO SUCH THING AS GHOSTS! ♪
HEEHEE
A FLOATING CREATURE WITH NO LEGS? THAT'S RIDICU-LOUS! ♪
WHAAAA

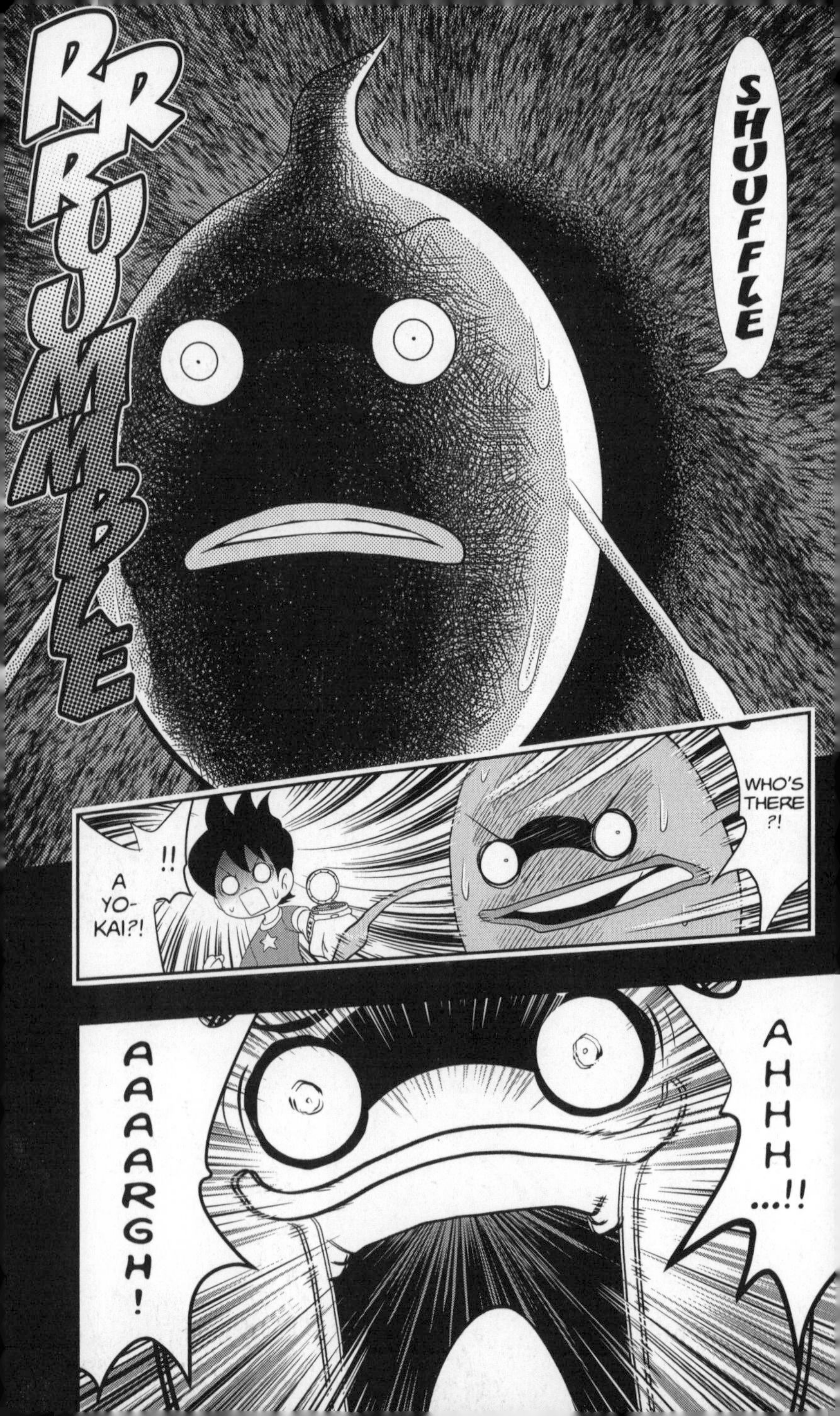
SHUUFFLE
RRRUMMBLE
WHO'S THERE?!
!!
A YO-KAI?!
AHHH...!!
AAAAARGH!

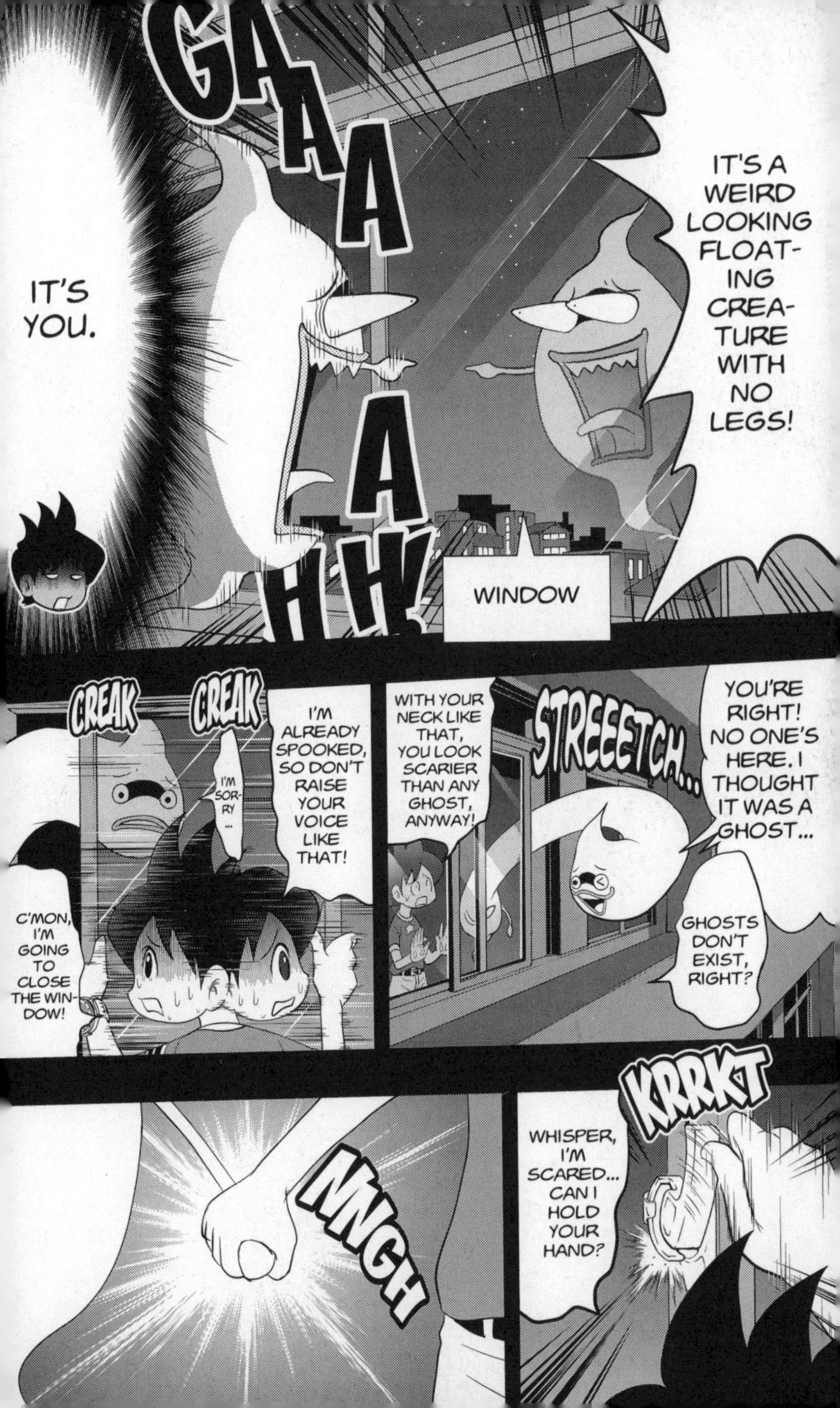
IT'S A WEIRD LOOKING FLOATING CREATURE WITH NO LEGS!
GAAAAHH!
WINDOW
IT'S YOU.
YOU'RE RIGHT! NO ONE'S HERE. I THOUGHT IT WAS A GHOST...
STREEETCH...
WITH YOUR NECK LIKE THAT, YOU LOOK SCARIER THAN ANY GHOST, ANYWAY!
GHOSTS DON'T EXIST, RIGHT?
I'M ALREADY SPOOKED, SO DON'T RAISE YOUR VOICE LIKE THAT!
CREAK CREAK
I'M SORRY...
C'MON, I'M GOING TO CLOSE THE WINDOW!
KRRKT
WHISPER, I'M SCARED... CAN I HOLD YOUR HAND?
MNGH

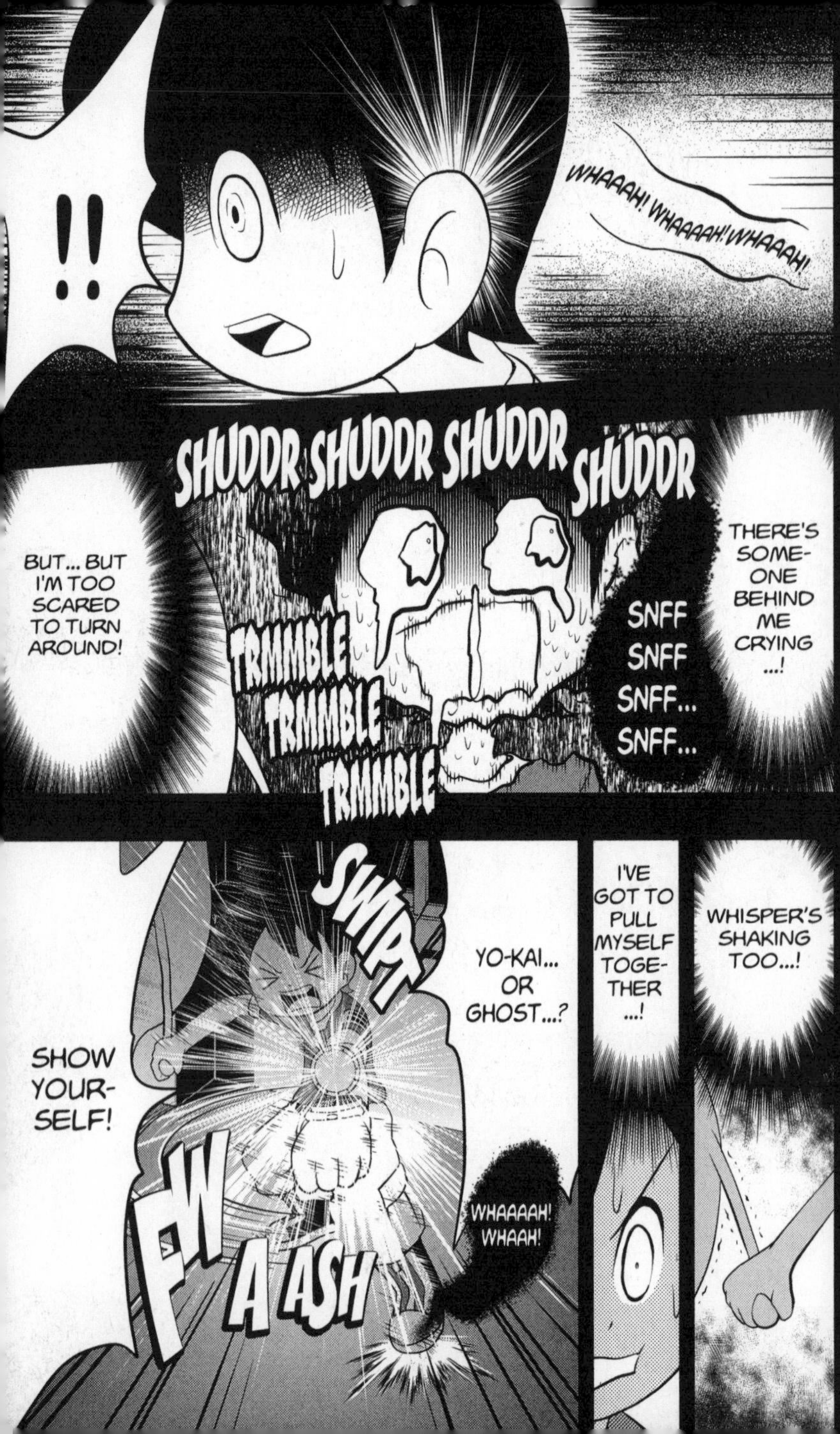
WHAAAH! WHAAAAH! WHAAAH!
!!
SHUDDR SHUDDR SHUDDR SHUDDR
THERE'S SOME-ONE BEHIND ME CRYING ...!
SNFF SNFF SNFF... SNFF...
BUT... BUT I'M TOO SCARED TO TURN AROUND!
TRMMBLE TRMMBLE TRMMBLE
WHISPER'S SHAKING TOO...!
I'VE GOT TO PULL MYSELF TOGE-THER ...!
YO-KAI... OR GHOST...?
SWIPT
SHOW YOUR-SELF!
WHAAAAH! WHAAH!
FWAASH

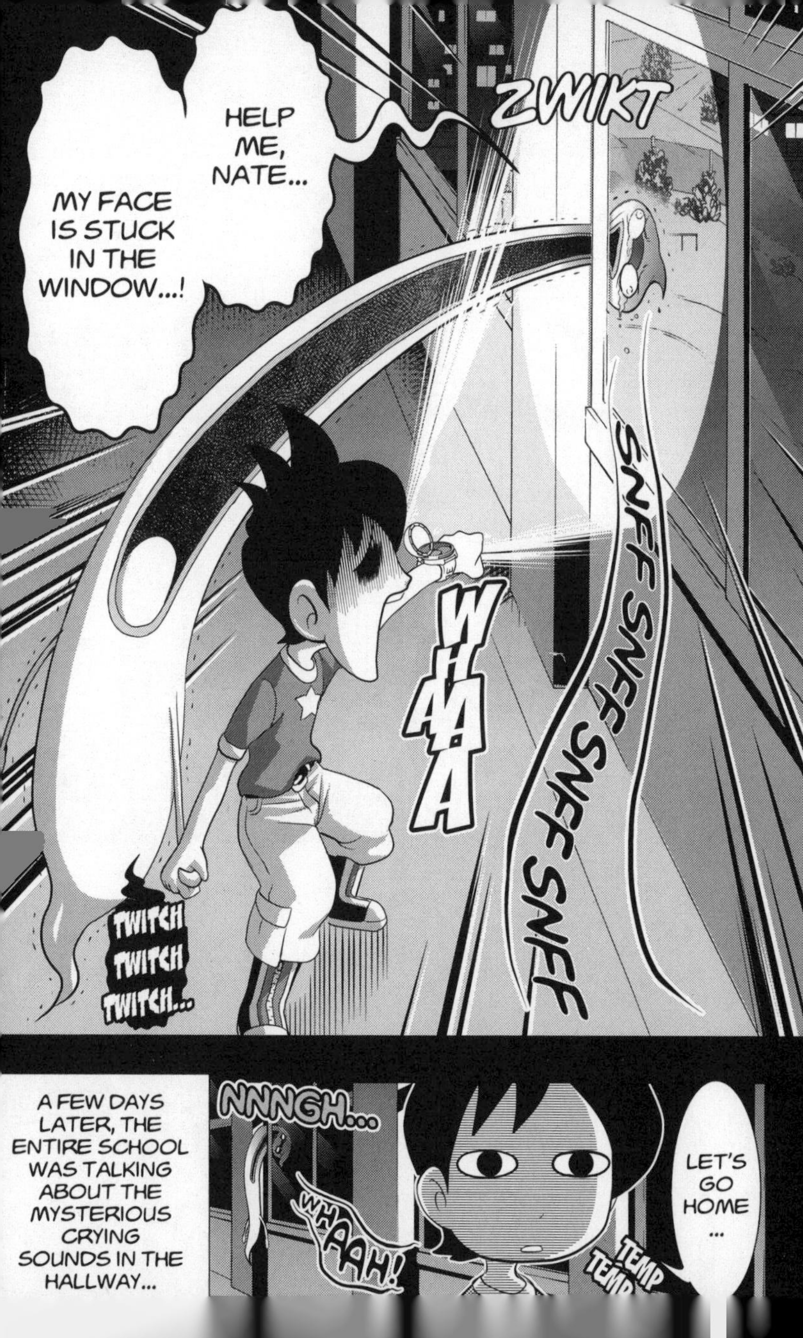
ZWIKT
HELP ME, NATE...
MY FACE IS STUCK IN THE WINDOW...!
SNFF SNFF SNFF SNFF SNFF
WHAAAA
TWITCH TWITCH TWITCH...
LET'S GO HOME ...
TEMP TEMP
WHAAAH!
NNNGH...
A FEW DAYS LATER, THE ENTIRE SCHOOL WAS TALKING ABOUT THE MYSTERIOUS CRYING SOUNDS IN THE HALLWAY...

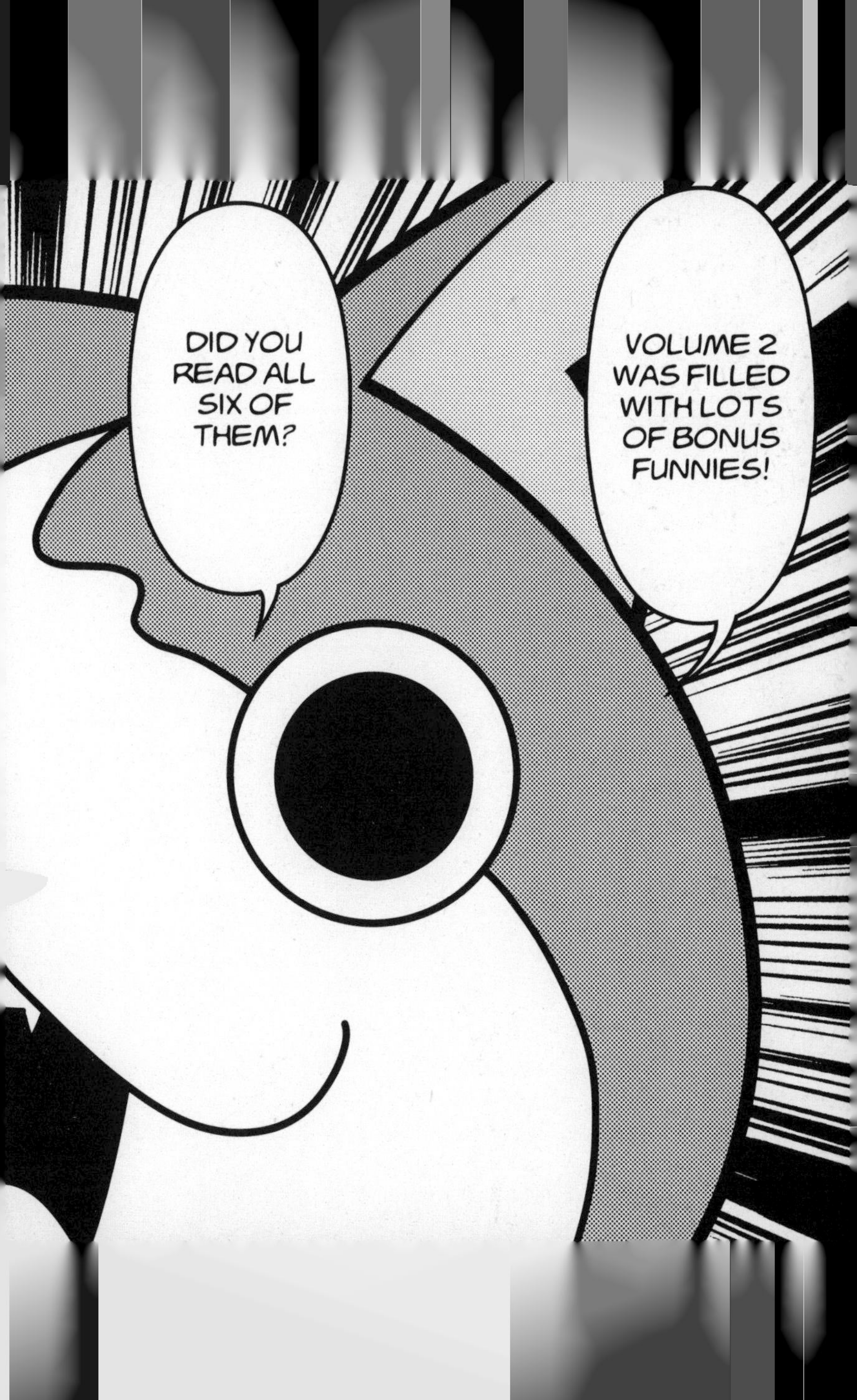
VOLUME 2 WAS FILLED WITH LOTS OF BONUS FUNNIES!
DID YOU READ ALL SIX OF THEM?

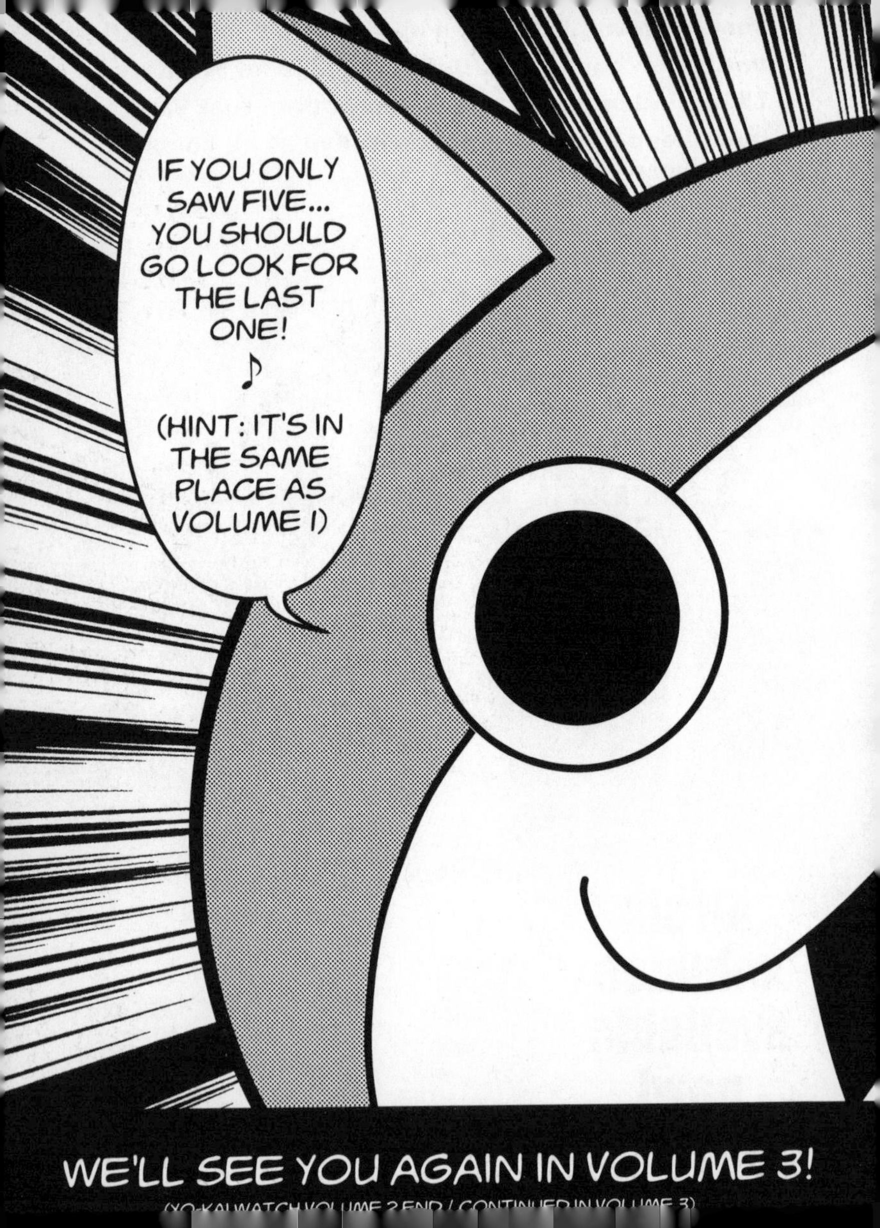

IF YOU ONLY SAW FIVE... YOU SHOULD GO LOOK FOR THE LAST ONE! ♪
(HINT: IT'S IN THE SAME PLACE AS VOLUME 1)
WE'LL SEE YOU AGAIN IN VOLUME 3!
(YO-KAI WATCH VOLUME 2 END / CONTINUED IN VOLUME 3)

Welcome to the world of Little Battlers eXperience! In the near future, a boy named Van Yamano owns Achilles, a miniaturized robot that battles on command! But Achilles is no ordinary LBX. Hidden inside him is secret data that Van must keep out of the hands of evil at all costs!

All six volumes available now!

DANBALL SENKI
© 2011 Hideaki FUJII / SHOGAKUKAN
© LEVEL-5 Inc.

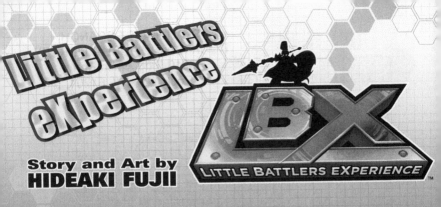

Little Battlers eXperience

Story and Art by HIDEAKI FUJII

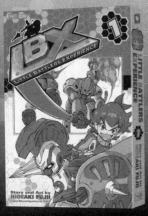

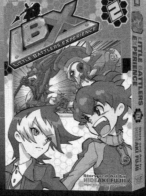

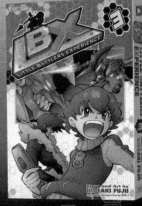

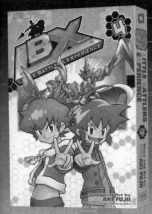

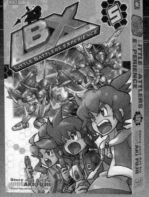

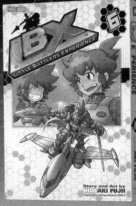

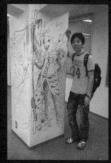

THIS IS THE END OF THIS GRAPHIC NOVEL!

4
3
2
1
2
1
8
7
6
5
4
3
9
5
FOLLOW THE ACTION THIS WAY.

To properly enjoy this Perfect Square graphic novel, please turn it around and begin reading from right to left.

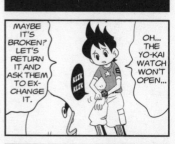

THE RETURN

OH... THE YO-KAI WATCH WON'T OPEN...
KLIK KLIK
MAYBE IT'S BROKEN? LET'S RETURN IT AND ASK THEM TO EX-CHANGE IT.
THE YO-KAI WATCH IS A ONE AND ONLY PRODUCT. IT CAN'T BE EX-CHANGED.
BUT YOU CAN HAVE IT REPAIRED BECAUSE ITS WAR-RANTY HASN'T EXPIRED YET.
OOH!
THERE WAS A CONTACT ADDRESS ON THE WARRANTY CERTIFI-CATE.
GREAT! LET'S CALL THEM!!
BUT I LOST THAT CERTIFI-CATE.
TEE-HEE♪
I WANT TO RETURN MY BUTLER...

AUTHOR BIO

When the Shogakukan building was scheduled to be torn down, artists came to draw on the walls as a sign of gratitude!

Hopefully, this series is still running long after the new building is finished!

—Noriyuki Konishi

Noriyuki Konishi hails from Shimabara City in Nagasaki Prefecture, Japan. He debuted with the one-shot *E-CUFF* in *Monthly Shonen Jump Original* in 1997. He is known for writing manga adaptations of *AM Driver* and *Mushiking: King of the Beetles*, along with *Saiyuki Hiro Go-Kū Den!*, *Chōhenshin Gag Gaiden!! Card Warrior Kamen Riders*, *Go-Go-Go Saiyuki: Shin Gokūden* and more.

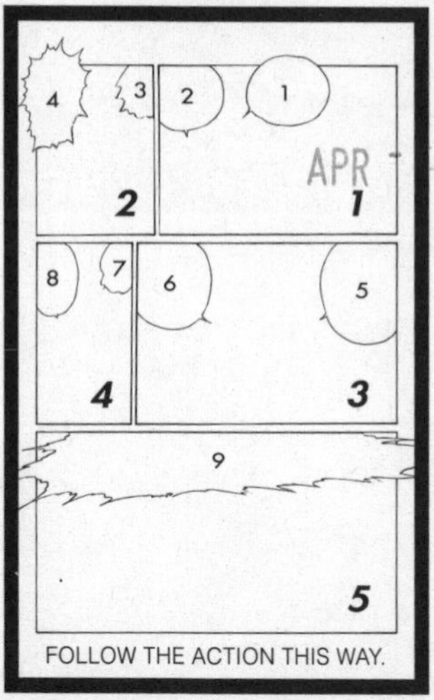

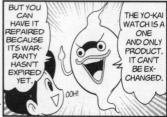

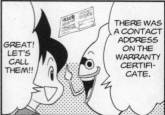

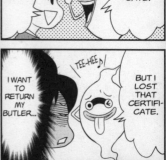